Royalist Rebel

For Clive, who always encourages me and gets neglected as a result.
For Mike and Alex, because they are too important not to mention at every opportunity.
For Jan, my most dedicated reader, but never a critic - so far.

◎

Acknowledgments

This is to pay tribute to everyone who helped me put this story together, from my critique group, who read every chapter and offered their valuable feedback, to Victoria Bradley at Ham House for turning me loose on the archives, and all the patient tour guides who endured my awkward questions with endurance. For my lovely agent Kate Nash who started the whole thing, and my fabulous editor Karen Selley, who polished my prose with her magic duster and whose telephone calls kept me focused. Not forgetting the unflappable Laura Hirst at Pen and Sword.

Royalist Rebel

Anita Seymour

CLAYMORE PRESS

First published in Great Britain in 2013 by
CLAYMORE PRESS
An imprint of
Pen & Sword Books Ltd
47 Church Street
Barnsley
South Yorkshire
S70 2AS

9781781590683

A CIP catalogue record for this book is
available from the British Library

Printed and bound in England
By CPI Group (UK) Ltd, Croydon, CR0 4YY

Pen & Sword Books Ltd incorporates the Imprints of Claymore Press, Pen &
Sword Aviation, Pen & Sword Family History, Pen & Sword Maritime, Pen &
Sword Military, Wharncliffe Local History, Pen & Sword Select, Pen & Sword
Military Classics, Leo Cooper, Remember When, Seaforth Publishing and
Frontline Publishing

For a complete list of Pen & Sword titles please contact
PEN & SWORD BOOKS LIMITED
47 Church Street, Barnsley, South Yorkshire, S70 2AS, England
E-mail: enquiries@pen-and-sword.co.uk
Website: www.pen-and-sword.co.uk

'...love her intirely but let her not know it, for all wifes are but too apt to take advantage of the fondness of theire husband, and upon it to growe insolent and imperious, and inclined to pevert the laws of nature by indeavouringe a superiority over the husband, and if shee getts the reignes in her own hands, away shee will runn with it, you scarce ever will stopp her in the whole course of her life.'

Sir Lionel Tollemache in a letter to his son, Lionel

She was a woman of great beauty, but of far greater parts. She had a wonderful quickness of apprehension, and an amazing vivacity in conversation. She had studied not only divinity and history, but mathematics and philosophy. She was violent in every thing she set about, a violent friend, but a much more violent enemy. She had a restless ambition, lived at a vast expense, and was ravenously covetous; and would have stuck at nothing by which she might compass her ends.

Elizabeth, Countess Dysart according to Bishop Burnet's History

Chapter 1

July 1643, Richmond, Surrey, England

Though the hour is early, my riding habit sticks to my back and moisture gathers on my upper lip. The air is thick with the scent of wildflowers, parched grass and sharp tang of silt. My mare high steps along the barge walk, where clouds of midges gather in the trees beside the river Thames that curls through lush fields in a silver ribbon toward Richmond town.

Two footmen ride escort, one ahead to clear the way of walkers, whilst the other steers his mount close to Nan's horse. The animal needs a firmer hand than my sister's, but he is a favourite of hers and at times, determination overrules her sense.

'Which goddess shall I be when Mistress Carlisle paints my portrait, Nan?' I ask.

'Why can you not simply be yourself, Elizabeth?' She grips the rein with a tight fist and the pommel of her saddle with the other. 'You have beauty enough without the enhancements of immortality.'

'It is for that precise reason, I fancy I would look well attired in the robes of the goddess Iris, do you not think?'

'You have never possessed much modesty,' Nan murmurs, though not low enough that I do not hear. 'I know nothing of this Iris. Who was she?' Her feigned disinterest does not deceive me and I cannot help but goad her.

'Because I study Ovid's Metamorphoses, while you still wrestle with elementary French.'

'Perhaps I too would enjoy Ovid,' Nan whines. 'How can I know if I have not tried?'

'And you shall not, until you have learned Latin, which I have not the inclination to teach you. As for Iris, she wore a halo of light on her head and trailed a rainbow across the sky.'

A pigeon bursts from a hedgerow causing Nan to shriek in alarm. Her horse half rears at the panicked snap, snap, snap of the bird's wings as it lunges into a tree above our heads.

A footman springs forward, grasps the bridle of her horse and murmurs an endearment that settles the animal. By some miracle, Nan is not unseated and the servant drops back again.

'I would like to dress for the portrait too.' Nan carefully nudges her mount close to mine. Her darting eyes probe the willows on the far bank, where swaying fronds dip lazily into the river. 'I know nothing of goddesses. Which one shall I be?'

I pretend to ponder for a moment, but have given the matter some thought. 'What about the enchantress Circe, who was also a witch, and turned those who offended her into creatures. Like pigs.' I raise a clawed hand and bare my teeth in a grimace.

Nan glares at me and falls back, her shoulders hunched in dejection.

Laughing, I guide my mare over a rut of dried mud on the path. 'Don't take my teasing to heart so,' I call to her over my shoulder, though her abject misery stirs my wicked tongue. 'Iris had sisters too, but they were the winged monsters known as harpies.'

'Elizabeth!' Nan's head jerks up. 'When we return home I shall tell Katherine and Margaret what you said. You can be so cruel at times.'

'Make way there!' The footman closest to me orders a figure approaching from the opposite direction. A man in a patched coat faded across the shoulders leads two laden donkeys, heads down and hindquarters swinging beneath their heavy loads.

The journeyman snatches off his hat and bows clumsily. His beasts bray in protest and strain against the ropes as he attempts to haul them onto the grass verge.

Inhaling with a sigh, I reign in my mount and resign myself to wait as the ragged procession moves past. My mare nips at the man's sleeve as he draws level. I throw back my head in a laugh at her naughty manners, then again at the journeyman's low curse.

My footman snarls at him for disrespect, but I signal him to desist. The journeyman's full knapsack reminds me today is Saturday; market day in Kingston. His animals already look tired and I don't envy the long day he faces beneath the summer sun at the market.

We set off again, but have gone less than a dozen paces, when a tremor runs through the ground. A scurrying of wings or feet erupts from the bushes and a flock of startled crows scatter from the branches above us. A rhythmic pounding of hooves and jingle of bridles sets my horse snorting in alarm, her head thrown up and ears flat.

A line of horses appears round the bend and canters toward us, the riders in sleeveless buff jerkins with baldricks slung over their shoulders, and short swords at their waists. The officer at the head of the column wears the round, blackened helmet that strikes terror into every Royalist heart.

'Rebels,' I growl in contempt, though at the same time a trickle of fear creeps into my belly.

Nan reins her mount in behind me. 'They're Onslow's men!' Her gaze darts in all directions as if in search of escape. 'I told you we wouldn't be able to avoid them on the towpath. Even you, Elizabeth cannot bluff and bluster with those men to get your way.' Her restless hands jerk her reins; her alarm transfers to her horse and the animal crabs sideways, tossing his head.

Timid she may be, but my sister is no fool.

'Be still,' I hiss, forcing calm into my voice. 'They'll not harm us.' Though my throat dries and my heart thuds uncomfortably beneath my doublet.

The second footman jostles to my side, his chin jutted forward and a hand on the pistol at his belt.

I shake my head at him and with ill-concealed reluctance he relaxes in the saddle, his hand slides from the weapon and he flaps his coat forward to conceal it again.

'Halt!' The Roundhead officer's raised gauntlet signals his untidy cavalry to draw rein. Harnesses jingle as the horses shuffle to a stop, whickering and champing at roughly pulled bits. A powerful stench of unwashed bodies, horse sweat and dung drift toward me on the breeze.

'What do we do?' Nan presses a gloved hand to her mouth.

I throw her a warning glare. 'You'll do nothing. I'll handle this.'

The officer dismounts with indolent slowness, pausing to examine a cluster of persistent dog roses that have survived the recent drought. I imagine he does so to demonstrate his authority over us. What heady power it must be for such a man to keep the Murrays waiting.

Broad and ungainly, he is not young; probably near two score in years. He peels a glove from one fleshy hand, and slaps it against his other palm. The nose guard of a lobster-tail helmet hides most of his face, but I recognise him. His father rose to be a justice of the peace, but his grandsire was a butcher.

His troop of soldiers spread across the grass. They look ill-prepared for conflict, and though several wear helmets, most are in soft, madder red Montero hats.

A patrol then, most likely a trained band sent from the stews of London to intimidate the fine folk of Kingston.

'Captain Fitton.' I use his rank with grudging respect.

He tucks a glove into his waistband, then plants himself beside my mount, his feet splayed.

'Mistress Murray.' His voice drips with contempt and he regards me with a lascivious leer, one bare hand pressed flat against my horse's muzzle.

Pity I did not choose to ride Saracen this morning. That beast would shear the man's fingers at the second knuckle for such presumption.

'Where are you bound, Mistress, looking so fine on this bright morning?' He cocks his chin at my footmen. 'And with two such well-armed men at your side.' His gaze roves upward in a slow, insolent inspection to linger on my bodice.

'Indeed, sir.' My hand drifts to my throat, recalling belatedly that my doublet is fastened to my neck and give brief thanks to the fashion of wearing male clothing on horseback. 'My business is private, and my men are no better armed than yours. With so many ruffians on the road in these troubled times, I have need of them.'

At the word 'ruffians', the captain's eyes narrow and he steps closer, his hand slides along my horse's gleaming neck and hovers close to my boot.

Once, I would have taken my whip to that hand. Instead, I console myself with a conjured image of my arm striking his helmet above his ear and sending it tumbling end over end into the river. The vision makes me smile, a gesture the captain responds to as if it were aimed at him.

'As to my destination,' I continue with deliberate slowness. 'That is not your concern.'

My horse grows restless. Her hooves paw the path and send the captain back a pace, a flash of apprehension in his eyes. I could calm her with a hand, but do not; instead I relish his unease.

'Hah!' He gives a derisive snort and paces an invisible line on the path. 'It won't be long before everyone's business in this realm is ours. Charles Stuart cannot ignore our demands forever.'

'I would think, sir,' I lick my lips and fight to keep my anger from showing, 'your commanding officer must be well aware of how the townsfolk view Parliamentarians. 'They give him enough trouble.'

The previous November, Sir Richard Onslow, the deputy lieutenant of Surrey, took control of the Kingston Magazine for Parliament, bringing the Southwark trained bands with him. Ostensibly this was to defend the town, but in truth caused a riot when he forcibly removed the king's favourite, Lord Digby. A mob crowded the market square to jeer at the interlopers, calling them 'Roundheads' and demanded they withdraw.

The locals don't easily accept a hostile garrison in their midst, and their continued occupation of Kingston remains an uncomfortable one.

Fitton swings round to face me, but I do not flinch. Neither my heritage, nor my pride will bear insult from someone who, a twelvemonth ago, would not have dared halt a Murray on the road, let alone demand their business.

His smile dissolves, mouth twitching with surly discomfort. For all his swagger and disdain, this cur of a man is more used to receiving orders than giving them.

'The Stuart has not your confidence, Mistress.' His uneasy grin reveals brown-tinged teeth. 'What with him scurrying to Oxford with his court of stragglers, he looks to be on the run. But then you'd know that, since your father is his whipping-boy.'

A snigger rises from the troop behind him, and my hand tightens on my whip. Designed for decoration, it is too short and light to cause damage. Yet for the second time in as many minutes,

I fight an urge to lash it across this whoreson's smug face.

Truth indeed rankles, for as a boy, my father, William Murray, accepted punishment for the transgressions of the young Prince Charles; but that is long ago history, and only spoken of amongst his enemies.

'My father,' I say through clenched teeth, 'is the king's envoy, and a Gentleman of the Bedchamber. You would do well not to underestimate the influence our family has.'

A gust of wind lifts the feather on my hat, cooling the heat of fury in my cheeks. I ease the cloth at my throat with one hand, uncomfortable beneath his scrutiny.

Fitton's skin darkens at his neck, the colour slowly spreading into his face accentuating pale marks left by the pox he must have contracted in childhood. He could be a handsome man but for those blemishes. And the double chin.

Our eyes meet and hold, but he is the first to drop his gaze.

How easy it is to cow men of low birth. Five yards of velvet and a few pearls have them quivering in their shoes. The rebel leader, John Pym, may imbue his followers with a sense of holy righteousness, but the mien of superior birth is strong. At heart, men like this upstart soldier know their place.

'I mean no disrespect, Mistress.' Fitton's voice turns obsequious, though his blank eyes betray a lack of sincerity. He replaces his glove, and tugs the front of his leather jerkin; his bravado replaced by calm duty. 'I am charged to demand where you are bound.'

'As I said, sir, my errand is no business of yours.'

Nan's hand creeps across the space between us and closes on my forearm. 'I beg you not to make a fuss, Elizabeth. Mistress Carlisle can paint our portraits another day.'

'Hush, Nan. No one in Surrey would dare lay a hand on us.'

Nan releases a whimper, and unwilling to reduce her to an attack of nerves, I paste on an ingratiating smile. 'Since you are determined to know our purpose, Captain. My sister and I are expected at Petersham Lodge.'

A cunning light enters his eyes. 'So, it is the Keeper of Richmond Park you speak of. Him and that unnatural wife of his?' He strokes his chin in thought, though I doubt contemplation is an activity familiar to this man.

'He's a poet and court dramatist,' I snap. 'His Majesty is his patron.' I do not add that Joan Carlisle is an excellent artist, but to this canting fool, any woman who can do more than wash, cook and suckle children is unnatural.

'Another cursed Royalist,' an ensign snorts, loud enough for me to hear.

The captain doesn't even glance at the man, much less reprimand him.

An insult I will not forget.

'I have my orders,' Fitton barks, his mouth curled into a sneer. 'To keep watch on Royalist movements in the locality.'

My fists clench on the reins. 'And why pray? Surely my sister and I are no threat?' But of course, I know very well why he does so. We Murrays are Royalists; 'delinquents' and 'malignants' and therefore enemies of Parliament.

The footman with the ready pistol eases closer, his glance flicking to the captain and then back at me. 'Shall I insist he lets you pass, Mistress?'

The man is new to our household, and impetuous. I am tempted to allow him to show his courage, but Mother would not thank me. Besides, a footman in Kingston gaol is useless to us.

At any other time I would challenge Fitton, and enjoy the scrap. However the sight of Nan's pinched face makes me relent. And yet, something has given Fitton his courage, though it only dawns on me at that moment to wonder what that could be.

'Very well, Captain. On this occasion, we will return home.' I nudge my horse in a tight circle. 'Yet be assured my father shall hear of your unwelcome interference.'

His gaze meets mine again and in an instant of mutual communication, we both know there is no substance to my threat. My father attends the king at Oxford, with no plans to return to Ham in the near future. Something the captain, and indeed the entire Kingston garrison, must know.

'Heed your sister, Mistress Murray.' He signals for his horse, his lips twisted into a parody of a smile. Leather creaks as he heaves his ample rump into the saddle. 'Your lady mother has need of you

14

at home.'

A cold hand grips my heart. We left the house not a half hour ago. What has happened in so short a time? And how would this man know of it? Their patrol approached from the Richmond road. They could not have passed by Ham House.

'Oblige me by explaining yourself, Captain.' My tone is soft but firm. 'What do you know of my mother?'

He turns his mount, presenting the horse's hindquarters in a gesture of blatant insolence. I fear he is not going to respond, but cannot bring myself to plead with him. He would like nothing better than to see me beg.

Fitton regards me over one buff-clad shoulder with a sly, mocking grin, his eyes devoid of interest, as if our encounter now bores him. 'A representative from the Committee of Sequestration calls on Mistress Catherine Murray this day.' He signals to his men to mount and line up in readiness to leave. 'She may need a daughter's comfort on hearing his business.'

Hooves dislodge gobbets of dry earth and the horses' rumps sway as the line of rebels gather speed to cross Petersham Meadows toward the main road to Kingston and the garrison.

I clench my bottom lip between my teeth, and stare after them, my hands trembling on the reins. I have to fight an inclination to shout that they cross Murray land, but I would surely be mocked, or worse, ignored.

'Elizabeth, what did he mean?' Nan gropes for my sleeve.

'I do not know,' I snap, shrugging her off. Immediately guilt softens my tone. 'Don't fret, Nan, it could be nothing, but we must return home.'

After our desultory outward ride, the footmen forge ahead with enthusiasm, while my restless mare needs no second command to stretch her neck and gallop back the way we came.

Nan's cry of dismay is swallowed by the sound of pounding hooves. With my shoulders hunched over the pommels of my saddle, I urge my horse on while the footmen at my side shout warnings to pedestrians on the towpath, who leap aside to let us pass.

Chapter 2

My horse takes the bend at a reckless clip, and with the familiarity of home, pounds across the stretch of grass between the river and the north front, scattering indignant sheep that graze indolently beneath the trees.

Dropping to the ground outside the red-brick façade of the house, I toss the reins carelessly at the stable lad who scurries forward. My boots crunch on gravel and I reach the door, where a footman inadvertently blocks my way. Seeing his mistake, he bobs and darts aside.

Despite her lame leg, an infirmity which often comes between her and less interesting tasks, Nan remains at my shoulder.

I halt in front of the closed door to the main hall and clamp a hand on her upper arm. 'No, Nan. Go upstairs and stay with Katherine and Margaret. If there is bad news, I will come and find you.'

Nan glowers, but obeys and trails up the wide staircase, pausing at the top to throw me a hard look over her shoulder. I turn away with a sigh, for I act not from spite, but good intention. My sisters are precious to me, but they are not strong.

A footman bows me into the main hall where my mother stands with a strange man in a plain black doublet and cloak. His thin, carroty hair hangs limp and greasy from beneath his hat, and his heavy boots have left a trail of dirt across the marble floor.

So this is what a Sequestration Committee Collector looks like? I might have known he wouldn't be a gentleman, though this drab creature could never be mistaken for anything but a toady to the Parliament army.

Mother's diminutive stature gives her the look of an exquisite child in a jewel-coloured gown that glows like sapphires. Her complexion is paler than normal, but she remains calm, her gown stretched tight over ample breasts that swell in indignation.

'Mistress.' He inclines his head, his bow shallow enough to be insulting, his thin-lipped mouth twisted into a sneer as his gaze slides over me.

My stomach plummets. His demeanour tells me he does not bring good news. We have already been ordered to hand over the rents our tenants pay on quarter day to finance the Roundhead army. How much more can they demand?

As if he reads my thoughts, the man pulls a sheaf of pages from inside his doublet and snaps them open. 'Says here the Murrays are of those delinquents and Papists who-'

'We are not Papists!' Mother's eyes glint with fury and for a second, I believe she might strike him.

This possibility must have occurred to him too, for he steps back a pace, easing his collar away from his throat with the none-too-clean fingers of his free hand.

'I only repeat what the documents state, Mistress Murray.' He holds the papers inches from Mother's face. 'A Master Calcott accuses you of accumulating rents from your tenants and sending them to the king.'

'That is an outrageous and untruthful claim.' Mother's chin lifts in defiance and her blue eyes harden. 'I have no acquaintance with this Calcott creature, and doubt he has knowledge of my affairs.'

'Aye, well, that's as mebbe. But you've been ordered to pay forty pounds to the Committee before the tenth day of August-'

'Forty pounds?' My outrage explodes in disbelief. I start forward but Mother's upheld hand halts me. With the other, she snatches the sheaf from the man's grasp.

Her plump fingers shuffle the pages, until she reaches the second one where she halts. Her cheeks blanch, lips moving as she finds what she seeks. The gaze she lifts to meet mine is dull. 'There's also a list of furniture here.'

'Furniture?' I take the pages from her with a trembling hand and run a finger down the list in neat script. Several of the best pieces Father bought when the king presented him with Ham are listed there, but nothing from the original inventory of the house; most likely because they are too old-fashioned to provide a good return for the vultures of the rebel army.

'I'm to take the specified goods to Captain Jennings at Hasall

17

Hayes for disposal,' the Collector says with unnecessary cruelty.

I tug at Mother's sleeve, praying silently for her to do something, anything, to stop this from happening.

'There's nothing I can do, Betty, and besides, the pieces shall not be greatly missed.'

'But, Mother-'

'Hush. It could have been far worse.' Her smile wavers and there is pain in her eyes which sends fresh fury through me.

Apparently satisfied, the Collector nods. 'My men will be here shortly with a conveyance.'

'Do what you have to, sir.' Mother's contempt is evident. 'But have the courtesy to take your men round to the servants' entrance between the stables and the kitchens. Labourers are not received in the grand hall.'

Taking my cue, I hand the papers back to Mother and stride to the front door. Ignoring the pain its considerable weight exerts on my shoulder, I haul it open.

The Collector hesitates, but is not dull-witted enough to miss my meaning. His sneer turns to a grimace and he stomps toward me.

'Master Ball,' Mother says loudly, holding the pages out to our steward, who must have been waiting behind a door, for he arrives instantly at the sound of his name. 'When the men arrive, see they take only what is on this list. And not a stick of firewood more, mind. When their duty is done, see them off the premises. Completely off the premises. Do you understand?'

He adopts an air of hauteur and dips into a low bow. 'Perfectly, Mistress Murray.'

I cannot see his face, though I suspect he is smiling.

The Collector, whose name I have no wish to know, throws a last, furious glare at Mother, before strutting past me.

The door slams shut and I accompany Mother up the wide oak staircase. 'I think it best we do not mention this to the girls.' Her voice is calm, but her hands tremble on the handrail.

'I doubt that will make any difference. They are sure to notice the empty spaces in the rooms.'

'I suppose so,' she says with a shrug. 'It's foolish of me to think I can protect them from everything, but a little pretence cannot hurt.'

'At least our beds are not on that list, so we shall have somewhere to lay our heads tonight.' My feeble attempt at levity falls flat at her wince.

'The furniture is one thing, my dear.' She releases a long sigh. 'There is still the forty pounds I must pay in less than a week.' Her lip quivers and I sense tears are not far away. For all her strength and bravado, I know every day without Father is a trial.

'Do we have it?'

'Yes, although I would rather throw it in the river than hand it to those rebels.' Her words are accompanied by shouts and bangs from the rooms below, along with the grinding creak that signifies heavy wooden objects being dragged across the floor. The Collector's men have lost no time in beginning their work.

'Have you done what they accuse you of?' I lower my voice and step closer as we reach her bedchamber. 'Did you send money to King Charles?'

Her lips part and I imagine she is about to take me into her confidence, but the moment passes and her blue eyes meet mine without artifice. 'Whether I have or not is of no consequence. The fact we have attracted the notice of the Sequestration Committee means our possessions are under close scrutiny. I fear their next demand will be that we relinquish this house.'

'And leave us homeless?' My voice rises in panic. 'But they cannot! You have four daughters to provide for, and Father needs money to keep himself in Oxford. Ham is all we have.'

'Hush, my love, the girls,' she says with a hiss, thrusting me ahead of her into her room and closing the door. 'I need to think, Betty.' She paces the Turkey rug between her bed and the fireplace, the knuckle of her thumb thrust into her mouth. A gesture I have inherited, or copied, I am not sure which.

While waiting, I stand beside a Chinese cabinet, its black lacquer doors decorated with images of strangely shaped trees and figures in flowing gowns fashioned in gold. I have always admired it, recalling when my childish fingers prised open its drawers in search of treasures. Safer, happier days.

'Evidence or no,' Mother says after a moment, 'I fear that whatever we surrender will not satisfy the rebels for long.' She taps her teeth with a fingernail, thinking. 'They have to pay for their army somehow. Where else will they obtain monies but from families like ours? We are Royalists, delinquents,' she spits the words with scorn. 'Our allegiance makes everything we have subject to forfeit.'

I swallow a protest, but what else did I expect her to say? That she had a grand plan to protect us all from an entire army bent on the destruction of its royalist enemies? Angry yet despairing, I swipe a stray tear from my cheek.

'You mustn't fret, Betty.' She rushes to my side. 'We have not lost yet. I will write an appeal to the Surrey Committee, and swear a holy oath that any money I send to Oxford is for your Father's use and never reaches the king's coffers.'

'Suppose they do not believe you?'

'There must surely be one compassionate man amongst them who will take pity on a woman alone with her children.' Her finger slides across my cheek. 'Trust me, my hen.'

Soothed by the childhood endearment, I close my eyes and lean into her touch.

Not once since Father left has she complained of the heavy responsibility she carries; nor has she ever blamed him for leaving her to raise four daughters alone.

'I fancy paying another visit to the Oxford court to see your father.' Mother straightens, smoothing her skirt with both hands as if removing some contamination.

'It is too dangerous!' I grasp her arm, horrified. 'Besides, Sir Richard Onslow would never let you go, not while we are watched so closely.'

'Hah! To the Devil with the rebels.' She throws up the lid of the chest at the bottom of her bed, kneeling on the rug in front of the crammed trunk. 'Send Anne Henderson to me. I shall need some sewing done in preparation for the journey, though I hanker for new things rather than these patched ones, but in these times . . .'

I hesitate and she turns on me. 'Do as I say, Betty!'

I step into the hallway and send a passing maid to fetch my cousin.

'I shall ask His Majesty to put in a kind word for us with

Parliament,' Mother continues when I return, pulling gowns and shifts from the chest and piling them in a silky rainbow of colours on the bed coverlet.

'The Committee answers to the Westminster Parliament now, Mother, not the king. Perhaps it is not within his power to stop them taking Ham House.'

Her head jerks in my direction, a cambric petticoat hanging limply from one hand. 'What can you mean? He is the king. If he commands it they will have to obey.'

'I merely thought . . . never mind, of course he'll help us.'

'The Murrays have always been his loyal servants.' Her voice rises and falls as she delves into the chest. 'And your Uncle Thomas was King Charles' tutor when they were children in Edinburgh. I shall apply to that turncoat Essex for a pass allowing me to travel.' Mother's face splits into a bright smile over a silk petticoat. 'He made no objection when I went to Oxford in the spring.'

Mother was always capable of charming the indolent, and, if rumour proved true, impotent Earl of Essex. The king had never trusted him, and when the Puritan John Pym was warned of the king's intent to arrest five members of Parliament the year before, it surprised no one that Essex was rumoured to be the culprit. He proved it by changing sides.

'He would spy on you?'

She hunches her shoulders, unconcerned. 'Let his men waste time if they wish. I will betray nothing.'

Her courage leaves me breathless. I may possess a sharp tongue, and a temper alert for disrespect, but the thought of the three thousand Roundhead soldiers less than a mile away at Kingston churns my stomach.

A light knock announces the arrival of Cousin Henderson, Mother's waiting woman and a distant cousin. Grunting with the effort, Mother rises to her feet. In her thirty-ninth year, she is not as sprightly as she once was, though she has more energy than any of her daughters.

'This argument the king has with his Parliament cannot last forever. These things have happened before, though no one ever imagined Parliament would carry their grievances this far.' She tuts

21

and shakes her head, then beckons to the silent figure at the door.

Anne Henderson bobs me a curtsey as she passes. Taller and scrawnier than I, her frizzy red hair is barely confined beneath a white cap, a coarse, tanned complexion betraying her country girl origins.

Mother proceeds to give detailed instructions for the repair of broken stays and tears in silk petticoats.

Forgotten, I wander to the window and stare at the empty river.

Once, a constant procession of wherries and barges passed by our house on any day of the year, going downstream to London, and upriver to Hampton Court, or the Palace of Oatlands at Weybridge, each craft outdoing the next with awnings, pennants and coats of arms; liveried watermen displaying their skill in the currents.

Only plain barges carrying soldiers, supplies and weapons glide past our house now, their guards hostile to curious watchers on the bank. Anyone who pays them too much attention is quickly ordered to move on.

We have few visitors, apart from a group of Mother's like-minded friends who despise the rebels as much as we do. Others avoid us, fearful lest their patronage opens them to accusation. I do not mind their absence, which I am determined will change once the king sets everything to rights again.

My fear is that Mother's skill and diplomacy may not be enough to keep our home out of Parliament hands until the king returns to Whitehall. Without brothers, I am my father's heir, and when he is gone, Ham will be mine. The notion that my destiny could be thwarted by the avarice of the Surrey Committee of Sequestration haunts my dreams.

I pause in front of a gilt-framed mirror on the wall and give a sigh. A visitor to the house once called me 'my father's jewel', only to condemn my three sisters as 'crook'd, poor things not worth their dowries.'

If that made me vain, it was surely not of my doing. I often ponder on that stranger's cruel reference to the fact my sisters have an affliction of their bones. Nan has a twisted hip and Katherine a weak spine. Margaret is only seven, but her hesitant gait is caused by one leg being longer than the other. There was another sister too, poor sweet Mary, lost to us when no more than a babe.

The future prosperity of the Murrays lies firmly with me, though I carry the burden willingly. My sharp tongue is legendary, and on occasion, I have been known to fly into uncontrollable rages. Above all, I am sworn to protect what is mine and no one can gainsay my care of my siblings.

As for my supposed beauty, I could never see it. Being small of stature, my shoulders slope and my hair is a shade of red-gold no one would own to happily. My eyes are as blue as Mother's, with a slightly sleepy look which is much praised, and I have what is described as a provocative mouth, though my weak chin is not much enhanced by its dimple.

What is beauty, anyway? A well-proportioned visage in a silvered glass? Or the passion within a heart of fire and the will to rise above life's misfortunes? True beauty should emerge from courage and a stout heart, and if anyone has that, it is my mother, Catherine Bruce Murray.

Where some women wring their hands and plead for their bairns and treasures, Mother guards what is hers with the ferocity of a lioness. 'You are descended from the Murrays of Tullibardine,' she reminds us often. 'The blood of James Stuart II, King of Scotland runs in your veins. When King Charles sends these canting Puritan rogues back to their farms and butcher shops, as he must surely do, the Murrays will rise again alongside those who kept faith with him.'

Most times her courage sustains me. But suppose Mama is arrested as a Royalist spy before she reaches Oxford? What if this man Calcott gives more false evidence against her? Or maybe it is not so false? If the Committee discover or invent crimes against us and seize our estate, what will happen to us all, to Ham? My inheritance?

'Such vanity, Mistress Elizabeth.' Cousin Anne blinks her rodent-like eyes as she passes me on her way out, her arms full of gowns and petticoats. 'Do you seek your future within the depths of that glass?'

'I-I had a smut on my nose.' I say, following her upright

back with my gaze as her footsteps echo along the hall.

My future in a looking-glass? For a Christian woman, my cousin has some unholy superstitions.

Chapter 3

August 1643

During our customary walk in the gardens before dinner, Mother announces her intention to visit Father in Oxford to my sisters.

'Again, Mama?' Kate's fingers pause in the process of shredding a rose. 'You have just returned this last April. And with Father away too, we are at the mercy of the rebels.'

'The rebels will not bother with you, child.' Mother avoids my pointed look. Kingston is but a mile away, and we are both aware that rogue soldiers frequently carry out raids on storehouses and farms for food and horses.

'If Father needs you, Mama, then we shall simply have to bear it,' Nan speaks with fifteen-year-old gravitas, her lips turned down in disappointment.

'I do not want you to go!' Meg's childish features twist in anguish.

Mother looks at each face in turn, finally settling upon me. 'Is that how you feel too, Betty?'

Unsure as to what response she requires, I hesitate. The days passed slowly when she was last away, and though I flew to the front door at every hoof beat, raking Ham Street in search of soldiers, none came to harass or threaten us. 'I cannot pretend I will relish your absence, Mama. But if you feel it is necessary. . .'

Mother blows air through pursed lips in a long sigh. 'Then there is nothing for it, but to take all of you with me.'

'Is that possible?' Nan's eyes widen. 'Go to the king's court at Oxford?'

'The exiled court,' I remind her. 'And I shall welcome the opportunity to see Father again.' A thrill of anticipation runs through me at the prospect; I have missed him.

'Well, naturally that is what Nan meant,' Kate says. 'What dutiful daughter would not?'

The pert look she directs at Nan is met with a protruding

tongue.

'Will the Princes Charles and James be there?' Meg bobs and twists in front of Mother in her excitement. 'And Elizabeth and Henry?'

'I'm afraid not.' A wasp hovers in front of Mother's face and she flicks it away, wincing. 'Princess Elizabeth and Prince Henry are being held under guard in St James' Palace.'

'They are prisoners?' Kate says, aghast. 'But Elizabeth is no more than my age, and Henry but a babe in arms!'

'Naught but children, indeed, held as hostage for the king's good behaviour.' Mother's deep sigh wipes away our smiles. 'What a wicked thing it is to keep such little ones from their mother.'

'I can only wonder on the effectiveness of such action,' I say. 'The king has not given way to any of Parliament's demands, whether they hold his children captive or not.'

The notion of seeing Prince Charles again appeals. He must be thirteen now, and was always a good-looking boy with a liking for the ladies. Prince James is not yet ten, and barely worth my notice.

'The House of Commons takes too much on itself,' Mother sniffs. 'I received word that the Queen's Capuchins have been arrested at her chapel in Somerset House.'

'What is a Capuchin?' Kate frowns, then leaps aside as another wasp buzzes beside her ear.

'A friar,' I explain gently, waving the offending insect away. 'Twelve of them were among Queen Henrietta Maria's attendants when she came to England to marry King Charles.'

'They have been here all this time?' Meg's voice rises to high-pitched indignation.

'Yes, Meg.' I cannot help smiling at her outraged expression. She may be only seven years old but she is a faithful Anglican. 'It does strike me an odd notion in a country that condemns Papism. But the Queen has always had a mind of her own in matters of religion.'

'Not for much longer if her confessors have been arrested.' Kate's derisive snort is reminiscent of Mother's.

'The statues and stained glass windows in Westminster Abbey and St Margaret's have been destroyed,' Mother continues without responding to Kate, 'and an altar-piece by Rubens thrown into the Thames.'

'Where did you hear all this, Mother?' Nan chews at a thumbnail, her limp more pronounced than usual. Like Margaret, Nan readily accepts the notion we are under threat from Rome through the Queen. Kate is more like me, outwardly devoted, but does not hesitate to demand explanations.

'Oh, here and there,' Mother answers enigmatically. 'Ah here is Cousin Henderson.' She indicates the figure who appears like a ghost on the path, with not even a whisper of leaves to announce her. 'It must be time for dinner.' She gathers the girls together and ushers them into the house.

Cousin Henderson lags behind, and when we reach the door, she steps in front of me.

'I visited Kingston Market this morning, Mistress Elizabeth. I heard something there your lady mother may choose not to mention in front of your sisters.'

An air of conspiracy clings to her like cobwebs, but she remains silent too long. Suspecting she relishes this minor power over me too much, I snap. 'If you intend to waste my time, I cannot allow it.' I stride across the terrace and grasp the door before it closes. Cousin Henderson and I conduct a constant battle of wills, fuelled by jealousy and my pride.

'Parliament plans to impeach Queen Henrietta Maria for high treason,' her Scots lilt rises behind me.

I halt with my hand on the door knob as the terrace tilts and blood rushes in my ears. 'Treason? How-how can they do such a thing to the queen?'

She touches a finger to her lips, lowering her voice. 'On the grounds she brought a Popish army into the country to wage war against Parliament.'

Without a governess, Cousin Anne good-naturedly harries my sisters into a routine of study and devotion; one I baulked at long ago, for I am too near her in age for her to exert much authority over me. She imparts housewifely duties adequately enough, but will never reconcile to my reading Greek, or to mathematical conundrums. Sewing and ale brewing are all very well, but my sisters and I shall grace a finer company.

I recall Queen Henrietta's year spent at The Hague, raising loans, buying weapons and recruiting troops by selling or pawning jewels. Styling herself, 'Her She-Majesty, Generalissima,' she returned to Oxford the previous month with the king's nephew, Prince Rupert at the head of a company of veteran professional soldiers.

'Prince Rupert is not a Papist,' I grab the stone balustrade and the rough surface grazes my palm. I pull my hand away and massage the torn skin with my other hand.

'That he is not,' she says, ever patient. 'But many of the soldiers the Queen brought with her are French.'

Impeach a queen? It is unheard of. 'Her Majesty only seeks to settle these troubles, not to wage war against her subjects.'

'May those who stand in judgement develop your clear sight, Elizabeth.' She glides past me with a murmured remark about seeing to the girls.

The door swings shut behind her, leaving me on the deserted terrace. With no other outlet for my fury, I aim my foot at a clay pot and send it skittering across the terrace, where it smashes into a hundred orange shards.

It soothes my restless mood not at all.

If Parliament believes itself powerful enough to impeach a queen, what do they have in store for His Majesty? And for his faithful servant, William Murray?

* * *

October 1643, Oxford

Cold and aching after three days in a coach on sodden roads turned to quagmires, I cross the threshold of the black and white timber-framed house Father has leased for the winter. My first inclination is to march straight out again and demand accommodation more suited to Father's rank as a Gentleman of the King's Bedchamber. Disappointment assails me as I search for

28

something complimentary to say, and fail.

Each room leads into progressively smaller ones across a wide frontage, and though stone fireplaces grace each of the principal rooms, no fires welcome us. Cupboards gape wide and furniture has been pushed haphazardly aside to facilitate the removal of the owner's possessions. Trails of dust cling to the woodwork and pale squares where paintings once hung are evident on shabby walls. The finger I slide along a windowsill comes away grimy.

'I would have done better,' Father says as he disentangles himself from Meg's clinging arms. 'But over two thousand soldiers are garrisoned in the city, all of whom must be lodged somewhere.'

'We aren't soldiers, Papa!' Kate rolls her eyes.

'Of course not, my love.' He gives a long-suffering smile. 'However, times are hard, and we find ourselves in unfortunate circumstances.'

An air of neglect hangs about him as he hovers between the front door and the salon, his reddish-brown hair lank on the shoulders of a black coat that sports shiny patches. Shadows of old stains stand out on his cuffs and lace collar, while the sight of mended hose above scuffed shoes jolts me.

'It is a fine house, my love.' Mother's obsequious tone is out of character. 'You're so clever to have found it for us, and we are grateful. Aren't we, girls?'

'Well, Betty, what do you think?' Father's tired eyes meet mine, and I can no longer hold my tongue.

'If one were a guild master or a merchant, Father, I might approve.' My gaze takes in the uneven floors and rough-hewn doorframes. 'But it is too small for all of us.' I step back as a line of servants troops past with our baggage. 'Do close the door,' I mutter to a passing servant. 'The wind is blowing all the dead leaves indoors.'

Father's gaze slides from mine, and he offers no response. He knows not to expect false compliments and half lies from me.

'I thought we would stay with you at Christ Church, Father?' Kate voices my next thought.

He pinches his fleshy lips together and steps aside to allow a heavily-laden servant to pass. 'If this is not to your satisfaction, you would scorn my apartment.' His light laugh is unconvincing. 'I sleep high in the attics, which is barely adequate for me and two servants.'

'We were surprised how few Royalist soldiers we saw as we rode into the city.' I hand my fur muff to a maid who bears it away with a curtsey. 'We counted less than a dozen blue uniforms on our way here.'

'The city regiment is here, as are two auxiliary regiments of scholars and strangers who form protection for the city,' Father says. 'His Majesty is in Newbury at the moment.'

'He is not here?' I look at Mother, but she is busy talking to our steward, and doesn't catch my eye. 'Wouldn't that leave Oxford open to attack from the Parliament forces?'

'Attack?' Kate's eyes widen.

'Now, girls.' Father grimaces and flaps his hands. 'There's no need to worry. We have ten regiments of foot and three of horse who keep the rebels away from the city. Once the king has re-taken London, none of us will stay here long. We shall all be back at Westminster.'

'The rebels are nearby?' I ask, suddenly fearful.

'They make occasional raids on our cattle and storehouses, but never gain a real foothold.' His casual shrug does not convince me, and I doubt he believes it himself.

Meg climbs awkwardly onto a wooden settle, feet swinging as she picks at the moulding with a fingernail. 'I thought we would be at Court, Papa. With you, and the king and queen.'

I sympathise with Meg, but suppress further complaint as Cousin Henderson's baleful gaze takes in our dismayed faces, her expression made comical by a nose reddened from the cold.

'How ungrateful you are, girls. Are you not aware that every inn and attic in this city is full to the rafters, whilst we have the advantage of an entire house?'

In no mood to be chastised for ingratitude, I escape into the next room, but she calls after me.

'Never mind that sour face, Mistress Betty. Be grateful for what the good Lord and your father provide.'

I inhale through gritted teeth. Only Mother calls me Betty, and besides, how can she see my sour face? I whip around to respond, but Mother's weary expression keeps me silent.

'We'll all feel much better when we're unpacked and settled.' She ushers the girls into the hall, looking near to tears with tiredness and the dent to her pride.

My boots echo on bare boards on the upper floor, reverberating as I march along opening doors. The bedchambers are all low-ceilinged and criss-crossed with heavy, uneven beams, the tiny fireplaces so cramped, I doubt they provide much warmth.

'I'll have this one.' Nan indicates a room overlooking the neglected garden. 'Unless you would like it, Elizabeth?'

'No, I have no preference.' I fling open a door opposite. 'This one will do. It has a view of Trinity Street, and what looks like a garden beyond the wall at the far end.'

'What's in here?' Nan throws open the door of a cupboard-like room that sits beside hers, where Cousin Henderson's luggage has been piled on the floor. The chamber, if that is what it is meant to be, has a tiny window high in the wall, below which sits a low, narrow bed.

Cousin Henderson appears at Nan's shoulder, her pinched face that of a nun about to accept a cruel penance. 'It will do me very well. We all have to make sacrifices during time of war.'

Nan's giggles cease abruptly, and I bite my lip to stop a smile. I almost feel sorry for Cousin Henderson.

Chapter 4

While Mother and Cousin Henderson squabble and my sisters tease, I escape the chaos of the upper rooms and venture onto the lower floor in search of Father, picking my way over boxes and packages yet to be allocated into the already crowded space.

I discover him seated in a small parlour, the distempered walls a shade of dirty yellow, and furnished with scratched oak settles and mismatched chairs. The massive wood lintel above a stone hearth is blackened and well-used over a cold grate where ash and leaves gather.

Huddled into the largest of the nondescript chairs, Father stares at the pile of dried ash with such intensity, I experience a pang of guilt for my uncharitable behaviour upon our arrival.

I approach slowly, aware that my feet make the floorboards creak, and come to stand beside his chair. 'This will be a snug and pleasant room with the fire lit, Father,' I whisper, in an attempt to make amends. I hope he will stay with us for a while, but dare not ask.

'I am afraid this is the best room the hoose has to offer.' He slips into his native Scots accent, which tells me his spirits are low.

'Oh, well, I doubt we'll do much entertaining, in any case.'

His lips tilt into a wry smile. 'Not quite what ye were expectin', eh, Betty, my love?' He tugs the loose ends of his cloak together and shivers.

I drag a tapestry-covered stool beside his chair and perch within arm's reach of him. 'Forgive my churlishness earlier, Father. I did not mean to be short-tempered, but everything has changed so much this last year, I hardly recognise our life anymore.' What I really want to say is that I do not recognise him, but it is an emotion I cannot express.

'I've been sorely neglectful of ye all, haven't I?' he says without looking at me.

'Not through lack of regard.' I try to recapture his attention, hungry for his smiles. 'We know how demanding the king is of your time and loyalty.'

His harsh laugh explodes into the room. 'My dear, ye canna imagine what my life is like now. I keep running everything through my heed trying to see where things could ha' been different. If only Edgehill had gone better.'

'Could it have?'

'Aye. Prince Rupert wanted tae take a troop of cavalry to London tae secure it fer the king.'

'I thought Lord Essex reached there first, which is why the king had to come to Oxford instead.'

'Exactly. King Charles insisted the entire army should make an entrance, which slowed us all doon tae a crawl, and by the time we got close, our spies told us Essex was in command.'

'It's not all bad news for the king though, is it, Father? There have been victories?'

'Nay, not all. The Marquess of Newcastle occupies most of the north, and Cornwall has mostly declared for the king. Prince Rupert has seized Bristol, but the South East is held by Parliament, who gain more ground by the day.'

'When will it all end, Father?'

A door closes out in the hall and the sound of girlish laughter reaches me, but no one interrupts us.

'The country is sickened by this war, and though the people love the king, they're angry wi' him, too. There are peace riots in London, and not only from the Puritans, either. I feel they no longer care which side is the victor.'

'And you, Father. How do you feel?'

'My feelings dinna count, Betty. How can I begin tae explain what it means tae have a royal master?' His voice drops to a whisper. 'Summoned at any hour of the day or night, and duty bound tae obey every ill-conceived order, nae matter how dangerous.'

'Dangerous? What have you been commanded to do?' I hunch forward, listening.

'Ah spend days on horseback through countryside filled with Parliament soldiers who would like naught better than tae wreak their anger upon the king's servant. I deliver messages, packets of orders, and bribes that go nowhere.' He stares into a dead fire, his thoughts far away. 'Only tae be sent straight back again with more letters and incriminating documents tha' could send me tae the gallows.'

'You are His Majesty's boyhood friend. He trusts you, and has never doubted your bravery, or your faithfulness.'

'Bravery involves choice, my love. And ah have none.' His smile is wistful, and I can only guess at the memories that slide through his head behind those mournful eyes.

Perhaps, as I do, he longs for simpler days spent at Ham, when he would gather us round the fire on winter evenings to listen to tales of his childhood in Edinburgh. When his Uncle Thomas was tutor to Prince Charles, and as a boy, William Murray was put forward as his companion. In those days, Henry was Prince of Wales, a dazzling, beautiful star everyone adored, but whose death at eighteen made the sickly, stammering Charles the next king.

He sighs and props his elbow on the arm of the chair, his head against his hand to look at me askance. 'Odd how fate stepped in tae make Charles the heir, only for him to lose his sister Elizabeth to marriage with the Elector Palatine the following year. A lonely young man he was then.'

'Until the Duke of Buckingham wove his way into the king's heart,' I say.

'Aye, that he did. 'His dear Steenie' the king used tae call him.' He sniffs in disdain at the memory. 'And when an assassin's blade found that blackguard's heart, not a tear was shed apart from His Majesty's. Hah!' His short laugh holds real mirth. 'None amongst us believed Villiers had a heart.'

I was no more than a babe when a disgruntled sailor named John Felton stabbed Buckingham to death, the assassin led away to jail amid the cheers of a grateful crowd.

'You are a good king's man, Father.'

He shrugs. 'I wouldnae know how to do anything else.' He looks at me then with a mixture of censure and amusement. 'You wonder if I toy with the idea o' changing sides? Tae trade my lord for an easier life as a Presbyterian? I'm a Scot after all, and have friends in Edinburgh who might protect me.'

Shocked by this suggestion I rush to disabuse him. 'I would

34

never suggest such a thing. None of us would.'

His raised hand silences me. 'Ah jest wi' ye, ma hen. That option is ne'er open tae a man who has pledged fealty tae King Charles. My destiny is tied wi' his, though my soul shrivels when I look ahead and see the outcome o' this war.'

'What do you see?' I dread his response, but need to hear it.

For a long pause I feel he is poised to say something momentous, then his face clears and he shakes his head, as if dismissing bad thoughts. 'Ah, ignore a jaded old man, Betty. Ma vision of the future has become blurred. I willnae burden ye with it.'

'It burdens you, so I would hear it. I thought we shared everything, you and I.' Shocked to hear him describe himself thus when he is only in his forty-fourth year, I hold my breath.

'If only His Majesty would gie a little.' He holds a clenched fist to his mouth. 'Listen tae those who want what is best for the country. He doesnae have tae agree tae everything Parliament wants, simply enough to appease them.' His fist shakes as if at the invisible face of the king. 'In his eyes, to make any concession would lead tae further demands that would strip him o' his God-given power. At least, the constant whisper in his ear tells him it is so.'

I know the whisper he refers to belongs to the queen, though even in the privacy of this room, to speak such thoughts aloud could be construed as treachery. A silence falls between us again, and unable to comfort him, I move onto more sturdy ground. 'We miss you at home, Father. *I* miss you.' I grasp his clenched fist in mine and smooth my fingers over a spattering of brown spots, trying not to react to the way the skin slides loosely over the bones of his fingers. He doesn't pull away, and grateful for this rare contact, I tighten my grip.

Our relationship has always been close, a bond formed from shared interests in such subjects as religion, philosophy and mathematics. Any hugs and kisses I received were Mother's, and Father's touch was never more than a gentle resting of a hand upon my head each morning in a gesture of paternal blessing.

'I miss the mathematical puzzles we shared, Father.' His hand is cool in mine and the nails bitten to the quick. 'Those you left for me to solve while you were away. The verses you set me to complete, the French verbs to conjugate. I have had no one to talk with about the stars.' My throat closes as emotion threatens to overwhelm me. What a void his absence has left in my life during this last year.

At Ham, we were always one, he and I. He loves us all, but I know his ambition for me is every bit as fierce as if I had been a son. 'You are my heir, Elizabeth,' he would tell me often. I haven't heard that lately, and I long to be reassured of the special place I hold in his heart.

'Is there anything you wish to convey to me, Father? Some wise words you wish me to follow while we are apart?'

His grip increases on my fingers. 'As for that, you would do well tae heed your mother.'

'She frightens me sometimes with her daring.' I have never said this aloud, especially not to him, but he appears unsurprised.

His leans forward so our foreheads touch. 'Magnificent though she is, she terrifies me, too. You can learn a lot from her, my dear. Though there is one thing I entrust tae both of you. Never let the Parliament men take Ham.'

'But how-?'

His raised finger stills me. 'I've put the estate in the hands of Lord Elgin my Scottish kinsman. He's a powerful Covenanter, and Parliament is still trying to negotiate with them. The Sequestration Committee will have to submit their claim to Elgin first, and, God willing, they'll find the task too onerous tae pursue when those Scots have tied them with legal strings.' He exhales noisily, but I cannot describe the sound as a laugh.

I wonder if Mother has told him about Master Calcott, but dismiss the thought. Of course she has told him, this is one of the reasons we came to Oxford.

'Father?' My voice is little more than a whisper. 'Do you wish I had been a son?'

'Ah, my lass. Does that bother you still?' The breath of his heartfelt sigh is warm on my temple. 'I tell you every man wishes for a son tae carry his name. But this last year, when I watch so many fine young men marching off tae fight, never to return. Then, ma hen, ah'm more than thankful tae be spared such pain.' He brushes my cheek with his other hand. 'I know full well the burden ah place upon you. There is only one way tae secure the estate for you and your sisters. You must marry, Elizabeth.'

The smile I summon in response is shaky. Dare I rebel? Refuse to embark upon a marriage in order to secure Ham? His gaze meets mine and I know he expects nothing less than complete obedience. He has raised me to have good sense, and accept that marriage for me will always be for status, land and fortune. Yet I cannot help the tiny voice in my head that asks, what of love? 'D-do you have anyone in mind?'

He shifts in the chair to stretch his legs, wincing as if they pain him. A stiffness from the cold, perhaps?

'I always hoped you would marry ma cousin, Robert Moray,' he says after a moment.

I hold my breath, unsure as to what reaction he expects. My cousin Robert is fifteen years my senior, and though my intellectual equal, he is not the husband of my girlish dreams.

'A marriage of two such excellent minds would bring you great contentment,' Father continues, his fingers kneading mine gently.

'He is Sir Robert now, Father. The king knighted him, remember?'

His smile turns wistful and he continues as if I have not spoken, 'he was a confidant of Cardinal Richelieu, you know, and made a successful spy for King Charles.'

'Hush, Papa. You do not know who might be listening.' I arch an eyebrow at the thin door and thinner walls.

He waves me aside. 'I cannae hurt him further. And since Richelieu's death, his successor, Cardinal Mazarin, took a dislike to Robert. Now with King Louis dead too, and replaced by an infant king, Mazarin is virtual ruler of the country. Robert lost his influence at the French court, so he joined their army. But that spiteful Mazarin had him arrested.'

'I have always held a special fondness for Cousin Robert,' I say carefully. 'Though, he has no fortune, and do you not think he is too much of a Royalist to be safe?'

'That is ma only regret.' His deep sigh confirms it. 'That and the inconvenient fact he reclines in a Bavarian prison.'

'I will marry where and whom I have to, Father.' The promise slips from my lips with ease, and I pray silently for the strength to keep it. 'Tell me who.'

He shakes his head with genuine regret. 'Would ah had the freedom or the time to apply myself tae such a task. You will have tae trust your mother tae find you a husband.'

'I do trust her. And I shall obey her.' I give a one-shouldered shrug and a wry smile. 'Unless he is older than you, and has bad teeth.'

'Hah!' He enfolds my hand in both of his, nodding. 'Ah hope we can do better than that. Though my duty keeps me from you and your sisters, do not doubt ah would leifer be at Ham.' He sighs again and stares at the ceiling. 'My beautiful Ham, how ah miss it. But as with everything, it came tae me through the patronage of my king. That is what ah owe him, complete loyalty.'

While his thoughts turn to images of home, mine are plagued with visions of hunchbacked suitors with warts and foul breath.

Our brief communion is broken by a discreet knock on the door, and a maid enters to tell us dinner is served.

I climb slowly to my feet, reluctant to forgo his company. 'You will dine with us, won't you, Father?'

'Aye,' He slaps his knees with both hands and rises with a grunt of effort. 'Ah think the council can spare me another hour or two.'

'When will you be able to come home to Petersham?' My childlike need for my parent overrides practicalities, for I know this is a question he cannot answer.

'Ah'll not mislead ye. This fight between the king and his people will grow worse before it gets better.' His arm closes round my shoulders, while hunger and the prospect of a warm fire quickens our steps toward the enticing smells of roast meats and fresh bread that invade the hall.

'The way things are going, I fear by the time His Majesty regains his throne, much of his power may be gone.'

'Surely the rebels must be the ones to concede?'

'When it comes tae it, what else can they do?' He shrugs. 'He is, after all, their king.'

'Don't walk so fast, Elizabeth.' Nan jerks my arm. 'You know I cannot keep pace with your long stride.'

My pattens slip on the wet cobbles, and I stagger against her. The maid accompanying us leaps forward to prevent us both falling, and clinging together, the three of us collapse against a wall, giggling.

'These objects are supposed to protect me from the muck, not cause me to break my ankles.' I snap, lifting a foot to glare at the offending block of grooved wood attached to my shoe.

'This city is so dirty and unkempt.' Nan pulls her shawl tight around her shoulders as if she can keep the eye-watering smells at bay. 'Do they not clean these streets?'

I ease past a handcart piled with wrinkled vegetables well past their prime, which brings me close to the overflowing kennel that runs along the middle of the road. The body of a rat as large as a cat bobs past me in the filthy water and shuddering, I turn away. 'From what Father says, most townsfolk are employed making weapons and uniforms for the soldiers.' I chatter as we walk in an effort to distract Nan from the less pleasant sights around us. Kingston was never like this. 'I doubt they have time to worry about the state of the roads.' I wrinkle my nose and hurry past a pile of ordure, unsure whether the sharp, clinging stench it emanates is animal or human.

'What soldiers?' Nan sniffs as we turn into the deserted high street. 'We've been here for days and I've hardly seen any.'

'The king's army stayed behind to defend the town. I hear them sometimes being paraded past the Magdalen College gatehouse.'

'Can we not return home now, Elizabeth?' Nan whines. 'We have been in every shop in the High Street and I doubt we'll find more meat.' She clutches the parcel of beef shin we found close to her chest.

'If you wish.' I acquiesce with reluctance. It is a relief to be out of the crowded little house in Trinity Lane for even a short while. We are even subject to the servants' petty quarrels through the thin walls. 'We do not have far to go, the eastern gate is just ahead.' I nod to where one of the armed guards who stand sentry eyes us with bored disinterest. The other one leans against the wall, his musket propped at his side.

I slip my arm through Nan's just as a shout comes from the direction of the gate. I ignore it, my attention on a piece of sacking that has stuck between the ridges of my left patten and refuses to budge.

'Open up, or I fire!' The loud command comes again.

'What's happening, Elizabeth?' Nan tightens her hold on my arm. 'Who's shouting?'

My patten forgotten, I gather Nan and the maid closer, but can see no one other than the two sentries, both of whom look frozen with indecision.

The head and shoulders of a man in uniform appears above the ledge, his musket trained on one of the sentries and repeats his terse call to open the gate. The sentry hesitates, then makes a grab for his own musket which lies discarded against the wall. He cannot move fast enough, and before his hand closes on the butt, the man on the roof discharges his weapon. The sentry freezes, one hand still outstretched toward his musket, open-mouthed in horror as a spurt of crimson erupts between his shoulder blades.

Nan shrieks, and air is sucked from my lungs as the man's legs crumple beneath him and he slumps to the cobbles. Shock pins me to the spot, but in my head, I disparage the fool for leaving his weapon out of reach.

The second sentry is no more than a boy, and drops his musket, both hands held up in surrender.

The man on the roof jerks his weapon meaningfully.

The terrified sentry obeys and swings open the gate.

Instantly the narrow street fills with the ring of hooves on stone as horses flood through the gate, their riders holding weapons aloft and shouting in triumph.

'Roundheads!' The word leaves my mouth with a mixture of incredulity and fear.

First come the mounted men with short swords and bucket topped boots, in stout leather coats and blackened, lobster tail helmets. Foot soldiers follow close behind, matchlock muskets hoisted in their hands as they march in swift formation. The powder charges slung from strings across their shoulders click and rattle as they move.

I have to think. What to do? Cower against this wall and wait for them to spot us, or run?

Nan seems to read my thoughts. 'If they do see us, what threat are three females?' she says with surprising calm.

The second sentry is overwhelmed by three foot soldiers, one of whom raises his sword to strike.

'Look away, Nan!' I say, glad that for once she obeys me, though the man's scream is something I doubt either of us will forget.

The entrance to Trinity Street lies twenty yards behind us on the opposite side of the road. To reach it, we have to pass in front of the troops, whose horses take up most of the street between us.

'Perhaps they will pass by and not notice us,' the maid whimpers.

The sound of approaching hoof beats from the direction of the bridge banishes this feeble wish, although this time the sight of the blue coated soldiers fills me with relief, despite the fact we are still in danger, being only a few feet away. If the two columns clash here, we are at risk of being trampled by hooves or peppered with musket balls in the crossfire.

'What do we do?' Nan demands in a high-pitched squeak.

I shrink back against a house, pulling Nan and the maid with me.

The girl presses her hands to her ears and gives a low, terrified keening. 'We shall die!' she repeats over and over in a high pitched whine.

I shake her roughly and the sound stops, replaced by a volley of firing as the king's men launch themselves at the rebels in an attempt to beat them back toward the gate.

A rebel braces an arm on a garden wall and takes aim, the slow-burning fuse in his left hand poised to light the priming powder. The weapon discharges and I duck my head into Nan's shoulder.

The ball meets its mark. A grunt and a yelled oath, followed by a thump as a body hits the ground, is muffled by the stamping of hooves. Gleaming hindquarters and spurred boots pass close to our faces. A man topples from his horse no more than two feet from where we huddle against the wall, blood gushing from a slash to his stomach.

'They will cut us to pieces, Mistress!' the maid shouts in panic, huddling closer.

The stench of burnt powder stings my eyes. Frozen in shock one moment, my mind races the next. At any second a blade could slice into one of us, or a horse might fall and we shall be crushed.

'We cannot stay here, Nan.' I twist her round to face me and shout to make myself heard. 'When you see your chance, run that way across the road and make for Trinity Street.'

She looks to where I point, but does not move. Her white face stares back at me, her head moving from side to side. 'I can't-I-'

'Yes, you can!' I shake her shoulders hard, hating myself for such brutality to my gentle sister. But if we are to escape this place unscathed, she must do as I say.

A clang of metal rings close to my ear. A man screams, a horse whinnies in fright and with an angry roar, a rider takes off in pursuit of a foot soldier. Amongst the flash of blue, red and buff coloured coats, I cannot tell who has the upper hand.

Then an angel approaches in the form of a Royalist soldier, his blue coat a beacon of hope as he lopes toward us on foot, dodging between struggling, slashing bodies. He pauses, sword raised to glance both ways along the street and then back at us. 'You must leave this place, Mistress!'

'I am well aware of that, sir!' I shout back, indignation overruling my fear. 'What do you suggest?' I cock my chin at the narrow alley. 'We live in that lane there.'

A musket ball pings off the stone wall to my right, leaving a deep pink scar in the stonework in line with my eyes. I stare at it, transfixed. Seconds later, the soldier is beside me, his urgent shake of my arm pulling me from my reverie.

'Heed me, Mistress.' He screams into my face. 'The rebels are pushing towards the bridge. They are moving away from us.'

'Y-yes, I see.' My response is perfunctory, my view blocked by the backs of horses as they snort and plunge against oncoming troopers. With a brusque nod that indicates we are to move, he pushes Nan and the maid in the direction of Trinity Street. 'Go now, I will guard your back!'

Nan hesitates, and throws me a beseeching look, her pinched face stark white. I nod in encouragement and finally, she grabs the terrified maid by the arm and together, they edge across the road in a series of spurts and stops until they reach the other side.

Our soldier waves me across and I take a tentative step into the filthy road, my pattens slip and threaten to tip me into the kennel. I assume the bluecoat is about to follow, but when I look back, he has stopped to fend off a rebel, who slashes at his unguarded shoulder.

'Run! Mistress!' He yells, his eyes bulging as he swings his weapon at the approaching rebel. Grunting with the effort, his sword slices into his adversary's upper arm. Yelling in pain and rage, the rebel staggers and stumbles backwards. My rescuer shoves him hard into the wall and gestures me to keep going.

Horrified and fascinated at the same time, I tear my gaze from the red stain spreading on the rebel's sleeve, and with the soldier at my heel urging me on, trip and hop along the lane until I reach our house.

There is no sign of Nan and the maid, but the front door opens after a single knock and I tumble inside. Gasping, I collapse onto a settle, my breath shuddering more from shock than exertion. Nan and the maid huddle inside the door, both white-faced and silent. Mother appears from the rear, her frantic questions reaching me from what seems like the end of a long tunnel.

'There are Roundheads outside, Mama!' Nan gabbles in near hysteria. 'They attacked the sentries and now the street is filled with murdering soldiers.' Her breath comes fast and her hands flutter in front of her. 'We only escaped by the grace of God and this man.' She indicates the young Royalist soldier who now huddles in the shelter of the doorframe, his gaze on the altercation at the end of the street

'I am grateful to you, sir,' Mother gasps. 'Are we invaded?'

I try to stand, but my knees threaten to give way and bile rises in my throat. I feel dizzy.

I want to urge her to bolt the door, this minute, but a surge of guilt rises in me for the poor man left on the doorstep, the thought immediately replaced by another. He is a soldier, it is his duty.

Cousin Henderson appears on the stairs, the shocked faces of Kate and Meg peering round her skirts.

'Lock your doors and stay inside,' the soldier commands. 'My men and I will try to drive the rebels back outside the city gates. Pray the Lord we can do so quickly.'

'How many of them are there?' Cousin Henderson asks calmly, though her hand on Meg's shoulder shows whitened knuckles.

'I know not, Mistress.' He adjusts his hat and steps back. I notice with detached calm that his sword has blood on it. 'The Parliamentarians must know most of our troops are laying siege to Gloucester, so take their chance with our numbers depleted. It will not work because most of the city is for us.'

A loud thwack sounds close to his head as a musket ball slams into the door frame, gouging into the black wood. Another shatters a window pane and splinters of glass fall onto the tiles.

'Keep your family inside, Mistress.' The man throws over his shoulder as he turns to leave.

'Aren't you going to stay and protect us?' Kate calls out, while Nan grips the newel post, her lower lip quivering as she recites silent prayers.

The soldier grins. 'Would that I could, but my commanding officer will have me whipped if I do not return to the fray. God keep you all.' He disappears and Mother leaps forward to slam the door shut and throw the bolt.

Frozen, we stand huddled near the door, listening to the growing clamour outside.

Chapter 5

October 1643, Oxford

Our rescuer didn't leave his name, and I doubt we shall hear from him again. After a subdued supper, we retire to the rear parlour to huddle over an inadequate fire.

'Perhaps the rebels have been driven back,' Mother says, her features sharpened by the glow of our single candle. Though I suspect she says so merely to comfort us.

'Or the rebels have flooded into the city and the king's men are being overpowered,' Kate mutters, earning a glare from Cousin Henderson.

'Why hasn't Father come?' Meg whispers accusingly. 'He should be here to look after us.'

I too, am worried for him, hoping the rebels have not breached Christ Church, but dare not voice my fear.

'He is better guarded than we are,' Mother says, though whether it is relief or resentment which prompts her words, I cannot tell. If the latter, she deserves no criticism from me, as again, she is left to fend for us alone.

'He might have sent soldiers to protect us, or a message,' Kate says sulkily.

'The fact he has done neither tells me he does not fear for our welfare,' Mother chides her, always alert for disloyalty in her daughters, even if her own loyalty slips at times.

'Perhaps we should discard our silks and dress in black,' Kate offers. 'Then they'll think we are Puritans and not hurt us.'

'And suppose the Royalists win and come to our door to find a family of Puritans?' I can barely contain my contempt at her suggestion. 'They would kill or evict us on the spot.'

'Now, girls,' Mother's fierce whisper silences us. 'I will hear no more nonsense. You all heard that soldier at our door today. They will drive the rebels out, you'll see.'

Time passes, and the street falls silent. No one is brave enough to venture outside for more wood, so our fire burns down, throwing ghostly shadows into the corner of the room.

Finally, Mother pulls Meg to her feet. 'There's nothing more we can discover until morning. We may as well retire.' She beckons to Kate, who reluctantly follows her to the door.

The worst of my imagination shreds my nerves, and I know I shan't sleep, but I comply. Mother is right. What else can we do tonight?

'Do you really suppose it is over?' Nan and Cousin Henderson follow me into the hall where I fumble with the tinderbox and light a candle. 'It's been quiet for a while, I think-' The sound of heavy footfall from the street freezes my hand on the taper.

Mother halts on the stairs, Kate and Meg a step lower, as the rhythmic sound of marching grows closer.

'Hide the light, Betty!' Mother says. 'They might shoot at a light.'

Hitching my skirt with one hand, I snuff out the taper with the other and kneel on the settle beneath the window, peering through the grimy glass into the street.

'What's out there, Elizabeth?' Nan asks in a whisper from the parlour door.

'I cannot see anything.' My eyes search the darkness, but the street looks empty.

William Ball emerges from the kitchens, a look of enquiry on his face, and holding an axe, while one by one, the servants arrange themselves behind him.

'Put that down!' I order him in a fierce whisper. 'If they are rebels and see you armed, they will kill you.'

His gaze sharpens for a second, but then he slides the weapon into the cubby under the stairs.

Satisfied, I turn back to the window, willing my eyes to adjust to the gloom. 'I think there are soldiers in the lane, but I can't be sure.'

A furious pounding on the door sends me jumping back.

Kate hugs Meg to her and Nan whimpers in fright.

'Open this door in the name of Parliament!' A gruff male voice hollers through the wood.

'Quiet, girls!' Mother says, her voice low but commanding, though her warning is unnecessary, we are all frozen in fear and could not speak if we tried.

A tense moment stretches into an eternity, then the same voice growls. 'Break it down!'

'Now, good sirs,' Ball addresses the door in response to Mother's frantic signal. 'There's no need for that. I will be but a moment.' He grapples with the cumbersome bolt, but barely has he lifted the thumb catch before the door crashes back against the wall, hurling him backwards.

Boots hammer on bare boards as six Roundhead soldiers in helmets and breastplates rush inside and spread out, filling the small space. Thin candlelight throws shadows across their unsmiling faces, and glints off dull armour and belt buckles. They loom above us, big and terrifying, their faces half-hidden by the nose plates of their blackened helmets.

No one speaks as a giant of a man follows the soldiers in: an apparition in a black coat and brown breeches. A sword hangs from a leather waist belt, the sheath glittering with silver fittings beside a brace of pistols and a small, spiked axe.

On his head is a wide hat with a felt brim, but no feather, merely a plain black band. A bulging knapsack is slung over his shoulder, cross-body fashion, indicating he has collected plunder of some sort on his way here. He is not an old man, but the weathered skin and the deep lines around his mouth tell me he has spent his life outdoors.

His flat gaze slides over us each in turn, his fleshy face devoid of expression.

This man will not show mercy.

'Your name?' he snarls at last, pointing at Master Ball.

Mother steps in front of the steward, dragging Meg with her by the hand. 'You address my manservant.' Her chin lifts in defiance, though the top of her head doesn't reach the man's shoulder. 'My name is Murray, and apart from my household servants, I am alone with my four young daughters. What is your business here, sir?'

His lips curl in a half smile, as if Mother's challenge amuses him. 'I am Captain Hudd, and we are here on behalf of the Parliamentary army. 'We are searching houses for recusants!'

His casual manner sends a shiver through me. This man makes

Captain Fitton look like a courtier.

Without waiting for Mother's response, he signals to his men with a curt wave. Two soldiers stomp toward the rear of the house, while two others shove past Cousin Henderson and climb the stairs. They force a wide-eyed Kate roughly against the wall, ignoring her high-pitched squeal.

'What right have you to do so?' Mother splutters. 'When the king returns, he-'

'If the king returns,' Hudd's fleshy lips split in a sneer, 'he'll find Oxford no longer welcomes him and his cavaliers.'

Mother opens her mouth, but I smother her indignant protest with a pressure of my hand on her arm. 'You cannot argue with them, or prevent them doing what they will, Mama,' I whisper at her shoulder. 'Let them do what they have to, and then pray they'll leave.'

She swallows and nods, the muscles of her shoulder relaxing beneath my hand, though her heart must thump every bit as hard as mine.

Heavy boots pound across the floor above in what I assume is a thorough search of the bed chambers. Screams and thumps come from the kitchens, where the servants fled on the soldiers' arrival, followed by the sound of breaking pottery as pots and plates are hurled to the floor.

Captain Hudd displays no reaction, as if he has gone through this ritual many times before. He merely glares at us, dead-eyed and uncaring. I imagine him in a pulpit, with that square jaw rigid and his cold gaze directed at a congregation while he administers dire lessons in mortal sin and the evils of bishops. I try not to stare at him, but his presence offends me.

A small hand slips into mine and I give a sharp gasp, but it is only Meg. In her nightshirt with a white wool shawl spread over her narrow shoulders and a frilled cap on her head, she looks like a tiny ghost. Her hand clasps mine tight as she peers at the massive officer from the shelter of my skirt.

'What is a recusant, sir?' she asks, her high, child's voice echoing in the silent hall. She must feel safe with me as her shield, but she cannot know it is by sheer will alone I remain standing and do not

48

crumple to the floor in a faint.

'Hey?' His eyes narrow and his gaze alights on my youngest sister. Meg blinks back at him, more curious than afraid. Her reddish fair hair falls to her waist beneath her nightcap, its ribbons tied under her pointed chin.

'A well brought-up, pious child would not have to ask that question.' His sneer betrays his apparent discomfort.

'Are you angry because you have no answer to my question, sir?'

'Margaret!' I whisper fiercely, kneading her fingers. 'Hold your tongue.' Yet at the same time pride fills me. She is indeed a Murray.

'But I wish to know,' she persists, fixing him with her innocent stare.

The officer bends at the waist and beckons her forward.

Mother gives a tiny gasp as Meg tugs away from me and stands before him, her head level with his.

'So, you wants to know what a recusant is?' His accent is one I do not recognise, but his words sit thick on his tongue. 'Have you a rosary in your box of trinkets, young maid?' His thick lips peel back from slightly yellowed teeth. 'Do ye believe the sacrament turns to blood and flesh?'

'How dare you, sir!' Mother's chest heaves and she holds her arms outstretched as if about to grab Meg and drag her backwards.

Hudd raises a hand the size of a shovel. 'Let the girl answer.'

Mother's hands freeze and she clenches them instead, chin quivering, and opposite me, Cousin Henderson's lips move in silent prayer. My teeth grip the inside of my cheek until I taste blood, and my breathing grows shallow.

Take care what you say, little sister.

He crouches low, his face close to Meg's. 'Then tell me true, little mistress. Do you gather with your mother and sisters in a private chapel to pray, or do you worship in a church like God-fearing souls?'

Meg shakes her head. 'I haven't been to church since we left Richmond, sir.'

A light of triumph appears in the officer's eyes, and he mouths the word 'recusant.' His head lifts and he levels his gaze at Mother.

'No!' Mother rushes to explain. 'We arrived from London only a few days ago, and the Sabbath is yet three days away.'

'We shall attend Anglican services on Sunday,' I add, frantically trying to recall the name of the church we passed earlier in the day. Then it comes to me. 'St Peters. Beside the East Gate.'

'Humph!' He places both massive hands on his knees and pushes himself upright as his men descend the stairs. The one in front gives a brief, but meaningful shake of his head. The two others appear from the rear with broad smiles, probably put there by the sport they have had in our kitchens with the serving girls. At one look from their superior, their mirth is wiped away, and they display similar disappointment. 'Nothing, sir,' one says.

My heartbeat slowly returns to normal, and then I realise the front door has been open all this time, and I am shivering from the cold.

Mother bustles forward and wraps Meg in her ample arms. 'If you've quite finished, sir. May I take this poor child to bed now?'

The poor child, however, hasn't finished. She turns to look at him from the bottom step, one small hand on the newel post and the other held in Mother's. 'Why does God mind so much where I worship Him?'

Captain Hudd looks at her over his shoulder. He has his back to me, so I cannot see his face. A pity, for I would give our week's candle allowance to see his expression just then, but I have to content myself with his dismissive snarl. The only response it seems little Meg shall receive.

A dozen feet pound the floor in marching rhythm as his men file out into the street. I retrieve my candle from the window sill, and for a heart-stopping second, the officer's bulk returns to fill the doorframe. Then with a final sour glare at me, he is gone.

I wonder what I have done to deserve that look of hatred, until I catch my reflection in the looking glass by the front door which reflects the wide smile on my face.

* * *

The knock on our door the following evening holds none of the urgency of the previous night.

'Forgive me for not coming to you sooner, my dears. But the city is in chaos.' Father stomps inside, sweeps off his cloak and pushes it into Ball's waiting hands.

'We are aware of that, Husband.' Mother draws herself to her full height, her ample chest heaving. 'I had four frightened girls to comfort after a visit from Roundhead soldiers last evening. We spent a dreadful night, and have not dared step outside all day. Our food stocks are low, and we-'

'I wasn't that frightened,' I interrupt firmly.

'Beg pardon, my dear?' Mother gives me a sideways glare. 'If that is so, then why did you share Nan's bed last night?'

'We were both cold, Mama.' I bustle importantly from table to dresser and back again, moving items that do not need attention. 'The fires had to be dampened early because there is little fuel.'

I am reluctant to admit how Captain Hudd upset me, or that leering men in blackened helmets filled my dreams, demanding I pray aloud. Faces that laughed in a humourless way I did not really understand. What disturbed me the most, was that I was naked before them.

'Praise the Lord ye are all unharmed.' Father enters the parlour, where we follow and arrange ourselves on stools and chairs round our first fire of the day. 'I would hae come earlier, but nae one dared venture onto the streets until the fighting stopped.' He examines our faces one by one, but no one speaks. 'Surely ye see there was noth'in more I could hae done?'

Mother remains silent, her lips clamped into a thin line. I sympathise, but cannot bring myself to chastise Father for his apparent neglect. Perhaps he really was unable to come to us.

'It seems,' Father flicks up the back of his long coat and sits, 'a small troop o' Parliament soldiers took advantage of lax security at the east gate and attempted tae seize the city.'

'That much we are aware of.' Mother plumps onto a chair with ill-concealed annoyance.

'We saw men killed in the street!' Nan's voice is high with remembered horror. 'Musket balls flew around us and there was blood-'

'Enough, Nan.' Mother gives a tiny shake of her head, and flicks a meaningful look at Margaret.

'They searched other houses for recusants, you weren't the only ones.' Father appears to think we would find this reassuring, and looks surprised when we are not. 'I doubt they'll be back.'

'Why were they not prevented from entering the city?' Mother says, disgruntled.

A vision of the shot sentry flashes into my head, and I blink hard to clear it.

Father looks sheepish, as if forced to admit something he has thus far avoided. 'The Mayor fled last night and some of the city councillors offered nae resistance to the incoming rebels.'

'Does this mean Oxford is in the hands of Parliament now, Father?' Kate asks, prompting cries of dismay from us all.

'Not at all, my dears. There were a few skirmishes, that is all. However the rebels have dared to fasten the city gates against the return of Prince Rupert, but we'll have them open again before the day is out, you'll see.'

'Is the prince on his way back to Oxford?' I ask from my precarious perch on a wobbly stool; the only seat left. Cousin Henderson stands behind them like a hovering crow, her nervous fingers picking at her skirt.

'I will try tae explain,' Father says, though his expression is doubtful. 'His Majesty planned to re-take London with three offensives. Lord Newcastle from Yorkshire, Sir Ralph Hopton from the West Country, and Prince Rupert and the king from here in Oxford.' He studies our faces in turn, perhaps to gauge whether we understand or not. 'Newcastle did well in the north,' he continues, 'and Fairfax was forced to seek refuge in Hull. Hopton made good progress through Devon, and Prince Rupert captured Bristol, having already beaten Lord Essex further west.'

'So the king has the upper hand?' I say, halting him mid-sentence.

'Well.' He fiddles with his lace collar, which I recognise as the same one he wore on his last visit, the stains still visible. 'The king's men dinna fight well when taken too far from their homes.' He lifts both hands in resignation. 'With victory in sight, they prefer to

52

remain on familiar ground. The Parliament garrison holds out at Plymouth, and makes threats tae the families the Royalists left behind. What with the northern army turning back at Lincoln, the plan has become fragmented.'

Now bored, Meg bounces on the settle and Mother checks her, a finger pressed to her lips.

'Ah'm not makin' myself clear am I?' Father smiles at the chastened Meg, while Kate frowns, confused.

I exchange a look with Nan, but she too looks bewildered.

'Father,' I say gently, 'Such details are a little complicated for some of us.' I do not count myself, for I have no problem following what he says. 'Simply tell us what this means for the king?'

He nods, relieved. 'The king has had to abandon his plan to re-capture London.'

'Is that why he marched to Gloucester?' I ask calmly, inwardly frustrated by men who throw away their advantage and reduce their victory to nothing. If I were a man, I would fight until every town, not simply my own, was in Royalist hands.

'He did indeed, and the siege was hard, I hear.'

'All sieges are hard. That does not exonerate the royal army.' I cannot keep the scorn from my voice. 'You mean they failed.'

'Betty!' Mother admonishes me but I am in no mood to be quiet.

'The intent was to control the River Severn,' Father says, without a trace of Mother's scorn. 'But when Lord Essex called out the trained bands, the royal army was forced to withdraw.' His shoulders slump, and I know he has more bad news. 'They are now bound for Newbury, where a tougher battle awaits.'

'You mean they retreated?' I say, shocked.

Mother's furious glare flits from me to the two younger girls and I mouth an apology at my outburst.

'How do you think Prince Rupert will fare at Newbury?' Nan asks.

'Who knows?' Father's shrug shows his disappointment must be as great as His Majesty's. 'The prince is a more prudent general than his detractors allow, but we are short of both ammunition and cannon shot.'

'Ought I to take the girls home to Ham, my dear?' Mother asks.

Father frowns, thinking. After a pause, he shakes his head. 'I doubt the route back to Richmond will be free of trouble. You would do well to stay here until we have news from Newbury.' He slaps his knees and rises in a well-worn gesture of dismissal. 'I must get back. The council meets tonight at Oriel College. The Parliament soldiers disarmed the university men and confiscated their plate.' He holds up a hand. 'But dinna worry. Our troops intend to reverse both those impertinences before the king returns.'

My sisters crowd around him and after a flurry of enthusiastic hugs and farewell kisses, Mother escorts him out.

The door closes, and I slump onto my stool in front of the indifferent fire, both arms wrapped around my midriff, unable to stop myself shivering.

Suppose Father is wrong and when the king returns to Oxford, the rebel numbers have grown and the gates remain shut against him? Are we to be trapped here at the mercy of the rebels?

'Elizabeth?' Nan's voice at the door makes me jump. 'If you intend to share my room again tonight, oblige me by coming to bed now. I have no wish to be woken by your icy feet.'

Chapter 6

October 1643

'Why could we not go out to greet the king when he rode into the city?' Meg's high, childish voice rises in petulance as she impedes Father's attempts to greet me at the front door.

'You know perfectly well that isn't possible while the rebels still wait for an opportunity to sneak through the gates,' Cousin Henderson says, disentangling Meg from his arms and ushering her into the dining room.

Normally, I would be the first to disagree, but the previous day, I heard shots coming from the Magdalen College field at the end of our lane. Shots that sounded nothing like a drill.

'Their attempts tae harass us grow less each day.' Father settles himself at the head of the table where dented pewter plates show their mistreatment at the hands of the Roundheads. 'Now the king is back, we have ample troops tae keep them at bay. Master Dennis, the new Mayor, is more sympathetic toward us than the last incumbent. Let's hope he's also more amenable tae the king's instructions.'

'I imagine His Majesty was less than pleased to find Oxford full of rebels and the gates fastened shut,' Cousin Henderson says. 'Will the fortifications be strengthened and a curfew instigated?'

I look up at her with interest. For someone whose time is spent immersed in the trivia of domesticity, her inquiry is well thought out. It appears I have underestimated her intellect. I resolve to push aside my lingering jealousy of Mother's regard for this plain Scots cousin; we have need of loyalty such as hers now.

'That situation has been rectified.' Father's appreciative smile makes Cousin Henderson blush.

Mother supervises the arrangement of the table, though there are few choices. The acquisition of fresh food is always a problem, and dinner tonight is obtained from a local ordinary.

After grace is said, Mother doles out lukewarm beef stew and onions, the meat heavily marbled with fat and gristle. At least the bread is plentiful, delivered from the royal bake house that morning. I sink my teeth hungrily into the soft dough, only half-listening as Father explains that the king has declared the Westminster Commons illegal.

'He has commanded the members must attend an Oxford Parliament in January.' He exhales in a long sigh that touches my heart with its sadness.

'You don't think they will come, do you?' I say gently. My gaze drifts to a small rip in the lace at his cuff, and his nails are dirty.

'I doubt it, nay, and many will have grievances to air, and demands of their own.'

'Isn't that what a king does, Father? Listen to his subjects' complaints?' Kate says, without a trace of irony.

'King Charles listens tae a privileged few.' Father's superior smile shows he considers himself amongst that company. 'Though whoever speaks last tends to make the most impression.'

'That's somewhat indiscreet of you, my dear.' Mother's darting glance goes to the door and back.

'I doubt anyone would bother to listen at the window, Mama.' I attempt a light-hearted joke as I chew, but it is only bravado. I too imagine black-clothed listeners at every door. I discard the stringy beef that has congealed in a pool of grease on my plate and reach for more bread.

'One never knows.' Father whips the cloth from his shoulder and wipes his hands. 'Our troops do well to keep the Roundheads out of the inner city, but there are pockets of resistance.'

Mother fiddles with a ringlet beside her cheek, a sure sign of nerves. 'This unpleasantness must end soon, I've heard nothing to indicate the king is not beloved.'

'Thass true.' Father looks thoughtful. 'Although no' everyone finds the rebels unwelcome. His Majesty's extortionate demands for food and ordnance where none is to be had causes constant disquiet. Some townsmen have offered their services as guards for the Roundheads. Scuffles between the two sides persist, so girls, you must avoid the Carfax.'

Mother shoots me a warning look I pretend not to see. The concept of staying within these walls through a cold winter is a dismal prospect.

'There was a fight there yesterday,' Father goes on. 'One of our soldiers was badly wounded. The man may lose his leg. I suggest you remain on this side of the river. The closer you are tae Christ Church, the safer I will feel.'

'I wish we had not come to Oxford at all,' Nan mumbles over her plate.

Father darts a look at Mother. 'I sent a message suggesting your visit here was delayed until we were more secure, but your dear mither insisted.'

'I received no message,' Mother replies, her expression bland.

I frown, recalling no mention that Oxford was in imminent danger from a rebel attack when we planned this journey. But then, the Sequestration Committee is no less a threat to us in Richmond.

The only sounds in the room are chinks of knives against plates and an occasional cough, our eyes cast down to the indifferent food no one is eager to consume.

'I must return to Christ Church.' Father's chair scrapes back, the sound harsh in the silence. 'No, do not look at me like that, girls. You'll be pleased to hear that now the Roundheads are subdued, His Majesty has planned a soiree tomorrow evening, and we are invited.'

At last my mood lifts, and I relax back in my chair. 'We've been here two weeks and thus far have not seen anyone!'

'I imagine there are many who feel as you do, Betty.' Mother pats my hand. 'A little social discourse will benefit us all.' Her smile disappears and a frown creases her brow. 'Although I do not think Katherine should attend.'

'Why should I not, Mama?' Kate's shrill protest stills the sudden excited chatter.

'You are not yet fourteen,' Mother says. 'I insist you remain here with Meg and Cousin Henderson. You are too young to witness the actions of the more brazen Court females.'

I raise my napkin to conceal a smile, recalling a Puritan pamphlet brought into the house by one of the servants that depicted a crudely drawn cartoon of Prince Rupert and the Duchess of Richmond.

'Something amuses you, Betty?' Father snaps.

I shake my head, and he narrows his eyes at me before continuing. 'Protecting the girls merely keeps them ignorant, my dear. However, if that is your decision, I will abide by it.' Having absolved himself of the responsibility, he bows and quits the room.

'There, you see! Father sees no harm in me being there!' Kate wipes damson juice from her chin.

'Your father,' Mother glares at each of us in turn, 'sees what he wants to see. You younger girls will stay here with Cousin Henderson and read the prayers you failed to learn on the Lord's day.'

While Kate complains and Mother holds to her word, I toy with a broken walnut shell on my plate and let my attention wander.

Tomorrow, I shall dress in my best silk gown for my presentation to the king and queen. With a shiver of pleasure, I anticipate a hall filled with brave cavaliers who risk their lives to fight for the king's cause. My next thought is how I shall discern those young men who have lost their fortunes from those likely to keep their estates. The latter I am eager to become acquainted with, the former are of no use to me if I hope to keep Ham away from the Parliament men.

* * *

Our carriage joins the queue of vehicles lining the High Street, where the pavements are four abreast with walkers, amongst whom stride soldiers in breeches and caps of blue and red, declaring their loyalty to the king.

In St Aldgate we are halted by heavy traffic, and unable to do anything but wait, I tap my fingers impatiently against the window frame. On the street beside me, a handsome man with flowing dark hair lounges against a wall. He does not wear a uniform, or at least none I recognise. He catches my eye, and embarrassed to be caught staring, I pull back.

He signals to his two companions and approaches our carriage, his face inches from mine on the other side of the window. He dips into a low bow and doffs a feathered hat that promptly slips from his hand and rolls into the gutter. As he bends to retrieve it, his sword clangs off the wall of the building behind him, which turns his nonchalant stride into a skip and stagger.

Aware Mother is watching this undignified display, I conceal a laugh behind my fan.

The gallant makes a vain attempt to lift a foot onto the step. Swaying unsteadily, he abandons the attempt. 'Where, might I ashk, is such a bevy of beauty bound?' The alliteration is too much for him and he mashes the words together, although his voice is cultured and deep.

'Be off with you. Rogues!' Mother snaps through the leather flap, then shouts to our driver to continue, despite that he is powerless to obey by the volume of traffic.

His two companions attempt to hold back the first man, issuing apologies and excuses for their friend. Judging by their exaggerated movements, the three are evidently quite drunk.

'Really!' Nan says, aghast. 'And it not yet six of the clock.'

The first man shrugs off his friends and makes a fresh attack on our carriage, but is again hauled backwards, while his friends gesticulate at me with apologies, waves and winks.

The breeze from Mother's fluttering fan intensifies. 'I am sorely afraid, girls, this will not be your first encounter with such creatures. I fear war has affected all young men, and not for the better.' High colour tinges her round cheeks. 'I cannot condone such behaviour, despite the fact that some of the best families in the country have been virtually ruined by the demands of Parliament.'

I detect worry in her eyes. Does she envisage such a fate for the Murrays? The image of Father's shabby appearance returns, and the ever-present question of money nags at the back of my mind.

Rogues? Perhaps. But how exciting this sojourn in Oxford will prove to be if all the king's men are so eager for our company.

I twitch back the flap enough to give me a view of the road. The young men's attentions have turned to two ladies in heavy cloaks with fur-lined hoods. Neither looks to be the sort of woman one would see on a public street, yet no maids accompany them.

Mother plucks at my sleeve. 'Do not stare at those reprobates, you'll only encourage them.'

'It is not they who interest me, Mama. Do you not think it strange those young ladies are unaccompanied?'

Mother balances her chin on her hand, following my gaze. 'Hmm. I recognise one of them as Lady Isabella Thynne, the daughter of Earl Holland. She married Sir James Thynne when she was barely out of the schoolroom.' Her glance at me intimates I have failed miserably by reaching seventeen and am not yet betrothed. 'It is indeed curious that she is on foot, and without an escort.'

'As a married woman surely she is allowed such freedoms?' I say a little enviously.

'Apparently so, and with carriages so scarce, she may have no choice but to walk.'

'We would get there quicker if we walked,' Nan mumbles, staring morosely out of her side of the coach.

I stop listening, my thoughts on Lady Isabella, envious of her superior height, which is such an advantage if one wishes to be noticed. She is quite beautiful, with a cloud of curly hair and an unconcerned air about her as if it is of no business but hers that she walks virtually alone on city streets. Her look is one I long to imitate - a mixture of affronted disdain and a hint of sensuality.

As she draws level with the three inebriated young men, I cannot look away. Surely they would not dare approach her? The thought has only that second formed, before our erstwhile admirers back away from her withering stare, the leading one the recipient of a flick of her closed fan across a hand that had the temerity to grasp hers. Her companion is equally disdainful, refusing even to grace the men with a look as the pair glide past our carriage and along the street.

I hope their direction is to the king's soiree, for I intend to seek an introduction to these two ladies. If Father is right and the rules of society are wholly abandoned in this city, I may need an ally or two to steer me through its more dangerous waters.

At Christ Church, we join a queue of guests in a chill corridor outside the reception hall. A footman takes our names with a sneer that tells me he would like to refuse us entry, but does not have the authority. With a sniff and a toss of his head, he minces before us and holds open the door to a long room, bowing as we pass through.

An effort has been made to transform an ecclesiastical style building into a courtly hall with portraits hung on the plain, panelled walls. A vast fire at one end goes some way to remove the winter chill, while a line of footmen hand out warmed spiced wine from tarnished trays.

A mixture of cinnamon, civet and male sweat lodges in my throat. We edge further inside and the stench increases, overlaid by heavy perfumes that fail to hide the more earthy smells beneath, but I refuse to recoil. If this is the aroma of power and ambition, I shall have to learn to live with it.

There is no sign of Father, so I wait with Mother and Nan, acknowledging familiar faces that file past, though most I have never seen before, united in an intense study of the door through which the king and queen shall appear.

A figure appears at Mother's shoulder, and my nose instinctively wrinkles at the musty, damp odour that emanates from his coat.

'My dear, Mistress Murray, in the absence of your husband, do allow me to act as your escort.'

'How kind, sir.' Mother blushes like a girl beneath his courtly manners.

The gentleman is not known to me, and as if he reads my thoughts, he grasps my hand in his warm, dry one and raises it to his lips.

'Sir John Harrison, at your service.' His bow halts halfway, as if he suffers from stiffness of the joints, though his lingering kiss is flirtatious. At close quarters, the lace at his sleeve looks yellowed. The shirt beneath his short coat displays food stains and his left shoe is split near the toe.

'I am surprised to see you back in Oxford so soon after your sojourn here in the spring, Mistress Murray,' Sir John addresses Mother. 'Such a tragedy that we have been confined to barracks, as it were, with the recent troubles.'

'Indeed, sir,' Mother replies. 'I brought my daughters here for the winter, but we have hardly set foot outside the house since arriving.' Mother lifts a hand to indicate the occupants of the room. 'I am distressed to see such changes in old friends.'

'You will find a great deal that is not as one would expect, my lady, nor what one might wish for.' His sad smile evokes my pity for this man has obviously enjoyed better days. A sense of quiet desperation pervades this overheated room, and despite my excitement at the prospect of the evening, I am strangely uneasy.

Sir John's gaze shifts to a point over my head, and his florid face relaxes into an expression of pure pleasure. 'Ah, my own daughters are here.'

I arrange my face in a welcoming smile and turn, coming face to face with one of the young ladies I saw walking toward the gates.

'Ann, Margaret, my dears.' Our new acquaintance beckons them closer. 'I would like to present you to Mistress Murray and her delightful daughters, Elizabeth and Anne.'

The sleeves of Ann Harrison's sage green gown reveal a soft yellow silk lining through artistic slashes, adding warmth to her eyes and glossy hair. The fact the garment is clearly not new does not distract from her charm. In some ways, it makes my gold silk appear overblown and extravagant.

'I am honoured,' she says, clasping both my hands in hers as if she had lived for this moment.

An indomitable spirit seems to shine from her clear brown eyes. Her pert mouth strikes me as the sort never pulled down in sulks. She looks to be the sort for whom nothing could dampen her animation and enthusiasm for life.

I accept her sister's equally enthusiastic greeting, but continually find myself drawn to Ann. She surveys the company with bright, intelligent eyes as if seeking someone of special interest. Her ringlets swing from side to side, and her feet shift in impatience as if she cannot keep still. 'Elizabeth, I insist upon introducing you to some people, although I am sure you know many here already.' Without waiting for my response, she drags me across the room.

'Is it proper for ladies to conduct introductions?' I whisper as we join a jostling crowd, whose focus of attention I am too short to see.

'Oxford is not as formal as London.' She snaps open her fan and gives a charming shrug. 'One may talk to whomever one wishes, for are we not all united by a common cause? Besides, of late we are starved of society. Your presence is doubly welcome.'

'Is it true that many of those here have lost fortunes due to their loyalty to the king?' I ask, prompted by the shabby coats and mended skirts that brush past me.

'Indeed, but there are worse losses than fortune.' Ann's lovely eyes cloud. 'My-ah, my brother William suffered an injury when his horse was shot from beneath him during a skirmish against Lord Essex.'

'My sympathies, Mistress. Was he badly hurt?'

'We thought not, at first, for he appeared to have no more than a dark bruise to his side. But he fevered and writhed in pain for days before he died.' She blinks rapidly. 'We buried him here.'

Not knowing what to say, I stare awkwardly at my feet. When I look up again, her bright smile reveals she requires neither comfort, nor condolences.

'Of course, Papa has been beggared by the war,' she whispers behind her fan. I fear I shall never step inside Montague House, our home in Bishopsgate Street again. It was seized, and Father taken prisoner.'

Instant fear for my own parent rises in my throat, threatening to choke me. I shoot a glance in the direction of my mother, reassured to see her smiling at Master Harrison.

'How did he escape?' I ask, the reason for his down-at-heel appearance clear.

'The soldiers demanded he hand over some writings he had in his possession relating to public revenue.' Ann bounces on tiptoe to see over heads. 'When he excused himself to fetch them, he slipped through a rear door.'

'He took a grave risk.' My gaze drifts to Master Harrison again. He looks so gentle, almost frail. Not the sort of man one would expect to defy a troop of armed Roundheads.

Ann leans closer to whisper. 'They threatened to put him on board a ship and send him to the plantations. Instead, he fled here and sent for Margaret and me. We arrived with no more clothes than we carried in our cloak bags.' The fan comes into play again, and her eyes twinkle above it. I detect steel beneath her light words, as if the pain is dimmed but harsher memories remain.

Shame warms my cheeks, and I dare not mention that Mother and I arrived with two carriages and fourteen servants, yet still I complain about our accommodations.

'Some days I wish we had stayed in London.' Ann sighs. 'Roundheads or no. Here, our circumstances force us to lodge over a baker's shop in a cramped garret, with scarcely any clothes or money. It's quite horrid.' Her misery does not last long, and the pert smile returns as she greets an acquaintance. 'In fact,' she continues, when the newcomers pass on, 'Father refused a baronetcy, saying he was too poor these days to do the rank justice.'

This admission has me stammering regret, but Ann seems not to hear me and waves to someone on the other side of the room. One unfamiliar face drifts away and another takes his place, though I find it impossible to recall their names.

Tightening her grip on my arm, Ann steers me through the crowds until we reach the same lady whom Mother identified earlier.

'Allow me to present Lady Isabella Thynne,' she says, breathless with pride.

Younger than I first thought, Lady Isabella's blue eyes take in everything with mildly bored indifference.

'I declare, Ann.' Lady Isabella waves her fan lazily. 'Should His Majesty fail to arrive in the next half hour, I swear I will quit the company.'

'You are too easily bored, Bella. Allow me to brighten your evening with new and delightful company. This is Elizabeth Murray, come from London.'

Lady Isabella's limpid gaze swings toward me, and transforms instantly into angelic prettiness.

'Ann, you're a marvel. A new and lovely face to chatter to. Fie, I have bored the stays off all these ladies here.' She tucks a slender arm beneath mine. 'Let us take a turn of the room.'

With no choice but to acquiesce, I am again steered around the floor, while bodies bump against us at every step. Lady Isabella works the room with aplomb, gliding on silent feet to bestow a gentle touch here and a smile there. Her long fingers linger on a cheek, or an arm, her eyes bright and deep as if the person before her commands her whole attention.

Is it any wonder she is so admired and gallants write poetry in her honour? My own beauty is of a different sort; borne of good health, a youthful glow to my skin and unusually good teeth, not to mention a grace developed with the help of a French dancing master.

I decide to waste no time envying Lady Isabella, for looks as startling as hers will surely goad her into unwise choices and reckless behaviour. Whereas mine shall be the means to obtain what I want, rather than my becoming the willing slave of handsome men.

'Do tell me the news from London.' Lady Isabella leans sideways to speak into my ear. 'But I have no wish to hear about those odious Roundheads.'

'My home is in Ham, my lady, some fourteen miles from-'

A fanfare of trumpets smothers my response. The crowd swivels as one toward the far end of the room, to where two footmen swing open a set of high, double doors. On the threshold stands the diminutive figure of the king. His beard trimmed to sharpness, the blue ribbon of the Order of the Garter across his narrow chest. My heart seizes at the dark shadows beneath his eyes. He has aged since I last saw him.

In a russet silk gown, with her tiny neck encircled with pearls, the queen follows her husband, flanked by her two eldest sons.

The royal procession moves forward to a fanfare, and as one, all heads in the room lower and a sea of skirts dip and rustle in homage to our sovereign. After the required pause, I lift my head again, while the king's gaze rests on a spot high on the opposite wall. I recognise this ploy. A trick born of his natural shyness as opposed to a wish to detach himself from the company, though his aloof manners can be disconcerting to those who do not know him well.

Prince Charles is less reserved, nodding and smiling at familiar faces in the crowd. At least a head taller than his royal father, but with the same dark and sultry looks. An old soul hides behind those magnificent Stuart eyes. But then is it little wonder? In his thirteen years, he has faced more than many men should ever see.

Beside him is Prince James, younger, shorter and more slender. With his fresh complexion and abundant light brown hair cascading over his shoulders, he might be a handsome boy without the superior sneer that pinches his long features.

Several figures push forward and are greeted by the royal entourage with condescending smiles. A man in a green doublet with dirty fair hair hands a leather pouch to a stout figure in black who stands behind the king. I recognise the second man as Edward Hyde, the king's closest adviser and someone not beloved of my father.

Hyde weighs the pouch in his hand and whispers something to His Majesty, who barely gives the object a glance, though he aims a slight nod at the giver. Now redundant, the fair-haired man is instantly jostled away from the royal presence.

'Now there's a pretty face that is familiar to me,' a male voice speaks softly at my shoulder.

I turn and, instantly dip into another deep curtsey. 'Your Highness.'

Chapter 7

'My dear Mistress Murray, welcome to our poor court.' Prince Rupert lifts my hand and brushes my knuckles with his lips. I cannot help noticing all eyes are drawn to his chiselled, Stuart good looks, though his smile remains on me.

His curly dark hair flows over the shoulders of his midnight black suit, its starkness broken only by a silver lace collar. A scarlet sash encircles his boyish waist, and beneath his aquiline nose sits a thin moustache that begs to be touched.

While my heart beats faster, I scorn myself for being so easily affected. Every woman in this room simpers for a look from this Palatine god, no matter how brief. Reason enough for me not to clamour to be one of them.

'A somewhat sad court I find, Your Highness.' I glance past him to where Sir Edward Hyde whispers earnestly into the king's ear, though His Majesty stares into the fire as if the conversation is of scant interest. The Chancellor's smooth face and penetrating brown eyes give an impression of easy charm, but I know him to be ambitious and cunning.

'Why should you think so?' The prince asks, bringing my attention back to him. 'Our victories have been sound in Yorkshire and Bath, though Newbury was less decisive.' He gives a dismissive sniff. 'But once my brother is fully recovered, we shall enter into the fray again.'

'And how *is* dear Prince Maurice?' Lady Isabella makes to tap him on the shoulder with her closed fan though no contact is made. 'Is he still laid low with the typhus?'

'He is weak, but the chirurgeons expect a complete recovery. Thank you for your concern, Lady Isabella.' He executes a gallant bow, more, I suspect, for the admiration of the watching crowd than his already entranced audience.

'And where do your travels take you in your service of the king, sir?' A light of mischief invades Ann Harrison's eyes.

I listen closely, wondering if secrets are about to be revealed and if he will succumb to the urge to boast of his achievements. His glance sweeps the room before he leans forward conspiratorially. 'Take full advantage of my presence here, ladies. For my cousin Charles has made a settlement with the Irish Confederates. Some fifteen thousand troops are gathering in Chester as I speak.'

'Catholics?' Lady Isabella's expression is sharp with renewed interest. 'Is that wise, sir?'

The prince's dark, arched brows lift. 'His Majesty has agreed to repeal anti-Catholic laws in exchange for Owen O'Neill's help.'

'Would that not encourage Papism?' Lady Isabella's shocked face must mirror my own.

Prince Rupert gives his throaty, sensual laugh. 'Have no fear, my uncle has no plans to make the country an instrument of Rome.' He glances at the queen and away again. 'No matter that it may be the dearest hope of some.'

I wonder at his flash of animosity, then recall that he escorted Queen Henrietta Maria and her continental army from York. Had Her Majesty agreed to certain conditions under which their help was pledged? Or had Father's gossip proved true, and Prince Rupert had quarrelled with virtually every member of her retinue?

'Ah yes, our dear queen,' he says thoughtfully. 'I confess, I have altered my opinion of her since our return from France. She is a more courageous soldier than ever I imagined.'

'Really? In what way?' There is nothing I like more, than for a man to admit he has misjudged a woman's cleverness.

'Did you not hear?' Lady Isabella resumes her superior air, and regards me down her nose, a stance most people take to meet my gaze. 'Her Majesty's ship was driven back to port by a terrible storm. Her party had to take to a fishing smack, and were so bruised and sore from the ordeal, they had to be carried ashore.'

I look to the prince for confirmation of this story, but his attention has strayed to a lady in peach satin who saunters by, her flirtatious eyes fixed on his face.

'She must be relieved to be reunited with His Majesty,' I say, fearing he will withdraw from me before my curiosity is satisfied.

The lady in peach is claimed by another and Prince Rupert turns back to me. 'More likely she didn't trust him to stand firm when he was out of her sight. And her lapdog Henry Jermyn got a peerage for his trouble.' He nods toward the man who hovers at the queen's elbow.

The fact he is not on friendly terms with his aunt-by-marriage intrigues me. Does she distrust him for his Protestantism, as most Catholics do, or is he perhaps too beloved of her husband? I would be interested to know.

'Someone else of whom you have a low opinion, Your Highness?' I say, unable to resist teasing him. He reacts so well; with a ducking of his head and a slight flush of his skin before the defiant smile appears.

'I am a soldier, not a courtier, or a simpering whisperer in compliant ears.'

'Perhaps you should learn to be both, sir.' Emboldened by his obvious discomfort, I continue. 'Then you would not make so many enemies.'

A flash of flint enters his eyes and I regret my forthrightness. He is after all, of royal blood and will not welcome criticism from a daughter of a Gentleman of the Bedchamber. Before I can summon an apologetic response, warmth returns to his expression.

'Perhaps you are right. However, should you repeat as much, my dear Mistress Murray, I shall hotly deny it.'

'Every lady in this room will cry into her pillow until you return to us safely.' Lady Isabella splays the ivory spars of her fan with a flick of her wrist and turns away, apparently bored with our conversation. Or perhaps she thinks I monopolise the prince?

'Flatterer!' The dark Stuart eyes flash again, prompting a sigh or two from a circle of female observers. 'And what of the divine Elizabeth?' The hooded gaze settles on me again. 'Shall you also pine while I fight to secure the country for your sovereign?'

'I admire your bravery, Your Highness, and indeed, my prayers go with you.' I stare up at him, aware I pander to his vanity. The effect those magnificent Stuart eyes have on my blood disturbs me, though his words concern me more. Has the king made a pact with the Devil to free us from Parliament control? Or as Father said, will the king agree to any terms put forward one day, only to change his mind later? If so, Owen O'Neill and his Irish army will be sorely disappointed, perhaps vengeful.

I shiver in my revealing gown, though not from cold, for the press of bodies and the tang of male sweat make the overheated room airless.

Prince Rupert leans closer, his wine-tinged breath an indication his tongue is becoming loose. 'Our spies tell us that despite being racked with sickness, the Puritan rebel leader John Pym has signed a pact with the Scots Covenanters, who have agreed to bring an army into England against us in exchange for religious reform.' He strokes my bare arm in an intimacy I did not invite before his hand drifts to my neck.

I paste on a smile and force myself to relax. I am told he is a man unaccustomed to rejection, and protestations of female modesty from me would appear tedious.

'What sort of reform?' I take a step back, thus putting myself out of his reach.

He shrugs, sweeps another glass of wine from a passing tray and downs half the contents in a single gulp. 'To bring Presbyterianism into England.'

'What a dreadful prospect!' Lady Isabella's mock horror shows she does not take this threat seriously.

The words 'Better that, than Papist' jump into my head, but remain unspoken. 'Who would wish such a thing?' I turn to the prince. 'I trust you choose your friends more wisely, sir.'

His sultry eyes widen at my boldness, though I retract not a word. I prefer he remember me as a woman with a mind of her own, not a weak, ingratiating female. The fact that Lady Isabella softens her expression for the Prince's benefit and peers at him through half closed eyes angers me somehow. Not because she is a married woman, but because I detected nothing weak or compliant about her when we were introduced.

'The Scots will soon launch their attack in the north-east, but we'll dislodge them, you'll see.' He slurs his words as the last of his discretion deserts him. 'You judge me over confident, Mistress Murray? Despite that I forced a truce from Colonel Fiennes at Bristol?'

'No one doubts you are a brave commander, sir.' I sip from my glass, savouring the moment. 'However, I hear your men are less disciplined than they might be. Rumour has it they have a penchant for plunder, which overrides their caution.'

Ann releases a shocked gasp, but Lady Isabella's gaze swings in my direction, openly admiring. Perhaps my desire not to be dismissed as a callow female clouds my good sense? Or is the wine stronger than I realise?

'Hah!' His lips pull back from perfect teeth in a wide grin. 'You English are too merciful when it comes to battle. What good is victory unless one enjoys the spoils afterward?'

'Because,' I continue, unabashed. 'The hunt for sport, as you call it, leaves your army open to attack when their guard is down.'

'My men never let their guard down.' He leans closer, his face inches from mine, but there is no anger in his expression, only the light of a lively debate.

'Do you think the people of Cirencester, or Birmingham regard what you did to their towns as sport?'

Shocking tales reached us at Ham, of the violent and rapacious sacking of those cities permitted by this man, who was chastised publicly by the king over the outrage, and urged to '*mingle severity with mercy*'.

'I've fought with the best.' He sways slightly on his feet. Either he doesn't understand criticism, or chooses to ignore it. 'Scots mercenaries as well as the French and Dutch. There's little I don't know about fighting men.'

'Oh, look at Captain Hudson!' Ann Harrison warns me with a look that says clearly I grow too bold. She stands on tiptoe, her fan pointed at the royal party. 'He's in uniform.'

I follow her gaze to where the queen's dwarf struts; a blue sash tied round his waist, his stumpy legs encased in riding boots, the tops turned down to form wide skirts. Her Majesty laughs open-mouthed in childish glee at his antics, her tiny hands clasped together beneath her chin.

'Hudson is a captain now?' I look to the Prince for an explanation.

'Humph . . .' He gives a loud belch and narrows his eyes. 'Her Majesty made the little wretch a Captain of Horse. He thinks it amusing to whip out his miniature sword and challenge better men

71

to mock duels.'

'He is only funning, Your Highness,' Lady Isabella says batting her lashes at him. 'He is Her Majesty's pet, and means no harm.'

'Even so.' Prince Rupert lifts his glass at the object of his annoyance. 'He'll challenge the wrong man one day. If he kicks my dog again, and then runs off to hide behind the queen's skirts, I'll have his head.'

'Poor little thing.' I say. 'If there is one thing I cannot abide it is cruelty to small, helpless things.' The prince slides his gaze sideways at me and I continue, 'I mean your pet, sir, not the dwarf. What sort of dog is he?'

The Stuart eyes flash with pure happiness. 'A white poodle, I call him Boye.'

'He accompanies His Majesty into battle,' Ann says. 'Is that not so?'

'Surely not?' I stare at the prince, aghast.

'Indeed yes, and Boye does not need your concern, Mistress Murray. He makes himself invisible and darts between pounding hooves to alert my men to both my position and direction. He is an able soldier.'

'An unusual animal.' I suspect he mocks me, which he confirms with a wide grin.

'I jest, Mistress Murray. The Roundheads have imbued Boye with mystical powers.' He shrugs. 'Who am I to disabuse them?'

Captain Hudson's performance ends, and I am about to take another sip of wine when a sharp nudge between my shoulder blades empties the contents onto the floor. I draw a quick, astonished breath, grateful that none of the wine has found its way down my gown.

The prince steadies me with a firm hand beneath my elbow, while he exchanges a sour look with the miscreant, my only glimpse of whom is the back of a tousled brown head as he saunters away with no attempt at an apology.

'Outrageous!' Lady Isabella's fan flaps beneath her chin like an insect on a quest for freedom.

'The blackguard! I'll call him out for his clumsiness toward a lady.' The Prince gives a curt bow and takes a menacing step forward.

'Please do not worry, sir.' I halt him with a hand on his arm. 'I am sure it was an accident. This room is so crowded we can hardly help bumping into one another.'

The Prince's jaw clicks and he glares at the man's back with a shrug. 'I fear I am the one who attracts his disrespect, Mistress Murray. Chandos is at odds with me.'

'Why so, Your Highness?' Lady Isabella's boredom is evident in the way she scans the room. I suspect she will drag him away to more frivolous company at the first opportunity, but I do not wish to relinquish him quite yet.

'I passed over his promotion for a man of lesser standing, but superior military skill.' Prince Rupert's breath warms my cheek. 'He has yet to forgive me. I imagine he'll depart our company before long, for I'll not reconsider.'

'Are not your officers selected from the most aristocratic families?' Lady Isabella frowns, evidently confused. 'How else can you finance your army?'

'Not so, my lady.' He waves a shaky finger. 'I choose men with the best credentials, not those with the longest titles and largest incomes. Skilled men, not flouncing lords. Men like Page and Appleyard are of more use to me than the Earl of Chandos, no matter what their origins.'

'And besides,' Ann fixes him with a hard stare. 'High born or peasant, their blood is the same when spilled on English soil in your service, sir.'

'What a cynic you are, Mistress Harrison.' His harsh laugh fills a brief, awkward silence and they stare each other down.

I catch Ann's eye and salute her with my near empty glass, admiring of her boldness. I glance across the room to where Mother beckons me from the circle clustered around the king, with Nan on one side of His Majesty and Father the other.

'Do excuse me, Your Highness.' I drop into a curtsey. 'I am summoned.'

Prince Rupert bows me away, eliciting a promise that I return directly.

I weave toward the group arranged around the seated king,

whose sleepy eyes drift over me, but before they move on to someone of more interest, light in recognition.

'My dear Elizabeth!' His genuine pleasure brings tears to choke me. The hand he reaches to grasp my own is too light, too frail. I ache for him, wishing I possessed the ability to remove part of his burden.

It feels wrong, twisted somehow, that we are brought to this: a poor, replica court in a strange city, exiled from London and all the riches that rightfully belong to King Charles. Each with a tale of either tragedy or ambitions unfulfilled; that form this island of outcasts in an impoverished sea. And yet are we not the elite? The measure by which every Englishman sets himself?

'You look well, my dear.' He traces a delicate finger across my jaw. 'I'm glad you are here. I know Will has missed his girls.'

'Especially my fairest jewel,' my father says. His words are slurred, and his eyes unfocused, but then few in this room can claim sobriety.

'Mistress Murray.' Sir Edward Hyde acknowledges me from the king's shoulder with a bow slight enough for disrespect, but I expect nothing else. Envy permeates this place as much as it ever did Oatlands or Whitehall, and Hyde has reason for his. King Charles tolerates the man but does not like him, a fact Hyde himself must resent in my father's company.

'We have arranged a small masque to be performed after supper.' The king speaks slowly, a ploy he uses to disguise the stammer he has suffered since childhood. 'One hopes it will help us put aside our troubles for a while.' His weary sigh tells me he regards the effort as futile.

'I 'ope you enjoy it, Mistress Murray,' the queen says in her little-girl voice with its charming French accent. She places a light, yet possessive hand on her husband's arm. 'Though, my dearest, we must not forget why we are all 'ere.'

'Ah yes, my loyal followers may flock to demonstrate their devotion, the king says, 'but I am well aware their main objective is to partake of a good meal.' His brittle laugh is met with a round of sycophantic murmurs and the odd awkward cough.

During this exchange, Father heads for a nearby table where tall leather pitchers of wine are laid out. At first, the bulging containers look strange, then I realise, they stand denuded of their silver edging and royal badges. Is His Majesty reduced to stripping the silver from his household items to finance his soldiers?

This fact strikes me a fiercer blow than all the displays of penury I have yet encountered. Then I am distracted as Hyde intercepts Father and whispers something into his ear. I am too far away to hear, and Father has his back to me, but his shoulders stiffen and he steps closer, his nose no more than an inch from Hyde's face. His cheeks redden and his mouth moves in what I can only interpret as a contemptuous barrage, a rigid finger thrust into the man's face. Hyde's sly grin doesn't waver, and he says something more, nods and withdraws. Father stares after him for a moment, then gives a light shrug, staggers and grabs the nearest pitcher, tilting the heavy object over his glass.

As I ponder the reason for their furious exchange, a tall, dark male figure appears at my side.

For the second time that evening, a prince lifts me from an instinctive curtsey and scoops my hand in his. 'Mistress Murray.' Prince Charles plants a firm kiss on my palm before addressing the king. 'Are we not to eat, sir? For many here tonight, this will be their only meal of the day.' He tilts his dark head toward me, my hand still captive in his. 'Are you not hungry, my dear lady?'

'Not very, Your Majesty. My family is among the more fortunate.' I thrill to the fact he uses my given name in company, drawing curious and admiring glances from the crowd that press round us in the hope of a word from the king.

The queen's indulgent smile at her eldest son does little to enhance her thin features, serving only to accentuate her protruding teeth. 'The king is aware of 'ow much his loyal subjects have sacrificed, Charles. We dine from no more than three courses ourselves.' Her penetrating scowl at this apparent indignity might have cowed a lesser man, but Prince Charles is dismissive.

'Then I suggest Father announce dinner immediately, for everyone is hungry.'

Instead of a rebuff, the king smiles at his son, a young man now who quite towers over him, and gives the order for the trumpeter to announce dinner.

Prince Charles cocks an elbow in my direction. 'May I escort you to supper, Mistress Murray?'

I slip my arm through his. 'If you possess sharp elbows, I would be honoured.' I indicate the crowd that now converges on the supper table in response to the royal command.

A wide smile transforms his brooding features to pure beauty. 'I do not need them, for when I appear, the waters part as they do in the scriptures.' He pulls me into line behind the royal party who lead the way to the table and take their seats. 'Sit with me,' he whispers, guiding me into a chair held by a footman at the head of the table.

I sit, unable to prevent a surge of triumph at both his irresistible charm and being elevated to royal status, even for a short time.

He rubs his hands together before taking the seat beside me, emitting a low rumbling laugh at our audacity that is taken up by those nearby.

How I wish all of England could see this magnificent boy prince. Surely then, they would not be so eager to dislodge his father?

Long coats flap and silk gowns swish as the crowd clambers into the remaining seats at the long table, while the doors are flung open to admit a line of servants bearing trays. Within seconds, the platters are buried beneath a flurry of reaching hands.

'They remind me of rats on a corpse.' I cannot help a shiver of alarm as I watch eager hands grasp, and bread, meat and fruit disappear with startling speed. I've not seen beggars in the streets fall on food in this way. The sight of silk-coated men with their hands full of torn meat sickens me.

Averting my gaze, I observe the progress of an elderly man in a dun-coloured velvet coat trimmed with ecru lace and diamonds on his shoes. He moves slowly, with a proud tilt of his head indicating a long life lived well. He pauses between the high backed chairs of the king and queen and drops into a low, obsequious bow.

The king dips his head in silent acknowledgment, but after a swift glance, the queen pointedly turns away and begins an animated conversation with a lady-in-waiting.

I can recognise a snub when I see one.

Prince Charles hands me a pewter plate piled with cold meats.

'You look decidedly uncomfortable, Mistress Murray. Is something troubling you?'

'Who is that man?' I nod toward the object of my gaze, fascinated.

He smiles. 'Ah. That's Henry Rich, the Earl Holland.' He lowers his voice, though our dining companions are too engrossed to eavesdrop on our conversation. 'The father of the notorious Lady Isabella Thynne.'

'Her Majesty appears to dislike him.'

The royal eyebrow lifts in world-weary cynicism. 'Indeed she does. No man can easily survive my mother's scorn after refusing a direct request from my father.'

I nibble a bread roll. 'What sort of request?'

'He refused my father's call-to-arms at York, and chose to stay in London and negotiate with the Parliamentarians instead.' His gaze shifts to the Earl and his face softens. 'For myself, I believe the man has good intentions, but going against the king's wishes is no way to win his favour.'

'Is he now here as a puppet of Parliament then?' I turn my head and study the proud-looking man from behind my fan. 'He doesn't look much like a Puritan.'

'I doubt it was religion that prompted his defection, but he has declared for my father now.' At my frown, he gives a boyish shrug, which reminds me how young he is. 'However, my mother dislikes him for his disobedience and for negotiating with the king's enemies. He thinks his road to redemption was to join the 'Peace Party'.'

'What is that?' I frown, feigning confusion. I have heard the expression before, but like to hear others' interpretation.

'Parliament is divided into those who would exert their regime by war and the lords who seek compromise with my father,' he says, with the air of a schoolboy superior in knowledge. 'Holland is of the second persuasion, but the fact he carries proposals from Westminster is reason enough for my royal parent to refuse to listen.'

I detect a simmering frustration beneath his facade of youthful charm, but it is gone in an instant.

Finally, the queen acknowledges Earl Holland's presence, though her lips barely move in her immobile face. Whatever she says brings a dull flush to the man's cheeks.

'My esteemed Mama,' Prince Charles goes on, 'has a long memory, and has not forgiven his lapse in loyalty. To spite Holland, she gave his post of Groom of the Stole to the Marquess of Hertford. As for Rich, rumour has it he will return to London to reclaim his seat in the House of Lords, though everyone doubts they will have him. He's a laughing stock now.'

Prince Charles's nonchalant shrug does not deceive me, for his eyes glint with fire. 'His mother was a Devereux and he has inherited the family pride. He takes insults to heart and rarely forgives a slight, especially from a Frenchwoman like my Mama.' His gaze sweeps the room. 'But I weary of these political squabbles and would talk of more interesting things.' His good humour returns and he taps my arm. 'Talking of which, have you heard of my cousin, Prince Rupert's scandalous dalliance with the Lady Mary, the Duchess of Richmond?'

My eyes widen in shock. 'You're over young to know of such things, sir, surely, much less speak of them?' I say, despite the fact I am only four years older than he.

'It's true!' His face puckers in childish offence. 'Rupert's in love with her. If you seek confirmation, watch them. They can hardly keep their eyes off each other, not to mention their hands.'

'Your Highness!'

He winks at me, rises and throws his towel onto the table. 'Do excuse me for a moment, I must find a close stool.'

He bows over my hand again and is gone in an instant, my attention immediately drawn to a scuffle further down the table where an argument is in progress over a boiled chicken. A man delivers a hard kick to the shin of his adversary, their faces dark with determination as their fingers dig deep into the scrawny carcass. Onlookers jeer and urge them on, until the taller man wrestles the now broken prize away from the other.

The grimness of the fight strikes me as sinister, and left isolated on a table amongst strangers, I discard my slice of roast beef on my plate, untouched. Disconcerted, I glance round, but Prince Charles has not yet returned.

'If you have no appetite, my lady, may I?'

I turn and face an enquiring eyebrow on the face of a stranger, whose grease-coated fingers already reach for my plate. Demurring without a word, I push my chair away from the table and rise, pushing through the press of bodies.

The smell of slightly mouldy clothes and sweat mixes to make my head swim, and overwhelmed by nausea, I determine to reach the door without fainting.

Outside, I dart along a hallway in search of a quiet corner, relieved to come upon an unoccupied alcove at the end with a window seat. Collapsing onto the wood, I press my back against rough stone that leaches damp through my shawl. I lean my burning cheek against the icy leaded window pane, relishing the sharp cold on my skin, and allow my eyes to flutter closed.

What are we doing here? The king's court should be at Hampton and Whitehall, not hidden away in Oxford while others less able tear this country apart. How low the once-dazzling courtiers have come is a shock, but what terrifies me more, is how much further we might fall if the Scottish church and the Roundheads take what little power King Charles has left.

Inside the hot, crowded Great Hall, where lives hang by a tenuous thread, I caught a glimpse of what might become of us all if the king fails to triumph over his enemies. Shall we be reduced to begging scraps from Puritan tables and sharing poor beds in attic rooms with nothing to do all day but bemoan our state?

Another shiver runs through me, though it is not caused by the frigid air that slices mercilessly along the deserted hallway.

* * *

December 1643

After a dismal autumn of fog and floods, where food is scarce and the fuel situation worse, we shiver through a frigid winter at Trinity Street. I have learned to curb my complaints of these challenges, grateful that at least we benefit from regular deliveries from the royal bake house. Unlike many others in this besieged city, we manage to keep hunger pangs at bay.

Mother reclines on a settle by the fire, where the last of the wood burns with a desultory flame. A rug covers her from waist to toes, and beside her, a lit candle softens the planes of her face. Another flickers on a table where Nan concentrates on a piece of sewing, biting her lower lip with small, even teeth.

We make a cosy scene sitting here in the half-dark of the afternoon, and for a while, I am able to forget the damp stains on the walls of the parlour, the worn and faded furnishings and the scrabbling of rats in the skirting.

Idly, I flick through a book of sermons left behind by the previous occupants. Its message of charity makes me think of those who suffer worse privations than the Murrays. In particular, a dismal Yuletide looms for Ann Harrison and her family, which prompts me to ask Mother to ask them to dine on St Stephen's Day.

'Why that particular young lady?' Mother frowns in disapproval.

'Why ever not, Mama?' My tone turns petulant at the implied insult. 'Ann Harrison has called on us twice this week, walking all the way here in freezing wind.'

'Without a maid, I noticed.' Mother flicks imaginary dust from her thick shawl pulled tight round her shoulders. 'That young woman is too closely associated with a certain other, and although I might approve of her family connection, I advise caution.'

'If you mean Lady Isabella, surely her rank shields her from any censure?' I let the book I am trying to read fall onto my lap. 'What has she done to engender your animosity?'

'Hmm . . . she has breeding enough, I grant you, but she and Mistress Harrison have allowed their boredom with society here to lead them into mischief.'

'What kind of mischief?' Nan's needle stills on her work and she tilts her head, eager for gossip.

Mother rises, advancing on an oak dresser to which she gives unwarranted interest. I am not fooled: it is a poor, misshapen thing compared to the furniture we have at home, and Mother was the first to remark on it upon our arrival.

'Lady Isabella,' her inhaled breath expands a generous bosom, 'together with Mistress Harrison, played a practical joke on the president of Trinity College, Dr Kettle. They draped themselves in garments resembling angels, and with a page and a singing boy, serenaded him on the college lawn.'

'That doesn't sound too scandalous,' I say, keen to mitigate Ann's sin, for this is not the first time I have heard the story. 'In fact it sounds not dissimilar to one of the queen's masques.'

'That is entirely different!' Mother's chin lifts haughtily. 'Their clothes were no more than transparent sheets, and therefore most inappropriate.'

'Mistress Harrison told me Dr Kettle hates women.' Nan holds her handiwork close to the candle glow and peers at it. 'He will not allow them inside the college grounds. Surely whatever he says must be tinged with prejudice.'

'It is not what Doctor Kettle *says* that is the heart of the matter, Nan!' Mother waves her away. 'They were seen!'

'I like Mistress Ann,' Nan persists, uncharacteristically defiant, applying her needle to the kerchief with brisk stabs. 'She has an indomitable spirit in dire circumstances.'

I am about to suggest Nan employ her skills in a more useful purpose other than useless fripperies. A shirt for one of the ragged soldiers who march past our window at all hours, perhaps. The words form on my lips, but I change my mind in case she asks me why I do not do the same. If there's one thing I detest, it is sewing.

'Also,' Mother continues. 'Ann Harrison is so enamoured of Master Richard Fanshawe as to be unseemly. And he nearly twice her age.'

'She is in love with him.' My tone is resigned, but I too find their love affair an odd match; his looks ordinary and his poetry unexciting. Or, is there another aspect to attraction between man and woman that has not yet revealed itself?

'Tush! What has love to do with marriage?' Mother wrinkles her nose. 'She should take a husband of her father's choice, produce an heir or two, and then if she must, think about love and Richard Fanshawe.'

'An heir to what, Mama?' Nan looks up from her sewing long enough to ask. 'The Harrisons lost everything, remember?'

'They'll get it all back again, and more when-'

'The king returns to Westminster,' Nan and I chorus together.

Mother's jaw tightens and her eyes shoot fire. 'Shame on you girls. Such disrespect would never have been thought of when I was a girl.'

'I promise you will never encounter me dancing on the lawn in front of the president's lodgings.' I roll my eyes at my sister, who ducks her head to her work to hide a smile. 'Will that satisfy you?'

Mother's look is sceptical. 'It is the least I expect from you.'

'I think I'll retire, Mama.' Nan gathers her sewing in preparation to leave. 'This room is so cold, my fingers won't work properly. I shall be warmer in my bed.'

We give her our combined blessings and the door closes with a firm click. Mother shifts into a sitting position, her feet not quite reaching the floor. She discards the rug and fiddles with the lace at her cuff, then meets my steady gaze.

I pick up my book, though I do not take in a word. We have played this game of wits often, and I am proud to say I usually win.

'Oh, very well, invite her if you must!' Mother says, with a martyr-like sigh. 'I like Sir John, and I expect the poor man would appreciate a good meal.'

A thought occurs to me, which might explain her reluctance. 'How bad is our own condition where money is concerned?'

Her shoulders slump and she rubs her palms along her knees, creasing her skirt. 'I hoped I wouldn't have to worry you with it, my dear. Our funds have dwindled somewhat. That's why I sent the carriages back to Ham - to save the stable fees.'

'You mean we've spent all of last quarter's rents?' Now I understand this morning's announcement that we shall travel home by hired barge instead.

'I didn't spend it, dear. Your father lent most of it to the king.'

'Lent? Hah! I doubt we'll see that money again,' I snort, cynical, though at the same time, pride fills me that we have extended this service to His Majesty.

'Don't be angry, Betty.' Dismay carves lines below her pretty eyes. 'When King Charles comes into his own again, he'll not forget the Murrays.'

No, he won't! I will make sure of that.

'Mother, you must ask the Sequestration Committee to have at least part of your income restored. Appeal to them as a mother of four daughters who need money to live, and to provide for Father here in Oxford.' I lean forward and grasp her arm gently, urging her to look at me. 'They haven't sequestered Ham, have they?'

'Not yet.' She bites her lip.

'That means you believe they might.' My breathing quickens, and an all too-familiar dread settles in my stomach.

She exhales a long, sad sigh that tugs my heartstrings. 'I think so, yes.'

'And all I've done is complain about bad food and having to dress in the cold.' I join her on the settle and wrap my arms around her, wobbling together as the lumpy upholstery sinks beneath us.

'It shames me to have no money to buy you girls new gowns for the Twelfth Night festivities.' She fumbles for a kerchief and blows her nose.

'As your custom is to summon the seamstress in October, and there has been no sign of her, I came to that conclusion myself.'

Her quivering lips split into a smile and she leans against me. 'What would I do without you, Betty? You are my strength, despite that whip-sharp tongue of yours.' She wriggles from my hold, her composure restored. 'Invite the Harrisons for St Stephen's Day. I am sure we can stretch to three extra guests for dinner. We are not paupers yet.'

Chapter 8

January 1644, Oxford

A blanket of snow falls silently upon the dirty Oxford streets, smoothing the edges of jumbled rooftops and lending the colleges and chapels a dreamlike beauty. I stand in my best gown amongst the same jaded faces gathered in the Great Hall at Christ Church at the start of the Twelfth Night festivities.

Ann Harrison waves to me from beside Richard Fanshawe, and not wishing to appear ungracious, I summon a smile and accept her silent invitation to join her.

'How are you, my dear Elizabeth?' I suspect Ann's beatific smile is not for me, confirmed when its scorching light sweeps to encompass her companion's face.

The admiration in her eyes makes me shiver, and although I have no means or experience of my own to offer her in warning, a heart so open is surely poised to be broken. Mother's opinion of her has softened since our supper party, and she now decrees that, if Master Fanshawe can remove her from the mischievous influence of the notorious Lady Isabella, maybe their alliance is no bad thing.

With his stooped frame and thin, unruly brown hair, Richard Fanshawe is not a handsome man, yet a kind soul lurks behind his plain face. In fact, their combined illumination threatens to burn me, and self-conscious, I cast about for someone else to talk to.

'Have you heard Richard's latest poem, Elizabeth?' Ann grasps my arm as if she fears I may escape. Ann has good instincts, despite her unwise heart.

'I have not. Do write it out for me and send it round to Trinity Street, so I may enjoy his verses at my leisure.'

'What an excellent notion.' Her girlish giggle makes me ashamed of my sarcasm, though I am irritated that her enviable intellect deserts her in Richard's presence. If love drains a woman of her sharp mind, I will have none of it.

Her smile disappears as quickly as it came. 'I'm sorry to hear you intend to leave us soon.'

'It would be sooner, but we have to wait for the thaw. Mother has affairs to see to at home and-' I break off, aware the Harrisons have nothing left but poor lodgings in this city and no prospects. 'Do be sure to call on us tomorrow. Nan and Kate would love to see you.'

'Margaret and I will be occupied sewing clothes for soldiers on the morrow, but we will be happy to visit in the afternoon. Many of the king's men are reduced to fighting in rags, which is no less than a disgrace.'

'I shall look forward to it.' I look away guiltily. I complied willingly when Ann inveigled me to traipse through snowy streets begging for contributions, but I have no intention of sewing shirts in the freezing halls of the music school.

The room has filled since my arrival, and Ann is in demand. At the first opportunity, I make my escape. Her eternal selflessness in the face of adversity makes me less comfortable with my own ambitions. If I were forced to repair my petticoats myself, I would not cope with nearly so much grace.

I spot the welcome face of Master Dobson and waylay the court painter with a greeting for the season as he hurries past.

'Mistress Murray.' He pauses and shows a fine leg. Rising he flicks back his abundant hair to reveal a boyish smile. 'Is there any opportunity I may paint your portrait? I am weary of soldiers and dour-faced courtiers. To capture a pretty lady's features would lighten my day.'

'I doubt there is time before we leave, sir. Though it is my one regret.' I lie, being loath to admit I cannot spare the fifteen shillings required for a portrait.

He lifts both hands skywards. 'As it is mine, dear lady. Yet with so many soldiers coming and going between skirmishes, I have several paintings half-finished. Besides, I have run out of canvases and there are no more to be had in the whole of Oxford. Neither do I have enough cerulean blue paint to do justice to those beautiful eyes of yours.' His gaze darts repeatedly to the far end of the room where Prince Rupert stands. Conscious he is eager to lay hands on his fee for painting the prince's likeness, I take pity and allow him to withdraw.

A fanfare sounds from the end of the room. Conversation halts, and feet shuffle into a wide horseshoe while heads lift in anticipation.

'The first dance is about to begin.' Mother appears at my shoulder with Nan. 'I am too old for such things, but Nan and I will be over there if you require me.' She indicates a line of chairs against the wall.

Nan throws me a wry smile over her shoulder as she and Mother weave through the lines of couples assembled in readiness to begin a courante. Sympathy for my sister wells at her awkward gait. She will never make a dancer. In fact, none of my sisters will.

'Mistress Murray,' a voice speaks at my shoulder. 'How are you enjoying our meagre Twelfth Night celebrations?'

'Good evening, Your Highness.' I rise from my automatic curtsey and turn to meet the compelling gaze of Prince Charles, in a black doublet and breeches, his satin-lined short cloak draped over one broad shoulder.

He indicates the lady beside him. 'I trust you are acquainted with my Lady d'Aubigny?'

I acknowledge the vision in a black and silver gown of mourning, whose honey-gold hair and light blue eyes declare her a beauty, despite her plain dress.

'Of course, Your Highness, we were introduced at a supper party Her Majesty gave at Hampton Court some time ago.' The words 'before the war began' hang in the air between us.

'I remember the occasion well,' she says in her low, seductive voice.

'Please accept my belated condolences, my lady.'

Her sultry eyes cloud and she blinks as if summoning painful memories. 'My dearest George died at Edgehill, Mistress Murray. Long enough ago for me to learn to live without him, but not so long his name fails to bring fresh pain. It is my two babies I feel the most sorry for.' She presses my hand before hailing an acquaintance. 'I will leave you two to talk, sir. It would not do for me to monopolise the handsomest young man in the room.'

'I fear I may have upset her.' I say when she leaves us, searching Prince Charles' face for signs of disapproval.

'Not at all. She is a remarkably strong woman and my father has forgiven her for eloping with George Stuart. In fact, he is exceedingly fond of her. But then there's nothing so appealing as a beautiful young widow.'

'I hope I am never so cynical, sir.' Determined to change the subject, I indicate the laurel boughs and clumps of holly draped across the roof supports. 'It is nice to see the old traditions kept.'

He gives a harsh chuckle. 'The Puritans might declare Twelfth Night as pagan superstition, but I hope we always have an occasion to eat cake and cause havoc.'

A portly man in a paper crown sits on a makeshift throne. Chin on chest, he dozes, the glass in his hand spilling dark drops onto his velvet-clad knee. His equally middle-aged queen for the night makes several snatches at a plum cake on a tray. After three abortive attempts, she gives up and slumps back in her chair. 'It appears your Lord and Lady of Misrule began their celebrations early and are now incapable of causing chaos.'

'I think you're right.' His loud, boyish laugh draws appreciative eyes from the female dancers, who twist round in their partners' arms to look at him.

'I never did like these French dances,' he whispers, chin cocked at the couples who prance across the floor with elaborate, running steps. 'I prefer the country ones.'

A hand slides to his slim hip to reveal a red and gold doublet. 'Gathering Peascods, or Parsons Farewell. Roistering tunes that are more like marches.'

'The Queen is so petite and graceful, I suspect she enjoys the sight of strapping Englishmen struggling with elaborate moves. It serves as amusement.'

'How astute of you, Mistress Murray,' Prince Charles whispers. 'But Mama isn't dancing.'

'No,' I say thoughtfully. He is right, Her Majesty has not moved from her chair in the last hour. 'I expect the festivities have worn her out.'

'If I can persuade these lute players to change the tune, would you take the floor with me?' The dark Stuart eyes flash as he drops a kiss on my knuckles before striding away to talk to the musicians.

He is half a room away before I realise he did not wait for my answer. Yet again, I find myself charmed by this man-boy. What a king he will make. I foresee every lady in the land will become his willing slave.

After two Rigaudons and a Bourrée, I am footsore, hot and breathless. Pleading fatigue to my latest partner, I go in search of the nearest close stool. A servant directs me to the far end of a corridor, so cold, a fine mist hovers slightly below ceiling height. I find the door with little trouble, but in my haste to return to the warmth of the hall, I take a wrong turn.

Two figures approach from the end of a corridor, and unwilling to be discovered in a place where I have no authority, I retrace my steps. Ahead are two full-length curtains fastened to the walls over an archway. I slip behind them and tuck my feet out of sight. Footsteps approach and I pray they pass by without noticing me.

As the two draw level with my hiding place, I spy Sir Edward Hyde through the gap in the curtain, in the company of a man I do not know.

'I do not trust Murray with the Scots,' Hyde says. 'Some of the Covenanters are his kin, and he's too close to them.'

I hold my breath and press my back against the cold wall, listening.

His companion murmurs something I do not catch and Hyde gives a harsh laugh. 'Nay, he has not enough standing to wield influence. The king and queen may harken to everything that creeps from his mealy mouth, but the incident troubles me.'

His emphasis on the word 'incident' implies something more than a casual reference.

Already their steady footsteps recede down the hall, and though the other man speaks again, his voice is indistinct.

I ease out from behind the curtain and follow them at a distance, preparing an excuse in my head should they chance to see me. I have gone but three paces before a door opens beside me, spilling colour and light into the hall. The sound of laughter and music halts me in my tracks.

'Betty, there you are, child.' Mother bustles toward me. 'Will you not step back inside? The masque is about to start.'

'Yes, Mother. I will return directly. The reception room is stifling and I need some air.'

'Well, do not delay too long.' Her tone turns impatient. 'The queen is fatigued and will retire soon. She is breeding again, you know.'

'I will return in a moment.' The door closes again, throwing the hall into chill darkness. My thoughts turn to Her Majesty. To bear another child in such uncertain times must be hard indeed. How much more can that brave woman stand?

I glance toward the end of the corridor to where I last saw Hyde, but there is no sign of him or his companion.

What *did* he mean about Father?

* * *

In defiance of Cousin Henderson's edict to save fuel, the fire in my room is banked high to relieve the damp chill, while I pack my boxes in preparation of our return to Ham. That is, my cousin folds and packs; I lounge on a chaise with a coverlet across my knees issuing instructions.

'Not that one, Cousin. I wish to wear it during the return journey.'

She raises her arms and examines the garment minutely, her gaze sliding to me with scepticism. 'Surely, velvet is too fragile for a river barge in February?'

'I'll wear my thickest cloak, and besides, it's my favourite gown.'

Mother looks up from a pile of neatly folded linens she has set beside an open trunk. 'You cannot wear that, you'll ruin it.' The curt nod she directs at Cousin Henderson is final. 'Pack the velvet. Elizabeth can wear the wool.'

Cousin Henderson smirks as she obeys.

I slump back against my cushions, resigned and slightly bored. I search for something more interesting to do than packing, when I recall the conversation I heard at Christ Church the other night.

'Mama?' I ask slowly. 'Have you ever heard of something called 'The Incident'?'

Alert as a squirrel, her glance flicks to my companion and away again. 'Where did you hear those words?'

'Why? What does it mean?'

Instead of an answer, she cocks her head toward the door in a gesture for me to follow, and bustles out. Abandoning my comfortable seat, I rise, ignoring the pained look of enquiry on my cousin's face.

'Did I say something wrong?' I ask, pulling the door closed behind me. The upper hall is so cold, I take a sharp breath and rub my arms with both hands, but it makes little difference.

'I will ask you again.' Mother twists her hands together and peers both ways along the hall. 'Where did you hear about the Incident?'

'At the Twelfth Night party, Sir Edward Hyde was telling-'

'Hah! I might have known.' She plants a hand on her hip, and with the other she fiddles with the diamond pendant Father gave her one year for a Yule gift. She stares at the floor for a beat, then shrugs with resignation. 'I may as well tell you.' She takes a deep breath and leans closer. 'Two years ago, Hamilton and his brother, the Earl of Lanark, were charged by the king with preventing an alliance between the Covenanters and the English Parliament. The king needed the Scots' support, but refused to relinquish control of the kirk.'

'That doesn't surprise me,' I say, cynically. 'And it makes sense he would not want both the English Parliament and the Scots factions against him.'

'Exactly, and to this end, he made promises to Argyll. Turning him from an Earl to a Marquis for one, although James Graham, Earl Montrose, believed this scheming would ultimately damage the kings intentions, and-'

'Wait,' I hold up a hand. 'Montrose was a Covenanter, but has now turned Royalist?' These facts crowd my head and I fight to make sense of them. I have learned more of the wars and its wrangles here in Oxford than I ever did at home.

'Indeed, though I suspect his hatred of Argyll prompted his change of heart.'

'I can understand why the Royalists might want to rid

themselves of a powerful Covenanter like Argyll, but aren't James and William Hamilton Royalists also?'

'Very much so, but they all suspected each other.'

'What does this have to do with Father, and this 'Incident' Hyde mentioned?'

She exhales a long breath while toying with a ringlet nestled against her cheek. 'In late forty one, the plan was to seize Argyll, Hamilton and Lanark. They were to be taken to the king's ship at Leith, and-'

'Seize? You mean arrested?'

She hesitates. 'Not exactly. Kidnap would be a better term, for they were to be, uh, disposed of. Oh, don't look so shocked, Betty. It didn't happen. Colonel Leslie warned them.'

'I'm not shocked,' I say, truthfully. Then her meaning becomes clear and the already cool air grows colder still and a chill creeps up my spine. 'Father was part of this plot?'

'Yes, and the king knew of it, though he denied it afterwards,' she says defensively. 'Hyde tells everyone who will listen that the scheme fell apart because your father warned them.'

'Why would Father warn them if he was involved?' My jaw tenses in anger, not that Father planned three murders, but that he was blamed for its failure. Plots and intrigue at court are commonplace, but Father would do nothing the king did not sanction. Of that I am certain.

Mother shrugs. 'It made no sense to me either at the time, and it was all to no purpose, for the English Parliament have signed the Solemn League and Covenant with the Scots against the king.'

'What about Hamilton and Lanark? I heard they refused to sign the Covenant and returned to Oxford.'

'They did, indeed,' Mother says. 'The king hates failure and is so angry, he has sent them to Pendennis Castle in Cornwall as prisoners.'

'So now the price of failure is imprisonment by one's own side?'

'Curb that acid tongue of yours, Betty. Having the Scots align with Parliament is a blow. These Covenanters are intransigent.'

'No less intransigent than the king himself,' I snap scornfully. The last thing we need is to be at war with the Presbyterian Scots.

My agitation grows and I pace the narrow hall, though I can barely feel my feet. Eyeing the door of my room, I long for the comfort of the fire there and edge towards it, but Mother's hand on my arm halts me.

'Your father doesn't want the Scots as enemies, he wants the king to negotiate with them instead, something His Majesty resists strongly.'

'Is Father at odds with King Charles now?' Her hand on my wrist is so cold, it is all I can do not shake her off. 'If the Scots march south, that may prove a good decision.'

'Perhaps. But His Majesty-' She breaks off and shakes her head as if this has been said many times before.

'Listens to no one except the queen,' I finish for her, equally despondent now, but I can understand why Father would attempt a compromise. 'Now John Pym is dead, perhaps Parliament wavers in their stern doctrines.' I do not believe this myself, but I have to say something to take the sad look from her face. 'After all, they gave him a state funeral in Westminster Abbey.'

'State funeral indeed!' Mother sniffs, her misery subsumed by contempt. 'For all their Puritan cant, they heap royal ceremony upon themselves.' Her furious breath forms a white mist in the frigid air. 'As for that hypocrite they have appointed leader, Oliver St John, pretended to work for the king when he was Solicitor General, when all the time he favoured Parliament.'

'Perhaps this St John will invite the king to return to London, and this war will end sooner than we think?' A flame of hope flares briefly in my head, but dies quickly. It cannot be that simple.

'A fine ambition but a futile one.' She straightens her gown and turns away. 'Now, enough of such talk. Your father will be here soon, and I don't want you to utter the word 'Incident' in his presence. Do you understand me?'

She doesn't wait for my response, and the rhythmic tapping of her shoes on bare floorboards echoes through the frigid hallway.

Thoughtful, I follow her slowly down the bare wooden staircase and enter the hall at the same moment the front door flies open. Father enters on a flurry of snow carried in on a gust of wind as he stomps inside. Melted snow clings to his hat, the flamboyant feather reduced to a bedraggled chicken tail.

'Disaster,' he mutters, shrugging out of his cloak, while his boots form dirty puddles on the floorboards.

'What's wrong, my love?' Mother flaps her hands at his wet clothes, her mouth turned down in a moue of disgust.

'Did it not go well, Father?' I say, recalling the king called his first Oxford Parliament that day.

'Most o' the lords turned up, but only a third o' the Commons.' He shakes his wet hair and lowers himself onto a settle in the hall. A servant scurries forward and Father lifts a foot. 'Many sent messages of apology, blaming the difficulties in travelling at this time.' He rolls his eyes in disbelief, waving his arms as he speaks, oblivious of the battle the servant wages with his stubborn footwear.

The sodden boots are finally removed and borne away.

'Feeble excuses!' Mother sniffs, bending to help Father into fur-lined slippers.

'Ah'm frozen to the bone,' he mumbles, shivering. 'If there's mulled wine tae be had, I'd appreciate some.' Rising, he rubs his hands together and strides into the salon, while Mother and I follow like ducklings in his wake.

He settles in his favourite chair in front of a newly made-up fire, while a footman places a tray with a pitcher of wine at his elbow, the tang of cinnamon filling the room.

The footman starts to pour, but Father waves him away and sees to the task himself. Eyes closed, he cups his glass in both hands and settles back in his chair as if intent on staying for the rest of the evening, though I expect this visit will be as brief as previous ones. A pity, because did we not come to Oxford with the purpose of spending time together?

'What does it mean?' I creep closer and lower myself onto a stool. 'This refusal of theirs to attend Parliament here in Oxford?'

'If all the members had come today,' he begins, 'the king could have declared the Westminster Parliament invalid and full power returned to him. As it is-' He breaks off with a shrug, disappointment etching deep lines round his mouth.

'Will the ones who did come stay, Father, or will they return to

London?'

'Don't badger him, Betty,' Mother scolds, but he ignores her and addresses me.

'Some waver, unhappy with the king's attempt to negotiate with the Irish Catholics.' He shifts sideways in his chair to face me. 'Sir Edward Dering ordered his lodgings packed in preparation for leaving.'

'Traitor,' Mother snaps, though with less fire than she once might have and sees to replenishing his now half-filled glass.

'There is more bad news than the stubborn MPs.' He drains the wine with a weary sigh, wrestles the pitcher from Mother's hands and pours another. 'Lord Leven has abandoned his camp in Berwick-on-Tweed and his Army of the Covenant has crossed the Tweed and marched into England.'

I exchange a horrified look with Mother, but he pays us no attention, his gaze levelled at the grate where flames take hold and yellow tongues lick round the sides of the logs.

'Where are they headed, and what will the king do to stop them?' Mother asks wearily, taking on his worry like a cloak.

'Newcastle, we think, tae prevent us getting weapons and supplies frae the continent. The Marquis of Newcastle has been ordered from York tae stem the advance. The king has also commissioned the Earl of Antrim to raise an army of Irish soldiers agin Fairfax in England and Lord Leven in Scotland.'

I recall Prince Rupert's promise that seeking Irish help would not make Papists of us, and hope he is right.

'I cannot condone the notion of having foreign soldiers on our soil.' Mother tucks strands of Father's damp hair behind his ear.

'It's either the Irish for us, or the Scots agin us, take your choice, my dear.' Father thanks her with a gentle smile, his head bent toward her. She reaches a slow hand and straightens his collar, their faces inches apart and softened by the firelight. Watching them, I recall long ago days at Ham, and similar domestic scenes in the company of my sisters and Cousin Henderson. I can even picture the room and where each of us sat. How I wish the war would recede into another place and time, but Father's voice brings me sharply back to the present.

94

'Then there is Lord Fairfax, who is on his way to Nantwich with near on five thousand men to break Lord Byron's siege of the town, where we have already lost five hundred men.'

'What of Prince Rupert, Father? Isn't he the one to see both the rebels and the Covenanters off English soil?' My question receives less enthusiasm than I expect.

'Rupert has been created Earl of Holderness and Duke of Cumberland so he may stand in the Lords, but for myself, I shall reserve judgement.'

'What do you mean?' I ask, surprised. He is a magnificent soldier.'

'Huh! He may see himself as the king's saviour, but he is capable of inspiring as much hatred as he is loyalty.' Father lowers his glass and smacks his lips.

'But I thought-' I scrabble for an explanation, but none comes to mind.

'Ach, I know all you young women swoon over his Stuart looks and those seductive eyes.' Father's eyes glint with amusement. 'He is proud, self-opinionated and argumentative. Someone should hae boxed his ears when he was a boy.'

'I am no empty-headed wench who cannot see beyond a yard of lace and a well cut doublet,' I say, affronted. 'I was speaking of his military ability.'

'I quite like his doublet.' Mother smiles. 'It fits without a wrinkle over his muscular chest. And he's one of the tallest men I have ever seen. And you are so right about those eyes, my dear.' She strokes Father's arm, and he gives a soft chuckle.

Neither of my parents seem to be listening to me. As an intruder on their intimate companionship, I silently seethe at their casual neglect.

'Prince Rupert is brave, there is nae question o' that.' Father sips his warm wine now instead of gulping it. 'However, his intolerance of the opinions of others is a serious obstacle. Lord Digby has already complained about it ' He chuckles again. 'But then anyone who disagrees wi' Hyde has ma favour.'

I open my mouth to ask another question, but Mother forestalls me.

'That's enough talk, Betty, your father requires some peace. Now, I'm sure you have plenty of packing to do.'

I rise and leave them, disconcerted that Prince Rupert's ability is in question. As for intolerance of others, that appears to be a Stuart family trait; one that the king in particular suffers from.

If the war is now being fought on two fronts, against Lord Fairfax's Parliamentarians and the Covenanters in the North, who will be the final victor?

Then logic prevails and I shrug my fears aside. Parliament will always have to negotiate with their sovereign. No matter which side triumphs. If the Murrays remain loyal to King Charles, surely nothing too terrible will happen to us.

Chapter 9

No matter how thickly I arrange the cushions at my back, the barge seat still cuts cruelly into my spine. Huddled beneath the canvas awning out of the icy wind, I am resigned to another uncomfortable day in this nausea-inducing boat.

'I wish you hadn't sent the carriages back to Richmond, Mama,' I say, unable to keep the whine from my voice. 'A river journey is hardly pleasant in this cold weather.' I punch the cushions into submission but it makes no difference to my comfort.

'You know why I had to do that.' Mother darts a quick look to where Nan and Kate sit chattering with Meg. 'The expense of keeping a carriage and horses in Oxford was nigh impossible.'

A gust of wind slaps at the awning, which tilts, showering me with icy water.

Nan giggles and I scowl her into silence, wiping cold wetness from my face. The weather is dreadful for so late in the year, and though spared snow, freezing rain bombarded us for days and only now, small patches of blue struggle through an overcast sky.

Our remaining servants occupy the open benches in the barge behind us, along with the luggage we require for the three-week journey. Is it my imagination, or do we attract more than the usual interest from the Roundhead patrols who line the river? They demand we halt the barge at every opportunity, on the pretext of examining our pass.

The fact that our papers bear the signature of Captain General the Earl of Essex gives me confidence, yet whenever those buff jerkins appear over a rise, my throat dries and breathing becomes more difficult.

Despite Mother's dire warnings when we embarked, that river men are of the lowest sort, ours has kept us entertained on the route with stories of the Thames valley. Giving his name as Master Warner, he is not only young and personable, but his manners and speech are that of an educated man.

We slide by a rustic church on the Buckinghamshire side, and daring a glance at Mother, I experience a moment of pure mischief. 'Do you have a story for us about this area, Master Warner?'

Mother narrows her eyes and inhales slowly, but says nothing.

'This is Marlow, Mistress, once the property of an Earl of Mercia.' He needs no further urging to impart his store of knowledge. 'After the Norman Conquest, the town became a possession of Queen Matilda, and later, of the King-Maker, who was buried close by at Bisham.'

'King-Maker?' Kate slides across the bench, her eyes wide with interest. 'Who might that be?'

'Richard Neville, Earl of Warwick,' I say, wrinkling my nose in response to her look of disbelief. Does my sister think I have no history at my command?

'I would hear more of the King-Maker,' pleads Meg, who having never read a history book in her life without the incentive of the birch, is not to be left out. But Warner's lesson has long since left the mercian Earl.

'Many years later, Marlow belonged to Lord Paget of Beaudesert,' our guide continues, 'he that signed Edward the Sixth's settlement of the crown on Lady Jane Grey.'

'I am surprised Paget survived such an undertaking,' Mother says lazily, apparently mollified by the young man's knowledge.

'He might not have, Mistress. However, being wiser than many, he made peace with the queen they called Bloody Mary. He received Marlow as a reward for arranging her marriage to the Spaniard, King Philip.'

'An act which, in itself, should have earned him the axe,' Mother says, smiling at her own humour.

A bend in the river removes Marlow from our sight, and Mother's head nods sleepily. The only sounds are the occasional alarmed rattle of a blackbird from the bank, and the rhythmic creak of the oars as I allow my mind to drift back to the lessons Oxford has taught me.

Since the indecisive battle at Edgehill, the ambition of all Royalists was a simple one; take back London and restore King Charles to his rightful throne, then punish the arrogant rebels for their presumption and show them they cannot change the natural order of things. Once Royalist supremacy is assured, it will only be a matter of time before everything is back to normal again.

The Army of the Covenant mustered at Berwick remained a far off threat, but since they crossed the border in January, I am no longer so sure.

Mother insists our men will soon see them off, but I suspect this assurance is for the benefit of my sisters. I do not accept it so easily.

The Parliament army is not simply a discontented mob, but a real and growing menace to our way of life. And Father has enemies; powerful men prepared to do what they can to destroy his position with the king.

A benevolent parent, my childhood at Ham was one of affection and indulgence. It is true that he is prone to odd flashes of temper on occasion, which even I find unsettling at times, but at Oxford, he subjected more than one man to a tirade of sarcasm and vitriol that had me wincing in embarrassment.

His habit of imbibing vast quantities of wine is less startling, for who in Oxford can claim to do otherwise? With little to occupy them but gossip against Parliament, creep as close to the monarch as they dare, and play cards until dawn, wine dulls the pain of an uncertain future as well as an empty stomach. When he drinks, there comes a quiet reserve, as if Father stores up all his mean thoughts and mulls them over to regret at leisure. If regret them he does.

Once, Hyde referred to Father's 'false and insinuating' ways in my hearing, though many of those close to the king do much the same; each prepared to slander others or alter his stance on any subject from Covenanters to the best way to cook venison, depending on the lead taken by His Majesty. That William Murray exhibits little discretion in his attacks, and then holds up the weaknesses of his peers for his master to see, is a side of his character I find less palatable.

Was that what happened with the Hamilton and Argyll plot? Did Father's enemies stand to gain more from the scheme than he did, so he chose to dismantle their plans instead? Or does he prepare the ground to ensure the Murrays are on the right side in the event of a Covenanter victory? I will not pass judgment on Father, nor shall I allow this new insight to taint my loyalty, though I mark everything I see for future use.

Goodness, honour and high morals have their place, but not, I feel, at court. Not this king's court at any rate.

We Murrays may lack royal blood and the influence others are born to, but we know how to further our own cause. If Father achieves his ambitions through intrigue and subterfuge, then that is what he must do. He will always be able to count on his 'jewel'. For who will look to the Murrays but another Murray?

'You look so serious, Betty.' Mother frowns, concerned. 'And you are monstrous pale. Are you unwell?'

'No, Mother. I am quite well. I know where I am going now.'

'Well, of course you do, dear. Where we are all going. Home to Richmond.'

* * *

Another early spring day brings overcast skies and frequent bursts of rain to accompany us on our slow journey. The countryside through which we pass lies depleted and worn, as if England has grown thin; its fields stripped of everything edible or beautiful. Meadows once filled with livestock look bereft, a half-lame ewe or an elderly cow the only occupants. Trees and hedgerows are strangely silent, as if they too have been plundered of all life.

I once looked on this river with a different eye, when gentlemen in satin coats arrived at the riverbanks in sedan chairs, and ladies in wide skirts and masks lounged on cushions, fanning themselves. Once afloat, the men would preen and call to each other in loud, affected voices, or cast derision upon walkers on the riverbank.

Now their awnings are folded away, their bright livery discarded lest they give offence to the drab uniformed soldiers who patrol the paths and fields. Barges loaded with sour-faced Roundheads loom out of the mist to order our boatmen to make way.

'How can a journey of a hundred miles take so long?' I mutter under my breath and adjust my fur-lined hood over my hair. 'I doubt my clothes have been completely dry for days.'

'Stop moaning, Betty,' Mother says. 'You're worse than your sisters.' She nods briefly at the bleak countryside sliding past. 'There are those who suffer far more than you as a consequence of this war.'

I retreat into silence, slightly comforted by the fact that others' journey is surely more miserable than mine. Having spent most of the morning squabbling, Nan and Meg are banished to the second barge with Cousin Henderson.

'The going is slow, Mistress,' Master Warner says, evidently taking pity on me, 'because we are forced to give way to troops and supplies being taken upriver.'

Mother's chin slumps forward and she snores softly, while Kate takes advantage of her inattention to ease closer to Master Warner. His open, friendly smile is that of someone who indulges a child, although if Mother saw, I feel sure she would order Kate back to the other boat with Cousin Henderson.

'Do you travel this river every day, sir?' Kate preens, ignoring my warning frown.

'Tis my livin', Mistress.' His shoulders flex with each lift and pull of the oars. He cocks his square, beardless chin at the curve ahead. 'Do ye know where you are now?'

Kate's enraptured gaze hardens, and she looks round, confused. 'I'm not sure.'

'Well,' he cocks his chin at the next turn in the river. 'About two miles round that bend is Windsor Castle.'

Her face brightens. 'We have been there to see the king, when-'

I shake my head in warning, and catching my look, Kate breaks off and clamps her lips together.

He angles his head toward me and meets my gaze steadily. 'I'm a royal bargeman, Mistress. My grandfather was Nowell Warner of Greenwich, bargeman to old King James.'

I nod, relieved. And to think I worried he was a Parliament spy. Not that I would recognise one if I saw one, but it is not an impossibility. 'You are far from London, Master Warner,' I say, relaxing again.

101

'Times are hard.' The tendons on his neck tighten. 'My father was King Charles' bargeman and an esquire, while I was a junior, but there's been little call for our services since Edgehill. We have to ply our trade wherever boats are needed now.'

Weak daylight fades into gloomy dusk and the wind drops as we glide through the tightly-packed houses and cobbled streets of Windsor, still busy from the remnants of market day trading. My dread at entering this Parliament-controlled town invades my peace of mind.

'I wish we didn't have to stop here.'

Mother yawns as she wakes from her doze, but doesn't appear to hear me.

'Royalist officers are kept prisoner at the castle,' Kate says. 'And the governor, Colonel Venn, allows his men to use the chapel as a stable. They broke all the stained glass windows, smashed the monuments and stole all the furniture.'

'I heard that too.' Mother comes fully awake. 'We plan to stay only one night. We shall be gone first thing in the morning, and tomorrow will find us in Richmond.'

The barges bump the quay, and a footman leaps from the boat behind us onto the footpath, and summons a carriage. We swap the rocking boat for the more solid, but equally uncomfortable seats of a hired hackney, squeezed so tightly in the small space, Meg has to occupy Mother's lap.

The minutes pass and still we do not move. I poke my head out of the window to see why. My mouth falls open in dismay at the sight of our servants lifting boxes and trunks from the barges into a waiting cart, while Ball stands in the road giving directions.

'You're not listening, Elizabeth,' Kate's voice rises in annoyance from the seat opposite.

Uninterested in further tales of vandalism, I hush her. 'Do we need all the luggage at the inn tonight?' I direct my question at Mother. 'It will take an age to unload it all, and I am cold and hungry.'

'I refuse to leave the boxes here where villains might steal them.' Mother strokes Meg's hair while my sister's eyes droop, her thumb firmly in her mouth.

'I hope it isn't far to Peascod Street and the *Garter Inn*.' Nan shifts on the seat but is immediately nudged into stillness by Kate.

'A good meal and a warm fire will soften those sharp edges you have on you today, Mistress Nan,' Mother says.

Finally the door slams shut, and the coach lurches forward and climbs the hill. I exchange a sympathetic look with Nan, for if anyone is being sharp today, it is me. Being confined on the barge all day with little opportunity to move must be torture for her, but she never complains.

'What chance is there the inn will avail me of a hot bath when-' I am cut off as the carriage comes to an abrupt halt, hurling me against the door frame. A shout goes up from above, followed by the slithering of hooves on cobbles and the sound of tramping feet.

'Why have you stopped here?' Mother raps hard on the roof, lifts the leather sheet that covers the window and calls to the driver. 'The inn is farther along the street. Do you expect us to walk?'

I rub my temple that has come into sharp contact with the wooden upright of the door frame.

Our footman's face appears beneath the flap, his features thrown into relief by the light spilling from the windows of a nearby building. 'We've been ordered to stand down, Mistress.'

'By whom? And whatever for?' Mother snaps, though her face shows mounting alarm.

At a shouted command, the footman opens the door and reveals a dozen or so soldiers surrounding our carriage, two hand-held torches held aloft that turn their already sullen faces into gargoyles. 'Step down if you please,' a gruff male voice orders.

'What do they want?' Nan cries, pressing a fist against her mouth.

'I don't know,' I whisper back, 'but we have no choice but to do what they say.' I glance past them to where, twenty paces or so farther on, the orange glow from a window of the *Garter Inn* beckons.

Our footman slides an arm around Nan's waist, and cradling her knees with the other, lifts her as if she weighs nothing, and sets her down on rain-slicked cobbles where a cold wind lifts the edges of her cloak. I follow onto the wet street, straight into a puddle that drenches my exposed ankles.

Mother shakes off a soldier's proffered arm, her sharp eyes latching onto the nearest officer, whom she approaches with the mien of a duchess. 'I assume you have a name to go with that uniform?' She rakes him from the top of his hat to his boots with an imperious stare.

'Major Buxton, at your service.' His haughty manner and omission of a bow indicate he is inordinately pleased with himself. 'Your pass, madam?' He avoids Mother's eye, his outstretched hand insolently close to her chin.

The urge to demand he show her due respect dies in my throat, and inwardly I vow that one day, the entire world will know who we are, and treat us with the deference we deserve.

'Of course, Major.' Mother chooses to disregard his lack of respect, and withdraws the pass from inside her bodice. By her pinched face I know how keenly she feels the insult, though she remains calm. 'I trust you recognise the name of Captain-General Lord Essex?'

His eyes narrow, but he says nothing as he takes the parchment from her hand.

A soldier holds a burning taper above the page to enable the major to read, which he proceeds to do with agonising slowness.

'May we not carry on to the inn, sir?' Mother gives an exaggerated shiver. 'My daughters and I have travelled all day, and we are cold and hungry.'

Without looking up, the officer continues reading.

Chafing against the delay, I huddle inside my cloak as a whip of cold wind is funnelled up the street between the buildings. I summon a smile for the second officer, but he looks straight through me and instead, jostles the maids into line with his staff.

'You are London bound?' the major barks.

At this, several pairs of hostile eyes turn toward us.

'To our home, near Richmond,' Mother says. 'It's in Surrey.'

He doesn't respond to her sarcasm, and continues to read, a task he could have completed five times by now. I assume this is deliberate, a ploy used in order to keep us waiting, and in our place.

At last, he jerks his head in the direction of the castle at the top of the hill.

'Thank the Good Lord for that,' I whisper, turning to address Mother, 'perhaps we can go now?'

'Mistress Murray,' Major Buxton's voice drowns my words. 'I order you to accompany us to the castle, where you will subject yourself and your party to a search.'

Chapter 10

April 1644, Windsor

Mother's arm closes around a yawning Meg, and she pulls her against her side. 'My daughter is but a child. She should be in a warm bed with a hot supper inside her, not standing in a frigid street being harassed by soldiers.' Meg's eyes are wild and her fingers clutch at Mother's cloak in terrified bewilderment, though she has no pointed questions for the rebels on this occasion.

'That is not my concern, Mistress Murray. I have my orders.' He jerks his chin at the waiting soldiers, who fall into a double line on either side, hemming us in.

My stomach plummets at his lack of compassion. He reminds me of the rebel who invaded the house in Trinity Street. Cold, self-righteous and condemning in his conviction we should be punished for our allegiance. I also suspect Major Buxton knows exactly who we are, and of our close connection with the king. Had guards been put out on the river to alert him to our arrival? And if so, what do they hope to find?

'This way, Mistress Murray.' He signals us to follow his men.

'I know the direction quite well, thank you.' Mother slings an arm around Meg's shoulder and ushers her past him without a backward look.

Cousin Henderson releases a shocked gasp in response to a burly soldier who shoves her hard for not moving fast enough. Kate rounds on the man, her mouth open, poised to deliver a reprimand. I pinch her arm and she redirects her venom at me, but I cock my chin at the pikes and swords the soldiers carry.

With a nod of resigned understanding, she slides an arm through Cousin Henderson's and continues their unsteady walk without a word.

The grooms in charge of our luggage cart follow a few yards behind, their shoulders bent against the incline and unheeding of the filth from the street that splashes their immaculate breeches.

Resentment surges into my throat, but the protest, so loud and arrogant in my head, goes unspoken. We are powerless against their authority.

Mother falters on the slippery cobbles and looks about to fall. Cousin Henderson rushes to her side, relieves her of Meg and lifts the sleepy child into her arms.

'Keep moving!' A soldier barks at them both, his face expressionless.

My cousin casts him a withering look, but silently obeys, while Meg's head lolls on her shoulder.

My shoes slip on the mud and sludge of a road slippery with recent rain, while wary and curious faces appear in upper windows to watch our progress, only to disappear again almost immediately

With Cousin Henderson encumbered with Meg, Kate falls back, slips her hand into mine and huddles close. 'What will they do to us?'

'I don't know,' I croak through a dry mouth. 'They may simply wish to examine our pass more closely.' I doubt she believes me, but it is all I can think of.

Mud and ordure squelch underfoot and I groan aloud. My shoes will be ruined. I release a choked laugh and Kate glares at me. I shake my head at her and press on. We are about to become prisoners and I fret about shoes!

The major signals the procession to halt beneath the Norman gateway, which I eye with growing panic. When those doors clang shut behind us, will we ever be allowed out again? Or are we to be locked away and forgotten? And for how long? Until the war is over. Until we die?

Fresh sympathy rises then for my father. Is this the stomach churning dread that he experiences every day of his life?

I have to fight an urge to turn and run, but there is no time to think before we are ushered through the archway and the massive doors swing closed, engulfing us in stagnant darkness within impenetrable walls. I would give anything to return to the frigid street with its biting wind, rather than the confinement of that dead space where all sound is turned inwards and stifled. Possibly forever.

'Wait here!' Major Buxton commands.

We shuffle to a halt in a courtyard open to the darkening sky, where scudding clouds obscure a misty moon. From behind me, the sob of a maid is quickly followed by the murmur of a male voice as one of the footmen comforts her.

'Move on!' a voice calls, making me jump. Another uniformed man appears to guide us into a smaller courtyard where a lone torch flickers in a sconce on the wall. A soldier raps with his staff on a door at the far side. It immediately swings inwards, hinges moaning in protest. Prompted again to move forward, we file inside the gloomy interior of what looks to be an entrance hall.

Glistening moisture clings to bare stone walls and a dusty, boarded floor echoes our hollow footsteps. The door slams shut with ominous finality. Bangs and scrapes follow as soldiers pile our luggage into a haphazard heap on the floor.

The jingle of keys in locks, and the clang of a metal door grates on my shredded nerves as we are ushered further into the room. A long desk sits at one end, upon which an oil lamp struggles to lift the gloom, while a door with a metal grille at eye level stands at the far side.

Meg stirs on Cousin Henderson's shoulder, who lowers her gently to the floor. Meg blinks and stares round, rubbing her eyes.

Mother utters a gasp and my breath catches as a man in clerical garb steps out of the shadows.

'My name is Christopher Love,' he says, his voice pitched low. 'I am Major Venn's chaplain.'

'I doubt we have much use for a man of God in this place,' Mother says, with only the slightest tremble to her voice. 'Dare I hope you are here to intervene on our behalf at this man's outrageous conduct?' She points a wavering finger at Major Buxton, whose skin darkens in rage, though he stays silent.

'Alas, no, dear lady.' Reverend Love's hands flap in agitation. 'I am here merely to see that the search is carried out in a proper manner.'

Mother sniffs, 'Then I can see further discourse with you is useless.' She gathers Meg and Nan closer. 'I trust, Major, that you will ensure this business is not unnecessarily protracted?'

I am stunned by her courage, but at the same time hope she does not persist in haranguing the major, or we may never get out of here. I throw her a warning scowl, but though I know she sees me, she remains stiff-lipped and defiant.

My hands are clammy, and I shiver inside my cloak, not from cold as much as sheer terror for what is to come. I cast a fearful look to where Cousin Henderson stands, her arms stiff at her sides and her lips moving in what I take is a prayer.

At a signal from the major, a soldier upends one of our boxes spilling gowns, gloves and stockings onto the boards. Kate squeals and I draw her backwards as two soldiers dart forward to pluck at cloth, lace and small shiny items that roll between their feet; like magpies at a lady's dressing table.

'Have a care with my possessions!' Mother wrests a none-too-clean male hand from a silk gown and stares the man down. 'I am aware you do nothing but your duty. However, you might treat your betters with some respect.'

Major Buxton watches with no emotion, perched atop the table while twirling a gauntlet glove in one hand. 'Mistress Murray.' His smile turns to a sneer. 'Kindly do not to interfere with my officer's duty.'

Mother advances on the major. 'If you would tell me what it is you expect to find amongst my petticoats, I may be able to save you some time.'

Uncertainty enters Reverend Love's eyes, which doesn't surprise me. How many furious women with the air of a queen has this man had to deal with? If he is a Christian as he says, surely he will do something to stop this travesty. I look to him for support, but he appears unable to meet my gaze.

Easing upright away from the table, Major Buxton tucks his glove into his waistband and clasps both hands behind his back. 'We seek evidence, madam. Evidence of delinquent behaviour and treachery to the Parliamentary forces.'

'My master is the crowned sovereign King Charles.' says Mother, drawing herself up to her full height. Her hood falls back to reveal round flashing eyes and a trembling chin. 'To serve him is not treachery.'

Cousin Henderson smirks and Nan groans.

I bite my lip, tempted to urge her to silence, but at the same time I cannot help a welling pride at her courage.

Major Buxton's eyes narrow, and he inhales slowly. 'I will not enter into futile political cant with you, madam.'

His air of contempt makes my fingers itch. I wear my warmest gloves with the raised stitching and anticipate with pleasure the red line they will raise on his cheek should I strike him. The image is but a daydream, for I lack the final burst of courage that moves my feet.

Major Buxton fixes us with a baleful eye that makes our housemaids huddle together in fear. 'Step aside and allow my men to complete their work, or I shall be forced to restrain you all in one of the cells until morning.'

Mother gasps, and her head whips round to Reverend Love, but there is no help to be had.

He flaps his feminine hands and shrugs. 'I am so sorry, Mistress, but the orders are clear. I have no authority to intercede.'

'Then what is the reason for your presence?' Mother juts out her chin. 'To pray for us?'

He folds his hands together in monkish pose. 'I am here to ensure that you and your daughters are treated with proper respect. That you have no reason to complain later of, um, inappropriate manhandling.'

I narrow my eyes, my fear smothered by fury. Let them dare!

'And my servants?' Mother waves at the line of household staff, some of whom have been ordered to remove their jackets and boots. 'I trust they warrant respect too?'

'Of course, Mistress Murray.' Reverend Love looks offended. Then a new enthusiasm animates his face. 'However, should you wish a short prayer-'

'I do not!' Mother sends him a glare that settles his neck back into his hunched shoulders.

The contents of the boxes and saddle bags lay strewn across the floor, rifled through and cast to one side by coarse, disrespectful hands.

My teeth worry the inside of my cheek until I taste blood, my fists clench at my sides, helpless to do anything but watch as my

110

gold silk is examined. If they knew I appeared before the king in that gown, would they show more reverence, or treat it with disdain?

One of the men makes a coarse remark about a linen shift that belongs to Kate, who flushes with shame. Another waves a brocade shoe in the air with an expression of mockery on his craggy face, lips pulled back as he makes see-saw stepping movements, before tossing it into a disordered pile on the floor.

Their casual manner makes me wonder if they actually believe there is something for them to find, or if they simply enjoy deriding us and our possessions? Christian, righteous souls they may proclaim themselves to be, but these are simply dull-witted men who make sport of their betters, for no other reason than that they can.

The major points at me and barks. 'Remove your cloak!'

I try to swallow, but this simple act is impossible with such a dry throat. He cannot mean me to disrobe?

I stare first at Mother, and then at Cousin Henderson, but they stand frozen, identical looks of horror and disbelief on their faces.

'Surely you do not intend to search our persons?' Mother demands after a moment.

The hard-nosed officer hesitates, and for a heartbeat I think he might back down. Then his jaw hardens, and he raises a cynical brow. 'Outer garments can be examined for illicit documents with no loss of respect, madam.'

'Illicit documents!' Mother's mouth flaps like a fish. 'How dare you imply-'

'Mother.' My voice is little above a whisper, but I send her a plea with my eyes not to say any more. 'The quicker we get this done, the sooner we can be on our way.' I level my gaze at the major, and slowly, untie the ribbon around my neck.

'A sensible attitude, Mistress Murray.' A sudden light of interest in his eyes shows he is not totally immune to me.

Forcing myself to keep his gaze, I slip the heavy, fur-lined garment off my shoulders, revealing my low-cut bodice. Damp cold slides across my exposed skin as I fight a shudder. I clamp my teeth together to stop them chattering, lay the cloak across one bare arm, and hold it out toward him.

He will have to take a step forward to claim it, and in that brief pause between my action and his response, a battle of wills takes place. Will he order me to come forward, or relent and take the steps necessary and come to me?

I do not move, my arm held straight and steady. 'If you want it, Major. Why do you not claim it?' Emboldened by the fact my voice does not quake, I lift my chin.

He eases his neck inside his collar and swallows, then takes the step. His fingers graze mine, and as the fabric whooshes through my hands, he gives a start and a slight flush appears on his cheeks, difficult to see in this low light, but I am sure it is there. Despite the overt threat of this awful place, exhilaration fills me at the effect I have on this man.

His lips twist in a smile as he hands my cloak to a soldier. Then he jabs a finger at Kate. 'Now you.'

True to his word, Major Buxton requests no more than our cloaks, whose linings and hems his men search with rough diligence.

'They will tear the fur trim,' Kate whispers, her round eyes fixed on the gangly youth who metes out careless treatment to her cloak.

'I will repair it for you.' I say, slipping an arm round her hunched shoulders, drawing her closer. She looks up at me with an incredulous but grateful smile. She knows how I hate to sew.

My glance sweeps the room to where Mother watches with barely suppressed fury as the men root through our belongings. She eases toward one of the boxes, a movement which to some may seem casual, but I sense there is purpose to it.

At first, I cannot see what holds her attention, but on further examination, something about the leather bound box strikes me as odd. As a result of rough handling, a soldier's boot has dislodged an ornamental strap and it lies askew, revealing what appears to be a gap in the base.

Mother's focus turns to Meg, and though the child shows no signs of distress, she rubs her cheeks and straightens her shawl, while at the same time sliding the strap of the trunk back into place with the toe of her boot.

I watch, transfixed, until Major Buxton steps in front of me, blocking my view, one hand outstretched in the act of returning my cloak. I slip it over my shoulders and fasten it gratefully, though the damp cold of the hall still cuts into my bones.

'The search is over,' he says. 'You may go now.'

The soldiers fall into formation and march out, followed more slowly by Reverend Love. He pauses at the door and turns back addressing Mother. 'I offer my apologies, Mistress Murray, but there was little I-'

'Hold your tongue, you poor excuse for a man.' Mother's anger returns in full flood and she rakes him with her gaze. 'How a cleric can stand by and allow such disregard for the sensibilities of gently-born young ladies is something I cannot comprehend. May your conscience trouble you for a long while, sir.'

The reverend ducks his head and scuttles away.

The door clangs shut, and left in the near dark of a single lamp, low murmurs of relief and indignation erupt.

The men amongst our servants are grim-faced, while the girls shake with shock. A footman nurses an injured shoulder from a blow with a musket butt, and a maid sobs, one hand gripping her torn gown against a half-exposed breast.

One by one, animation returns to the servants, and at a signal from a stiff-lipped William Ball, they retrieve our belongings from the floor, right the trunks whose linings have been slashed and re-pack them as best they can.

The carriages await us outside the castle gates, and leaving the servants to their task, we clamber back inside and continue our short journey to Peascod Street.

'Mother? Do you think-'

'Hush!' she cuts me off, her gaze flicking upward, a forefinger pressed to her mouth. 'There are soldiers on the box.'

At the door of the *Garter Inn*, I hang back until the others file past us through the door and out of earshot. 'There was nothing for the soldiers to find, was there, Mother?'

'Whatever do you mean, Betty? What could there be for them to find?' She pats my cheek with a slightly clammy hand, her smile one of utter confidence as she ushers me toward the dining room. 'I hope they haven't run out of roast beef. I'm quite famished.'

* * *

By morning, the wind has dropped, but the cold turns our breath into white clouds when we respond to Master Warner's greeting as he assists us into the barges. Instinct tells me he is aware of the humiliations we suffered at the hands of Major Buxton, but nothing is mentioned. The events of the previous evening are locked into the dark recess of my mind where I intend them to reside, though they leave a sour taste in my mouth.

The oars slap the grey water as we glide through country both beautiful and familiar, until a large, square red brick palace floats into view.

'Old King Henry built Oatlands Palace to receive his new Queen, Anne of Cleves,' our boatman says for the benefit of Meg and Kate. 'But he liked not the look of her, and the poor lady was sent elsewhere.'

'The poor queen,' Meg mutters.

Oatlands, the scene of so many memories, slides away to my right, its sylvan slopes interspersed with elms, oaks, and pines. Then Major Buxton's face looms into my head and I wonder if the king will ever receive us there again.

Long, trim lawns slope down to the water from the rear of country houses along the bank. Trees line the route, their leafless branches reflected in the water. The river twists sharply to the left and then sweeps to the right as we approach Penton Hook, Chertsey and Shepperton.

'You've been silent a long time, Master Warner. Do you have no tales of this place to entertain us?' Boredom prompts me to ask as the turrets of Hampton Court Palace drift into view over the trees.

'Perhaps.' A smile tugs his lips. 'They say the ghosts of Jane Seymour and Katherine Howard roam the halls.'

Meg stares from the boatman to me and back again.

'I've never seen them,' I say, mainly to reassure her, though I know of such stories.

'Then there's Mistress Penn.' He signals to the second bargemen in the stern to slow for an oncoming boat. 'Her that was nursemaid to the baby King Edward.' His blue eyes crinkle at the corners. 'And Queen Mary spent her honeymoon with Philip of Spain at the Palace of Hampton.'

'You're a romantic, Master Warner.' Convinced this conversation about past royals must be overheard, I glance at the other bargees who manage the sails, but their bovine eyes remain blank and uninterested.

'It is this river, Mistress. It invades your heart and won't never let go.'

Hampton Court Palace slips by, where vines entwine the locked rear gates. In my mind, I walk through the arch with its oriel window and perforated parapet, the embattled walls, pinnacles and fretted chimneys, where the royal children once ran across the grass, calling to me that I am too slow.

Then we are at Twickenham, and I catch my first view of my beloved Ham, and my spirits lift as we berth at our own jetty. Master Warner hands me onto firm ground where the house greets me like an old friend, its solid red-brick facade glowing in the winter sunlight. I feel the sting of tears in my relief to be home again.

Meg scrambles onto the bank and Mother beckons with a wave of her muff. 'Come along, Kate, Nan. Don't dawdle.'

Master Warner bows to me in deep respect, then turns away to fix part of the awning without taking leave of Kate, whose face falls. He's a handsome man in a rough, yeoman way, and his rejection stirs a pang of sympathy for my sister. Perhaps lady and yeoman will never be friends, but whether Mother likes it or not, times are changing.

The servants unload the luggage, while we cover the distance to the house, the girls keeping up a stream of animated chatter. Cousin Henderson walks with Nan, whose pace is slower than the rest of us.

A few feet short of the gates, a shout brings my gaze to the stable yard entrance.

'Mistress Murray!' Our housekeeper bustles across the grass, red-faced and with her arms waving. 'We wasn't expecting you today. We wuz hoping to get things in order before you came home!'

'What things? What has happened?' Mother demands, as the woman curtseys to a halt.

'Soldiers came, Mistress.'

'What soldiers?' I step between Mother and the housekeeper, who flaps her arms like a fat, brown hen.

'They came to the 'ouse two days ago.' A frown puckers the rough skin between her eyes. 'Leasaways, they looked like soldiers. They 'ad jerkins and boots and carried pikes. Not cavalry, that's certain.'

'Did they have documents with them?' Mother shakes the woman's arm, but releases it immediately, her lips pursed in distaste as if touching something unpleasant. 'What did they say? Did they take anything?'

'They carried no papers, Mistress. Not that I could'a read them if they 'ad. They wanted food.'

Master Ball's shrewd gaze assesses the situation with one sweep of his pebble eyes. 'Now, Sybil,' he addresses the bewildered woman. 'Take your time and tell us everything. Did you grant these men entry to the house?'

Sybil grasps his proffered arm and sags against him, evidently more comfortable answering his questions than Mother's or mine.

'We 'ad to, sir. But as I said, they didn't bother much with the 'ouse. They took some of the chickens, then ransacked the pantry and the dairy.' She lifts a trembling arm and points to where the drive meets Ham Street. 'They lit a bonfire beneath the trees last night. Drinking our cider and ale 'till all hours, they were. We wuz terrified they'd come back and demand more.' She sniffs and wipes her face on her apron. 'But they wuz gone by morning.'

'Did they come from the Kingston garrison?' Mother asks, her eyes calculating. If they were sent by their superiors, maybe we should expect more of them.

'I dunno where they come from.' Sybil's features twist in confusion. 'But there weren't no officer with them.'

'Renegades,' Master Ball mutters. 'Deserters probably. What else did they take?'

116

Fat tears slide down Sybil's round cheeks, her crumpled apron a creased rag in her hands. Three maids have emerged to watch us from the rear door, whispering together and darting fearful looks in our direction

'Oh, Master Ball.' Sybil's lower lip trembles. 'We couldn't stop them. Not with a few ancient gardeners and a coupl'a footmen.' Her voice rises to a screech. 'They 'ad muskets!' As if this fact explained everything.

'No one would expect you to fight them, woman,' Mother says, her face tight. I suspect she would like to shake her, but restrains herself.

Sybil takes a deep breath as if summoning courage. 'They bashed the head groom over the head and took three of the 'orses, Mistress.'

'Not the horses!' Kate's face is a mask of indignation that reduces Sybil to noisy tears.

'Did they take Saracen?' I ask, praying for a miracle that somehow our prize stallion was spared.

The flat eyes search for mine amongst the faces around her, and she smiles. 'Nay, Mistress. They tried to, but that beast was hav'in none of it. He bit one o' them on the shoulder, so's they made do with the others.'

'I hope he drew blood,' I mutter beneath my breath, my remark met by a smirk from Mother.

'Has anyone discovered how the groom fares?' Cousin Henderson asks.

Master Ball holds up his hands at another rush of apologies from Sybil. 'Allow the Mistress to come inside and get settled. It has been a long journey.' He turns back to Mother, emanating his usual calm efficiency. 'Once I've discovered the extent of the damage and losses, Mistress Murray, I will report back to you presently.' He gives a curt nod, effectively dismissing us all and ushers the distraught housekeeper away.

They present a comical sight, walking side by side toward the house. The lean steward in his black suit and white hose, hands clasped demurely behind his back, while beside him Sybil waves her arms and keeps up a stream of shatter as she relives her ordeal.

Soldiers at Ham? Who could think such a thing? And thieves too!

The loss of the horses is a blow, but we can surely survive that. Nor did it sound as if they were acting on Captain Fitton's orders.

'I shall complain to the garrison!' Mother says, apparently coming to the same conclusion. 'Perhaps they'll get our horses back for us.' Then the fact we all stand about on the drive in a cold wind seems to dawn on her. She gives an exaggerated shiver and beckons Cousin Henderson. 'Take the girls inside.' Then turns burning eyes on me. 'This is a fine homecoming, Betty.'

I gape as her angry stride carries her across the gravel. Anyone would think it was my fault.

Chapter 11

Despite our recent raid by what Ball is convinced were rogue soldiers taking advantage of unlawful times, order is restored with minimal fuss. The household swiftly settles back into well-worn routines, though the servants who accompanied us to Oxford rapidly adopt superiority over those who remained behind. Amongst it all, Mother skitters from room to room smoothing hurt feelings and settling disputes.

Today I leave my lace-trimmed morning gowns in the press and wear a plain black dress and white apron in preparation for a morning in the stillroom, one of my favourite places where I spend many happy hours amongst the shelves of herbs, dried flowers and exotic bottles and jars.

I push open the rear door, only to have it whipped from my hold by a fierce gale. My shoes slip on wet cobbles and my skirt billows as I make my way across the yard where the kitchens and domestic offices stand. Brushing raindrops from my gown, I step inside, dismayed that even after such a short distance, my skirt is soaked.

'When I am married to a wealthy man,' I grumble, shaking water onto the slate floor. 'I shall have the kitchens and storerooms moved inside the house.'

'A fine ambition, Elizabeth,' Cousin Henderson says, the only witness to my complaint. 'Though as the wife of a rich man, you will most likely never be called upon to visit them.' Her hands lift to her cap, and she studies me beneath bent elbows.

'Perhaps, but one day I would like to eat my food when it is piping hot instead of lukewarm.'

'Have you come to assist me today?' She stands at a scrubbed pine table laid out with small pots, miniature pans and metal instruments.

'If you wish, Cousin.' Although I had no firm purpose in mind other than to spend time amongst the aromatic herbs and colourful powders.

'Good. In our absence, no one has thought to distil any herbs or make infusions. Our stocks of medicines are low.'

'What do we need?' I survey the gaps in the once closely-packed shelves.

'The cook's eyesight is not as good as it once was. She burns herself often and thus I thought to prepare her some salve.' She picks feather remnants off two hen's egg shells, adds them to the water in a thick-bottomed pan balanced on the fire.

'I've never prepared a burn remedy before, how is it done?'

'I should roast these, but boiling would do as well,' she says, poking the eggs with a stick. 'When hard, the yolks are fried with oil and then blended to a pulp.' She adds more wood from a box in the corner to the fire. 'Then,' she slaps her hands together scattering the dust. 'Take a pig's bladder soaked with sallet-oyl, spread the pulp upon it and place the whole on the burned area to reduce the pain.' She glances up at me and smiles. 'I don't expect you to remember all that. I have a book of receipts I could lend you.'

I nod gratefully, glad to have more concoctions to add to my journal along with my measurements for infusions of feverfew for headaches, and my flint stone with small beer for ague.

'Is there something I might help you with?' She cocks her head to one side to meet my gaze and her lips tilt into a smile which does little to enhance her appearance. Her nose is too heavy and she possesses a patchy complexion that rapidly discolours in both heat and cold.

'What makes you think so?' I shrug, but there is something I would discuss with someone. And why not her? My sisters are of no help with their childish giggles and I dare not broach the subject with Mother. She may think me unmaidenly, for what daughter urges her parents into securing her marriage?

'I know you well, Elizabeth,' Cousin Henderson says. 'You always come in here to think as you pound away with pestle and mortar. Now, tell me what it is that drives you to be alone in this place of industry?'

I inhale slowly and summon my courage. 'At Oxford, my father said I must marry soon. Not for myself, you understand, but to

120

secure the future of Ham.'

Round brown eyes regard me speculatively. 'Indeed, your mama has mentioned her hopes in that direction.' I open my mouth to demand more, but she lifts a hand to forestall me. 'In a vague, general way, you understand.'

I groan inwardly at having revealed my soul to a servant who, as it turns out, appears to know nothing.

'I don't know what I expected.' I see no harm in expanding now she knows what is on my mind. 'Not one from amongst the impoverished rabble gathered in Oxford anyway.'

'Elizabeth!' She pulls back her chin in surprise. 'Those young men come from the best families in the land.'

'Families whose fortunes have been plundered once by the Sequestration Committee, and again by His Majesty. I fear we Murrays may be next, for Parliament has already taken most of our Richmond and Kingston rents for last year.' I fold my arms and lean against a dresser, annoyed at myself for having let my frustration show.

'Ah yes, I see.' She holds a finger to her lips in warning, flaps her hands at the open door as if shooing someone away.

I turn to see who is there, but they have already gone.

'My worst fear,' I continue, reassured our conversation will remain private, 'is that some Roundhead officer will throw us out of Ham to make room for his pallid-faced wife and Puritan children.'

The water in the pan has halved and she lifts out the eggs with a wooden spoon, laying them on a bunched up linen cloth.

'I will leave those to cool.' She replaces the hot water with cold from a nearby bucket. 'Our conversation is more entertaining.'

'Pray God it never comes to that.' She leans a hip against the table and fixes me with her bland stare. 'What kind of husband do you dream about?'

'Dreaming is a futile pastime, Cousin.' My sharp tongue responds for me. 'What I require from a husband is purely for the sake of my family.'

'A selfless ambition indeed.' She taps the top of one of the cooled eggs and peels off the cracked shell. 'A pair of kind eyes in a handsome face perhaps? Not to mention well-muscled calves that look to advantage in hose.' Her fingers pick bits of broken shell to reveal a bone-white interior. 'Do not those masculine qualities appeal?'

'I had not given such things any consideration.' Warmth floods my face at the lie, for I have thought of little else since Father first mentioned it. 'I shall accept whomever my parents choose.'

'You are not suitable for martyrdom.' Amusement lights her eyes and she lays down the shelled egg and plucks up the other, inserting a fingernail into a crack. 'You are a passionate creature who should have made a grand marriage by now, were it not for the uncertain times in which we live.'

This is the longest speech I have heard her make, apart from quotations from the bible to my sisters. I stare at her, amazed that she has given such thought to my predicament. She calls to a maid who passes outside in the courtyard. The girl jumps, her ferret eyes blinking rapidly in anticipation of rebuke. 'Fetch me a heavy pan would you?'

The maid bobs a curtsey, exhales in relief and darts away.

'Now what was I saying? Ah, yes. I imagine John Stuart would have suited you very well, or perhaps you prefer his younger brother, Bernard?'

'They are both handsome, charming young men, but I prefer Mary Villier's husband, James Lennox.' We slip naturally into the camaraderie of two friends. 'He's a duke, so would suit me better. Though on second thought, he has pretty looks but perhaps not a strong enough character for me.' I recall Prince Rupert's smouldering looks directed at Lady Mary, and Lennox's apparent unconcern. Had James married me, I would never dally with another man. Prince or not.

'Apart from the Lennoxes.' She pauses to accept the pan from the returning maid. 'Is there another who has caught your eye?'

The image of brown eyes beneath a head of soft, glossy curls on broad shoulders comes to mind. 'No, no one.' I shake my head, loosening a few strands of hair from my cap. I did not know Charles Cavendish well, but such a beautiful young man is hard to forget. What a waste that he should survive Edgehill, only to be killed in a skirmish at Gainsborough. Too many wonderful young men have been lost, and how many more will die in this war, leaving a string of widows and spinsters to mourn them?

'Your Papa would like to see you marry a Scotsman.' Cousin Henderson's voice brings me back to the present. '

Robert Moray springs to mind, but I dismiss him. 'I have lived in Richmond all my life, but at heart I am still Scots, so I would have no objection.' Though it occurs to me that few Scots of our acquaintance are either Presbyter or Royalist.

'However,' my cousin continues, 'if you are to avoid the more rapacious Royalist on the one hand, and the pious Covenanters on the other-'

'Not a Covenanter!' The words are out before I can stop them. 'That would be worse than marrying a Roundhead!'

She throws back her head and laughs, dislodging strands of reddish hair that fall in a soft frizz on her temples. 'In truth I cannot blame you.' She purses her lips and sweeps broken pieces of eggshell into a tidy pile. 'There is always the Tollemache family.'

'Who?' The name means nothing to me. 'I thought you had no names?'

'I did say that, didn't I?' Her flat eyes glint with mischief. 'I admit, I heard this one by accident. A lady spoke of the family to your mother, who repeated it to me.'

'Mother has never mentioned them.' The notion that Mama has discussed prospective bridegrooms with her waiting woman sharpens my voice. 'What else did she say?'

'That the Tollemaches own a vast estate in Suffolk, and the present baronet's great-great-great grandfather was Sheriff of Norfolk and Suffolk during the reign of Henry VIII.' A flash of unease enters her eyes. 'No one has gossiped about him to me, I promise you. But who can prevent the speculation of servants? I trust you not to repeat what I say to your mother.'

'No-o, at least, not if you tell me everything you know.' Aware I now have the upper hand, I fully intend to exploit it. 'You said he is the present baronet. Is he an older gentleman then? A widower perhaps?' Images crowd my head, most dominated by the infirmities of old age; a crackly voice, a hunched back, drooping jowls beneath coarse white whiskers and rheumy eyes.

'Are you quite well, Elizabeth?' She moves the pan with its sizzling egg yolks to one side and wipes her hands on her apron. 'You've gone quite pale.' She extends a hand to my forehead and then presses my cheek. 'You have no fever.'

I slap her hand away, suspecting she is trying to mollify me for having spoken out of turn. I doubt my colour has changed at all but for my burning cheeks. 'I am never ill, as well you know. Now, about this ancient baronet.'

She applies a wooden whisk to the yellow mass with unhurried strokes. 'Sir Lionel Tollemache,' she says after a pause, 'is, I am told, but nineteen, having inherited the title three years ago when his father died.'

Nineteen! The shrivelled husk in an armchair fades, replaced by a hope of affection, and the possibility of children. My breathing quickens. 'He owns a vast estate in Suffolk, you say. Is he Royalist?' Or is that too much to hope for?

'Apparently neither he nor his late father declared allegiance to either side. He is, what do they call it? Politically neutral.'

'You jest!' But her expression is clear and I cannot help a smile.

It's almost too good to be true, and maybe it is. How could anyone not aligned to the king's cause be equally as ambivalent to Parliament? What would such a family believe in?

She transfers the cooling yellow pulp into a clay dish. 'I have finished here for now.' She wipes her hands on a cloth and places a firm hand on my shoulder. 'Let us return to the house, it must be time for a nuncheon.'

Suddenly hungry, I acquiesce, intending to go straight to Mother with a dozen questions.

Outside, the gale has all but blown itself out, though above the suck and roar of the wind in the trees comes the unmistakeable pounding of hoof beats. Too many for a carriage.

Cousin Henderson and I exchange a glance of mutual bewilderment as we skirt the kitchen garden and cross the back of the house to the west side where the main entrance stands.

Captain Fitton stands at the door, his clenched fist raised to knock.

My gaze shifts to his other hand where he clutches an official-looking packet. My stomach plummets. I'd be willing to wager half my dowry he does not bring good news.

Chapter 12

'How many soldiers can you see?' Cousin Henderson's chin touches my shoulder as we crane round the corner of the house, the view of the gates obscured by shrubbery.

'No more than five,' I shout to be heard above the wind. 'It's not a patrol.'

She taps my arm and signals in the direction of the south front. Like two thieves in the night, we retrace our steps through the shrubbery and enter through the terrace door into the salon.

Mother turns from the fireplace as we enter. 'Close the door, you've brought the cold wind in.' Her face softens into bemused surprise. 'Betty, dear, you look ready for a Quaker meeting in those clothes.' The tremulous look I exchange with Cousin Henderson dismantles Mother's smile. 'What's wrong? Has something happened?'

'I am not sure, Mama, but Captain Fitton is at the front door.'

Her hands fall to her sides and her eyes close. She slumps onto the nearest sofa like a puppet with its strings cut. 'What can that brigand want from us this time?'

The door opens to admit William Ball, who advances into the room, a packet of papers in one hand. I look past him into the hall, but it is empty. 'The Captain has gone, Ball?' My heart leaps at this positive sign.

Ball gives a jerky nod. 'I asked if he wished to be announced, but he said it wasn't necessary. He instructed me to give you this, Mistress Murray.' Silently, he hands the packet to Mother.

Mother dismisses him, waiting until the door closes before her fingers pluck at the wax seal.

'What does it say?' My restless fingers twist my still slightly damp skirt.

'Give her a moment, Elizabeth.' Cousin Henderson's hand rests on my shoulder in gentle warning. 'The message will not alter for your exercising a little patience.'

Mother reads the two closely scrawled pages and looks up with a deep sigh. 'They are not satisfied with the rents. Parliament wants

Ham and all the lands this time.'

'They would take everything?' My voice rises as my fragile control threatens to spin away from me. I grasp a table to support my weakened legs. 'What are we going to do?'

'Would they allow you to compound?' Cousin Henderson addresses Mother.

'They haven't stated that as an option.' Mother scans the paper again, a finger to her lips. 'Only that they intend to sequester the estate of Ham House, and all its lands, rentals and income.'

'What does compound mean?' Katherine's voice says from the door.

'Kate!' Mother summons a smile. 'How long have you been there?'

'Not long. I saw the captain leave. Now are you going to tell me? I hate it when you speak in terms I do not understand.'

'You may as well explain,' I say with a shrug. 'We shall have to anyway if we are eventually forced to leave.'

'Leave Ham?' Kate's voice rises. 'What can you mean?'

'That will not happen, Betty.' Mother says with a see-what-you-have-done tone and turns to address Kate. 'To compound means we have to give the Committee what they decide the estate is worth.'

'Then can we stay here?' Kate's ringlets bounce on her cheeks as she looks from Mother to me and back again. 'Why don't we do that?'

'Because,' Mother begins, swallowing. 'I am sorely afraid they will value it too high.' Her eyes moisten and she swallows noisily. 'If we cannot pay, we would certainly lose the estate.'

Images of Ann Harrison and her father invade my head. Her family were deprived of Balls Park with no notice at all. Soldiers stood in Sir John Harrison's hall while he escaped through a rear door with only the clothes on his back. That cannot happen to us. I won't allow it.

'This is a letter of intent,' Mother says more slowly. 'They have to send to Lord Elgin to state their case against us as, 'Malignants' and 'Delinquents'.'

'You left out Papists and Recusants,' I say, attempting a laugh which comes out hollow. 'Is there nothing we can do?' I pace the floor, biting my lip.

'I can only appeal to the Committee.' Mother's jaw is set, which reassures me she has not lost heart for the fight.

'What good will that do?' I snap, reverting to childish sulks.

Kate's face twists in anguish. 'I don't wish to hear any more of this. How can you bear to let them take our home?' She flings out of the room and slams the door.

'I will go to her,' Cousin Henderson rises and follows.

'What are we going to do?' I take my frustration out on a thumbnail, chewing until it is sore.

'Perhaps I could press your father to take the Covenant, as it has now been made law for every man over eighteen.' I gape at her, but she merely shrugs. 'He can rescind it later.'

'Yes, yes, of course he can. Father will take any oath he has to in order to save Ham. It is only the king who dares hold out against such a law.' I stare at the red, torn skin of my cuticle, and fresh annoyance rises. The discomfort will bother me all evening. As if I had not enough irritations.

Mother claps her hands to get my attention. 'Do come and sit down, Betty dear. Your pacing makes me nervous. I have something serious to discuss with you.'

I slump obediently into the chair opposite. 'I think I know what you are going to say.'

'You do?' Her arched eyebrows raise in enquiry.

'Cousin Henderson told me about Sir Lionel Tollemache.'

'I see.' She folds her plump hands in her lap, unconcerned. 'I was going to tell you myself, but it appears the matter has gained some urgency.' She indicates the document in her hand. 'If you could put your prickly temper aside, how do you feel about this match, Betty?'

'I-I have had no time to feel anything. I heard the name not an hour ago.'

'Your father has already made preliminary approaches to the family, and thus far they are agreeable. To a discussion at any rate.'

I rub my arms with both hands and stare round. 'Why haven't the servants lit a fire in this room, it's so cold.' What I want to say is, will a family like that accept me, the daughter of an enemy of Parliament, but both pride and my shaky nerves keep me from voicing my fears aloud. If Ham is seized by the sequestors, I shall have no inheritance and no dowry. Without that the Tollemaches are unlikely to consider me a suitable match.

'In the event of a betrothal, the Committee are bound to withdraw, or they risk alienating the Tollemaches, which is something they would wish to avoid. They are an important and very ancient family. Thus we must have you betrothed to Sir Lionel by the end of the year.'

Evidently Mother has considered every detail.

'Have you met this Sir Lionel? What does he look like? Does he have brothers and sisters?'

'Well,' Mother stares at the ceiling. 'He does have seven elder sisters.'

'Seven!'

'The product of more than one marriage, I believe.'

The image of a spoiled, indulged boy with his mouth curved in a superior sneer appears in my head; the result of being feted all his life by so many doting women. 'Anything else?'

'I'm afraid the young gentleman's countenance is unknown to me.' Mother says, her lips pursed. 'That he is healthy, young and strong is more than enough to recommend him.' She lifts both hands and laughs. 'How ill-favoured can he be?'

I recall a woman of over sixty in the village, whose sixteen-year-old son engenders repulsion in all who see him. Youth is no guarantee of bodily perfection. My own sisters have physical flaws that might render them ill-favoured in some eyes.

'The Tollemaches own Helmingham Hall near Stowmarket,' Mother continues, 'a beautiful and ancient house I am told.'

Suffolk! My stomach drops into my shoes. How could I have overlooked the fact I would be expected to live in my husband's home? Suddenly, the notion of being Lady Tollemache isn't quite so attractive. I cannot bear the idea of leaving Ham.

'Would my marriage make such a difference to the Committee?' I ask, worried now that this may not be a good idea after all.

'If your father entrusts the estate to your future husband, most

129

certainly, yes.'

'In which case this Sir Lionel could take every penny we have, and we could still be homeless.'

'The Tollemaches do not seek to add Ham to their assets, my dear, they are rich enough.' Mother pats my hand and rises to study her reflection in the mirror above the mantle. 'Your father still regrets he cannot marry you to Sir Robert Moray.'

'Mother, he is penniless and at this moment resides in a Bavarian prison.'

'I am quite aware of that. However, your father has hopes he will be released soon. Sir Robert has some influence through that society they are all members of.'

My chin jerks up. 'What society?'

She plucks at her skirt with nervous fingers and avoids my gaze as if she realises she has said too much. 'It is merely a gentlemen's club,' she lowers her voice, despite there being no one but myself to hear. 'The members take an oath as Royalists, and swear to further the cause.'

'Further–? You mean they work against Parliament in secret?'

She shrugs, but my insistent gaze finally penetrates her veneer of reluctance. 'It's a Scots organisation, though Robert Moray was initiated in England. They call themselves stonemasons. Do not look at me like that, Betty. I know very little about it. Besides,' the plump shoulders rise in dismissal, 'I said it was secret. Why would they discuss something like that with a mere woman?' Her light laugh does not convince me.

'Is that why Robert Moray is a prisoner, because he is a spy?' Enthralled by this talk of secret societies, I push Sir Lionel to the back of my mind

'Oh, dear, I shouldn't have mentioned it, your father–'

'Father is a member?'

Her deep flush confirms it, though I am not surprised. Deceit and subterfuge are the tenets he lives by. 'Why do they call themselves stonemasons?'

'I have no idea, only that they form some sort of brotherhood, and that once the king is back in Westminster, their titles and income will be restored, and we shall all reap generous rewards.'

'I applaud your faith, Mama. Have you considered the Committee might beggar us long before then, and the king could lose his fight with the rebels?'

Her spine stiffens and her eyes glint with fury. 'How could he lose? He is our crowned sovereign. No one outranks him.'

The thought strikes me that thousands of rebel troops who lay down the law not a mile away at Kingston might argue with her, but for once I hold my tongue.

'I have never doubted the king, and you should not either.' She leaves the mirror and returns to her seat, her fists clenched on her knees. 'Forget stonemasons, your thoughts now should be on your prospective bridegroom. Is that not enough to occupy you?'

'I apologise, Mama. You are right, but consider how awful it would be, to keep our home out of the clutches of the Committee, only to hand it over to a careless spouse instead?'

'Sir Lionel comes from an ancient and noble family who can trace themselves back to the Norman Conquest.'

'Which side?' I murmur beneath my breath.

'Hold your cynical tongue, girl.' Her eyes sparkle with tears and I am filled with remorse.

'I am sorry, Mama. I do not mean to doubt you or Father.' I take the place beside her on the sofa and wrap my arms around her shoulders. 'I am simply afraid that no matter what we do, we cannot stop the rebels taking everything we have.'

Her nose is cold against my cheek, and her clothes smell faintly of jasmine and honeysuckle, conjuring happier days of my childhood. Days when I didn't have to worry about advantageous marriages and threats to our home. 'I will summon a servant to light this fire, and you can tell me more about Sir Lionel Tollemache.' I rise and pull the bell rope.

A watery smile appears on Mother's face and she dabs her cheeks with a scrap of lace pulled from a pocket. 'His mother is Elizabeth Stanhope, whose father was John, Lord Stanhope. Sir Lionel's wealth does not depend upon the auspices of the crown.'

'I did not know such men still existed.' I resume my seat and lean my forehead against hers. 'And he has seven sisters as well as a mother still living?'

Mother waves a hand in dismissal. 'That should not worry my Betty? You will enchant her, my darling. As for the sisters, they are all older and most are likely safely married off.'

'I hope you are right,' I say with a sigh, not looking up as Ball enters.

'The gentleman is here, Mistress,' he says, pinch-mouthed. 'Where do you require him to wait?'

'What gentleman?' My glance slides from Mother to Ball and back again. 'I didn't know we expected anyone.'

Mother's face clears and her eyes sparkle with recollection. 'Oh, I had quite forgot. Show Master Lely into the small salon, Ball. Mistress Elizabeth will be with him in a moment.'

Ball withdraws, leaving me gaping like a landed fish. 'Who? And why does he need to see me?'

'Your father arranged everything.' She announces this fact as if further questions are unnecessary. 'Master Peter Lely is from The Hague, and likely to become the next court painter, or so your father says.' She bustles toward me and pulls me to my feet. 'The king thinks most highly of him, and because he is as yet unknown, he does not charge the outrageous fees most artists do.'

'I'm sure, Mama,' I inhale slowly, summoning patience. 'But what does he have to do with me?'

'Oh, did I not say? He's come to paint your portrait.'

Leaving the young man from The Hague kicking his heels in the salon, I hurry upstairs to change into my pale blue silk. Partly to annoy Mother for having failed to inform me of the occasion, and also because I looked far too shabby to be immortalised in a portrait designed to endure for future generations of Murrays, and hopefully Tollemaches.

The reason for Ball's prior distaste is plainly evident in the figure who springs to his feet on my entry into the salon. A strikingly handsome face with soulful dark eyes sits beneath a battered hat brim, cocked up at the front and from which straggly, ill-cut dark hair falls in mahogany curls to below his shoulders.

Belatedly he snatches off the hat and crushes it to a stained doublet with fingers rimed with either dirt, or paint. His full lips do not so much as quiver into a smile at the sight of me, and his bow is

132

curt rather than courtly; both facts I find disconcerting. Evidently irritated at being kept waiting, he sets to work arranging his easel without waiting for my greeting.

'Where shall I sit?' I ask through clenched teeth.

'No sit. Stand by here.' He reaches past me and tweaks the curtain into a curved line. He gazes round for a moment then lifts a finger and darts to roll a round table in front of the curtain on which he balances a vase shaped like a Greek urn. He ponders the arrangement for a moment before moving the table a fraction to the left.

Annoyed at being ignored, I am about to speak again, but before I can do so, he beckons me to the curtain with swift, curt movements of his long fingers.

Apparently satisfied, he steps back to his easel and picks up brushes and sticks of charcoal, paying me no more attention than if I were a chair.

'Do I look at my best with this drape behind me?' I try again to instigate some sort of civil exchange.

'Iss goot. The light ees better there,' he replies without looking at me. 'Be still eef you please.'

Chastened, I fall silent, the only sound in the room the scrape of charcoal on canvas.

* * *

June 1644

Since Captain Fitton's last visit, I scan the road each day in anticipation of more riders with damning news about our fate. It is five weeks since that first notice arrived and the Committee appear content to keep us in mortal fear of their next action.

Master Lely no longer calls at the house each day from his Kingston lodgings to work on my portrait. In a way I regret his absence, for I became accustomed to his silent way of working, using the time to think and reminisce.

His taciturn ways persisted, but the portrait itself surprised us all, and was completed after only three weeks. In my best blue silk gown with Mother's pearls around my throat, I look pale, ethereal and maybe more serene than I am in real life.

I feel sure Sir Lionel will like it and hope Mother is right when she predicts Master Lely will replace the late Master Van Dyck as the next court painter. I also hope the fee Mother pays him allows him to purchase the services of a barber.

A letter from Father he concealed in a packet of flour, informs us that Rupert has left to join Lord Newcastle against the Scots Covenanters and the rebel army laying siege to York. Then almost as an afterthought, he adds that the Earl of Essex's army left London to join forces with Sir William Waller and Oxford is under siege.

While Mother and I fret over how Father would fare in a siege, another letter arrives to say he has left Oxford with the queen. He made no mention of my friend, Ann Harrison, and I worry for her safety, hoping she and her family have found somewhere to be safe from Roundheads.

Then my thoughts turn to Queen Henrietta Maria, pregnant and ill, according to Mother. Where she obtains her information, I do not ask, but she appears sure of the fact that with rebels approaching Oxford, the king decided to send her to Exeter.

'She gave birth to a daughter at Bedford House,' Mother's announcement comes one sultry afternoon. It is too hot to go outside, where even simple tasks drain our energy, so we sit in the salon.

'Is she in Exeter still?' I ask, aware the rebels are on their way there.

'No, she has fled to France, leaving the child behind.' Mother delves into a pocket and removes a packet she holds out to me. 'Before he left Oxford, Ann Harrison gave this to your father for you, dearest.'

'Thank you.' I take it from her, the parchment softened and much stained. I wander to the window seat and perch in the corner where the fierce summer sun falls into shadow, open out the page and begin to read.

24th May 1644
Oxford

My Dearest Elizabeth,

I hope this letter finds you well. I write to inform you of some marvellous news that you will not be surprised to hear from me.

Master Richard Fanshawe and I were married on the eighteenth day of May at Wolvercot Church. A blissful, though quiet ceremony with none in attendance but my dear father, my sister Margaret, who is known to you, and also my brother and sister Boteler. Master Edward Hyde, and Sir Geoffrey Palmer were gracious enough to stand as witnesses. I was married with my mother's wedding ring, which was long her desire.

His Majesty the king has promised my dearest Richard preferment as soon as occasion offers. Before this terrible war, my portion was 10,000 pounds, but now we are to be merchant adventurers, for we have not twenty pounds betwixt us.

I cannot grieve for it, being the happiest of women now I am the wife of my dearest Fanshawe. It is all I can wish for.

My compliments to my Mistress Murray and to your dear sisters.
Your affectionate friend
Ann Fanshawe, Harrison as was.

I pick out snippets to read out to Mother, who looks less than enthusiastic at Ann's news.

'I cannot help but feel she will live to regret her choice,' Mother says.

'I am happy for her. Never have I seen a girl so in love.' My voice teases, for secretly, I agree.

For Ann to marry under such circumstances is reckless. In her situation, I would have sought out the richest man I could find, love or not.

'Tush!' Mother arranges her skirts on the sofa beside me before settling down with her embroidery. 'In such times we have not the luxury of marrying where our hearts lie.'

'Ann does mention they have no money,' I say.

'Hah! Wait until the babies come. She'll have reason to grumble

135

then.'

'She does no more than we all do, Mama. She hopes for happier times, and Sir Richard is best placed to receive royal largesse when the war is over.'

'Except that His Majesty is now on his way to the west country. There will be few honours to be had in Oxford until he returns. And maybe not even then.'

'What else have you heard?' I keep my tone casual, but my nights are plagued with faceless visitors coming to the door with fresh orders to dispossess us.

'From the Committee, you mean?' Mother's brow lifts, her lips pursed. 'I admit, a messenger arrived this afternoon when you were out riding, sent through the garrison at Kingston.'

'Only a messenger, not a troop of horse?' My attempt at sarcasm brings a curl to her lips.

'No, no troop of horse.' She shoots me an uneasy smile. 'The Committee applied to Lord Elgin, as we thought, but they have not yet made a decision.'

'Lord Elgin is an influential Covenanter, and Father told me the Puritans would not wish to alienate him.'

'I like that fact even less, my dear. With the king now set against the Scots, I doubt the Covenanters dare assist known Royalists. It implies they have divided interests. We may not be able to count on their support indefinitely.'

'Lord Elgin must have some power, or the Committee would have already seized the estate.' I study her expression closely. How did I not notice the purple shadows that sit beneath her eyes before now?

'I believe they do, but suppose things go badly for the king in the north? Lord Elgin will be forced to take the side of Parliament.'

'He is your kinsman, Mama. Surely he wouldn't throw us on the mercy of our enemies?'

'He may have no choice.' Her hands still on her lap and I cover them with my own in silent comfort. Her skin is dry, papery and her bones so fragile, I fear they might snap if I grip too hard. How small she is, and although we are of the same stature, I feel robust beside her.

The room darkens around us, the orange and pink dusk beyond the window leaches to a pale grey. The servants haven't been in to light the candles, but as soon as this thought comes to me, so does another. Mother must have left instructions not to do so in order to save money. Going to bed at sunset and rising at dawn has become second nature.

All we can do now is hope the York campaign is a success, and Prince Rupert proves himself the great commander he wishes us all to believe.

Dare I pin all my hopes on a handsome prince and a small white dog? A dog that the rebels claim can turn invisible? I am too worldly to believe in one, but I may be able to put my faith in the other.

Chapter 13

July 1644

The meadow between the north front and the river is covered with camomile flowers, flourishing where few cattle now graze. Willow fronds bend to brush the water. Despite its lush beauty, summer is spoiled for me by the fact we have not yet heard the Committee's decision on our fate. Like Mother, I am at pains to keep distressing news from my sisters, but each day brings fresh worry that we will soon be ordered out of our home.

One sultry afternoon, wherein no breath of wind stirs the trees and the ducks spread their wings on the riverbank to keep cool, Mother and I set off for Petersham Lodge, and dinner with Lodowick Carlisle and his wife, Joan. An event I always anticipate with pleasure, the prospect made no less agreeable when we are stopped on the road by Captain Fitton.

He must hide in the shrubbery, for as we turn into the gate to Richmond Park, his patrol appears out of nowhere and demands our direction. Some huffing and deep thoughtfulness ensues on the part of the Captain, while Mother smiles benignly and I seethe; but after a frustrating delay, he has no choice but to allow our progress.

'The man resents all this beautiful acreage being reserved for the king's hunting,' Lodowick Carlisle says by way of explanation when we arrive and explain our tardiness.

Our host struts before the fireplace in wide petticoat breeches and a crimson coat embroidered with gold thread. I wonder if he will ever concede to less flamboyant attire to appease the Puritans, but as a lifelong courtier and close friend of King Charles, I doubt he will do so willingly.

Though he must be upwards of forty, he bows over my hand like a young gallant, a sparkle of youthful exuberance in his eyes. 'Fitton would rather see the land turned over to common grazing for sheep and cows, with a few crooked cottages for crofters.' His high laugh breaks off as his wife enters the room on the arm of Master Justinian Isham, another friend my heart lifts to see.

A widower in his thirties, Justinian is one of the most attractive men I know, and despite his reputation for preferring his own opinion to any other, I cannot help but like him. He reminds me of myself.

'Whom do you laugh at, Lodowick?' Joan greets Mother with affection, and then her delicate hands enfold mine and we buss each other's cheek.

'No one of importance, my dear.' Lodowick waits until the formalities are observed before waving us to an arrangement of sofas set in a horseshoe facing the bay window overlooking the park.

'I did not realise you still resided with the Carlisles, Master Isham.' I allow my hand to linger in his longer than politeness allows. 'Are the circumstances not yet right for your return to Leicestershire?' Mother had mentioned to me some time ago that he fought a similar battle to our own with the Committee.

'Betty!' Mother nudges me. 'It is inappropriate of you to enquire as to a gentleman's circumstances.'

'Dear Mistress Murray, do not chastise your lovely daughter.' Master Isham regards me with an attention which I can only describe as admiring. 'To my chagrin, the Sequestration Committee hounds me to death. Fortunately dear Lodowick and Joan's hospitality allows me to travel to London to fight my case.'

'Hush, Justinian!' Joan shoots him a hard look. 'No talk of the wretched Committee this evening. We are here to dine in pleasant company, not wallow in our misery.'

'It will take more than the likes of Sir Richard Onslow to dislodge me from my position as Keeper of His Majesty's Park,' Lodowick interjects from Justinian's shoulder.

'What's this? Are you in fear of being evicted, Lodowick? Surely not!' a male voice says from the door. The newcomer is a grandfatherly-looking man in a dark blue clerical gown, with a plain crisp white collar, and cap. 'I do hope not, Ludo. The social discourse of my friends offers the only respite from the world's troubles.'

His blue eyes shine with gentleness from within a long face that bears a beard similar to all the Van Dyck paintings I have often admired at Hampton Court. Every hair on his head, from the thick brows, the fringe that covers his top lip, to the locks falling onto his collar, are a dazzling snow white.

'My Lord Bishop. How nice to see you again. I trust Oxford is no worse than when we left it?' Mother drops instantly into a curtsey and I quickly follow.

'No, no, my dear Mistress Murray.' Bishop Brian Duppa pulls us both upright again with gentle, almost feminine hands. 'But I am afraid bishops are nowadays unpopular in that city.' He inclines his head, both hands clasped in a pose I imagine he uses to give benediction.

'Bishops are no more popular than baronets!' a voice says from behind the clergyman.

Joan rushes past me to greet the newcomer. 'Sir Thomas, I did not hear you come in, do forgive me.' She turns to Mother. 'Mistress Murray. Are you acquainted with Sir Thomas Knyvett?'

'I do not believe so.' Mother extends her hand to a kindly faced middle-aged man. 'I am honoured to make your acquaintance, my lord.'

'I've learned to silence my footsteps of late,' he says, lazily. 'Rebels lurk round every corner.'

My turn comes and his gaze lights with interest as he takes the ends of my fingers in his. I return the greeting politely but snatch my hand from beneath his too-wet kiss. Despite my curt rejection, he regards me intently from beneath beetling brows whilst at the same time accepting a glass of Rhenish from a tray borne aloft by a footman.

Lodowick plants both feet in front of the empty fireplace, knees bent. 'These days we must keep our opinions and allegiances to ourselves. Which is why we Royalists congregate in groups to bemoan our situation.'

'I may as well forget making claim to my family title,' Justinian's mouth turns down like a sulky child. 'Perhaps I should turn my attentions to something more useful.'

'What pursuit did you have in mind, Justinian?' Joan presses his arm as she passes to take the empty chair beside me.

'Perhaps I might found a school. In Northamptonshire maybe.

What say you, Lodowick?'

'What say I?' Lodowick laughs. 'I cannot see you as a headmaster of unruly boys, Justinian. But if it keeps you out of trouble, it would be obtuse of me to disapprove.'

'With four motherless daughters,' Justinian says, 'perhaps it will stand me in good stead to ensure their future husbands are well-educated. When the Sequestration Committee has decimated my estate, I doubt I will be able to offer them dowries.'

'What did I say about forbidden subjects in my house?' Joan wags a finger at him and he splays his hands in apology.

'I do not wish to appear a bad host, Joan.' Lodowick rubs his hands together and stares pointedly at the clock above the mantle. 'But if dinner isn't announced soon, I swear we shall all faint from hunger.'

'A poor jest, Ludo.' Joan scowls at him. 'When there are families in Kingston and Richmond who'll have little enough on their tables tonight. Ah! Here's the steward to announce our meal. Now, my Lord Bishop, do escort Mistress Murray, and you, Justinian may take in Mistress Elizabeth.'

To enter the dining room at Petersham Lodge is to step into a woodland glade below a starlit sky where Joan has applied her artist's skills to devastating effect. The columns supporting the ceiling are painted to look like tree trunks that spread branches of lush green across the ceiling. Interspersed in the leaves nestle fruits, birds and small animals, through which peeps a midnight blue sky with twinkling stars.

Candlelight glints off glass, silver and the tiny mirrors strategically placed on the table and walls. Although it is only six of the clock on a summer evening, the gloom of the richly decorated room requires the candelabra to be lit.

'Do tell us what news from the north, Mistress Murray,' Joan asks as the food appears. 'I am sure you have more intelligence than we do. We promise to keep your counsel.'

As one, all eyes rest on Mother in eager anticipation.

'I am afraid I have nothing new to tell,' Mother says. 'Other than the Earl of Derby and Prince Rupert are bound for York to relieve the siege there.'

'Most of Lancashire is under Rupert's control, I doubt he'll encounter much opposition there.' Sir Thomas' gaze sweeps the table, looking pleased when no one contradicts him.

'I have to claim superior knowledge, Mistress Murray,' Lodowick says, helping himself to onions and cabbage. 'It seems that at Knaresborough, Prince Rupert discovered he was outnumbered, so planned not to engage until the Marquis of Newcastle arrived to join forces fourteen miles west of York. Realising that he was heavily outnumbered, Rupert wanted to avoid engaging the Army of Both Kingdoms until the Marquis of Newcastle's infantry join him from York.'

'Then let us hope he curbs that restless spirit of his and waits.' Justinian says, passing Mother a plate of buttered peas.

'What about the dear queen?' Joan throws a wide-eyed look at her husband, who spreads his hands.

'I know nothing of it, my dear, Mistress Murray is telling the story.' Lodowick spears a slice of pink fleshed lamb from a platter and transfers it to his plate.

With an annoyed 'tut' at her husband, Joan turns to Mother. 'Is it true the king sent her to Exeter, a distance of over a hundred and fifty miles in her delicate condition?' she asks, horrified. 'I do hope her health improves.'

'I thought pregnancy could only be enhanced by the appearance of a babe, dear lady.' Sir Thomas searches each face for a response, but receives none.

Mother narrows her eyes at the miscreant, who flushes and stares at his plate. 'Her Majesty has been in considerable pain not attributed to her condition. I witnessed her extreme discomfort whilst in Oxford this last spring.'

I sip my wine, only listening with half an ear as she recounts the queen's flight from Oxford, a story she has told me several times.

'An Exeter princess!' Joan clasps her hands together in delight. 'And what have they named the child?'

'Henrietta after her mother,' Mother leans across the table to an enraptured Joan. 'And Anne, in remembrance of her third daughter, who died as an infant.'

'Rupert has enemies who are envious of his recent success,'

Lodowick says, confirming my impression that the male contingent in the room have lost interest in babies, royal or not. 'I fear at this moment they profit by his absence to excite the king's distrust. Lord Goring wrote he was ready to join the prince with eight thousand horse, but the king demanded Goring's instant return.' He rests his gaze on each of us as if gauging our reaction. 'What did Rupert do? He disregarded the order saying that Goring's services were more necessary to himself.'

Bishop Duppa steeples his hands on the table. 'May the Lord grant them a good outcome in York.'

I bite my lip to resist an urge to enquire if he intends saying grace for the second time that evening.

'Amen to that.' Justinian moves aside as a servant sets a large oyster pie on the table, transforming the bishop's serene expression to an eager smile as he helps himself to a generous portion.

'I wish you would show more confidence in His Majesty, Ludo.' Joan says, while I wonder which Majesty she refers to, Prince Rupert or the king. 'The Royalist army is bound to triumph in York, then everything will be back to normal again.'

Sir Thomas wipes his hands vigorously on the towel draped over his shoulder. 'Whatever sends these pious churchmen off the battlefields and back to their prayers would suit me.' He glances at the man on my left and gives a startled blink. 'Oh, pray forgive me, my Lord Bishop, I intend no offence.'

'None taken here, sir.' Brian Duppa waves a gracious hand. 'I have long since lost both patience and understanding of the Presbyterian gentlemen.' His white brows draw together. 'Though I abhor the state of affairs that has condemned Archbishop Laud to his fate.'

Despite the fierce prosecution by Parliament at Bishop Laud's trial last March, the lords adjourned without coming to a vote. Even his most bitter enemy could not stretch the law enough to prove the man guilty of treason.

'Will the archbishop be released, do you think?' I ask, in an attempt to distract myself from Sir Thomas' penetrating gaze, which is upon me every time I look up.

'I very much doubt it, my dear.' Justinian's eyes dull with regret.

The ensuing silence is broken only by the scrape of spoons and clink of glasses, together with the odd cough. Sad faces and averted eyes tell me what fate everyone believes the rebels have in store for the Archbishop.

'Last year,' Sir Thomas breaks the silence. 'I came up against one of those 'Eastern Association' fellows at the siege of Lowestoft. If you think the local Roundheads are fanatics, you ought to see *these* men.'

'If you insist on regaling us, Sir Thomas,' Joan gives the forced laugh of a hostess trying to reignite her dinner party when the men insist talking politics. 'For the benefit of those who are sorely ignorant, what association is this?'

'It is some sort of union of country militia from Norfolk, Suffolk, Essex, Cambridgeshire and Hertfordshire.' Lodowick holds up his knife in gleeful triumph at his knowledge. 'Huntingdonshire and Lincolnshire joined last year.'

'How clever of you to know, Ludo.' Joan taps his hand, though his jaw jerks in a way that tells me her touch was not a gentle one.

'Don't imagine they are simple country peasants, my dear sir.' Bishop Duppa holds up a finger. 'This alliance makes the Parliament army better organised, and a force to be reckoned with.'

'Allow me to finish my story, if you will,' Sir Thomas holds up a hand for silence. 'While awaiting a ship to cross to Holland, a handful of Royalists attacked the Parliamentary forces, only to be rapidly defeated. The rebel commander ordered all strangers in the town, of which I was one, to surrender ourselves.'

Joan signals the servants to serve the fruit and nuts, though the gentlemen are more interested in the newly arrived carafes of wine.

'I shan't forget him in a hurry.' Sir Thomas sniffs and downs half a glass of wine in one gulp, smacks his lips and looks up at our expectant faces. 'Fella called Cromwell. First name Oswald, or was it Oliver? Yes, that was it. Oliver Cromwell.'

'What did you do, Sir Thomas?' Taking the footman's place, Lodowick circles the table, filling glasses and smiling at his guests while he pats shoulders and arms.

'I was arrested, and endured an uncomfortable ride to Windsor Castle as a prisoner. Fella thought I was involved!'

144

My glass hits the table with a sharp click as memories of Major Buxton resurface.

'Are you unwell, Elizabeth?' Justinian's brow puckers. 'You are quite pale.'

I steady my glass before the contents spill on the polished surface. 'I am quite well, sir. Really.'

He straightens with an if-you-are-sure smile and turns back to Sir Thomas.

'I had not a change of clothing,' Sir Thomas continues, oblivious of my discomfort, 'and one bed had to serve for seven persons.'

'How dreadful!' Joan's hand clutches at her thin neck.

'It was. And but for the fair ladies of the town who attended us, it might have been much worse.' He spreads both hands across his midriff. 'My wife was much aggrieved. Not for my incarceration, you understand, but the company I kept.'

The room erupts into delighted laughter and this time when Sir Thomas glares at me I glare back, at which he flushes and turns away.

'I have had no occasion to meet Colonel Cromwell myself,' my Lord Bishop dabs his lips slowly, eyes cast down. 'However, there was a certain incident at Oxford when his men captured some cattle on university grounds.' He nods at me. 'It must have been after you left, my dear. I was quite convinced the rebels were about to storm the city again. It quite had me in a confusion.'

'Elizabeth?' Lodowick asks when the laughter dies down. 'Have you had an opportunity to read the play I wrote and dedicated to your dear father?'

'I have indeed, sir, and found *The Deserving Favourite* to be excellent.' For the benefit of everyone else in the room I continue, 'It's a tragi-comedy with a romantic cast.'

'Does your Mama condone you reading love stories?' Bishop Duppa balances his chin in his hand and regards me with a direct blue gaze.

Mother flushes and I spring to defend her. 'Is there such a thing as delicacy in these times, sir?' I return his stare. 'I have seen more in these last two years than a matron of five and forty.'

'Ah! There you have me, dear child.'

'Ludo, you are so vain about your writing,' Joan taps his hand again. 'Leave Elizabeth in peace; she may not even have read the thing and only says so to please you.'

A footman appears at the door and beckons to our host, who gives his excuses and leaves the table.

'I confess,' Mother says as the door closes. 'I was fortunate enough to see *The Deserving Favourite* performed by His Majesty's servants at the little Blackfriars Theatre some years ago.'

'As did I, dear lady.' Justinian looks down his elegant nose. 'However, I had to pay a shilling for the privilege.' He pauses to allow the merriment to subside before continuing. 'Alas, that delightful venue has been closed down, so I know not when we shall have the pleasure of watching any play there again.'

Lodowick's return brings all eyes toward him. His face has lost all colour and he gropes for the edge of the table, his knuckles white.

'Ludo?' Joan rises to her feet. 'What is it? What's happened?' She scrapes back her chair and runs to her husband's side. 'Oh, Ludo, say something, you're frightening me.'

Justinian circles the table and presses a glass into his host's hand. 'Here, drink this, man! You look as if you are about to have a seizure.'

Lodowick takes a long gulp, heedless of the wine that dribbles down his chin. 'News from the north,' he gasps, swallowing. 'The-the Royalists are slaughtered!' He sprays the table with blood-red droplets. 'Four days ago, on a moor somewhere outside York.'

Gasps and murmurs of dismay erupt and someone tips over a glass, but no one takes any notice. I glance at Mother, but her eyes are squeezed tightly shut.

'Prince Rupert and Newcastle took on Lord Leven's Covenanters, the Earl of Manchester's Eastern Association and Lord Fairfax's Parliamentarians outside York.' Ludo lowers his empty glass and Justinian fills it again. More, I suspect for something to do for his hands shake, and the crystal clinks hard enough to break.

Joan releases a frustrated sob. 'I thought the intention was to relieve the siege of York, not launch into pitched battle!'

Justinian holds up a hand. 'I doubt Prince Rupert got that far, Mistress Carlisle. Lord Manchester and the Eastern Association joined the besiegers of York in early June, taking the unguarded northern sector between the Ouse and Foss.'

'Please, sir!' Joan snaps. 'I beg you not to dwell on the geography. It means nothing to me.' Her eyes shoot fire, the distress adds years to her features. 'Forgive me, I did not mean-'

'Quite understandable.' Bishop Duppa shifts position to pat her hand. 'Do go on, Lodowick.'

Our hosts's hand trembles as he takes another sip from his glass. 'It was late afternoon when Prince Rupert gathered his men on the field. He assumed no attack would happen until morning, so he quit the field in search of his supper.'

'So much for the invincible commander!' Sir Thomas grabs the wine carafe from Justinian and pours himself a generous amount before passing it into the bishop's reaching hand.

My attention drifts, and I wonder why men always rush for the drink while women grow pale and sniffle. I could do with some wine myself, but am reluctant to wrestle it from the bishop.

Mother's face is immobile and her eyes dry, but I imagine she thinks the same as me, that this is the end of our hopes and the Royalists could never recover from such a blow.

'What went wrong?' I ask, hoping Prince Rupert survived.

Lodowick focuses on me with mild surprise, as if he had forgotten my presence.

'Ah, well, Newcastle's men had not been paid for some time and mutinied. Many of them were drunk and looted the city for food and money. Prince Rupert demanded Newcastle prepare for battle, but the order was not received well.'

'Rupert never could discipline his men.' Justinian slumps in his seat, his wine glass cradled in both hands and tapping the glass with his fingers.

'Go on, my dear sir.' Bishop Duppa leaves his seat to place a hand on Lodowick's shoulder. 'It was a massacre, you say?'

Lodowick nods. 'Four thousand Royalists, dead. With fifteen hundred taken prisoner.'

Mother's cry is smothered by an anguished wail from Joan.

'And the rebels?' I ask. 'How many did they lose?'

Lodowick's shrug moves the gold thread on his coat so it shimmers in the low light. 'Three hundred.'

'Is that all?' Sir Thomas groans. 'But Prince Rupert's army are-'

'Lying dead on a moor.' Lodowick shakes his head again. 'All the Royalist ordnance, gunpowder and baggage captured, along with a hundred regimental colours. It was a disaster.'

'What did the king say when he heard?' Joan's hand hovers above her husband's shoulder, but she retracts it without making contact.

'Prince Rupert's failure has set him against the man.' He curls his lip, and this confirmation that Rupert still lives makes the breath leave me in a rush. One cannot be angry with a dead man. 'And Newcastle, who spent his entire fortune on the Royalist cause, says he refuses to 'endure the laughter of the Court.' He plans to abandon the cause and leave the country. Lord Ethyn goes with him.'

'Cowards!' Mother mutters, but with less force than I expect.

The room falls silent as the footmen file into the room to remove the covers and clear the table.

'Let us retire to the drawing room, so we can continue our discussion.' Our host rises and with despondent steps, we troop down the hall.

The sunset outside tall casement windows floods the room with soft coral light. Silhouettes of fallow deer stroll between the trees in the park to make a scene of beauty untouched by death and defeat. My throat closes with emotion and I blink away tears at the tragic absurdity of it all.

I occupy a sofa with Mother and Joan, while Sir Thomas lounges on a straight-backed chair and resumes his scrutiny of me. I am tempted to change my seat, but realise I cannot do so without attracting questions from Mother.

'Please go on with your story, Master Carlisle,' I venture, hoping to hear of some shred of good news amongst the bad.

'Forgive me if my information is patchy.' Lodowick's voice is steadier now, and his hands no longer tremble. 'The messenger was in a hurry to take the news to Richmond. I only hope I can recall everything he said.'

'We may have to await the next issue of *The Intelligencier*.' Joan sniffs into a handkerchief. 'I am sure there will be a full report there.'

'Maybe so, Joan.' Justinian paces the floor. 'But we would like to hear the rest of Ludo's account.'

'Oh, yes of course. I apologise. Do go on Lodowick.'

I give Joan a sympathetic look at being chastised by her own guest, though I too wish she would let Lodowick speak.

'The Parliamentarian cavalry cleared the Royalist garrisons around York, and the Scots stormed the city defences, demanding the Royalists surrender. Newcastle opened negotiations for a treaty.'

'He must have been playing for time if he was outnumbered.' Justinian pauses beside the fireplace, one elbow on the mantle and a foot on the fender.

'I believe so too.' Lodowick gives a wry smile.

'It all sounds truly horrible.' Joan cannot sit still and leaps to her feet when a servant enters with porter and more wine.

'Then what happened, Master Carlisle?' Mother's intelligent gaze probes his face.

'York is back in Scots' and Parliament hands, and the Royalists surrendered.' Lodowick gives a weary shrug. 'They were permitted to leave the city with their arms and colours.'

'Well, that's something,' the bishop says with a benevolent smile.

'Not really.' Lodowick sighs. 'Most of them have since deserted.'

'Will York resist the rebel occupation?' Sir Thomas asks.

'I doubt it.' Lodowick ushers Joan back to her seat then resumes centre stage by the windows. 'Lord Fairfax earned the thanks of the city by refusing to allow religious zealots to vandalise the churches and the Minster.'

'And Prince Rupert?'

'Dreadfully disheartened at losing so many men.' Lodowick sighs again. 'And it appears someone forgot to tie up his dog. The animal followed him onto the battlefield, where it was found dead hours later.'

'Poor Boye,' Mother says, echoing my own sentiments.

'Prince Rupert has given Colonel Cromwell's men the soubriquet, 'Ironsides'.' Lodowick's mouth twists into a cynical smile.

'What will he do now?' I ask. 'The prince, I mean.' The thought of Prince Rupert cowed by a Roundhead officer is not reassuring.

Lodowick shrugs. 'I imagine he intends to rebuild a new Royalist army.'

'I wish him well,' Justinian says. 'Yet I cannot help thinking he embarks upon a hopeless task.'

'Have you lost faith too, Master Isham?' Bishop Duppa's silver brows meet on his forehead in a troubled frown.

Justinian offers a weak smile. 'I was going to say I'll never keep my estate at this rate, but that would be disrespectful to all those men who died.'

'Does anyone know what is happening in Cornwall?' Bishop Duppa surveys the room expectantly. 'They are still for the Royalists, I understand.'

'I heard a rumour in Kingston yesterday,' Sir Thomas responds. 'There are anti-Parliament riots in London.'

'Discontentment with Parliament grows daily,' Lodowick confirms. 'Their bullying tactics over religion are more unpopular than their oppressive taxes. Desertion is rife amongst the rebels.'

'That is encouraging, is it not?' I say, examining each male face in search of reassurance, while wondering how this defeat will affect my father in France. 'Do you think the king can take advantage of this discontent?'

Justinian examines the remaining wine in his glass, takes a sip and regards me with a world-weary smile. 'In truth, I doubt it, Elizabeth. Not when the rebels have a new commander everyone fears.'

'You mean this Cromwell fellow?' Sir Thomas nods. 'You could have a point. At Lowestoft he was well respected by the soldiers.'

Justinian sighs. 'Cromwell has emerged from nowhere to become a brilliant cavalry commander. The entire Parliament army listens to him, and he has plans.'

'What sort of plans?' Mother asks.

'I heard rumours he intends to create a regularly paid force under the control of a single commander.'

'A sort of model army?' Lodowick says.

Justinian's silk clad shoulders lift slightly. 'Possibly. Probably. He also advocates tolerance of religion, which would endear him to many.'

'Tolerance?' Lodowick frowns. 'I took him for a Puritan, like all of them.'

'He is, but the Presbyterians have more radical views, and like to exclude men from the army who deviate from their rules. Cromwell wants no such exclusion. Though I fear if he gains control. . .' He holds both hands palms upwards.

The room falls silent, each of us occupied with our own thoughts. As if the Royalists didn't have enough in Essex and Fairfax to worry about, now there is this Oliver Cromwell. I cannot visualise what sort of man this 'Ironsides' might be, but pray I shall never have the misfortune to encounter the man.

Chapter 14

Sated by the Carlisles' good food, and with Joan's affectionate farewell kiss still warm on my cheek, I wait on the front porch for our carriage to be brought round. Wheels crunch on gravel and our footman leaps from the rear to open the door.

I turn to inform Mother, who stands in an alcove with Justinian Isham. His head is bent toward her, lips moving rapidly while Mother nods and frowns as if taking instruction. The intensity of their exchange makes me pause, and as I watch, Justinian reaches inside his coat and withdraws a packet which hurriedly disappears into the folds of her cloak.

She presses Justinian's hand and brushes past me on a whisper of silk, settling into the seat beside me in our coach, and snaps down the leather flap.

'A breeze would be welcome do you not think?' she says, rapping the roof smartly with her fan as a signal to the driver to move, then rests her head against the seat back, her eyes closed. 'I appear to have had more wine than is my custom, I feel quite fatigued.'

'You appear untouched by the tragedy at York, Mama?' I say, refusing to comply with her excuse. A few moments ago she looked anything but tired.

Her eyes snap open and she rakes me with a hard look. 'What good would it do for me to wail and cry about what has already happened?' She gives a feigned yawn. 'Messengers are not always reliable. I shall await the official report from London before I consign Prince Rupert to the ranks of the defeated.' Her facade of calm is admirable, but I don't believe it. Surely she is as devastated as me?

'Have-have you heard anything from the Sequestration Committee?' I ask, changing the subject.

She shakes her head. 'Nothing at all. Perhaps our friends in Scotland managed to intervene for us.'

With that particular demon returned to its box, at least temporarily, I change the subject. 'I like Master Isham. Do you know much about him? I mean apart from the fact he is widowed?' My question is pure flummery, to disguise my interest in the packet inside her cloak, but I cannot think of a way to introduce the subject into the conversation.

'He's handsome and charming, certainly, but not a suitable match for you, my love.' Mother's head lolls against the upholstery in time to the rhythm of the carriage.

'You do not think so?' I feign disappointment, though he is no more than a mild flirtation who panders to my vanity.

'After the death of his first wife, he wooed a lady who refused him on account of Master Isham being too pompous.'

'Pompous?' I am about to express my disbelief, but then recall a sideways look down a long nose, and smile. 'I see what you mean. Now, Sir Thomas, I found less than amenable. He stared at me all through dinner, as if I were a horse at market.'

Mother abandons her pretence of dozing and eases upright in her seat. The movement reveals a corner of the packet beneath her cloak. My fingers itch to touch it, but I pretend not to see.

'While you discussed paintings with Master Isham, I talked with Joan about their strange guest. Sir Thomas is, apparently, looking to marry his son to an heiress. He told Joan he is so enamoured of your charms, he intends to write to the young man about you.'

I am thrilled and aghast at the same time. Despite his penetrating looks, Sir Thomas is a well-made, handsome man. Perhaps the son does not suffer from the same lack of subtlety. I turn to stare out of the window, dismissing him and his faceless offspring.

'I have not yet lost hope of our baronet for you,' Mother says.

'You read my thoughts, Mama.' I often contemplate Sir Lionel Tollemache and wish I possessed an image of the man on which to base my dreams and make them more satisfying. Or not.

Mother's soft laugh reverberates in the enclosed space. 'Are you so eager to rid yourself of your maidenhead, Betty?' Her wine-fuelled giggle indicates her tongue is looser than normal, which may suit my purpose. She leans forward to tap my knee and the packet dislodges. 'As your devoted parent, I warn you against wasting your charm and intellect on such as Justinian.'

'I wasn't wasting my intellect, merely practising.' I tear my gaze away from the packet. 'Does not the mind improve when one exercises its abilities?'

She turns to study the darkening scenery outside the window, but I doubt she sees much of it. 'Your father's removal to Paris has slowed the negotiations with the Tollemaches, which is most unfortunate. Let us hope this dreadful war does not also turn you into a lonely spinster. I cannot have my ripest prize wilt on the vine.'

'I'm hardly an old maid, Mama.' My tone is pert but unease creeps into my head. Weeks have passed with no word about an alliance with the Tollemaches.

A row of torches illuminate the trees along the carriage drive to Ham House, though the familiar sense of wellbeing at the sight of home is absent. Has Sir Lionel reconsidered aligning himself with known Royalists whose estate is under threat? Am I to be rejected without my suitor ever laying eyes on me?

The wheels roll to a halt and a footman springs forward to open the door.

Mother leans toward me as we approach the house, all previous signs of fatigue forgotten. 'Before you retire, come to my room, I have something to show you.'

Visions of my invitingly soft bed dissolve, and I am wide-awake. 'What is it?'

She presses a finger to her lips. 'When we are alone, not before.'

I am about to point out that we are alone, when she raises an eyebrow at the upright figure of William Ball by the front door. Then with a backward flick of her head, she indicates the carriage driver, and two footmen still clinging to the back of the coach.

How foolish of me to imagine they are as oblivious of us, as we are of them. Who knows if their loyalties align with ours?

A servant hands me a lit candle in the hall, and I mount the stairs, unable to contain my impatience. I enter the room while Mother's maid unfastens her stays and removes her skirt and bodice. With no sense of urgency, Mother arranges herself before her mirror to have her hair uncombed, while I chew a fingernail to the quick with frustration.

At last, the girl leaves by the hidden servants' door in the corner of the room.

'This is what I want you to see.' Mother opens out several pages of thick parchment and places them by her elbow beneath a lit candle.

Words fill the top sheet in an unfamiliar, but graceful hand, together with combinations of numbers and letters.

A trickle of excitement trails along my spine. 'This looks to be a cipher, Mama.' Then another thought jumps into my head. 'Is this what you concealed in your bodice during the search at Windsor?'

Mother's lips twitch. 'It is not the same one, but quite similar. Forgive me for keeping that from you, but I was afraid you might let something slip.' I am about to protest, but she stills me with a raised hand. 'Had you known I carried something like this.' She taps the pages, and my gaze fixes on it. 'Would you have been able to disguise your fear when Major Buxton ordered you to remove your cloak?'

'You are probably right.' My hurt pride dissolves into relief as memories of that cold, dank room at the castle return. A place as close to a prison cell as I would ever wish to be.

'What is this, Mama? A message about the king's next campaign?'

'Nothing so exciting, I'm afraid. It's a list of names.' She points to a line of letters with a number beside it. 'These marks represent those loyal to the king at Oxford, and others we may count on in the country.'

'His Majesty doesn't trust those around him?' I recall the smiling faces and obsequious bows of the followers at Christ Church, and a chill runs through me. 'There are traitors there?'

'Maybe not yet, though allegiances change. Look at Lords Essex and Dering. Both loyal men once.'

I regard the pages with new reverence. 'We must keep this safe.' My thoughts go immediately to her maid, but the girl is but fifteen and cannot read, let alone decipher a code.

'Do you think I would leave it on my bureau for anyone to see?' Mother pats my cheek, and I wonder if my childhood belief is true and she can read my thoughts.

'I keep my papers locked in a cabinet to which only Cousin Henderson and I have a key.' Resentment returns at the thought I am not trusted as much as Mother's waiting woman. 'Don't look so despondent, Betty. The reason I show this to you now, is because the time is right to take you into my confidence. With this defeat at Marston Moor, communication between our friends is more important than ever. I foresee a time when I shall be called upon by His Majesty to leave England.'

'Leave? Where will you go?'

Her plump shoulders lift. 'Wherever I am sent. To France, or Holland, perhaps.'

'How will you contrive to do so without being watched? Or be subjected to searches like we were at Windsor?'

'I will be careful. Besides, your father and I have friends in Scotland amongst the Covenanters. No one will question my presence if I am seen in their company.'

'It is still very dangerous. I shall worry for you.'

'You know about the cipher now. I will leave it in your care when I go. Should I include one of these marks in my writing, you will know the person it represents has either gone over to Parliament or has taken the Covenant, and can therefore not be trusted by the king.'

The implications of sending such vital information must show in my face, for she grasps both hands in mine. 'I have no plans to leave just yet. In the meantime, you must memorise this code so you will recognise the names by the marks alone.'

'You can trust me, Mama. I will not let you down.' Although, I hope I can keep my promise when the time comes.

'I never doubted it. I hate to put your life at risk, but Parliament grows impatient with the king's refusal to negotiate, and he makes promises to everyone he has no intention of keeping.'

'You speak as if you do not trust His Majesty, Mama.'

'Discerning right from wrong is easy at your age, but becomes more difficult as one grows older.' The candle flickers, throwing her features into sharp relief, making her look old and weary. 'Suffice it to say, the fate of the Murrays is inextricably linked to our royal masters.'

156

'Father said the same thing in Oxford.'

'It is true.' Her grip on my hands increases. 'Parliament no longer trusts the king, and if things continue to go badly, or if he is captured-' She inhales and flaps a hand as if she cannot bear to say the words.

'Parliament would do that? They would imprison His Majesty?' An image of the slight monarch with his sharp pointed beard held in manacles floats into my head.

The very thought of such a travesty makes me feel sick, but the notion that my own mother might be arrested and locked away in a cell terrifies me more.

* * *

April 1645, Ham House

My sisters are out of the carriage almost before it halts, while I follow behind with Cousin Henderson, glad to be back indoors where it is moderately warm.

'I wonder why we bother to go into town at all.' Kate says to no one in particular. She runs to the fire where she crouches and rubs fiercely at her arms.

'Nor do I, for the market stalls have hardly any goods to sell.' Nan nudges Kate aside in her quest for a share of the inadequate flames. 'What they do have is of poor quality. Besides, the sight of so many soldiers in the streets make me uneasy.'

'We were all uncomfortable, Kate, now kindly move aside a little.' I hover behind them, hoping some of the warmth will transfer to me. 'That's why I insisted we return home early.'

'I had a token to spend at the cordwainer for new shoes,' Kate continues, 'but Master Hubbard said he had no nails or glue.' She holds out her foot, displaying a hole in the toe.

'I don't hold with tokens,' Cousin Henderson sniffs. 'What's wrong with pennies and farthings is what I say.'

'Nothing at all, Cousin. If you can find any.' I rub my hands together and blow on the space between my thumbs. 'Like everything else, coin is in short supply. Most of the traders use

157

tokens or they would never sell anything. Master Fielder offered me one made of leather at the chandlers the other day, and he had the gall to charge me five farthing tokens each for candles.'

'This war is making villains of every shopkeeper in the town,' Cousin Henderson says. 'Now where is that girl with the firewood?'

This talk of shopkeepers is but a distraction from what really bothers me. The soldiers in Kingston might annoy Kate, but they fill me with a more insidious dread. No longer are they all old men with ill-matched clothing and an indolent manner. Now there are new companies of dragoons, young conscripts in pristine uniforms, who walk with a swagger and a light of fanaticism in their eyes.

These are Cromwell's new army; a fighting force where troops can be sent to anywhere in the country. Called the new model, it is made up of full-time professional soldiers instead of the part-time militia of the trained bands. He intends to rid himself of the Peace Party, those who prefer to negotiate with the king rather than force his hand by conquest. To this end, he had a Self Denying Ordinance passed which prevents the officer corps from holding posts as either members of Parliament or sitting in the House of Lords. Thus Lord Essex and the Earl of Manchester have resigned their commissions. In future Mother will have to apply to Sir Thomas Fairfax for her permits. I wonder if he will be as sympathetic to her escapades as Lord Essex?

'Then should not Oliver Cromwell resign as member of Parliament for Cambridge?' I demanded of Captain Fitton when he called at Ham, ostensibly to check we attend church on Sundays, but whose purpose was surely to goad us.

'Nay, he's far too important as a soldier and is therefore exempt.' Fitton sneered at me. 'Our new force is designed for efficiency, with a professional officer corps promoted on merit.'

I stalked away from him then, convinced he quoted the words by rote and had little understanding of what they meant. These soldiers may have strong arms and the ability to march all night, but their mental acuity will never match that of a son of a noble family.

These days, I occupy my time supervising the household staff, though the servants greet my interference with sideways looks and deep sighs behind my back.

Abandoning the fire, I settle on the window seat with an ever-present shawl wrapped tightly round my shoulders. Once, fires burned in every room, but we have fewer staff now to collect what little firewood the rebels have not requisitioned for themselves. I check myself at that thought, for I doubt I will get away with calling them 'rebels' again. These days they are referred to by Prince Rupert's soubriquet, 'Ironsides', because they cut through all ranks with ease.

On the morning of Mother's departure in February, she gathered me into her arms in a hug, though I top her by at least an inch nowadays. 'I intend to make a call at a certain house in The Strand before I go to Edinburgh,' she said.

Wrapped in my misery I paid no attention to her conspiratorial smile.

'Do you not wish to know why?' The mischief in her eyes turned to impatience. 'Why, I am to see Lord Tollemache of course. He was in London during Yuletide, dismal though it was with the shopkeepers ordered to remain open and no special church service allowed on Our Lord's birthday.' Her eyes lost their focus as her thoughts drifted away. 'I remember when Christmas was a public holiday with all the buildings in Kingston dressed with rosemary, holly and ivy. Your father and I would entertain our neighbours on Twelfth Night with roast beef, plum porridge, minced pies and special ale. How I loved it.'

'Forget Christmas, Mama,' I snapped, my irritation exacerbated by memories of the poor time we had with Father absent. 'Mama, promise me you will not shower the Tollemaches with exaggerated descriptions of my virtues? Boasting will do more harm than good to any marriage negotiations.'

Mama pulled in her chin and blinked at me. 'My dear, I have to offer him some encouragement. Every man wants a pretty wife as well as a well-bred and virtuous one.' She held my gaze in her I-know-what-I-am-doing way, and the subject dropped in favour of details of the preparations for her journey.

'I shall order some refreshments,' Cousin Henderson says,

rising. 'I am sure some biscuits and wine can be found in the kitchens.' Her oblique reference to our unsuccessful shopping trip prompts my sympathetic smile. 'Thank you, Cousin.'

Since the Marston Moor last summer, a nervous anticipation hangs over us all. The streets and alleyways between black and white timbered buildings in Kingston, once pretty and welcoming, now hold menace. Soldiers patrol with an arrogant swaggering gait, confident of their increased superiority over those they must know resent them.

Townsfolk still offer respectful bows to both neighbours and acquaintances, but now these are accompanied with wary expressions, while those who gossip at water conduits and on street corners scurry away when soldiers walk by. Men and women alike hide their faces, or duck into doorways at the sight of a uniform. Everyone looks nervous, even frightened.

Discretion comes hard to me, especially where I am accustomed to being treated with respect. Now I have to grit my teeth and pretend not to hear their coarse remarks and sly looks.

'The house feels so empty without Mama.' Kate crouches before the fire with a pack of pasteboard cards and proceeds to build houses on the turkey rug.

'She had to go, I suppose,' Nan says. 'We need the rents from our land in the Low Countries. At least the Sequestration Committee have no claim upon them.'

Meg huddles in a sofa, a coverlet on her knees poring over a book with rapt attention. How can a child of eight be content to read sermons?

She scratches at her hand with the fingernails of the other, which reminds me I must remember to mix an unction to ease her painful chilblains. Nan abandons an attempt at sewing, and stares into the fire, lost in her own thoughts. Kate's tongue protrudes through her lips as she layers the playing cards, tutting with annoyance as her attempt collapses onto the floor.

Outside, a light dusting of fresh snow covers the parterre. Bare branches reach white claws into a watery sky where no birds fly. They must all have fled to a warmer, more hospitable place than Richmond and have yet to return while this unseasonable cold persists.

My eyelids grow heavy, and my chin drops, then the sharp click of the door latch brings my head up to where Cousin Henderson hovers on the threshold. Her cap lies skewed on her frizzy red hair, her cheeks flushed from running. I frown at her empty hands, but she ignores me and instead, presses a hand to her breast and fixes me with a breathless stare. 'You have a visitor.'

I rise from my chair as despair grips me. Not today. I simply will not deal with them today.

'If it is Captain Fitton, tell him I am indisposed and will receive no one. I don't care how many patrols he has behind him, I simply refuse to receive them with Mother away. I-'

'Elizabeth!' Her voice is a low hiss. She throws another glance at the door and then skitters to my side. 'It is Sir Lionel Tollemache. He is in the hall.'

Chapter 15

Kate's card house tumbles to the floor, and too shocked to speak, I stare at the squares of pasteboard scattered on the rug.

I must think. How can I meet this man for the first time today? I am not ready.

'Did you not hear me?' Cousin Henderson says, throwing a swift glance over her shoulder.

'In the hall, you say?' I stare down at my gown, which is not one of my best. The russet velvet is elegant enough, but the hem where it brushes the floor is worn and faded. I tweak the lace at my elbows and rearrange the bertha at my neck, but give up in frustration. Nothing I do will make my clothes suitable for receiving a prospective bridegroom.

'Who is he, Elizabeth?' Meg looks up from her book. 'He must be important, for you have gone all red. Is he handsome?'

'We have never actually met,' I reply through a dry mouth, aware that all three of my sisters are now staring at me.

'May I make a suggestion?' Cousin Henderson's conspiratorial tone tells me she is enjoying the situation. 'I will have him shown into the library, which will give you a clear path to go upstairs and change your gown.'

'There is no fire in there, it's freezing,' Nan protests. 'Besides, it hasn't been dusted for a week. You cannot receive him there, Elizabeth. He would drive off and never come back.' Her eyes widen comically, mocking me, and Kate giggles.

'She's right.' I grip Cousin Henderson's arm. 'But this is the only warm room in the house, so he will have to come in here.'

'In that case, forget changing your gown.' Ever practical, my cousin bustles to the door. 'I don't know a man who notices such things on first meeting in any case. You are pretty enough to captivate him whatever you wear.' She claps her hands and motions to the girls. 'Come along girls - out.' She turns back to me. 'I will return to chaperone you.'

'No, Cousin. I will see Sir Lionel alone.'

She halts, one hand on the door handle. 'Are you sure that is wise?'

'I'll be perfectly safe.'

'If you are certain,' she sniffs.

Nan sighs and Kate pouts, but they discard their amusements and follow her out. Meg reacts more slowly, until Cousin Henderson half lifts her and guides her from the room. Poor Meg. When she gets comfortable in a chair, it takes a great deal to dislodge her. The damp winds torture her poor joints.

I hope Sir Lionel Tollemache is worth all this disruption.

The door closes firmly. I barely have time to take a calming breath, let alone check my hair, before it opens again and a footman appears.

'Sir Lionel Tollemache,' he says with a deeper bow than he has offered Mother in years, disappearing before being dismissed.

I try not to sigh. The servants grow lazy with Mother away. I must try to keep better discipline, or by the time she returns, the house will have descended into chaos.

When she returns.

I swallow and prepare to offer a polite greeting to a richly dressed stranger with a strutting gait and superior expression. Instead, my smile freezes as the footman's place is taken by a soft-faced boy. He sidles into the room and makes a clumsy, apologetic leg before throwing a look of panic at the closing door.

His plain coat is expensively cut, with gold embroidery at the sleeves and buttonholes, its simplicity cleverly contrived to flatter his slim frame. My gaze slides downwards to spotless white hose and a pair of heeled kid shoes I cannot help but envy.

I hold out a hand in invitation, but he remains barely a pace or two inside the threshold, his jerky glance taking in the windows, the carpet and the furnishings. Finally, his gaze settles upon me with a start of admiration. A slight flush floods his cheeks, putting me squarely in charge of this interview.

I conjure my most charming smile; the one Mother says puts a dimple in my left cheek and makes my eyes shine brighter.

His coat covers a dun brown suit, making him look more like a sparrow than the peacock I had expected. He looks impossibly young, no more than a schoolboy. I remind myself he is two years my senior and already a baronet, yet at the same time know I have nothing to fear in this boy-man with his turned-in toes and hesitant stride.

'Good day to you, my lord. Welcome to Ham.' My initial nervousness dwindles beneath his obvious discomfort.

He ducks his head and smiles shyly from beneath unruly, sandy-coloured hair that kinks and falls softly over a high forehead.

'And to you, Mistress Murray.' His voice is pitched low, and clearly masculine, but soft. 'I hope you forgive this impromptu visit. Especially as I am aware Mistress Catherine Murray is not at home.' He stares round as if searching for something. 'Might you prefer a chaperone to attend us? For propriety's sake?'

'I assure you there are four footmen within call, sir.' My voice is calm, but I hope pleasant. I indicate a sofa and invite him to sit. 'What brings you to Ham House?'

His light brows lift above candid brown eyes. 'Why, you do, Mistress.'

I allow myself a triumphant smile, confident I will not have to convince him of either my suitability, or attributes. At least not my physical ones. As to the others, I trust my ambitious parents to make those irresistible.

He twists his hands in front of him, then smoothes a thumb and forefinger down both sides of his narrow nose. 'I mean, er- your lady mother called upon mine at our house in The Strand before she left for Edinburgh.'

'Is that so? I was not aware she had such intentions, Sir Lionel.' I smile to cover the lie, and flutter my eyelashes.

'Indeed, yes.' His soft brown gaze roves my face in a way that is not at all critical. 'She enjoyed a most delightful interview with my parent.' Somehow I doubt this, but my smile persists, encouraging him to continue. 'My esteemed mother suggested I call upon you to establish the veracity of such a reputed paragon.'

I'll wager she did. Check I wasn't a hunchback and possessed of all my own teeth, no doubt.

I indicate the sofa at my elbow and he starts, as if the idea of sitting is novel to him, then flicks up the back of his coat. This close, his skin looks smooth and juvenile, with the barest fluff of growing beard scattered over a slightly weak chin and top lip. His features have not yet acquired the sharp, rugged look of a man of experience. Not a handsome face in the traditional sense, but pleasant nonetheless. If his estate and fortune is equal to Mother's report, I imagine I could learn to care for that face, even admire it.

'Our property in The Strand belongs to my grandfather.' His foot collides with a chair leg, bringing him up short. He glances behind him, then back at me, sidles into position in front of the sofa and sits. 'Well, it is mine now of course.' Uncertainty enters his eyes, making him look even younger. 'I take it you are aware certain negotiations have begun as to-' I am still in the process of taking my seat, and noticing, he bobs upright again.

'Please be comfortable, Sir Lionel. I apologise for our simple surroundings, but your arrival is something of a surprise.' I conceal a pang of irritation that he has given me no time to prepare for his visit.

He slaps his forehead with a hand, frowning. 'I am remiss. I should have realised that to descend upon you without prior warning puts you in an invidious position. I hope you will forgive me.'

'The disadvantage is due only to the absence of my parents, sir.'

Is this me talking? I sound like a governess. Worse, I sound like Cousin Henderson.

'For myself, I am delighted at your unexpected visit. My sisters and I have lately been bereft of polite company.'

He coughs, runs both hands down his thighs to his knees and back again as he stares round. 'This room is quite charming. And what a magnificent garden.'

I follow his gaze through the bay window to the terrace. 'Somewhat depleted by the harsh winter, I'm afraid. I hope you will return and see it in summer, when the flowers are in bloom.'

'That is my hope also.' He clasps and unclasps his hands and coughs again.

'You are quite correct about the discussions between our families, Sir Lionel.' Tired of this meaningless trivia, I bring the subject back to the practicalities. 'However, I had no idea the talks were at the stage for visits.'

He slaps his thigh. 'I knew it. It was presumptuous of me to have come.'

His obsequiousness begins to grate. I hope I will not have an apologist for a husband.

'Not at all. Your impulsiveness is indeed an attractive quality. May I offer you some refreshment?' I ask, hoping that Cousin Henderson has located some wine.

His face visibly relaxes and his hands come to rest in his lap. 'That would be most agreeable.'

I rise to pull the bell-pull in the corner, and he is on his feet again. A footman appears at the door. Biting my lip to prevent a laugh, I issue my request.

The footman withdraws and Lord Tollemache resumes his seat. 'I hope I am not being indiscreet, but William Murray informed me that your inheritance is, ah- in some peril.'

I try not to groan. 'My father is a Scot, sir. He believes in plain speaking. I trust you did not find his manner offensive?'

Flushing, he holds up a hand. 'Do not take me wrong. I admire him for it, and think nothing less of the family for his candour.'

'That is generous of you.' My jaw is clenched so hard my teeth hurt. 'Though any betrothal is still a way off.' I hope he is about to disabuse me. A speedy marriage would suit me, but is surely not something a lady should press for.

'Allow me the sin of pride in that I am in a position to weather whatever the Sequestration Committee might have in store for your estate. My own is more than able to compensate.' His Adams' apple bobs nervously. 'My family is an ancient one, and my ancestors have been Sheriffs of the county for over a century.'

My stomach plunges. I don't want compensation! I need a man who will protect Ham. Keep it for me, not shake his head in mild regret as he hands it on a platter to Parliament. My gaze goes to the door, willing the footman to reappear. I doubt my prospective bridegroom would enjoy my throwing a tantrum at this stage of our acquaintance. I will have to make my position clear in a different way.

My guest appears to dislike silences and rushes to fill it. 'Master Murray made you sound so wonderful, so-er, perfectly suitable for a man in my position, I was determined to see you for myself at the first opportunity.'

'I hope you regard his promise as fulfilled.' I lower my chin and peer up at him through my lashes. Lady Isabella Thynne would have been proud of me.

His mouth opens and closes in silent discomfort. 'Oh, yes. I mean, you are every bit as gracious, and well-formed as I was told.'

Well-formed? I glance sideways at him, assuming this to be an allusion to my sisters' infirmities, and force a smile through gritted teeth.

He shifts forward, so only an inch or two of his breeches is in contact with the sofa. I pray he has a good sense of balance. If I have to pick him up off the floor I know I will not be able to contain my mirth.

'I -I wish you to know that I am not averse to a contract between ourselves. If-if you are agreeable, that is.'

Tempted to reveal I have few options at my disposal, I incline my head graciously instead. 'Indeed, now I have made your acquaintance, Sir Lionel, I feel we have a good basis on which to proceed with negotiations.' I cannot let him think I am a prize already won.

His cheeks flush again and he studies a marquetry table at his elbow with more attention than the object deserves. 'Naturally, I-uh, shall not burden you with the financial arrangements made between myself and your esteemed parent.'

'No burden, Sir. Both my parents are quite open with me as regards the dowry and provision they have made for me.' Another blatant lie, for Mother has revealed no details of my settlement, only my prospective husband's name. 'Nor am I ignorant of my inheritance, or the steps required to retain it. Or is Ham too trivial for you to be bothered with?' His disinterest would be an obstacle I could do without.

'Do not distress yourself. Master Murray has made it quite clear how vital your inherit-'

His response is interrupted by the footman bearing a large tray with wine and a plate of small biscuits.

I glare at the man with a where-have-you-been look, but he

merely dumps the tray unceremoniously on a table and retreats.

Serious conversation thus postponed, I pour wine for us both while my guest nibbles a biscuit and puts forward the merits of Venetian glass over English. He accepts the wine, but asks me to dilute it with water. 'Wine at this time of the day upsets my digestion.'

I hand him the almost colourless liquid without comment. Is this a warning of future ill-health, or merely a result of nerves brought on by our meeting? A sickly husband is less likely to provide me with heirs, and could be more trouble than a parsimonious one. Unless his constitution carries him off within a year or so, and then I shall be back where I began. Only much richer.

Aware these acquisitive musings border on the vulgar, I change the subject, but resolve to bring them out for further examination later. 'Sir Lionel, may I ask your opinion on wives who oppose their husbands' views on certain matters?'

'Op-opposing views? In what, pray?' A clarity enters his eyes and he nods. 'Ah - er Master Murray's position as Gentleman of the Bedchamber to His Majesty leaves me under no illusion as to your family's loyalty.'

'Forgive my mentioning the subject,' I take a sip of wine to bolster my courage. 'But I would have you know I cannot in all conscience become any man's wife under false pretences.'

'False pretences?' The term seems to confuse him.

'Men often marry believing they can temper their wives' opinions to align with their own. If that is your intention-'

He holds up a slim, girlish hand. 'To entice your allegiance away from the Royalist cause could not be further from my mind. I merely offer you the protection of the Tollemache name. After all, Parliament and the Scots Covenanters may fight over the king now, but they will have to negotiate with him in the end. I doubt anyone believes the country's future excludes King Charles.'

This speech alters my opinion of his maturity. My relief must show in my face, for his gentle brown eyes meet mine and for a second we are in total understanding.

'I understand your caution,' he says gently. 'Enemies are easily made, and in these times we can rely on only a few close friends.'

'Forgive me, you have not come to debate politics, or lament the Royalist position. As long as we understand each other, that is enough.' I place my glass on the table and lean toward him, noticing with pleasure how his breathing grows rapid at my closeness. 'Now, do tell me more about yourself.'

'Well, um- I am now in my twenty-first year, having inherited the baronetcy from my late father some four years ago.'

'So young, and yet you bear the status well.'

'Th-thank you,' he stammers. 'My rank is indeed a great responsibility.

'Your estate is in Suffolk, I believe,' I say, my sympathy for this gauche young man piqued. I am not much younger than he, but a wealth of experience sits between us, and I feel far older.

'Helmingham Hall, yes.' A ring of pride lifts his voice. 'There has always been a house on the site, but the current property is not so ancient, and yet most elegant. I also own a manor in Northamptonshire, and of course houses in Suffolk.'

'Of course. And you have sisters, I believe?' His habit of putting the glass down after each sip begins to annoy me and I have to suppress an inclination to mention it.

His face lights up at my question, and he eases forward again.

'Yes, yes indeed. I have seven sisters. All older than I. Jane is the eldest, who is now Mistress Cholmondeley, Elizabeth Lady Alington, and my favourite sister, Anne.' He mentions several more, but I lose track of the names. How much influence do his doting Mama and a bevy of beloved sisters have upon him?

When he marries me, I intend to be the only woman in his life.

'What say you, Mistress Murray?'

I blink, horrified at not paying attention. 'I'm so sorry, I missed what you said.'

He leaps to his feet as if scalded. 'I apologise, I'm tiring you. Please forgive me.'

'Not at all. I enjoy your company,' I say truthfully. 'My tedious afternoon has taken a fascinating direction. I hope this will not be your only visit?'

'I am sure not, once I have presented Mother with my favourable report of your person.'

I knew it. He has to get his mother's approval first.

'I am somewhat surprised then, that you did not bring the dear lady with you?'

'Mother regards this visit as unnecessary.' He runs both hands down his thighs, and avoids my gaze. 'In her view, physical appearances are irrelevant to a good marriage. Her concerns focus on the settlement negotiations between your father and your kinsman, Lord Elgin. I-' He takes a gulp of watered down wine, his face suffuses a deep red and he gasps for breath.

I leap to my feet intending to summon a servant? I am half way to the bell pull before he stops me with a raised hand.

'There is no need. I am quite well now.' He dabs at his mouth with a kerchief and shoots me a self-conscious smile, rising. 'Perhaps it is I who tires.'

Choosing not to argue, I summon a footman to show him out.

'Your carriage has been brought round, my lord.' The footman's announcement breaks an awkward silence, and propels my guest into the freezing hall. He makes an elegant leg, displaying none of the shyness he exhibited on arrival.

'I hope we meet again soon, Mistress Murray.' He looks right and left, but makes no move toward the front door that stands open to the cold wind. Instead, he grabs my hand with both of his and crushes my fingertips to his lips in an almost lover-like grasp.

Goosebumps appear on my exposed arms, and I try not to shiver. 'As do I. Good day, Sir Lionel.' I firmly disentangle my hand and walk him to the door.

Perhaps he thinks the warmth that floods my cheeks is due to maidenly modesty, when in fact what I experience is a surge of power that I can affect him so deeply on such a brief acquaintance.

Before Sir Lionel has taken three steps outside, Ball slams the door.

Chastisement springs to my lips, but I hesitate as the gale howls round the house. Perhaps it was the wind that took the door from his hands.

The command of a driver and the rumble of wheels comes from the courtyard as my future bridegroom departs. I narrow my eyes at Ball, who waits to be dismissed, an expression on his face I have grown used to lately; a mixture of exasperation and uneasy tolerance. 'Is there something you wish, Mistress?'

I am no longer an insignificant substitute for my mother. I am heir to Ham House and practically betrothed to a baronet, and a rich one at that. And in my parents' absence, mistress of this house. Mistress of Master Ball, whose mildly resentful manner would never be tolerated by my Mother.

'There *is* something, Ball.' I halt him in mid retreat. 'I wish the household ledgers brought to me in the salon this evening.'

His head swivels and his gaze meets mine, one brow raised.

'But, Mistress Elizabeth, I manage the accounts myself when my lady is away.'

'I am aware of that. However in her absence, I will oversee the household expenditure.' I cut off his spluttered protest with a hand. 'After supper, Ball. And bring two candles, I need a good light to see by.'

I do not watch him leave, but can imagine his sigh of exasperation. While revelling in my new-found confidence, footsteps on the stairs alert me to the reappearance of my sisters. I look up and sigh at the sight of them crowded around the landing window.

'Did you see his carriage, Elizabeth?' Kate throws over her shoulder. 'And those horses! Six of them no less, and all perfectly matched. Can you imagine?'

Cousin Henderson regards me over the balustrade above them, her amused gaze evidence she has revealed the identity of my caller to the girls.

'There are lamps on the windows!' Nan chatters excitedly. 'He has a footman runner too, something I haven't seen since the war began. He must be very rich.' Her sigh is tinged with longing.

'Did you think I am going to hang out of the window to gawp at him?' I adopt a terse tone to disguise the fact I intended to do exactly that. 'I have seen fine carriages before.'

'Not like this one.' Nan pushes past Kate her nose to the window. 'The footmen's livery is embroidered in gold and his lordship's coat of arms is on the doors.'

'Nan! Come away, he might see you.' I imitate Mother's

imperious tone but to no avail.

'He cannot possibly see us.' Kate rubs her upper arms with an exaggerated shiver. 'He is half way to Kingston by now. She descends the last flight of stairs behind the others slowly, hampered by her awkward gait.

'May we take supper by the fire?' Nan asks as we re-enter the salon. She surveys the empty pitcher and the biscuit crumbs. 'If, that is, you and your Sir Lionel haven't consumed everything left in the kitchens. Then you can tell us all about him.'

'There's not much to tell.' I feign nonchalance and resume my seat.

Nan and Kate exchange a knowing look that says I fool no one.

A sharp tug on my skirt alerts me to Meg's presence. 'Is he a nice man, Elizabeth?' She alone seems uninterested in horses and carriages. 'Would he be kind to you and your sisters?'

'Yes, Meg.' I cannot help but smile into her earnest blue eyes, so like my own. 'He is a very nice man, and I am sure he would be kind to you.'

'Then you may marry him,' she slips her slim fingers into mine.

'Thank you, Sweeting. I think I shall.'

Chapter 16

The wind moans round the house like a lost soul, with bleak skies and the clashing of tree branches that keep me awake at night. Preparing for bed by the light of a single candle proves a challenge. We are almost out of fuel and the fires must be extinguished early. With candle wax such a luxury, I guard my hoard jealously.

The maid sidles through the door with such well-practiced silence, her reflection looms in the looking glass at my shoulder before I realise she is there.

I jump, startled.

'I'm sorry, Mistress Elizabeth.' She indicates the gowns piled haphazardly on top of a chest. 'Your lady mother has kept me busy today. I've had no chance to help you. I'll do better tomorrow.'

I am so happy to have Mother home again, I cannot summon ill-temper over an untidy room, though my casual dismissal of the disarray appears to surprise her. I no longer care what happens to a few gowns. If the Sequestration Committee succeeds in its threat to take Ham, there will be nowhere to put them in any case.

Murmuring her gratitude, Molly turns to leave. The door has not closed properly before Mother appears from the hall.

'If you aren't too tired, my dear, may I speak with you?' Without waiting for a response, she crosses the room and plucks at the items on my dresser with restless fingers. The fact she makes no mention of the disarray tells me she has something on her mind.

Her carriage arrived not two hours ago, with no time for her to do anything more than take a hurried supper and send us to our beds with a promise of stories in the morning.

Approaching my bed, she arranges the cushions against the headboard and climbs the two wooden steps, settling beneath the coverlet. Her profile is softly lit by the yellow glow of my candle, and a familiar fragrance of roses emanates from her silk gown.

'Come, sit with me, Betty.'

This is the way we always share our night time confidences,

tucked up beneath the satin padded coverlet of my bed or hers. On colder nights, we draw the bed curtains to shut out the draught and whisper into the dark.

Eager for confidences, I join her, tucking the thick coverlet round our legs like two mummies in a sarcophagus, our shawls pulled tight round our shoulders.

The house quietens around us, and apart from a door closing somewhere and the scrabble of rats in the skirting, we might be entirely alone.

'Where have you been, Mama? You were gone for weeks.'

'Oh, France and Holland, and Edinburgh too. Though I think I discomposed my kinsman, Lord Elgin, who demanded of my friends to know what was my purpose there.'

'And what was your purpose?'

'Why, renewing acquaintances and seeing to our family affairs, nothing more.' Her face shines with innocence but I know her better. A trivial visit is not reason enough for Mama to leave us alone for so long in these times.

Busying my hands with tying the ribbons of my nightcap, I wait for her to reveal more.

'Had you heard,' she says as if she has this moment remembered. 'That Charles, the Elector Palatine has arrived in London?'

'Prince Rupert's brother?' I nod. 'Joan called on us yesterday.' I press a finger to my lower lip and adopt Joan's pensive expression. 'Charles Louis has not only taken up residence at Whitehall, but the Covenant too.'

Mother giggles in appreciation and I tuck her arm through mine, forgiving her for keeping secrets. 'There is talk that Parliament might offer him the crown.'

'Huh!' Mother tosses her head. 'They wouldn't have him, no matter how much he fawns over the rebels. The king hopes he will return to his mother at The Hague and stop interfering with English politics.'

'How did the Queen react to such a rumour?'

'The Lord knows Her Majesty bears enough malice toward Rupert. A shame, for she forgets how fond King Charles is of his

174

sister, Princess Elizabeth and her sons. Despite that they have not seen each other since he was a boy.'

'And how is Father?' I ask, jealous she has been with him so recently, when I have not laid eyes on him for more than a twelvemonth.

'Her Majesty calls him 'Little Will', she is that fond of him.' Mother's face shines with pride. 'The Queen has sent him to tour the courts of Europe, including the Papal Court to garner money and support for the cause.'

I stiffen in alarm. 'Won't that put him in greater danger?'

'He has no choice, my dear. He must do what he is told.' Her expression softens. 'And we had some time together at the Louvre, which was wonderful. King Louis is most kind to his sister, despite our queen's temper tantrums. She still grieves her separation from the little Princess Henrietta.'

'I expect she misses Princess Elizabeth and Prince Henry too. Keeping them prisoner makes the rebels appear heartless. What use are three children to the Parliamentarians?'

'Well,' her forehead touches mine. 'The day I left Paris, I heard that Lady Dalkeith, who has cared for the baby Henrietta since her birth, is on her way to France.'

'They allowed her to leave?'

'Indeed not!' Mother's snort conveys her contempt. 'They wanted to take the lady and her charge to St James' Palace, but before they could do so, she disguised herself and her servants in peasant clothes and absconded. The last I heard, she had reached Dover and awaits a ship for France.'

'I do hope she succeeds and the queen is reunited with her baby.'

'I too, although I fear Her Majesty will wear out her welcome at her brother's court. Her demands are seen as a burden, and her latest scheme to marry Prince Charles to the Duchess of Montpensier is causing scandal. She can be somewhat obvious in her approach.'

'The queen's niece? That would be a coup for Her Majesty. Anne Marie Louise d'Orléans is reputed to be the richest woman in France.'

'Which is the poor girl's main attraction. Her looks are average to say the least with those piggy eyes.' Mother turns a wry smile on me. 'Not that most young men see such faults beyond her fortune.'

'I thought all rich, single women were beautiful, Mama?' I nudge her playfully with my elbow. 'I also suspect the young men of the French court leave you cold.'

'Huh! Those boys wear too much face paint for my liking. Hardly like men at all. King Louis was most gracious to me, I'll have you know.' She preens and her plump cheeks redden slightly. 'I saw him once outside the Louvre. I am sure he was about to hail me, when he saw his sister approach and what did he do? He turned and walked away.'

'I thought you said the king was kind to his sister?'

Mother shrugs. 'He is, her apartments are luxurious and he pays all her bills. However, her pushing for a match between Charles and Mademoiselle has strained his temper. I could tell King Louis' snub bothered her, for though she made an excuse, I could see her distress as she leant on Henry Jermyn's arm. That man is too much in her company for seemliness.'

'You have reason to be suspicions of Sir Henry?'

'Nothing definite. However, now he is governor of Jersey and plans to cede the Channel Islands to France in exchange for military aid. There are those who resent Jermyn's influence. Sir Edward Hyde for one. But forget the war.' She turns sparkling eyes on me. 'I have news of your cousin, Sir Robert Moray.'

A sense of loss envelops me at the sound of his name. I have not seen him for a long time and miss the stimulation of his lively company. He is one of the few men of my acquaintance who treat me like an intellectual equal rather than a mere girl.

'Last autumn,' Mother continues, 'Sir Thomas Dishington offered to pay the German government the ransom they demanded for Sir Robert's release.'

'I thought Prime Minister Mazarin was happy to let him rot in Bavaria?' resentment sharpens my voice. 'Despite him being captured while on campaign for France.'

I recall Father's pride that his kinsman served in the Garde Écossaise, the personal bodyguard to the French Monarchy.

176

'He was,' Mother continues. 'But the First Minister of France has seen sense and decided Sir Robert may be of use to both the French and Scottish causes, thus he arranged the ransom to be paid to the Duke of Bavaria. Sir Robert is on his way to London as we speak.'

'I am glad for Sir Robert, Mama. When he is settled, I shall write to him.' My smile dissolves as a thought occurs to me. 'With Cousin Robert under suspicion as a spy and Father in Paris, were you followed by Lord Essex's agents?'

'I suspect so.' She shrugs, unconcerned. 'Lord Elgin asked a few pointed questions from our friends about the society I mixed with in Edinburgh.'

'You gave him no reason to-' I break off at her cynical stare. 'No, of course you didn't.'

Mother removes a velvet pouch from the pocket of her gown. 'I made sure they had no knowledge of this, or I would have had some explaining to do.' She loosens the thread around the top and spills a rainbow of coloured stones into her hand. Rubies, diamonds, sapphires and emeralds glisten against her skin; their depth of colour makes me gasp, even beneath the poor light of the candle.

'Where did you get them?' I stroke a finger reverently over a sapphire the size of my thumbnail. I have a particular fondness for my birthstone.

'The queen entrusted them to me.' Mother purses her lips. 'Would they were a gift for my devotion to the cause, but I promised to sell them for her. No one gives her full value for her jewels, you see, knowing who she is and why she requires funds. She thought I might do better.'

She returns the bag to her pocket and delves into another. Her hand emerges clutched round a coloured bottle. 'The queen gave me this as a gift.' Her grimace shows she is not impressed. 'I daresay she imagines I may find it of use.'

I remove the stopper and peer inside the dark blue glass where sits a fine powder. 'What is it?'

'The bark of some South American tree.'

'A strange sort of gift.' I hand the bottle back.

'Indeed. The French friars brought it back from their travels in

Peru. It is well thought of in France, though I expect most here would see it as a Popish medicine. It is purported to cure marsh fever. I would much prefer the jewels, but forget about that now.' She replaces the stopper and returns the bottle to her pocket. 'I will tell you what a dreadful journey home I had. I imagined myself so clever arranging to travel on the same ship as George Gillespie and Robert Baillie, both Roundhead sympathisers and ministers of the kirk.'

'They were not suspicious of you, Mama?'

'Of course they were, but I was as charming as I could be.' She pulls her shawl tighter round her shoulders and huddles closer. 'Then what do you think occurred?' Before I can answer, she rushes on. 'A dreadful storm blew up and we were driven off course and took shelter in a Dutch port. I had to send to England for permission to return home. Fortunately Master Baillie lent his support and the Admiral of the Fleet, Lord Warwick, signed my pass.'

I jerk upright. 'You were shipwrecked?'

'Don't exaggerate, Betty. Of course not. Well - almost.'

'Why did you not send word?'

'To what purpose? To pile more worry onto your shoulders?' She lifts a dismissive hand. 'There was nothing you could do.'

'I know, but. . . You must have been afraid.'

'Of the storm or the rebels?' She slews her glance sideways at me. 'Neither, and both. I did a lot of praying, though I imagined I would die from cold rather than drowning. My main fear was that my letters would be lost in the sea and never reach their destination.'

I am instantly alert. 'What letters?'

She flicks a sharp gaze towards me. 'I brought messages from the families of Royalist refugees stranded in Paris.'

'Suppose they had been found?'

'Well, they were not.' She pats my hand. 'I have them safe and will send them off by a trusted messenger on the morrow.'

I marvel that this diminutive woman with the face of an angel can be so brave. Facing treacherous seas and self-serving men who would betray her in an instant, and yet she defies them all.

I want nothing more than to be exactly like her.

'Never mind about shipwrecks, Betty.' She purses her lips in feigned innocence. 'Cousin Henderson tells me we had an unexpected visitor while I was away. I wish to know every detail.'

* * *

August 1645, Ham House

A knock at the door precedes the arrival of our steward, who wears a stiff disdainful pout as he drops the household ledgers onto the desk, where they land with a dull thump.

'Thank you, Ball,' I say, bracing myself for his inevitable question.

'Do you still require me to bring the books to you each Friday?' His expression reminds me of a hound denied his dinner. 'My duties leave ample time for me to control the accounts.'

'The arrangement stands, Ball.' I dismiss him with a nod.

He backs toward the door, head bowed and withdraws in silence, probably to complain bitterly to the housekeeper that I have usurped his position. I am loath to back down now.

What a dreadful year it is thus far for us Royalists. News from Father is so infrequent as to be useless, though I suspect he has made more than one visit to England in the last year. Mother claims not to know where he is, but she avoids my eye when I ask, so I have my own suspicions.

I hope and pray he stays safe.

Despite our Richmond set making light of the fact the New Model army soldiers sang psalms before battle in June, all my misgivings about them were horribly fulfilled. News of a dreadful defeat at a place in Northamptonshire called Naseby made me think for the first time that perhaps the king may not, after all, win this war with his people. They are a different breed, these men, in their thick leather jerkins instead of full-plated armour; they use speed and surprise to hit the royal soldiers hard before moving on.

'If our men leave the field, Cromwell's men don't ride after them like Prince Rupert's Blews would,' Justinian Isham told me one afternoon at the Carlisle's. 'They stay until the battle is won and then gather up the stragglers afterwards.'

I accused him then of admiring them and their ruthless leader, but he assured me it was possible to acknowledge a man's expertise without agreeing with his beliefs.

'On the other hand,' Justinian went on, much to my chagrin. 'When the Model Army are ordered to pursue, they never break ranks to loot abandoned baggage like the Royalist horse.'

'Hmm,' Lodowick Carlisle murmured thoughtfully. 'And we all know how Prince Rupert likes his spoils. Perhaps you are right, Justinian, and this man Cromwell knows what he is doing.'

I made an excuse then and left them, but even I had to face the fact that four thousand Royalist prisoners were captured at Naseby, and almost as many killed. They say fleeing Royalists were pursued and slaughtered all along the road to Leicester. The tide of the war is certainly turning - and not in our favour.

At summer's end, more bad news arrived when Prince Rupert surrendered Bristol, though plague had drained the people's enthusiasm for the town's defence, so I cannot believe he did so lightly. When Lord Fairfax, the new Rebel Commander and the Puritan Colonel Rainsborough broke into the town, they massacred the city's defenders.

What savages these God-fearing Puritans are, though is any army merciful in victory?

With tears in her eyes, Mother said King Charles was convinced Prince Rupert had betrayed him in allowing Bristol to surrender. Despite Rupert's pleas, the king refused to talk to his nephew, withdrew his commission and sent him away. I cannot help but feel his treatment was unjust. The Prince may be slow to listen to more experienced men, but he holds his uncle's cause close to his heart.

When I think of that beautiful young man flirting with me at the New Year soiree, I feel the pain he must have endured at such rejection. How cruel of the king to let his sister's son risk his life for him, and yet withdraws his favour so easily.

What will the Prince do now? He is a soldier, born to a soldier's philosophy. I cannot imagine him following another life. Perhaps he will go in search of the next fight and another cause? Whatever he chooses, I hate to think I may never lay eyes on him again.

Mother spends her time writing appeals in response to the constant demands from the Sequestration Committee, thus she has relinquished the household accounts to me with some relief.

Cocooned in the quiet, orderly world of figures, I transcribe amounts from the list of receipts at my elbow. The task appeals to my need for control, and enables me to pretend that life here at Ham goes on as it ever did.

Chickenfeed appears to be more expensive this year, though we have fewer birds to feed, and the income from the eggs we sell to neighbours has dropped again. I notice the hay delivery is short. 'Hmmm, if Master Bowan thinks I shall settle that bill in full, he is very much mistaken.' I total the column, but before reaching the end, a sharp knock at the door makes me lose count.

'Enter!' I snap, without looking up. Halfway through re-totalling the column I sense movement, but ignore the intruder. I hate to be interrupted.

'Elizabeth!'

That one choked word on Cousin Henderson's lips alerts every nerve in my body. 'What is it? What's wrong?'

She releases the doorknob and steps inside, but doesn't close the door. 'The Collector has arrived from London.'

'Where is he?' I fight to control the tremor in my voice. I heard nothing. Occupied with my ledgers and receipts I am lost to the world. 'Where is Mother?'

She twists her hands in front of her, her gaze darting to the door and away again. 'My mistress has the headache this morning and is still abed. She instructed me to tell him to wait, and is at this moment dressing.'

My hastily dropped quill makes inkblots on the white page, but I ignore it and make for the door. 'I will go to her.' The Sequestration Committee informed us they would make a decision in nineteen days. Surely they have not come to execute the order today - without notice?'

'The Collector has soldiers with him.' Cousin Henderson's voice halts me.

I can hardly breathe as my gaze darts to the corridor from which come purposeful male voices, followed by heavy footsteps. Doors open and close, accompanied by shouts.

'What are they doing?' Sudden fear grips me. 'Have they invaded the house?'

'Yes.' Her fear conflicts with her affront and her face darkens. 'They crowded into the stables and the dairy as if they were under orders. They are bullying the lads and being offensive to the maids.'

I cannot spare a thought for the maids. My main concern is for my sisters. 'Where are the girls? They will be terrified to have soldiers tramping through their chambers.'

'I sent Master Ball to the salon to sit with them. The housekeeper ordered the soldiers to wait outside, but they took no notice. Do you think-?'

'How can I know?' Instantly I regret my harsh tone, for no one deserves it less than Cousin Henderson.

'Elizabeth, would you talk to the Collector? Perhaps try and dissuade him from allowing his men to ransack the house?' She steps further into the room. 'At least to give your mother time to finish her toilette?'

Cousin Henderson's dilemma is now clear. Mother wants to keep the men waiting, but their manners are not equal to her own and they have taken it upon themselves to violate our home.

I hover at the door, listening with mounting fear at the approaching footsteps. 'Why would they listen to me?'

'You are a woman, and a lovely one. You could try to reason with this officer. Make him retrieve his men, even if it is only for a short while.'

Her eyes bore into mine, and I know I must not appear weak. 'Come with me?' I ask through a dry throat.

Her skin flushes, but at her nod, I sweep from the room before I can summon a reason not to.

The man in the hall paces from the front door to the marble mantel and back again, tapping his whip rhythmically on his thigh. He looks impatient. Does he have other families to terrorise today? Or am I keeping him from a good meal? Not that he appears to need it. His black coat is stretched to its limits across bulky shoulders, and drops to massive knees encased in brown stockings that resemble tree trunks.

The face below sandy-coloured and thinning hair is exactly what I would expect on such a bloated frame, its features obscured by too much flesh. A misshapen nose above flabby bee-stung lips that sit clumsily above triple chins.

His eyes narrow when he sees me, almost disappearing into the folds of his cheeks, but his comical appearance does nothing to lessen the rapid beating of my heart. He may be a travesty of a man, but he could hold my future in his hands.

'Mistress Catherine Murray?' His voice is scratchy and uncertain. More folds of skin appear on his forehead as he looks Cousin Henderson over, only to dismiss her and settle his gaze on me. He is still not satisfied.

'I am Mistress Elizabeth Murray.' I fold my hands before me, keeping my gaze steady, though my voice is higher than I wish. 'My mother will be with you shortly.' Heavy footsteps traverse the ceiling and I clench my jaw. 'May I ask why your men wander at will around my house?'

'Your house?' He wipes his bulbous nose on the turned back cuff of his coat, and then clears his throat with a wet cough. 'Not for much longer, Mistress.'

Cousin Henderson gives a sharp gasp, and I swing round in time to see her wrest a silver candlestick from the hands of a soldier who stands behind us.

The miscreant looks to be no more than a boy. Cousin Henderson's hard glare cows him enough to make him scurry, shame-faced, behind his comrade. My cousin returns the candlestick to the table with measured calm as if she had simply been dusting it.

There is still no sign of Mother.

'You have documents to justify your insolence?' I say, and hold out a hand that trembles, so I drop it again.

His brows lift into a low hairline, which gives him a moronic look. How does such a man elevate to a position of trust and responsibility? I would not employ him to feed my sows. He looks positively dull-witted.

At last, the Collector withdraws a sheaf of documents from his coat and hands them to me. I play for time, reading the words slowly. My hands shake so much, I cannot hold the page still, and the words jump and blur against the white paper.

'You have ten days' notice of possession,' the Collector says, growing impatient.

He has yet to give me his name.

My head jerks upwards in shock. 'Ten days?' The parchment slips from my fingers and Cousin Henderson rescues it from falling to the floor. 'We cannot pack our things and be away from here in so short a time. You cannot do this!' Panic lends urgency to my voice. 'We are not noblemen, and have no resources other than what you see around you. We own no other properties in which we might take refuge. If we are turned out of this house, we will be homeless.'

A flash of uncertainty enters the Collector's face, but is instantly gone. 'I only deliver the orders, Mistress. I do not make them.' He reverts to the adage of all dullards who excuse their outrages as the desires of another.

'We must leave this house in ten days?' I repeat the words automatically, trying to take them in. My voice is little more than a croak, my stomach fluttering so badly I cannot think straight.

Cousin Henderson's lips move as she scans the page. 'No, wait, Elizabeth.' Her hand closes on my forearm. 'It says here their final decision to sequester the entire estate will be made in ten days. Not seized.'

Relief floods through me, followed by fury, and I whip round to face the Collector.

'Is this a jape, you imbecile? Have you been sent here to torment us?' I snatch the paper from my cousin's grasp and wave it under his porcine face. 'You bring your rabble of soldiers to rampage through my house with no more authority than that a decision is yet to be made?'

The man steps back in alarm, and behind him, the boy-soldier sniggers.

Contempt escalates my rage, though I am aware this is only a reprieve. How can I tell Mother she must pack her belongings and seek shelter amongst our friends? And what friends? Ten days! It is not long enough. What can we do in so short a time?

The Collector's face twists in contempt. 'I do not write the orders, Madam. I merely serve them. And you have been served.'

The sniggering soldier plucks a Chinese vase from a shelf with both hands and tilts it clumsily to examine the underside. Another soldier in a coat faded across the shoulders delves in a chest by the front door.

'Take your hands off our property!' I raise a shaking hand to the man beside the chest. He turns to look at me with an insolent smirk, at which I leap forward and slam the lid.

He snatches back his hand only just in time. His eyes widen and a small growl erupts from his throat.

Anger seethes beneath my skin like a fever, and untouched by this implied threat, I turn to face the Collector again. 'You have done your duty and delivered your document, now you and your men may leave. Immediately.'

The three soldiers in the hall exchange looks of astonishment mixed with disbelief, but no one appears to take me seriously. One folds his arms and smiles, and another shrugs at his companion, while above, the sound of rapid footsteps makes me want to scream at them all to get out.

The Collector is a foot taller than me and twice my width, maybe more. He looks uncertain and I wonder if he contemplates restraining a woman. I care nothing for how he feels or what he thinks, I simply want them to remove their contaminating presence from my house.

While it *is* my house.

'Do you have difficulty understanding me, sir?' I lift my chin in defiance, but my hands tremble. I crumple the written orders between them, not as a mark of contempt, though there is plenty of that in me, but to hide my fear from this vile man.

He regards me steadily before hooking his chin at one of the soldiers, who bows and disappears in the direction of the stairs.

The hall falls silent, broken only by the Collector's intermittent cough, while I pace up and down in front of the fireplace and throw withering glances in his direction.

The rumble of footsteps grows louder and troopers appear from every door like a colony of ants before they file out through the front door. The Collector follows, pausing to glare at me round the frame, a finger held up in warning.

'Remember, Mistress. Ten days. And expect no mercy, for I and my men take possession of this house and everything within its walls. Not to mention the animals in those fields out there.' He nods vaguely in the direction of Petersham Meadows and the river.

In final condemnation, he turns on his heel, his vast bulk weaving away from me like a ship on an ebb tide.

I take the five paces to the door at a run, slamming it shut with an echoing thud. I turn and lean my back against the wood, my breaths short and fast, a hand clutched to my middle as dizziness threatens to overcome me.

'That was very brave of you, Elizabeth,' Cousin Henderson says gently. She has not moved from her position in the centre of the hall.

'Brave indeed, Betty.' Mother's face appears over the balustrade above me. 'However, you showed a lack of breeding by losing your temper.'

'Mother! Where were you? I needed you!' I want to throw myself into her arms and cry like a child, but cannot exhibit such weakness in front of Cousin Henderson. 'I'm sorry if I acted badly, but I didn't know what to do!' The child inside me that longs for approval and safety rises to the surface.

She descends the stairs and bustles towards me to wrest the crumpled document from my stiff fingers. Her touch is not the embrace I desperately need and disappointment wells in hot, angry tears.

'I was dressing when they arrived,' she offers by way of explanation. 'I assumed they would wait upon me at my leisure like gentlemen.' Her papery cheek brushes my own. 'How could I imagine you would deal with them on my behalf?' Her high, nervous laugh falls flat.

'My efforts were useless.' I delve in a pocket for a kerchief and dab at my cheeks. 'He says he will return in ten days.'

'Not necessarily.' Mother smoothes out the parchment with both

186

hands. 'Their decision may be made in our favour. And even if it is not, we shall be given a reprieve to make preparations. Do not panic, Betty.'

Do not panic? Didn't she listen? Is it possible she does not understand the gravity of what she holds in her hand? 'But the Collector said-'

'I know what he said. However, I will not take the word of a servant of Parliament as Holy Scripture, Betty, and neither should you.'

Like cool water over hot stones, her calmness drives away my terror. Where does she get her courage? Not ten minutes before, soldiers ran their disgusting hands over our furniture, laughing at us. Now she stands in her hall like a queen telling me all is not lost.

'I really believed they were here to throw us all out!' My voice hitches.

She pats my shoulder again. 'I know, dear. Now, Cousin Henderson, would you have some breakfast sent up to my chamber? Some bread and butter will do, and perhaps some buttermilk. I have letters to write.' With the paper still clutched in her hand, her plump face creases into an untroubled smile. 'Oh, and Betty, have you finished the accounts yet? I wish to pay the bills before tomorrow; you know how I hate to incur debt.'

'Um-almost, Mother, they will be done by noon.' I stare at her departing back, admiring, yet infuriated at her ability to separate devastation and trivia into compartments and deal with each equally.

Cousin Henderson's expression mirrors my amazement. Then she shrugs and disappears in the direction of the kitchens.

I trail back upstairs, where, alone again, my dread of the Collector returns. We have been given a short respite, but may still be ordered out of our home.

Where would we go, with winter coming?

Chapter 17

November 1645

In search of solitude, I choose the windswept bank of sodden grass beside the deserted river over hours of empty confinement in the house, where inadequate fires make no impression on the damp chill. Sheets of ice form on the inside of the windows come morning, and even the rats have fled the cavities in the walls for warmer nests. Either that or they are dead of starvation, for I have not seen a scuttle of dark fur or heard scratching in the skirting for over a month.

Each day that passes with no word from the Sequestration Committee is a small agony, while every hoof beat on gravel quickens my breathing and makes my hands tingle with trepidation.

Waterlogged turf sucks at my boots, but I am reluctant to return to the house. Unlike Mother, who conceals her melancholia behind a facade of brittle calm, I succumb to ill-temper and tantrums that help no one. Least of all me.

Driven by images of warm fires and mulled wine, I start back along the grey ribbon of the river. The wind quickens and bites through my clothes, throwing a spray of frigid water into my face.

Ahead, a lone soldier canters along the path between the river and the house. I recognise him as one of the Model Army dragoons, his cloth gaiters designed to protect his legs while riding. He reaches the north front, slows and turns in at the gates. His leather jerkin is black across the shoulders from the rain.

My pulse races. Hampered by my damp skirt, I dart forward to close the distance between us. What bad news does he bring? Have the Committee made their decision? Are we to be banished from Ham with all our belongings? If so, why is he alone? Where are those who would carry out their orders?

The rider reins in his horse at the door and dismounts. He looks up at the windows and down again, as if unsure of his mission.

My boots squelch on the wet gravel, my hooded cloak a wet

twist of rag on my shoulders, but I pay no attention to my discomfort as together, we reach the front door.

The soldier tugs off his sodden hat and ducks his head. 'Good morrow to you, Mistress.' Uncertainty crosses his face and he pats his left breast. 'I have a document for Mistress Catherine Murray. Are you she?'

Taken aback at his friendliness, I return his greeting. 'My mother is at home. Shall I take you to her?'

He shakes his head. 'I am but a messenger.' He removes a folded square of parchment from his jerkin. 'If you would give her this.'

I reach for the paper with a trembling hand, its yellow surface poxed with drops of water during the brief exchange.

He bows again and climbs into the saddle with youthful agility, turns the animal in a tight circle, and with a brief salute, canters back the way he came.

Clutching the document, I sit on a bench inside the front door while the footman removes my dirty boots. I smile at his attempt not to grimace as clinging mud works its way under his pristine fingernails. His task complete, he bears the offending objects away at arm's length.

'Why were you out in this dreadful weather, Betty?' Mother appears on the first landing. She hurries down the last steps and draws me into the hall. 'Come inside and get warm. You will catch a chill.' She slips my wet cloak from my shoulders and hands it to Ball with a sneer of distaste.

Word has spread and the hall fills with footmen and attentive maids who flick dusters over clean shelves and arrange logs that do not need arranging, their faces alert. Sometimes I forget their lives are bound with ours, and if we lose Ham, they face being scattered to the winds.

'Here, take it.' I push the parchment into Mother's hand as if it might burn me. 'A soldier brought it,' I say unnecessarily, convinced her appearance is no more a coincidence than the servants'.

She won't even look at the paper, much less take it from me. 'Come and warm yourself by the fire. I wouldn't send a dog out in

189

such weather. Even a rebel dog.' She sniffs, confirming my suspicions. Mother misses nothing.

I follow her into the salon where a fire is lit, but still she merely stares at the folded parchment in my hand, postponing the moment of revelation. Then she snatches it from me with a sharp 'tut'. 'Procrastination is useless, we may as well know the worst.'

She slips a thumbnail beneath the seal and opens out the page. Her gaze slides rapidly over the scrawled lines. 'The Committee has made their decision,' she says, her voice calm.

A lance of fear shoots through me. I want to tell her to stop. I don't wish to hear what the decision is, but cannot force the words past my thickened tongue. A scuffle sounds outside the door. The servants eavesdrop, but I do not care. If there is bad news, they may as well hear it too.

'When must we leave, Mother?' My voice cracks in the face of her stoicism.

'It says,' Mother raises her voice. Has she too heard the whispers at the keyhole? 'The Committee has withdrawn the execution of sequestration.'

My mouth falls open. 'What? Are you sure?'

A chorus of murmurs and squeals come through the door, which bursts open. My sisters crowd in and surround Mother, their hands snatch at the paper as each of them insist on reading the notice for themselves.

At the open door stands a group of maids, murmuring into their cupped hands in excitement.

Meg tugs at my skirt, her pale eyes clouded with confusion. 'What does it mean, Elizabeth?'

'That Ham remains ours, silly.' Kate bends until her face is level with Meg's. 'We don't have to leave Ham. Ever.'

'We are saved!' Nan hugs Kate, happiness and relief clear in both their faces.

Mother's gaze flicks to meet mine. Uncertainty sits in her eyes, but I sense her reluctance to introduce doubt into this happy occasion. The Committee has given in this time. But who is to say they will not make further attempts to seize the estate?

Meg tugs my skirt again. 'I knew His Majesty wouldn't allow

the Parliament men to take our home from us. He gave it to Father after all.'

I stroke a ringlet of pale gold hair from her cheek, but cannot summon words to explain that the wishes of the king have ceased to wield any power at all.

* * *

February 1646

Six long months pass, and with no renewed threats from the Committee of Sequestration, my thoughts turn to marriage. I can scarce believe it has been almost a year since Sir Lionel Tollemache came to Ham to inspect me as his future bride.

'If Father tarries too long, Sir Lionel will find another wife!' I snap at Mother when yet another letter arrives from Paris with no mention of the gentleman.

'Have patience, my dear.' She slides the parchment into the secret drawer in her bureau where she keeps his letters. 'These things take time, and with your Papa in France, the task is more difficult.'

How long can marriage negotiations take? I dare not ask too often for fear of seeming over eager. My sisters already make pointed remarks that I am in my twentieth year with no betrothal in place.

I pace the room, careful not to put too much space between me and the fire. These harsh winters do little for my complexion. I do not wish to have coarse, reddened skin like Cousin Henderson. 'If he doesn't agree soon, I may find myself another husband!'

'From all the suitors who queue at our door?' Nan's sarcasm is followed by a sniff, while Kate snickers behind her hand.

'The Dowager Countess,' Mother says, her tone leaving no doubt of her impression of the lady, 'insists there must be no restrictions to the estate should her son agree to marry you.'

'What does that mean?' I halt in front of her, my gaze flicking briefly to the drawer. Is there more written there than she admits?

'Exactly that. She says she is willing to exchange her son's hand

191

for Ham, and all the lands.'

A shiver slides down my back as again I imagine Ham slipping away from me. 'That's outrageous. Lady Tollemache cannot expect me to hand the estate to Sir Lionel outright. What about a settlement for me and dowries for my sisters?'

'I agree that we must tread carefully in these matters. There is no point in keeping Ham from the Sequestration Committee, only to give it to the Tollemaches.'

In the corner of the room, Cousin Henderson's gaze remains on her needlework, though her hands are still. I no longer mind that she hears everything. She has witnessed more than squabbles over my marriage settlement. I am willing to wager she will hear far worse yet.

Mother sighs. 'The Tollemaches seem amenable. After all, they have enough wealth of their own not to grasp ours like a hungry dog. Your father insists the estate is held by your husband, but in trust for you. Did you think he would give away his most prized possessions so easily?' She shakes her head, lips pursed. 'Without the agreement in place, your husband will own every stick of furniture in the place and your sisters will have to rely upon his charity until they are married. He will have no obligation to give them dowries.'

Self-conscious warmth floods my cheeks. I am behaving like a petulant child. I cannot help it, I am tired of waiting. If I am to marry, let it be soon.

'Or were you only thinking of yourself, and being Lady Tollemache?' Nan says.

Kate regards me steadily from Nan's shoulder. Their combined sense of betrayal stabs me from across the room. They have nothing to fear, for I would never abandon them. They should know me better than that.

Stung, I make for the door, eager to be out of the stifling atmosphere of this room and their accusing faces. How could they think I would do anything to hurt them?

'Where are you going, Betty?' Mother tuts, 'You are so restless today.'

Without answering, I pull the door closed and stalk down the rear hall, fury propelling every step. Since I was small, Father instilled in me the responsibility I bear for the Murrays.

With an adequate dowry, my sisters' physical imperfections should not be a bar to their marriage. But without Ham and its income, what would happen to them?

Their sly looks and barbed remarks may be partly due to envy, but they still cut deep.

Given our brief acquaintance, I can barely recall Sir Lionel's face, so it is not the man I desire. Pride and duty spurs in me this obsessive need to marry. Not my own vanity. I am like a reed blown this way and that by the fates. And those three muses in the salon do not even appreciate what I do for them. Serve them all right if I elope with the first handsome cavalier who asks me.

I leave the house and traverse the cobbled yard that leads to the stillroom. There I may be able to expend my nervous energy on something useful.

'What are you making, Mistress?' asks Mary, the maid I summon to fetch and carry. She hovers at my elbow, eager to please. Small and undersized for a girl of fourteen, she moves quickly and doesn't get in my way.

'A mixture for digestive complaints.' I do not mention that I labour on behalf of Master Ball. Our steward would not thank me for announcing his weakness to the lower servants.

I remove Mary's inquisitive fingers from a pot of poppy seeds. 'Can you find the conserve of roses?'

She darts away to search a high shelf, while I unlock the cabinet on the wall where precious items are kept. Carefully, I remove an ornate china pot with gilt curlicues on its sides.

'That's a beautiful thing, Mistress.' She hands me a ceramic jug that contains the conserve. 'Is it so precious you keep it under lock and key?'

I set the container gently on the bench. 'It is mithridate, and must be used sparingly. Two drams only for this remedy.'

'What it is made of?' Her scrawny face is transformed by a look of awe.

'A universal antidote to many illnesses. In ancient Egypt, a piece the size of an almond was given in wine as a guard against poison.'

The deep brown powder is slightly gritty and yet smooth at the same time. 'Fifty-two ingredients make up this compound. Its powers lie in the precise amounts used in its compilation.'

'What is in it?' she asks again. I frown and she flushes bright red. 'Beg pardon for my impatience, but it looks a wondrous thing to be so powerful.'

'There is costmary, sweet flag, hypericum, acacia juice, cardamom, anise, iris, parsley. And other things.' Components with which I am not acquainted, but do not admit. I pour an amount of rose water into the bowl with the mithridate, and hand it back to her. 'While I combine these together, fetch me some hazelnuts.'

Mary darts away and returns with the nuts. 'Do I put them in with the mixture?'

I blink Lionel Tollemache's face from my head and focus on her question. 'Er-no. The afflicted person chews them after they have swallowed the concoction. It helps dispel wind and ill humours.'

'I like working with you, Mistress.' Mary's brown eyes are alight with rarely seen enthusiasm. 'I learn such a lot.'

I grant her a benevolent smile, hoping I look something like my mother, whose handling of the servants is masterly; a combination of stern management combined with maternal care. They would do anything for Mother.

I return the precious pot back to its shelf in the corner cupboard alongside the exotic-looking blue glass bottle Mother brought back from France.

'What is in that, Mistress?' Mary reaches a hand to touch it.

I bat her fingers away and she yelps, more in shock than pain.

'That is- nothing at all. Something for rare illnesses. You will never have need of it.' I hold her frightened gaze. 'Never touch it, do you hear?'

'Yes, Mistress.' Her eagerness shrivels beneath a meek expression.

I lock the door and slip the key into my pocket, silently promising myself not to ask for Mary's help again. It would not do for her to become too curious about the powdered bark. Servants tend to gossip, and I am loath to let it be known we have what is known as 'Devil's Dust' in the house.

I leave the stillroom and step into the cobbled yard filled with cold winter sunshine, pausing as a line of cows are herded into the milking shed. With the clay dish in one hand, I nod to the cowman, whose cheery response reveals a gap in his front teeth. The cows look thin, and their hip bones protrude as they lope along. Our best bred heifers have already been sold, eaten or stolen.

Master Ball appears from the side door and I hold up the dish, about to tell him I have the remedy for his complaint. In a way I hope it compensates for having deprived him of the accounts. If he has not already forgiven me, I am sure he will.

He scowls and nods meaningfully toward a group of idling soldiers on the other side of the wooden gate before joining me.

'What do they want?' I say, narrowing my eyes.

'Grain, and a sheep, though it is hardly a request.' He holds up a hand at my indignant protest. 'They brought money, Mistress. They offer a fair price.'

'Can we spare a sheep?'

'Better that than a cow. The milk is more useful.' He releases my arm and steps back. I get the impression he wants to say something more.

'Take care, Mistress Elizabeth,' he says after a pause, keeping his voice low.

'Careful of what, Ball? Has something happened?'

'No, Mistress. I feel I ought to mention that your visits to the stillroom do not go unnoticed.' He nods again at the soldiers.

'Huh! I care nothing for that rabble.' I toss my head and turn a shoulder to the gawping men. 'They can watch me all they like.'

'Brave words. However, I advise circumspection.'

'What can you mean, Ball?' Impatient now, I make to brush past him but he halts me with a hand on my arm. I stare down at it for a second, dumbfounded, then into his face. His expression is serious, brooding.

'I warn you for your own good, my lady. Those rebels look for an excuse to betray you to their superiors. Don't give them a reason.'

'Betray me? Why? We have done nothing to resist the occupation of Kingston. Nor do we complain when they treat our

195

land as if it were theirs.' I glare again at the uniformed men lounging insolently beneath the trees. 'If there is something I should know, Ball, I would hear it. Now.'

'Very well, my lady.' He tugs down the front of his coat and inhales. 'An interest in healing and knowledge of remedies might be reason for suspicion among less enlightened types of persons.'

'You mean Puritans?' I cannot resist a smile, amused by his reticence but not yet alarmed.

'Puritans believe in witches. They seek them with as much fervour as they worship their God. They need no proof. Suspicion alone is enough to condemn anyone, no matter her rank or fortune.'

'This?' I indicate the clay pot. 'This harmless potion is enough to condemn me?'

'Perhaps, Mistress.' He flushes and stares at the ground. 'And, I mean no disrespect, but you have three sisters who have not been blessed with physical perfection.'

His words are like an icy wind that leaves me gasping. 'You cannot mean it?'

'I do.' He nods toward the soldiers again. 'Given the flimsiest of excuses, they would grasp the implication in an instant.'

'What implication?' Though I know exactly what he means. One relative with a disability is unfortunate, but three might signify the influence of a darker sort.

'I will tell them they can have a ewe,' Ball says, pre-empting me. He bows and backs away, his steps taking him toward the soldiers in an unhurried stroll.

I watch his receding back in disbelief. Did I hear him aright? I could be accused of witchcraft on the basis of a few stomach powders and a tincture or two? I refuse to entertain the slight to my sisters. But in truth, I have heard such things before.

Money changes hands between the soldier in charge and Ball, while the others stride across the grass to startle a group of woolly sheep grazing beneath the trees. The animals bounce away in all directions, and I hope the stupid things evade their captors for a good long while.

Before he follows his men, the officer casts me a hard glance. Despite the sun-filled courtyard, I shiver at the menace in his eyes. Are there not enough threats in my life without fear of witchcraft? I try to convince myself Ball panics over nothing, but cannot still the tremble in my hands.

There is more reason now than ever to marry Sir Lionel. No one would dare make such an accusation to a member of his family.

The sound of a coach rumbling closer distracts me. Tucking the clay pot out of sight, I hurry round the side of the house to the north front, where a familiar equipage now stands.

Justinian Isham steps onto the gravel, his handsome face pushing all thoughts of witchery away. Then my gaze drops to my housewife gown and my stomach plummets. It is too late to hide and pretend I have not seen him.

Why does he have to call when I look so homely?

He looks in my direction, makes an elegant leg, to which I respond with a curtsey.

'My dear Elizabeth, how delightful to see you.' He adjusts a glove and retrieves a silver-topped cane from the coach seat, his light blue satin coat and silver embroidery fit for any drawing room.

I smooth my free hand down my badly dyed woollen skirt and push back my cap. 'Do forgive my attire, sir. I had no idea you would call today.'

'No need for apologies, and besides, you always look fresh and pretty, no matter what you wear.'

'What flattery, sir.' I take his proffered arm with my unencumbered one, skirt the house and approach the main door.

'What have you there?' His glance slews sideways to the clay dish. 'Something delectable perhaps?'

'Nothing so interesting.' I nod to the footman who bows us into the hall. 'I have applied myself this morning to concocting remedies for the body, not delights for the tongue.'

An uneasy smile trembles on his lips instead of the witty response I anticipate.

This is not a social call. He brings bad news.

Mother would be furious if I received a caller so dressed. Impatiently signalling to a passing servant, I hand over the clay pot.

'Show Master Isham into the salon. Then go and tell your Mistress he is here.' Turning to Justinian I summon my most charming smile. 'I shall leave you for no more than a moment. Do excuse me.'

'I will await your return with anticipation, Mistress Murray.' Justinian bows and I leave the hall at a run.

In my room, I tear off the offending gown and subject Molly to a tirade of 'hurry' and 'do not bother with that', until I am finally attired for the morning room in a cream silk gown, my hair pulled into a hasty arrangement of ringlets on my crown. There is no time to tease curls out at my temples, so brushing Molly's pleas aside I rush downstairs to the salon.

Justinian stands with one elbow on the mantle, a lace-cuffed hand beneath his chin and his brooding gaze on his own reflection in the gilt mirror. A reflection I doubt he sees.

Mother sits on a sofa, her head down. Nan is perched on the edge of a straight-backed chair, her face in her hands, sobbing quietly.

A lump settles in my throat. 'What has happened?' My voice is little above a croak.

Master Isham takes a step toward me, his face softened in sympathy. 'I am sorry, Elizabeth, I am here at the behest of Lodowick Carlisle. He returned from London last night with some bad news of your father.'

'How bad?' I demand.

'He's been arrested,' Mother says. She delivers the news with such remarkable calm, I could swear she expected something like this.

Nan breaks into fresh, noisy sobs and Mother's hand clamps down on her arm.

'Quiet, Nan.' Her back is straight. She regards Justinian with a steady gaze. 'Now, Master Isham. What do we do?'

Chapter 18

'What charge have they brought against Father, Master Isham?' I fight to keep my voice calm though my palms are clammy and tears threaten.

He coughs into a fist as if the admission pains him. 'Willliam Murray is accused of spying.'

My legs no longer feel strong enough to carry me, and I reach for the curved back of the nearest chair. My shock dissipates quickly, followed by a certainty of Father's guilt. I wonder he has not found himself in similar peril before now.

Cousin Henderson scurries to Mother's side and grasps her hand, but she snatches it away, her lips clamped together and her eyes closed. Kate's stoic silence is in sharp contrast to Nan's noisy distress, while Meg huddles on a stool beside the empty fireplace, her childish features a mask of confusion.

Justinian passes close by me on a stroll between the windows, his gaze averted from this bevy of distressed females. I can hardly blame him. I pluck at his sleeve and he turns wary eyes upon me. 'Where and when was he arrested, Master Isham?'

A spark of hope leaps into Nan's red-rimmed eyes. 'Yes, where? The rebels cannot arrest him in France. Can they?' She turns for reassurance to Mother, who shrugs.

'He landed in Kent two days ago, Nan.' Justinian sighs as if relieved we are not about to collapse in a heap at his feet. 'He was recognised at Canterbury, and has been taken to the Tower to be tried by martial law.'

'A military court?' Mother looks up sharply. 'Why, sir?'

'Perhaps because it is the army who accuses him,' Cousin Henderson speaks for the first time.

'Or because they are the faction who fear him the most,' I mutter beneath my breath. 'He has the king's ear, and when they cannot bend him to their will, they would separate him from his master.'

'He will have to appear before the Lords.' Justinian presses my shoulder in comfort before turning kind eyes on my cousin, prompting a self-conscious flush to creep up her neck.

Justinian may be called pompous by some, but he is a rare creature who treats all ladies with kindness, having total disregard to their station in life. We depend more and more on friends like him, and I am beginning to understand how valuable such relationships are. I count off a mental list of our most influential friends. It is dismally short. Most are known Royalists. Then a harsher, more selfish thought chases the others from my mind.

Will Sir Lionel Tollemache be willing to marry the daughter of a Royalist spy?

'Most of the Lords are Royalists, and would surely be sympathetic toward my Will,' Mother says thoughtful. Her eyes remain dry, but a nerve jumps at the corner of her mouth. 'He is His Majesty's faithful servant, not a soldier.' Agitation hitches her voice, and I long to reassure her, but have no words to make this situation any less terrifying.

Justinian caresses a porcelain figurine on a table at his elbow. 'You may need to prepare yourself, Mistress Murray. Should sufficient evidence be found against him, the Lords will have no choice but to hand down a conviction.'

What has Father done?

Words like 'prison' and 'execution' crowd my head and make me nauseous. 'And you think they possess such evidence against him?'

'I do not know, Elizabeth.' Justinian gives a theatrical shrug. 'Lodowick has sent his running footman to London to await further news. As soon as anything is known, we shall be informed.'

Master Carlisle's footman, though small and wiry, runs like a deer. Father has won considerable sums wagering on him in foot races on the riverbank in Kingston. He even tried to buy him once, but Lodowick refused, albeit with considerable charm that made it impossible to take offence.

'Why did they choose Father to arrest?' Nan asks between sobs. 'There are plenty of people better placed to be called a spy.'

'The French are negotiating a treaty with the Scots,' Justinian says. 'Parliament knows how influential your father is with both the king and the Scots. That he comes into England straight from France and the queen's court is reason enough to suspect him. His

200

capture is a triumph for them.'

'Please, Master Isham,' Mother pleads. 'Don't frighten the girls more than necessary.'

'I apologise.' Justinian balances a hand beneath his chin as if giving her question polite consideration. He has made no extravagant promises, nor does he try to minimise Father's danger. It occurs to me he would rather be anywhere but here, discussing a situation he must himself dread. Does he fear being associated with us?

I let the thought die. Doubts about Justinian's allegiance can only work to my detriment. We have enough enemies, I cannot distrust our friends as well. Besides, Justinian is one of the 'Richmond Royalists', as the army call us, and has as much trouble with the Sequestration Committee as we do.

'I feel most of their proof is hearsay,' he says after a moment. 'Yet damning enough for all that.' He replaces the ornament and clasps both hands behind his back. 'They say Will made promises for terms with the French and the Scots Covenanters to allow Papism back into England.' His gaze rests on Mother. 'Master Murray is considered important by both parties, and that alone speaks against him. They will have most certainly searched his person for documents.'

'My Will would never be so indiscreet as to be caught with anything incriminating,' Mother snaps, throwing me a hard look. 'He must have passed them on to another messenger.'

I cannot help but smile at her failure to deny Father's duplicity.

'Someone must have betrayed him,' Nan insists tearfully. 'How did they know he would be arriving in England at all?'

Betrayed? Is it possible someone might want him put out of the way? Then I recall Edward Hyde's disparaging words at the king's soiree in Oxford, and Father's involvement in 'the Incident'.

I drag my thoughts back to Justinian, who is still speaking. 'The Lords do not need firm evidence, Nan. All they require are two reliable witnesses willing to testify against him, whether they speak the truth or not. Your father has enemies.'

Nan's tears seem to make Justinian uncomfortable and he eyes the door. 'I must return to Petersham Lodge to await news with

Lodowick.'

'Of course.' Mother rises and summons a footman to show him out. With a brief nod in my direction and swift kiss on Mother's hand, he is gone.

'If Father is found guilty of treason, he will hang.' Nan half rises, her voice choked. 'He will be drawn and quartered, and his head displayed on a spike on London Bridge as a warning-'

I want to slap her, but Mother forestalls me. 'Nan! I do not wish to hear such things.' Her gaze rests on each of us in turn. 'From any of you. There is to be no more talk of hanging.'

Kate sniffs into a kerchief and Nan's thin lips twist as she murmurs an apology. Meg creeps to her side and they sit holding hands, Meg's still and white, while Nan's knead the child's thin fingers with short, anxious movements.

My throat closes and tears prick the back of my eyes as I pray Mother's optimism is not misplaced. Where would we be without Father? I doubt the king would be able to help us, and there is no guarantee Father's Covenanter friends would speak up for him? Would they throw him to the wolves rather than spoil their own negotiations with the rebels?

* * *

May 1646

I rise in a cool half-light, my room chilled from an unusually late spring. As I dress, Molly informs me that Mother is confined to her bed with migraine, which comes as no surprise. Justinian Isham called again last night to discuss the latest progress of Father's situation.

Mother was right in that no incriminating documents were discovered, either on his person or in his cabin on the ship that brought him from France.

Reconciled to another difficult day of waiting, I descend the stairs.

The front door stands open, the corners of the staircase hall thrown into deeper darkness by the weak shaft of sunlight that cuts across the tiles. Cousin Henderson stands by the open door, her face devoid of colour, and a hand pressed to her breast.

She catches sight of me and her lips open, then close, but she appears unable to form any words.

'You look so strange, Cousin,' I snap, alerted to the sound of bits jangling and male shouts from outside. 'What is happening? You look as if the entrance to Hell lies on the other side of that door.'

I attempt a half-hearted laugh. Surely nothing worse could happen after the news of yesterday? My boots click on stone as I hurry forward, my intent to demand she either close the door or explain herself.

The sight that greets me sends my stomach plunging and my breath hitches.

What looks like an entire regiment of Parliamentarian soldiers line up on the other side of the gates. Two officers on horseback ride hard up and down beside the river, shouting orders, their mounts scuffing the turf with their hooves, scattering the sheep.

I release a low groan at the sight of Captain Fitton, who dismounts a massive horse that must be one of the few animals alive able to carry his substantial weight. Despite the hard times visited on the rest of us, the man looks to have increased his girth considerably.

He approaches the gates with slow, deliberate strides, his sour grin firmly in place.

'May God have mercy on us,' Cousin Henderson whispers and grips my arm so hard, I wince.

'I'd pray to Lord Fairfax if I were you, Cousin.' I disengage her fingers and stride forward. 'He is more use to us now.'

I reach the gates before the captain, and without the thought fully formed in my head, I slide the bolt into place, narrowly missing my thumb.

'Now, Mistress Murray.' The captain's sing-song voice echoes across the courtyard, followed by an insulting guffaw, its echo taken up by the men behind him. 'No slip of a girl shall disobey Sir Richard Onslow's orders.'

'And what orders would those be, sir?' I ask, playing for time.

What do they want? Is their appearance due to what has

happened to Father? Are we all to be put under close arrest?

I think of Mother, ill in bed, and hope one of the servants warns her.

I have no idea why or how I will achieve it, but it comes to me that if I can delay whatever they have in mind, even for a short while, a solution will present itself.

Captain Fitton plants his shovel-sized hands on his hips, and breathes onion fumes harsh enough to melt the wrought iron bars.

'This property is to be put to the use of my men here.' He waves a hand at the assembled soldiers. 'You should be grateful, Mistress. Our presence will offer protection to your family.'

'We don't require protection, Captain.' My voice is steady but my knees shake. 'Until the army came to Kingston, we were perfectly safe. We are law-abiding people.'

'Hah! Not our law. Not Parliament's law.' He looks to his officers for approval which comes in nods and murmurs of assent before turning back to me. 'Besides, the matter is not open for discussion.' His ingratiating voice turns to a growl. 'Now, stand aside and allow us through.' He waves the troopers on before turning aside to talk to a man on horseback.

'You say you have orders, Captain,' I shout above the sound of booted feet scrambling into formation ready to begin their approach. 'May I see them?' Panic lifts my voice an octave higher, but I hold my ground. Despite his coarse manners, surely Captain Fitton would not revert to force? I am half his size and to drag me bodily away from the gates is bound to diminish him in the eyes of his men. Yet a doubt lingers. If only I had a stout padlock for this gate!

Fitton narrows his eyes. 'You've a brave mouth on you, Mistress Murray for someone whose father is in the Tower as a spy.' A gleam of malice appears in his eyes and I have to resist the urge to spit in his face.

'My father will be released soon. He has powerful friends who-'

'Friends who could not keep him out of gaol in the first place. Put not your trust in them, lady.' His heavy features harden with angry contempt. 'Now, get this gate open.'

The lines of foot soldiers halt, murmuring in mild confusion. A voice says something I do not catch, followed by a shout of coarse laughter that sends warmth into my face.

Fury keeps me defiant, though I doubt my feet would move even if I wanted them to.

'I will not prevent you, Captain, if that is what Sir Richard decrees. However, I insist you show me your orders so I may see how many are to be quartered here, and what is required of us.' I am gabbling, unsure of my ground, but determined not to give in without a fight.

He lifts his arms and lets them fall again. 'I don't have the documents with me. You will have to take my word they exist. Now if you would stand aside.'

'No! I demand to see the papers first.'

His eyes widen, then dull with anger. He utters several incoherent sounds, most probably curses, and lurches at the gate. His fingers resemble fat sausages as he grips the bars on either side of his scowling face. The sight so ridiculous, it is all I can do not to laugh.

'Would you defy the Parliament army?' he bellows, 'I order you to allow my men to pass!'

I lick my lips, fearing my voice is about to desert me altogether. 'I defy no one. I merely ask that you allow me to see your written orders.'

My quiet tone seems to anger him more, and his lips curl cruelly upward.

A soldier sidles to the captain's shoulder, glances briefly at me, then whispers something to the captain.

Captain Fitton's skin turns a dull red and he cocks his chin at me in contempt. 'You tell her!' He throws me a contemptuous snarl, and then stomps away to join his group of officers, all of whom regard me with similar disdain.

The man before me is young and athletic-looking. He removes his lobster-tail helmet, gives a polite bow and regards me with intelligent eyes.

Immediately I relax, knowing I can reason with this man. Then I wonder what makes someone like him join the New Model Army. His coat is well made and fits him without a wrinkle. His boots are new and highly polished, and his short sword is obviously the work of a master craftsman.

'I apologise for this unexpected intrusion, Mistress Murray,' he says, his voice smooth and courtier-like. 'Captain Fitton appears oblivious of the fact that your household may not be prepared for the invasion of forty extra-er guests.' He indicates the captain, who glowers at me from a distance.

'Forty?' I stare at the young man, open-mouthed. 'How are we expected to accommodate so many?' I envisage eighty booted feet scuffing our floors and wiping dirty hands on the bed hangings. My ears start to buzz and I swallow noisily.

He shrugs and offers a deprecating smile. 'Our requirements are quite basic. I am sure we shall manage.' He fixes me with a direct gaze. 'Besides, Mistress. You have no choice.'

'I do not mean to thwart you, or Captain Fitton.' I hesitate, 'I'm sorry, I do not know your name.'

'It is Carter, Mistress. Sergeant Robin Carter.'

'Well, Sergeant Carter. Are we to be given no opportunity to prepare? Apart from the servants, we are five women alone. Surely you would allow us time to organise our accommodation to allow for the presence of so many men?'

'If you would wait but a moment, Mistress.' He blows air through pursed lips, his gaze on the knot of officers. Then he turns and strides to where Captain Fitton stands.

I clench my fists at my side as they hold an earnest conversation, which Fitton punctuates with jerky arm movements and a permanent scowl.

What am I doing? They will occupy the house whether I fight every officer in the troop or not. I will have to let them in eventually, so why humiliate myself?

I cast a look behind me and have to suppress a laugh. The horrified faces of my cousin and my sisters line up behind the upper front windows. The lower ones display Master Ball, the housekeeper, and that of several nervous-looking maids and footmen.

A gentle tap on the gate brings my attention back to Sergeant Carter.

'Um-Captain Fitton has agreed to return at this time tomorrow with the documents you requested, Mistress Murray.' I am about to thank him when his smile dissolves. 'We concede you triumphed today, however, he will be less accommodating on the morrow.' His voice drops to a whisper. 'Whatever you feel you gained by this action, I hope it is worth it.'

So do I.

With a curt nod, he turns and saunters away.

The scuffle of hooves and a shout of orders precedes their withdrawal.

Unable to hide my triumphant smile, I walk slowly back to the house, my head held high, though I resist breaking into a run until I reach the step. The door opens at my approach to reveal the astonished faces of Cousin Henderson, Ball and my sisters.

'That was very brave, Elizabeth, but dreadfully foolish.' Cousin Henderson's expression reproves me, but her lips twitch in amused admiration. 'Whatever made you do such a thing?'

My shrug serves well to hide my shaking. 'I cannot give in to Roundheads without a fight.' I mount the stairs and she follows me, my sisters behind her like a row of ducklings.

'What have we gained?' Nan endeavours to keep up. 'They will not be put off forever.'

I reach the top just as Mother appears on the landing, a hand held to her temple and displaying a frown. 'What is all this noise? My head throbs so. I am trying to sleep.'

'Elizabeth saw off the Roundheads!' Meg says, sidling between me and Cousin Henderson. 'They wanted to come in, but she sent them away!'

Mother's hand falls to her side. 'Explain!' she snaps, using the clipped way of speaking she adopts when troubled by the headache.

'Hundreds of soldiers came.' Meg tugs at Mother's skirt, earning a weary smile of doubt.

'More like a hundred, Meg,' I say, then address Mother. 'It looks as if they intend to quarter soldiers in the district. We are to accommodate no less than forty men.'

Her lips purse as she thinks, but the frown remains. Her

headache must be bad today. 'You did well, Betty dear. I take it they shall return?'

'Yes. Tomorrow.'

I expect her to be distressed, or even angry, but she merely nods her head. 'One day may be enough.'

'Enough for what?' Kate asks.

Mother doesn't respond. Instead, she leans over the balustrade to where Ball's upturned face displays rapt attention, a group of interested servants at his back.

'Ball. Summon every able-bodied man we have and move all the best pieces of furniture to the upper floor. Wrap all the paintings in sacking and put them in the attics. When that is done, do the same with the silver and gold plate.' As if as an afterthought, she adds, 'Lock the room we use for family prayers lest they take it for a chapel.'

Ball nods and disappears.

'Why must we lock it?' Nan asks, perplexed.

I recall the soldier who searched our house for recusants in Oxford. 'Puritans disapprove of private religious ceremonies, Nan,' I tell her gently. 'They see Papism in every gold chalice and candlestick.'

Her frown lifts and she looks from Mother to me. 'Why do we not simply invite them to worship with us so they can see we are as Anglican as they?'

'A clever thought, but Puritans and Anglicans do not worship in the same way.' Mother twists the fringe of her shawl in her fingers. 'As I said, we shall keep our private prayer room locked. You girls, hide all your jewels. We'll give them no excuse to seize gold crosses and missals.'

'Will we have to give up our chambers?' Nan asks.

'They can't have mine!' Kate shouts, indignant.

'No, girls you shall not give up your bedchambers,' Mother assures her, though anxiety dulls her eyes even more than the migraine. Her face is paler than a moment ago, but I know she would resist me if I tried to force her back to bed.

'I don't want soldiers in the house!' Meg pouts. 'They cannot have my bible. It has jewels on the cover. Papa gave it to me.'

'None of us do, Meg.' I crouch in front of my sister, taking her trembling hands in mine. 'If we cannot stop them, we must protect what is ours. Do what Mother says and hide anything of value.'

'Come along.' Cousin Henderson ushers Meg along the corridor. 'I will help you put your bible away. I have a plain pigskin bound one you may use in the meantime.' She beckons to the other two. 'You too, Nan, Kate.'

I accompany Mother on her agonisingly slow progress back to her room, where her rumpled bed shows signs of a restless night. I retrieve the heavy coverlet from the floor and drape it across the mattress. 'What about food, Mother?

Her brow puckers and she turns unfocussed eyes on me, dull with pain. 'What do you mean?'

'Soldiers have to eat. I doubt the army will bring many provisions with them. Is that not why they are being quartered here? Part of our punishment for being Royalists will be to feed and keep them warm.'

'I doubt any live in such luxurious surroundings as this.' She waves an arm to encompass the elegant room. 'Besides, it is May, so keeping them warm will not be a concern. For a while at least.' She plucks a discarded petticoat from a chair, but appears not to know what to do with it.

I take it from her gently and guide her back to the bed, but she breaks away from me to throw open drawers and chests in panic.

'Mother, Molly knows what to do.'

'I know, but I must - have to make sure-' She sways on her feet, and I rush to her side in time to prevent her falling.

'Must what, Mother?'

She seems incapable of speech, merely points to the open drawer of a small bureau that sits in the corner. Inside lie a stack of papers, letters with unfamiliar seals and a small black leather-bound notebook.

I exhale slowly. 'You wish me to hide these?'

She nods, but even that small action makes her wince with pain.

'I understand. Now you must lie down until your head is better. I will fetch you an infusion of feverfew.'

Apparently reassured, she slumps onto the bed with a sigh and whispers. 'What did you ask me?'

'Don't talk, Mama. I will see to everything.' I lift her feet and swing them onto the mattress. Being trusted with her coded correspondence and precious notebook fills me with new resolve.

'We can do little about the livestock in the fields.' I visualise the flock of sheep and the cattle that occupy the ground between the house and the river. 'We are bound to lose them. However, we may be able to keep some things for ourselves.'

'What do you propose to do?' Mother lays passive as I cover her legs and tuck the soft sheets around her.

'The larders are not very full, but we have preserves and sacks of grain, cheeses, herbs and spices, plus the contents of the stillroom which are quite valuable. Then there are the wine stocks.'

'Is it possible to hide all that from them?' Mother's voice weakens as sleep claims her. 'If they find out what you have done, there could be serious reprisals.'

'We hardly have enough to feed our own family, let alone forty Roundhead soldiers. Why should they benefit from our labours?'

Her hand lifts to her temple. 'So many? Where will they all go?'

I perch on the edge of the bed as her eyes grow heavy and slide shut. 'I was wondering that myself. I am sure they will tell us.'

'Pre-empt them, Betty,' she murmurs, her head lolls on the pillow and in a moment or two she will be asleep.

'How?' I whisper, hoping she will tell me before she drifts off, but her gentle snore tells me I am too late.

Thinking fast, I rise and sweep all the contents of the drawer into my arms. I doubt the rebels would search the house, especially Mother's room, but she is wise to be cautious. But where do I hide the evidence my parents have been at such pains to keep from rebel hands? Evidence they are indeed carrying information between the king and his loyal subjects in England: evidence enough to hang them both.

My gaze scans the room until it alights on the black and gold Chinese cabinet, that stands as if on guard in the corner of the room. The base looks solid but there is a drawer behind the baseboard. If I can only remember how to open it.

I glance at Mother but she is snoring gently, so there will be no help there for a while.

Dropping the papers on the rug, my fingers probe the gap between the cabinet and the floor, but meet only smooth wood. Then I find an indentation and I give a gasp of triumph as the baseboard swings open.

My heart hammers as if the soldiers are at that very moment outside the door, my breathing fast and shallow as I cram the papers and book inside the cavity, pushing them as far to the back as they will go. I replace the baseboard gently and click it into place.

Pleased with myself, I straighten the rug and go to the bell pull to summon Molly, using the time until she arrives to straighten Mother's covers and smooth her damp hair from her forehead. She doesn't stir.

Molly arrives and I issue instructions. Before leaving, I remind her to work quietly, and that she is not to leave Mother's side except to collect food or drink when she asks.

'Of course, Mistress,' Molly murmurs assent and curtseys, but as I leave, her reflection in the mirror by the door shows a very different expression. How does anyone poke a tongue out that far? She must be related to an ox.

Unable to spare the time or the inclination to reprimand her, I storm off down the hall. What did Mother mean by pre-empting the soldiers?

In the lower hall, I instruct a passing maid to send up an infusion for Mother. 'She's sleeping now, but these headaches tend to last for days, so prepare one ready for when she wakes.'

Turning away, I almost collide with Ball. I swerve to avoid him but he holds up a hand to gain my attention. 'Mistress? Will we be expected to provide beds for these men?'

'I-I have no idea. I imagine they will bring their own.'

'Or maybe not. That is, after your altercation with the captain today-' Ball swallows and clamps his lips together as if gauging my reaction to his implied criticism.

'Yes, Ball, I am quite aware of what I did today, and you probably feel I was unwise. What have you in mind?'

He takes a deep breath before speaking. 'If we clear some of the

211

outbuildings and lay out truckle beds in readiness, it may indicate we are prepared to co-operate.'

'And why would we wish to do that? I intend to let them know at every opportunity that they are invaders in our home.'

'Not a wise or diplomatic stance, if I may say so, Mistress. I was going to suggest arranging accommodation in the dining room for the officers.'

'What? Let that rabble ruin a beautiful room with their muskets and boots? What can you be thinking?'

He gives a mock innocent shrug. 'It occurred to me that if the officers are pleased with their quarters, they are not likely to demand better ones for the men. Not when we are being so amenable.'

'Where do you suggest putting the enlisted men?'

'In the dairy and outbuildings.'

Soldiers in our house, the very idea makes me shake with rage, but I make myself calm down. My displays of temper would only give them a reason to make us more uncomfortable.

'I understand your distress, Mistress,' Ball says gently. 'May I suggest you concentrate on caring for your mother and sisters and leave the soldiers to me?'

'Your practicality staggers me, Ball.' Though I am not surprised. Ball has smoothed the rough path of our lives for years. I press his arm briefly and watch his brows rise at the unexpected contact. 'See to it immediately.' I turn away, but then something occurs to me. 'Ball, do we have somewhere to store the contents of the larders?' A light enters his eyes and I know I was right to ask. 'Somewhere we can access, but keep secret from the soldiers?'

He bows almost to the waist and backs away. 'I have the perfect location, Mistress. Leave it to me.'

I am about to return to my room and find a safe place for my own valuables, but a thought strikes me and I reverse my steps and race through the rear hall to the still room. I must find a safe place to put Mother's bottle of powdered bark.

Chapter 19

June 1646, Tower of London

On a stifling hot day, Mother and I travel to the Tower on a rarely allowed visit to Father. The fields of Richmond give way to the western edge of the city where the stink is at its greatest. Thames Street throngs with sedans, pack ponies, carts and pedestrians, with an occasional fine carriage jostling with costermongers and link boys. Drovers manoeuvre flocks of sheep, geese and an odd lumbering cow into fields between half-timbered buildings and stone churches.

It takes me a while to discern what is different, until I realise it is the sound. The city no longer rings with the shouts of traders, drovers and farmers. Instead it murmurs. An atmosphere of dread hangs over the people who keep their faces averted, hurrying along with their heads down, looking neither right nor left.

Drivers of carts and packhorses do not demand their fellows make way or exchange light-hearted abuse, but gaze from face to face as if expecting trouble. Shoulders turn away from direct glances and chins drop to chests as if hoping not to attract notice.

The Venetian red uniforms of the New Model Army straddle every street corner, but even they look surly.

London is afraid.

I shiver on the hard seat as the carriage climbs Tower Hill and the wheels rumble hollowly over a wooden drawbridge that swallows us into the depths of the fortress. Towers and walls merge together with narrow alleys that meander off in all directions.

'Take heart, Elizabeth,' Lodowick says from the seat opposite, gauging my mood. 'We are doing everything we can to have your father released.'

'I know.' The words stick in my throat. If only I could do more than wait and hope.

We roll to a swaying halt and a soldier yanks open the carriage door. I jump with nerves as he orders us out. A warden hovers behind him and demands to see our papers.

After a brief examination, he points to Lodowick. 'Only the women can see the prisoner.'

I shudder. *The prisoner.*

Mother looks about to argue, but Lodowick stills her with a hand. 'I shall wait for you here.'

Another guard signals we follow him through the stone archway. Before following, I cast Lodowick a regretful look. He flicks his fingers to bid me move on, and I take strength from his sympathetic face through the carriage window.

Mother strides ahead into a square stone hall, with tiny windows high above our heads. Every sound echoes, making me feel enclosed and breathless. I keep close to Mother's swaying skirts and pray I do not become lost in this maze, for surely I would never find my way out again.

She follows the guard through a door at the far end, which leads to a smaller hall with a steep, curved staircase where little light penetrates. My heart plummets at the thought Father is being kept like this - in cold darkness that smells of mildew, rotting vegetation and dust.

Our guide neither pauses nor turns to see if we are behind him, his booted feet moving upward in a purposeful rhythm.

Hitching my skirt, I watch my feet, taking care not to slip on stone stairs that bear indentations from years of use. A door bangs shut above us, followed by a dull thump and a sharp cry cut off in mid flow. Suddenly dizzy, I brace a hand against the stone wall that feels slimy beneath my fingers.

'Come along, Betty,' Mother hisses, urging me upwards to where a single square of blue beckons from above.

At the top, the guard halts and throws open another door, steps to one side and cocks his chin.

Silently obedient, we enter a spacious room with walls of exposed stone.

My first sight of Father comes as a shock, until I recall his thin frame and shabby clothes are much the same as in Oxford. Strange that my recollection of him is from happier times, when his cheekbones held more flesh and his clothes bore no worn elbows or ripped lace. Perhaps this is because I pass his portrait in the hall at

Ham each day, and it is the well-fed man with the heavy-lidded eyes I conjure when I think of him.

His head is bowed over a desk so small, the chair he sits upon does not quite fit beneath. The door opens soundlessly, so unaware of our presence, he does not look up.

A waist-high window with wooden shutters reaches to a plastered ceiling. A patterned rug, its colours faded and worn in places, covers bare floorboards. The bed looks sturdy and comfortable, if a little small, with heavy velvet hangings to keep out draughts. A pot-bellied stove sits in the corner closest to the bed, a pile of ash beneath it on the stone floor. An incongruous sight in summer, but then at night, thick stone walls must be cold at any time of year. The chamber looks the same as that of a middling inn or yeoman's home.

'What can I do fer ye, ma man?' Father says. The goose quill pen in his hand flaps in time with his rapid writing.

'Vis'tors,' the guard snarls.

Father looks up, the frown of enquiry slides off his face, to be replaced with an eagerness that brings tears to my eyes and a prickle to my throat.

He discards the quill without looking to see where it lands; the chair scrapes the flagstones and he jumps to his feet and opens his arms in welcome. 'My dears!'

I imprint every sound and gesture into my brain so I may relive it later.

He greets Mother first, who holds onto him for a long moment during which I am sure she is whispering something.

Then she releases him abruptly and he enfolds me in familiar arms, where I greedily inhale wood smoke mixed with old wine and damp wool.

'Father!' I release a nervous laugh. 'And I imagined you in a damp dungeon with a tiny barred window and straw on the floor.'

He takes a step backwards, slides his hands down my arms until he holds both my wrists.

'Ma dear child, I feared so m'self for a wee while.' His gaze flicks to the door and back again. 'These gentl'men say such places await me deep in the bowels of this building, should ah be unlucky

215

enough to be convicted.'

I turn my head, only now aware of the two Roundhead soldiers who stand either side of the oak door. I step forwards with every intention of slamming it in their faces, but Father stops me.

'They insist it stays open,' he says gently.

Mother flicks at a stool with the fringe of her shawl, then changes her mind about sitting. 'How long will they keep you here?' She wanders to the window to stare at something in the ward below, but I doubt she is as detached as she appears.

'The Byward Tower is more comfortable than most,' Father says. 'Ah have been fortunate.'

'I shall complain to the Lieutenant of the Tower,' Mother says, her voice shrill. 'How dare they keep you here when you are plainly an innocent man.'

'You have books,' I say with some surprise, hoping to distract Mother from her tirade. 'And writing materials.' I nod toward the miniature desk where sits his half-completed letter and a box of quills.

Father follows my gaze. 'Thanks tae you and yuir mother. I ken things are difficult at home, but the money ye send me is much appreciated.' His laugh does not reach his eyes. 'And it is more than enough tae stop the guards spittin' in ma food.'

'How can you be so flippant, Father?' I snap, unable to hide my distress. Does he not know how worried Mother and I are? Apart from the threat to his own life, if he is executed, our entire estate would be forfeit.

Father leans close. 'I ken what troubles ye,' he whispers beside my cheek. 'I thought this possibility might occur some time ago. To guard against such an event, I made Ham over tae yuir mother.'

'I-I was not thinking that.' The lie slips easily from my lips, but I cannot meet his gaze. 'Tell us you have a plan to get out of here?' My gaze strays to lines that sit at the corners of his eyes and creases on his upper lip I am certain weren't there before.

'Ah hold out hopes still for the fruitfulness of yuir mother's letter writing,' he says gently.

'Letter writing?' Exasperated I flounce away from him over to the small window which gives a view of the river. The same river I see from my chamber every morning.

He follows me and taps my arm, then flicks his gaze at the door and away again, where the guards are plainly visible, and then back to me.

We are being overheard. How could I think otherwise? 'I'm sorry', I mouth silently at Mother, whose pointless complaints and examination of the furniture now make sense.

Her mouth tilts in a wry smile and she trails her fingertips along the bed rail. 'We are all well at home,' she says loudly. 'The girls all miss you of course, and would love to receive a letter from you.' She gives me a hard, direct look as if in warning to watch what I say. 'They wanted to come too, but I felt it unwise. It was trouble enough to obtain permission for Betty to accompany me. As it was, the guards insisted dear Lodowick wait in the carriage below.'

'He is with you?' A light enters Father's eyes. 'I give thanks daily for such a steadfast friend.' His nod and smile make me think he would like to say more.

Mother says something I cannot hear, her hand lifted to stroke his chin and their gazes meet. I am about to turn away to allow them a moment of privacy, but freeze as Father slips a folded packet into Mother's hand that disappears into the pocket of her gown so fast I might have imagined it.

'We would have come sooner.' Mother rearranges his cravat and strokes an over long strand of hair from his brow. 'Had it not taken so long to obtain a pass to allow us to travel. Then a week more for leave to visit you here. I dread to think how long we will have to wait for another occasion. Perhaps I shall have to be smuggled in next time dressed as a maid.'

She keeps up a tirade of nervous chatter while Father whispers low beside her ear. I would give a great deal to know what he is saying, but instead, I glance behind me at the two guards. One is out of sight, but the other peers into the room, frowning. I give a cough to alert my parents to his presence.

Mother immediately pulls away and moves to examine a wooden crucifix attached to the wall above the bed. The guard appears to lose interest, and after a brief, murmured conversation with his associate, moves away.

'Have you been questioned?' Mother says, keeping her voice low.

Father nods. 'Fellow named Thurloe quizzed me for hours soon after I got here.' He lowers his voice. 'One of Oliver St John's eager young lawyers, but nae an experienced questioner in ma view. He demanded to know everything the queen has said or done since reaching Paris.'

'I am sure he does.' Mother bites her lip. 'I take it you told him nothing?'

'The queen likes familiar faces around her,' Father speaks louder now, which I assume is for the benefit of our listeners, as he has not answered Mother's question. 'His Majesty wanted to ensure her wellbeing, so chose me tae accompany her. All I could tell Thurloe is that she pines for her husband and children and spends a great deal of time on her knees, praying.'

Mother's glance at me mirrors my own astonishment mixed with admiration at this blatant lie. The queen has more schemes in place to take back her husband's throne than he has himself.

'Is there a date set for the trial?' Mother asks.

'The Lower House has sent Sir Henry Mildmay to urge the Lords to expedite matters.'

'That Puritan!' Mother sniffs. 'Another who benefited from the king's generosity, only to turn against him.'

'Hush, my dear.' Father glances at the door and away again. 'His influence with Parliament might serve our purpose. Should he be successful, the trial will most likely take place sometime next month.'

Mother's face twists in anguish. 'July is a plague month! Should you cheat the scaffold, Will, we may yet lose you to fever and boils!' She holds one hand to her forehead, a sign one of her headaches threatens.

'Now, ma love. Dinna fash yer'self. It won't come tae that.'

'How can you be sure?' I murmur under my breath, but neither of them appear to hear me. 'Why have they taken so long to set a date?' I ask the question Mother and I have discussed endlessly since news of his arrest came.

Father strokes his chin with one hand, his bitten nails moving slowly through a fine layer of reddish-brown stubble tinged with grey. His eyes cloud with uncertainty.

'I can only think they are busy gathering evidence from their informants in France.'

Informants? This world Father inhabits of spies and traitors fills me with as much exhilaration as fear. Eager for more, I start to ask the nature of this evidence, but he taps a finger against his top lip in clear warning.

My questions will have to wait. The guard has returned and stands blatantly listening.

'Our friends in the high country are glad to hear from you,' Mother says, calmer now.

'Lord Elgin and Master Baillie?' Father mouths. 'I'm certain Lennox and Lauderdale will speak up for me as well.'

Lord Elgin is a name often heard at home, and Robert Baillie is a minister of the kirk whom Mother befriended on the ship from Edinburgh. Lauderdale is unknown to me, but I spend no time on speculation. No doubt, there will be opportunity enough to enquire about him if his efforts on Father's behalf prove successful.

'They have it all wrong, Will dear,' Mother says, patting her hair. 'This Thurloe creature will soon realise you would never act against the interests of the country. You are entirely innocent.'

Accustomed now to their playacting, I perch on the hard bed, the coverlet rough and scratchy beneath my hands. Father is unlikely to have come to England empty-handed, a fact Mother knows as well as I. The queen is bound to have entrusted him with papers, or letters to deliver for her husband.

What I would give for a few private moments with Father. I am certain his gentle expression belies a wealth of interesting plans where important men plot to destroy the rebels for good. I want to ask him when we might expect an invasion, but hold my tongue.

'I cannot believe it has come to this.' The fragile control Mother maintained all the way here dissolves. She flounces across the room, cheeks flaming and lips moving rapidly. In no more than four strides, she reaches the wall and is forced to turn round and pace back again. 'What will happen to us all?'

Stricken, Father lifts a hand in her direction, but she flicks it away and resumes pacing. He lowers his arm to his side with a sigh and attempts a weak smile.

'She will be calmer when we get home,' I say, stepping closer, my fingers stroking the slightly greasy sleeve of his coat. Her restless nerves I attribute to tiredness, for Mother sleeps badly, evidenced by the burned down candle stubs that lie beside her bed most mornings.

A shadow falls across the floor and I turn my head to where a man I do not recognise fills the door frame.

'I wish to question the prisoner again,' he says in a bland, unsympathetic tone. 'Kindly leave now.'

'Ah, we meet agin, Master Thurloe,' Father says, purely, I feel, for our benefit.

In his mid-twenties, he sports a prominent jaw, light, colourless eyes and thin, sandy hair worn quite long. His clothes are dark and nondescript but he is no soldier.

'You are to bully him again?' I say, though he looks straight through me. 'He has told you all he knows.' His indolence makes my fingers itch to slap across that impassive face as a reminder that he deals with a Gentleman of the Bedchamber to the king. Instead, I place myself squarely in front of him, giving my parents an opportunity to take their farewell in relative privacy.

Lawyer Thurloe makes a gesture of protest that he abandons mid-way. With an expressive sniff and a click of his heels, he waits by the door with his back turned.

After a moment of whispering, Mother breaks away and hurries past me, her face averted, no doubt to hide her tears. I take her place and reach up to give Father a fierce hug, hating to let go. Leaving him there with his gaolers is harder than I ever imagined.

He squeezes my upper arms and plants a soft, lingering kiss on my forehead with a whispered, 'Ye must not fret aboot me, hen. The king will save me and I will see you before too lang.'

I turn away with a silent nod. I cannot tell him that it will be Mother's appeals to his friends and a good defence that will save him if anything can. Not the king.

* * *

220

Lodowick sprawls on the carriage seat very much as we left him less than an hour before. Despite the heat, he looks quite comfortable in his brown velvet suit and white hose, his wide brimmed hat at an angle on chestnut curls only slightly tinged with grey and he fans his face lazily.

'I am sorry you had to wait all this time, Master Carlisle.' I tuck my damp kerchief into a pocket and offer him a bright smile.

'Don't worry about me, dear girl.' He twists his silver-topped cane between manicured fingers. 'Used the time to meet with a friend of mine who has the Tower Lieutenant's ear.'

'How enterprising of you,' Mother says. 'Did you discover anything?' She fixes him with an eager look as she arranges her skirts, all brisk efficiency and not a trace of a tear in sight.

The carriage lurches back across the drawbridge, and I can breathe freely now I am out of that place.

'You may rest easy, dear Mistress Murray, though it appears that since Will's arrest, the king is concerned that Parliament might discover his plans with regard to certain promises he made to the French. Information Will Murray possesses.'

'He thinks my Will would betray him?' Mother's mouth forms a round 'o' of shock.

'No, no, dear lady, I did not mean to imply such a thing.' He inches forward on the seat and plants both hands on his knees to regard us both steadily. 'Three days ago, His Majesty escaped from Oxford in disguise with two attendants.'

Our combined gasp seems to suck the very air from the confined space of the carriage. Hot and airless before, it is now stiflingly close. I fumble with the leather flap and let it down, not caring that the street odours are far worse than the stale air inside.

'The king has abandoned my Will?' Mother's lower lip trembles.

Lodowick lifts a hand that he lets fall back against his knee, his face twisted in anguish.

Poor Lodowick. He tries so hard to break bad news gently, and each time he has to deal with feminine emotions.

'Mother,' I reach across the space between us to press her arm. 'Let Master Carlisle finish.'

'Of course.' She gives me her best don't-patronise-me look. 'My nerves are shredded today. Do continue, sir.'

'My friends in Westminster believe His Majesty has been urged by the French envoy to seek help from the Scots to secure the release of your husband.'

'I *knew* the king wouldn't desert him.' Mother tosses her head and beams, contradicting her initial conclusion.

I return her smile but I am less convinced. If the king is on the run from the rebels, he has his own neck to worry about. My father's is surely of less urgency. 'Where has he gone?' I ask.

'North, although he didn't go purely because of what happened to your father,' Lodowick seems to read my thoughts. 'Oxford is under siege by Parliament.'

Images of the king's friends struggling to survive in the overcrowded lodgings and colleges of that city return to me with startling clarity. Freezing and half-starved in winter, and threatened with plague in summer. 'What about all the Royalists in Oxford? What has happened to them?'

Lodowick shrugs. 'Lord Fairfax ordered that no one be allowed out of the city, though some escaped at the same time as His Majesty. Others have been arrested. I have few details.'

'Was there any bloodshed?' I ask, my mouth suddenly dry.

'I only know the death penalty has been issued against soldiers found taking food from civilians. The city will sign a formal surrender once terms are established. I am sure of it.'

'The king left them,' I murmur under my breath. I conjure the face of Ann Fanshawe, whose husband is secretary to Prince Charles. Her last letter came from Truro, but Sir John and Ann's sister Margaret may still be in Oxford. I wonder where Ann is now if the Prince has to keep moving to elude the rebels, and if she is safe? If I remember correctly, Ann's second confinement is due any day and she has already lost one child.

'The king must have had no choice, Betty.' Mother must sense my distress as her voice is soft. 'He would not have left Oxford had there been an alternative.'

'Prince Rupert and the Duke of York were captured,' Lodowick continues, apparently deciding to deal out all the shocks at once.

'Prince Rupert is to be sent into exile and the duke is on his way to St James' Palace.'

'What about Prince Charles?' Mother's eager question makes me squirm. To my mind there are those closer she might enquire about. The Royal family will always be able to take care of itself.

'The last I heard he was in Jersey,' Lodowick says. 'Now that his father is on the run, I assume he will join Queen Henrietta Maria in France.'

I am willing to wager that is where Richard and Ann are too, but stay silent.

Mother withdraws the paper Father gave her from her muff and holds it out. 'Will wanted you to have this.'

The thick paper crackles as Lodowick opens it out, his thin fingers tapping his chin as he reads. 'Ah! I thought as much. Will says he was followed in Paris by a Parliament spy.' He swiftly re-folds the paper and hands it back. 'Should you ladies encounter a man named Robert Wright, be on your guard.'

'You and Father correspond?' I ask astonished. 'Is that not dangerous?'

Mother's smile mirrors Lodowick's. 'Who do you think devised the code your mother uses, my dear,' he says with a wink.

'Oh, I see.' Why did I not think of that? Then I recall the list of names Mother was given at the Carlisles' house on the night of the dinner party. It stands to reason they would communicate in this way.

'My request for money has also been answered,' Mother says dully. 'I have been granted three hundred and seventy pounds out of the rents.'

'Is that all?' I sit bolt upright. 'That will not last long in an estate as large as Ham.' I twist in my seat and frown at her. 'Why did you not tell me?'

Mother's shrug is philosophical. 'I see it as another burden I must bear alone, for how could you make the situation better?' She leans across the seat and pats my hand. 'Perhaps I could shut off a few rooms and discharge a footman.'

'We are overcrowded as it is with all the soldiers there, Mama,' I snap. 'The rebels steal our sheep and raid the storerooms at every opportunity.' I slouch against the rough upholstery, angry that after everything, she still keeps things from me.

'Betty! How can you complain of our situation with your father in a dungeon?' Her gaze slides meaningfully to Lodowick and away again.

Warmth floods my cheeks. 'I apologise.' Though I do not bother to mention that Father's accommodation is not a dungeon, but a well-appointed bed chamber with a stove and a private close stool.

We revert to silence, occupied with our own thoughts as the carriage sways and rumbles over dirt roads through Kew and Sheen, then into Richmond Park. The soft greens and golds of the countryside after filthy streets and cold stone are a welcome change, though there are fewer roe deer than expected at this time of year, and hardly any fawns; poached, no doubt, by those hungry enough to risk the severest penalty. I cannot blame them.

The carriage disgorges us in front of the house, where Mother sweeps past the soldiers who loiter by the door without a look in their direction.

Less brave, I sidle past, convinced they must know where we have been. There is sure to be gossip in the dairy tonight. Much of it malicious.

'Forgive me for a poor hostess, Lodowick,'Mother says, swaying a little. 'But the heat is stifling and my head pounds.'

'Of course dear lady.' He turns to me. 'I will wait for you here,' Lodowick says for the second time that day.

I assist mother up the stairs, though I am absent longer than I intend, due to a search for feverfew by an incompetent servant. Fortunately, Cousin Henderson arrives while I am castigating the wretch, and I leave the task in her hands.

True to his word, I return to find Lodowick occupying the high-back chair where I left him. It is almost dusk, and an amber glow bathes his face. Athletic and healthy for a man of almost fifty, he sits with one hand supporting his chin, his faraway look directed over the garden.

'This is a difficult time for her,' he says, without meeting my eyes.

'For all of us.' I perch on the edge of a chair not three feet from his. 'How much danger is my father in?'

Lodowick sighs, but I know well that he would not try to deceive me, whether for my good or not.

'The king's flight makes your father's situation more grave. I am sure you realise by now he not only carried messages, but also actively negotiated with the Covenanters and the French to reach terms with the king. Parliament is very angry.'

I inhale slowly as the implications of these actions settle into my brain. 'The Scots and the French have disparate religious aims. The king cannot submit to both.'

'You think that will prevent King Charles from appearing to agree with what they want in order to get his way?' His lips curl cynically. 'With your father's capture, they are now certain of the king's intent. They simply cannot prove it.'

'And yet, I am confused. How can His Majesty be accused of treachery? His word is law and any man who stands against him is the traitor.'

'Ah, Elizabeth. Your intellect is sound, but your youth and inexperience betray you. Everything is different now. Parliament has established their position and have the army behind them. The days when the king's wishes are the only law are over. Do you think after all this bloodshed, Parliament will crawl back to the Commons, beg the king's forgiveness and let everything return to the way it was?'

'Why cannot it be like that again?' My childlike yearnings for our old life return with a pang.

'The world is turned upside down. Parliament will force His Majesty to accept terms or lose his crown. In such a fight, do you think men like Will Murray stand a chance?'

My disappointment must show in my face, for he lifts his hand away from his chin and rests it gently on my arm. 'I do not mean to add to your grief; however, you must face facts. The king is stubborn and will not bend to save himself. To rescue your father could be beyond him.'

'We have friends in Scotland.'

'Then it is to them your mother should appeal. Do not give up on him.'

I lift my chin and meet his gaze steadily. 'I will never give up on Father.'

He pats my hand and rises to his feet. 'I know you will not. Will Murray is a lucky man to have you and your sisters.'

'He has Mother too.'

'Ah, yes. He married well.'

'As I propose to do, Master Carlisle. It may be the only way I can save us all.' I follow his ambling stride to the door. 'If the young man in question will still have me.'

His relaxed laugh echoes round the empty entrance, stripped of anything of value to save it from the Roundheads. The sound brings a footman running to open the door.

'Amen to that. We Royalists have a stubborn streak.' He performs a theatrical bow and twirls one hand, grabs mine and drops a kiss onto my knuckles. 'Look at me, I scribble plays for the queen in the vague hope the old Blackfriars Theatre might open again.'

'Her Majesty loves your plays. What is this one called?'

'*The Passionate Lovers*, though it progresses slowly. Perhaps I ought to compose another about the plight and triumph of the common people. To be on the safe side you understand.' His kiss lingers a second longer than politeness requires and when he looks up, his eyes are warm with encouragement.

His horse bears him away while I watch from the step, a hand held up in a wave and a smile on my face, while despair drags at my heart.

Chapter 20

September 1646

The late afternoon sun drapes shafts of golden light through the open windows onto the rug in my chamber, throwing the corners into deep shadow. Discarding our satin gowns, Nan and I sit in our shift and petticoats, sipping at glasses of chilled lemonade.

Boots crunch on gravel and an occasional male voice drifts up from the garden below; sounds we have become accustomed to, but will never welcome. Captain Fitton treats the house like his own, our lives disrupted in many small, mean ways that leave me frustrated but powerless.

Mother insisted a houseful of women not be subject to the scrutiny of so many men, and reserved the entire floor for our own use. It is a source of some disappointment that thus far I have been deprived of seeing any soldiers flogged, for they obey their officers with as much fervour as they pray to their cheerless God.

Nan lifts her glass and laughs. 'I know not how Ball managed to find these lemons, let alone conceal them from the Roundheads.' She sips the slightly tart liquid with relish. 'It makes everything taste better knowing we have foiled them at something.'

Ball took my instructions to heart that day, and our enforced guests have no idea how much food finds its way into our storerooms. Not that the quantity is anything close to what it was before the war, what with money short and few fresh provisions to be had. May the Lord punish me if I ever again turn up my nose at a plateful of wilted lettuce or a day-old-loaf.

How Ball contrives to find supplies in the first place is a mystery, but he appears to revel in the subterfuge. Whenever I venture to enquire where he finds such treasures, he places a finger against the side of his nose and sidles away.

'A pity we cannot keep the soldiers away from the cows,' I say, lifting damp hair from the back of my neck to allow the breeze to caress my hot skin. 'Another one died yesterday.' I glance at Nan with narrowed eyes. 'One of our best heifers too. That officer with the scar on his cheek told me the animal fell in the river and drowned.'

'Utter nonsense!' Nan picks up the nips to chip a tiny chunk from the sugarloaf and drops it into her drink. 'They could at least share it with us.'

'One cow will not go far between forty men. Ball says he will wait until the officers attend evening prayers, and see if he can locate the carcase. That is a lot of meat to hide.'

'I could do with some red meat instead of a constant diet of vegetable pottage and gruel. My teeth have forgotten how to work.'

'You exaggerate. We had rabbit yesterday.'

'Oh, yes. I forgot.' She twists a ringlet against her cheek and slews her eyes sideways at me. I know what is coming and brace myself for the question. 'Elizabeth, where do you suppose Father is now?'

I try not to sigh.

After several weeks of nail-biting fear, Father's trial ended happily. Without firm evidence and with many witnesses willing to plead his innocence, the Lords acquitted him, though it cost us five thousand pounds in fines, which Father had to beg and borrow from our friends. How we shall pay them back is something that gnaws at my joy in his freedom.

Even this triumph was spoiled when Parliament appeared reluctant to release him. It was only Mother's impassioned plea that he not be kept where plague could take him that finally worked. To my dismay, and I am certain Mother's, though she said not one word against him, as soon as Father stepped outside the precincts of the Tower, he went straight to Newcastle.

'You know where he is.' I conceal my disappointment behind airy superiority. 'He is with the king.'

'I hoped he would spend some time here with us.'

'You know as well as I that part of the agreement for his release was that he should try and persuade King Charles to yield to Parliament's demands.'

'I know all that, but surely he could have spared us a day or so.'

I have no answer to a question I ask myself daily. Instead, I shrug and slide off the bed close to the open window and rest my forehead against the frame, hoping to capture a breeze. The air remains impossibly still. My skin feels sticky and my hair clings uncomfortably to my neck. 'How unseasonably hot it is for September.' The lemonade in my glass is warm and no longer refreshing. 'If only we could harness the winter ice and keep it, ready to cool us in such stifling weather.'

'And how do you suppose that can be achieved?' Nan laughs. 'The sun would dissolve it straight away.'

'In Italy, peasants collect ice from the mountains to keep food fresh inside caves.'

'There are no caves in Surrey,' Nan says. She flaps her hand at a wasp, leaping from the chaise with a high-pitched shriek when it buzzes closer.

I turn away to hide a smile, and from the corner of my eye, see something move in the jumble of trees and bushes in the wilderness beyond the parterre. 'A brick lined hole in the ground might serve as well. I am sure there are grander manors than ours who have them. Perhaps, when I am mistress here, I will build one in the garden.'

I screw up my eyes against the sunlight, searching the line of bushes. Whatever it was is too large for an animal, yet too purposeful in its route toward the house. It must be a person. What would soldiers be doing loitering amongst the trees?

'Oh, Elizabeth, you are always making plans to change Ham.' Nan slaps at her skirt for good measure, but I could tell her the insect flew past me seconds ago. 'You talk endlessly of sweeping away the box and lavender garden to plant cherry trees.'

'I also plan to install a sheltered walk of pleached hornbeam, so I may examine the scarlet fruit as it grows ripe enough for me to eat.' I can almost taste the sweetness on my tongue as my teeth puncture the firm flesh. 'It's been such a long time since I tasted a cherry, and sometimes I find myself dreaming about them.'

'Dreaming of cherries, how fanciful.' Nan laughs, but I do not join in, my focus being on the movement below.

The figure is closer now, and definitely a man. In a black hat pulled low, his cloak tight to his knees. The fact he is not dressed for the hot weather alerts my interest, as well as the way he checks left and right before darting from one bush to the next.

The garden between the trees and the house is deserted now. The soldiers set to dig up the flowerbeds and plant vegetables discarded their tools and left for evening prayers some time ago.

'Then on your head be it.' Nan relaxes back on the chaise, and folds her arms behind her head. 'If you remove the box and lavender, the moths will devour our clothes. Now you want a house for ice. Whatever will you think of next?'

'We can move the lavender somewhere else.' I plant both palms on the sill and lean as far as I dare out of the window. The figure is closer now, and sidles along the wall toward the rear of the house. 'Never mind that now. Nan, take a look there. I am sure there is a man cowering under that hedge.'

She slides off the chaise and joins me at the window. 'His head is down so I cannot see his face, only the top of his hat.' Nan shields her eyes with a hand, then she turns wide eyes on me. 'Perhaps he is an intruder. Shall we call Captain Fitton?'

'An intruder? With all these soldiers about? Only a brave or foolish soul would attempt such a thing.'

The man has reached the terrace and sprints up the steps, pressing himself against the wall.

He looks up and my heart turns over.

Nan gasps and brings both hands to her mouth. 'Father!'

* * *

Father's anxious expression splits into a relieved smile. He points to the side door and then at himself.

Darting back into the room, I scoop my robe from the bed and throw it around my shoulders. 'I'll go down and let him in, you tell Mother he is here.'

'Where shall you take him? The officers will be at supper in the main hall soon. He will be seen.'

'There is still time. I'll bring him up to Mother's room.' I turn back at my bedroom door. 'And find Cousin Henderson. Tell her to bring the girls to Mother's room too.'

Sending up a silent prayer that God might keep the soldiers at

230

their prayers a little longer, I speed down the back stairs and into the hall where the long table is set for the officer's supper. At the sight of Father's face, distorted by the wavy glass of the garden door, my heart lifts and in my eagerness, my fingers grope clumsily at the lock.

He looks both ways along the terrace while gesturing for me to hurry.

My heart hammers as my fingers fumble with the key. The lock gives and his grin warms my heart as he steps inside and closes the door behind him.

'You are a good lassie.' He looks me up and down with a frown. It occurs to me then I am hardly dressed to receive visitors, but explanations will have to wait.

There is no time for even a hug before we hurry to the hidden door in the panelling. 'How did you get here? Where is your horse? Are you sure you weren't seen?'

I throw questions over my shoulder as he climbs the narrow servants' stairs behind me. With each step, I scrape the support post with my hip, or misjudge the rise and bang a toe. It occurs to me now to wonder how the maids manage them whilst encumbered with buckets of hot water or arms full of linens.

'Ah'm on my way tae London and thought tae call in and see you all,' he says, puffing a little as he disentangles his cloak from a nail. 'I left ma horse at the smith's in Ham and will go back fer it later.'

Mother throws open the concealed servants' door to her room and with a finger to her lips, ushers us both inside. Tears spring into her eyes, but she instantly takes command, drawing Father to a chair set by her dresser. There she bombards him with the questions I have already asked.

Discarding his cloak and hat with obvious relief, he patiently goes through the same litany of responses. His wide brimmed hat leaves a ridge of sweat round his shoulder length hair that clings damply to his temples. He runs the fingers of both hands through it and scratches his scalp. Now in shirtsleeves and breeches, his shoes shed a light film of grit on Mother's best rug. He gives a deep sigh and briefly closes his eyes.

'Ah'm that weary. Wuild ye help me tak' off mah boots.'

Nan giggles at his thick Scots accent, which always returns at times of exhaustion or stress.

'I will do it,' Mother says, bending to remove the offending items.

'I have missed ma girls.' He flicks back his dirt-encrusted hair and pinches Meg's chin gently between thumb and forefinger. Nan pulls up a stool and perches at his knee, earning a kiss on the cheek.

I wrap an arm round the bedpost and wait for him to begin his story. The fact he arrives in such secrecy tells me he does not plan to stay, something that escapes Nan, for already she urges him to come home.

'Why not?' Nan begs when he shakes his head. 'Does the queen still need you?'

'It's a mite complicated,' Father says, then stops, examining each of our faces. 'Where is my Kate?' he asks after a moment.

'I could not find her when Nan came to fetch us.' Cousin Henderson gives the room a swift glance. 'I have set Molly to keep an eye out for her. I am sure she will be here directly.'

Mother approaches the bell-pull. 'I will have Ball bring us a light supper. You must be hungry, Will.'

'Always,' Father replies grinning. 'It is indeed a lang road frae Newcastle.'

'How fares His Majesty?' Meg asks.

A cloud passes across his face, instantly replaced by a wide grin that does not reach his eyes. 'He is still smaller than me and his beard is sharper. Now, my lamb, would you bring me something to drink? Ah'm parched.'

Nan and I exchange a look at this strange answer, but he looks away from us, mildly impatient.

'There is a jug of lemonade in my chamber, Meg. Bring that,' I say.

Meg scrambles to her feet, eager to comply.

'I did what Parliament asked,' Father says quietly as the door closes on Meg. 'I took the Newcastle Propositions tae the king, as they demanded.'

'What do these propositions say?' Mother pours water from a

pitcher into a bowl on her dresser, dampens a linen cloth and dabs it on the grime that clings to the lines on Father's face.

'That the king must take the Covenant in exchange for their help.' He sighs as trickles of water make tracks in the dirt on his skin. Mother's hand pauses in her task, and he catches it in his and drops a swift kiss on her knuckles. 'Together with the abolition of episcopacy, the establishment of Presbyterianism in England for three years, more laws against the Roman Catholics. They also insist on full control of the army. Not tae mention a long list of Royalists they wish to persecute with nae chance of pardon.'

'His Majesty will never agree to those terms,' I say, scornful.

Father's low, cynical laugh comes as no surprise. 'Indeed he did not.' He dips into an inside pocket in his coat and withdraws a folded document a finger's width thick. 'The king has written his own terms and sent me tae take them back tae the Lords.' He slaps the packet down on the table, the Royal seal stark against the cream parchment. 'I don't doubt they'll reject them oot o' hand too. But what can I do? He's also dealing with the French and the Irish, hop'in tae keep them fighting amongst themselves.'

'Will that work?' I ask. Though after all the king's broken promises, who can trust him?

'Nay, the Scots will have their way over the kirk, or I can see them washing their hands of him, and removing the Army of the Covenant from England.'

'What does the king want of the Scots, Father?' Nan asks. 'I thought this was a war against the English Parliament?'

'It was, once.' Father sighs. 'Montrose's victories in Scotland kept up the morale of the Royalists in England. After Naseby, the king's plan was tae join forces wi' him. When Montrose moved into the Lowlands in preparation for an advance into England, his troops began to desert. He scans our faces again. 'After the defeat at Philliphaugh, where David Leslie and the Covenanters outnumbered Montrose, they didnae bother with proper sentries so were taken by surprise. It was a bad fight, with five hundred Irish cut tae ribbons.'

'Savagery always happens in war, it cannot be helped.' Mother appears unmoved by the plight of the Irish.

'Nay, lass. This was after they were offered quarter and had surrendered.' He sniffs and wipes a hand over his brow. 'The slaughter was a disgrace. To make it worse, the Covenanter ministers incited the violence. Men o' God, bah!'

Pensive, I remove the bowl of dirty water and replace it with a clean one. This dreadful war has gone on too long. There has been too much spilled blood with not enough progress made. Parliament rules us from Westminster and the king appears willing to sacrifice all his friends to his cause. Will Father be next?

'Now the king has surrendered his'self to the Covenanters and Montrose has gone into exile. Leslie is sick of the fight and may pledge tae do nae more until his men are paid. They hae had nae coin for months, the poor wretches.'

Meg returns, the jug of lemonade clutched in both hands, her tongue protruding slightly from between her lips. She pours the cloudy liquid with slow, careful movements and with a smile of triumph, hands the full glass to Father, who squeezes her shoulder in thanks.

A quiet knock comes at the door and Ball enters, ushering in two footmen with trays, jugs and goblets. 'Master Murray, I am so pleased to see you well.'

'Aye, Ball, but weary as a dray horse,' Father says laughing.

Ball holds out a large pewter plate on which sits a slab of cheese, several hunks of fresh bread, a ham bone with an inch of flesh clinging to it, and a pile of early apples.

'Pardon the simple fare, sir. I had no warning.' Ball snaps open a linen cloth and drapes it across Father's shoulder as if he sat at the head of the dining table. 'Captain Fitton and his men are taking supper downstairs, so I had to be discreet.' He retrieves the dirty boots from the floor. 'I will polish these for you, sir.'

'You had better not,' I say, removing them from his hands. He stares at them with faint longing, his duty denied. 'We cannot risk them being seen.'

'I understand, Mistress.' He sighs, but bows and retreats.

Despite the oppressive heat having robbed me of my appetite, I fall on our meagre supper with relish.

Mother refuses food for herself, but instead picks morsels from the items spread on Cousin Henderson's kerchief on her lap and from that of a less than gracious Nan.

'If the king has surrendered to the Scots, does that mean the war is over?' Nan asks.

'Many may think so.' Father plucks at the upholstery on the arm of his chair. 'But nae King Charles. He will ne'er give up.'

The shadowy presence of Sir Lionel Tollemache looms in my head. If the Royalists are truly defeated, what will happen to us? Could a marriage between us still be effected to save Ham? But with no word from the man in weeks, I dare not hope.

'Mother, may I have another apple, this one is all wormy?' Meg holds the offending object up for scrutiny, and in silence, Mother complies.

Father's arrival has mellowed her, for on any other day she would have told Meg to cut the worms free and eat the untainted flesh, and accompany it with a sermon about those with far less than we have.

'Don't look so despondent, ma hen.' Father pats Mother's hand, eliciting a weak smile.

'I am simply afraid Parliament may decide to take out their impatience with the king on you. They may even send you back to prison.'

'They tried that with the spying charge.' His lip curls in contempt. 'Ma duty is clear. Ah must take the king's plan to Westminster,' he points a knife at the paper that sits at his elbow, 'then it's back tae Paris fer me.'

The door opens again and Kate enters. 'Father, I'm sorry for not being here when you arrived.' All eyes turn toward her as she limps past me to throw her arms around Father.

'Here's my Kate, at last.' He kisses her noisily on her cheek.

'Where have you been, girl?' Mother scolds.

Something enters Kate's eyes I cannot define. Defiance? Pride? Unaccustomed to deceit from her, I do not at first recognise it.

'I was in the garden and did not see Molly until I came back inside.' Kate licks her lips and avoids my eye.

'Do not rebuke the lass, Catherine.' Father pats Mother's arm. 'She is here now and at last I have all my girls around me. Even if it is only for a short time.'

Mother bids Kate sit and Cousin Henderson fusses around her, ensuring she has something to eat. Kate's smug air and enigmatic smile stirs my suspicions.

Where has she been? I doubt the garden as she says, for surely we would have seen her, or she would have encountered Father there earlier. She is so restless lately, I worry there may be something wrong with her. I must remember to ask Cousin Henderson if she has noticed anything untoward.

The contents of the platter rapidly disappear, along with the jugs of wine and the rest of the lemonade.

'You will stay the night?' Mother pleads.

Father's sad smile answers her question. 'I cannae. With so many Roundheads in the house and patrols in the district, 'tis too dangerous. Especially with these papers I carry. I hae arranged tae stay the night at an inn near Putney under a false name. They dinna know me there.' He brushes crumbs from the front of his shirt and retrieves his coat and hat. I hand him his boots and he accepts them with world-weary resignation.

'I will see you out,' I volunteer, before anyone else can. I long for a private word with him, however brief.

He bestows rough, lingering kisses on my tearful sisters, then together, we retrace our steps along the hall and down the servants' stairs. The table in the main hall is clear but for a few fruit remnants and empty nutshells, and not an officer in sight.

I regret the long summer, for it is almost nine of the clock and yet the evening sky is still light, making our route through the hedges more hazardous.

No soldiers loiter beside the trees smoking clay pipes and chatting, nor do they stroll between the newly dug vegetable patches. Assuming they must be in their quarters, we reach the wilderness without mishap.

'Those bastards ha' ruined my garden!' Father growls, indicating the turned over beds and the spoiled parterre. He catches me up and tugs at my sleeve, bringing me to a halt. 'You didnae have to come this far, Betty. I can find ma way to Ham easily enough.'

'I know.' I glance back to make sure we are sufficiently hidden from the house. 'It is so long since I have had you to myself, I wanted to take my own farewell of you.'

'Aye, I've missed you too.' He halts me with a hand on my shoulder. 'Keep this to yerself, lass. But there's a rumour that an apartment is being readied in the Tower for a royal prisoner.'

'For the king?'

'Who else? Once there, even the Scots could not help him. Sir Robert Moray is back in Scotland, and we have a plan to spirit His Majesty away from Newcastle and out o' the hands of the Scots. I have a ship ready to meet us as Tynemouth.'

'I knew it. You are both too loyal to allow His Majesty to become anyone's prisoner.' I reach to tie the ribbons of his cloak. 'When will it happen?'

'It wulnae. His Majesty says he will not run because the plan is to dress him as a woman. He says he won't risk being caught in such an undignified manner.'

My hands go limp and drop from the perfect knot at his throat. 'What? But he must.'

Father shrugs and pulls the dust-caked material round him. 'The king still refuses to take the Covenant, so now General Leslie regrets accepting his surrender.' His laugh is scornful. 'Perhaps we could suggest Leslie looks the other way and lets him board the ship we have gone tae all the trouble tae arrange.'

'Are the Scots really tired of him?'

'Aye. They believed King Charles went north to support them and the kirk, but he demands unconditional co-operation which leaves them frustrated at every turn.' He wraps an arm round me and pulls me close. The combined smells of dirt, sweat and manure cling to him, overlaid by horse. I do not care. He is my father and he is going into danger. Again.

'Why then did the king go to the Scots camp in the first place?'

He massages my shoulder gently. 'A question we all ask ourselves, hen. Perhaps he believed that as a fellow Scot, all he had tae do was ask and they would return him to his throne.'

'Why should they?'

'Exactly!' He tucks my chin with a finger. 'I doubt he trusts me

237

as much as he used to either.' I open my mouth to protest but he stops me with a look. 'My aen fault for agreeing to get him tae negotiate. He regards those who attempt tae sway him from his Godly mission as the unholy.' His hollow laugh does not quite hide his dismay.

We reach the gate onto the footpath that leads to the village, where Father turns to me with a smile. 'There is something I didnae mention at the house for fear o' upsetting yuir mother.'

'What sort of thing?' Distracted, my response is perfunctory, for I am busy raking the woods and garden with my gaze in search of soldiers. Seeing none, I pluck a few stems of lavender that have survived the scores of boots, tucking them into his pocket. 'To remind you of Ham and to take away the stink of the road.'

'Thank ye, lass.' He plants a brief kiss on my forehead. 'That scheme I mentioned, the one Moray and I devised tae help the king escape?'

'What of it? You said the king refused to run away.'

'Aye, he did.' He smiles and pats the pocket where the lavender lies. 'A lad by the name of Tobias Peaker revealed our conspiracy to ah- certain other interested parties.'

'What interested parties?' My stomach clenches and I have difficult swallowing.

'It matters not. Suffice it tae say, I shall have tae appear before the Lords in Newcastle at a hearing.'

'Father! Not again!' I clutch at his coat with both hands.

'There's nae reason tae fret.' He pulls away from me and reaches to adjust his hat with a nonchalant shrug. 'Peaker is a thief who stole ma watch and forty shillings. It's nae just me he accuses. Lord Elgin, Sir Robert and Colonel Leslie will have tae appear also.' He speaks as if such exalted company will protect him.

'What will Mother say if you are imprisoned again and I have to tell her I knew about it?'

'Trust me, ma dear, it will go nae further.' He strokes his stubble with his free hand and stares off across the ruined garden. 'It breaks ma heart to see what those rebels ha' done tae my hoose.' He lifts a finger as if something has that second occurred to him. 'I almost forgot, I have some good news for ye, lass, in a letter that found its way tae me from Sir Lionel Tollemache.'

'Indeed?' I feign nonchalance, but the name brings a brief flutter to my chest.

His eyes soften and a low chuckle sounds in his throat. 'He congratulates me on my acquittal and looks forward tae finalising negotiations for your betrothal.' He disentangles his arm from my grasp. 'Ah have tae go now, or that smith will think I am nae coming, and close up fer the night. I dinnae relish a night in the fields, though I have slept in worse places.'

He turns and disappears into the thick evergreens of the wilderness garden, the faint smell of sweat mixed with gorse and cut grass drifting back on the wind.

With Sir Lionel Tollemache filling my thoughts, I make my way back through the trees toward the house. The south front is no more than twenty feet away and I relax and increase my pace. As I round a corner, a shadow breaks free of the bushes and a figure steps in front of me.

Strong hands grasp my arms and a black jerkin fills my vision as a hard voice demands, 'Who was that man?'

* * *

'I will ask you again, Mistress Murray. Who was that man?' Straggly clouds slide across the moon, throwing pale light onto the stern expression of Robin Carter, who glares down at me from his impressive height.

My first instinct is to kick him and run, but instantly I dismiss the thought.

I recall his kindness the day the troopers came to Ham, and decide I can use the gentle soul he hides within his fierce stare.

'What man would that be?' I do not flinch, indignant that he presumes to lay hands on me.

His eyes narrow, and uncertainty flickers within. 'The man you spoke to a moment ago. I saw him only briefly. By the time I reached you he was gone.'

'Dusk often plays tricks on our eyes in this dense undergrowth. You are mistaken. Now release me!' I shrug off his grip. 'There was

239

no man. And what right have you to question me in my own garden?'

'The right of Parliament!' As if he did not notice my attire before, his glance drops to the low neckline of my skimpy chemise beneath a light cloak. He gives a start and swallows, a self-conscious flush creeping into his face. He is either a good Puritan or a man of little experience with women. 'I-I know what I saw, and insist you tell me who that man was.'

I bundle the collar of my robe up beneath my chin in a display of affronted pride.

'Insist all you like, Roundhead. I shall explain nothing.' I make to brush past him, but his hand shoots out to grasp my forearm. I look down at his fingers and arch a brow, then lift my eyes slowly to his face. 'Remove your hand.'

He swallows again, and to my astonished relief, obeys. A light of interest enters his eyes that shows me he is not immune to me. A fact I shall use against him if I can.

I take a step toward him, thrilled when he inhales sharply and backs away. 'This heat is oppressive do you not find? I wished to take the air and the flowers are so sweet in the evenings.' I smile into his face. 'Is that not why you are here, rather than chanting prayers with your comrades?'

'I urge you to answer my question, Mistress Murray.' His voice croaks and he licks his lips. 'Unless you wish me to rouse the sentry and begin a search?'

My mind races. How far has Father got in the last few moments? I hope far enough. 'Maybe I have a lover?' The thought comes from nowhere. But then why not? Carter may be the plain soul his name implies, but is not illicit love something even he can understand?

His lop-sided smile tells me he rejects the explanation. Never mind, it buys me time.

He cocks his chin toward the house. 'Is she aware you cavort half-dressed with a stranger who does not present himself at your door?'

'You would accuse me to my mother?' I force appeal into my eyes that rove his face. 'With no more evidence than a shadow in the trees?'

His mouth opens and closes again. 'It-it would be no more than my duty.'

'Then I shall tell her the only man here was yourself. That to my horror and distress you accosted me. And of course, at my mother's insistence I would have to repeat my story to your commanding officer.'

His jaw clicks and his nose thins with anger. 'They would not believe you.'

'Even with the evidence of their own eyes?' I blink up at him and smile. 'With a defenceless girl in a house full of invaders, standing before them in a flimsy, torn gown.'

'Torn?' A glint of suspicion darkens his eyes. Such pretty eyes, I almost regret goading him. Almost.

Slowly, I lift the sleeve of my muslin robe and hold it away from my body. With my other hand, I grip the lace tight as if I am about to tear it.

His hand rises in a quick, defensive gesture. 'No! I cannot have such an outrageous slur on my reputation.' He drops his hand from my other arm and scans the surrounding shrubbery, his breathing quickening. I am certain he will not take the risk.

I drop my hand from my sleeve while giving silent thanks for guileless creatures such as he. 'Of course you cannot, Master Carter. And I suggest you have not seen me. Then we could both pretend this encounter never took place and neither of our reputations would suffer.'

'Unless this-this lover you speak of is a Royalist spy.'

My laugh is easy, genuine and full-throated.

So, his spirit has not completely deserted him. He still thinks he is in control.

I press a hand to my face in mock horror. 'Spy indeed. Let us see how many Roundheads a woman's scream would summon. I-'

'No!' He covers my mouth with a hand, but drops it instantly. 'You treat me with levity, Mistress Murray.' He inhales and glares at me. 'I have the authority to question whoever enters these grounds, and you react by threatening me with false accusations?'

Unmoved, I cross my arms, remembering at the last second that the action only serves to accentuate my breasts.

He blushes again and the moment passes when he might have denounced me.

'I use whatever weapons I have, as a woman and as a loyal subject of His Majesty.'

'The Stuart! That man of blood!' He curls his lip in contempt, apparently more at ease with a subject he can understand. 'You have not yet given me the man's name.'

'Enough of this banter.' I skirt round him, relieved when he makes no move to prevent me, but at the same time bored with his indignation. 'Now if you will excuse me, I shall return to the house before I am missed.'

'I will find out,' he calls after me. 'Make no mistake about that!'

I know he hasn't moved from the spot, but as my steps crunch on the gravel path a sweat breaks out on my upper lip. At any second, he will curse himself for being duped and summon his superior.

I do not turn back to see if he watches me. I do not need to. His furious gaze burns into my back all the way across the lawn. I wonder what he would think if he knew I fully intend to tell Mother every detail of my encounter with Robin Carter, and that she will applaud every barb and threat.

When I reach the relative safety of the house, I close the door and lean against it, the hard edge of the frame cutting into my back. Had it been Captain Fitton who saw us, the outcome would have been very different.

I must take more care in future.

Chapter 21

November 1646

Despite the damp cold that creeps into every corner of the house, and the fact our waking hours are spent huddled round meagre fires, I love these crisp, clear mornings where the trees along the river turn to shades of red, ochre, brown and flame.

As the days shorten, the leaves reach their most brilliant hues, then are shed into a crunchy carpet on the soggy grass. For want of something to fill the hours beneath a lowering grey sky, my sisters and I assist the gardeners sweeping them into piles for burning.

I rarely see Robin Carter's purposeful stride in the house and grounds, but when I do, I cannot help but be aware of his eyes following me. I give him no reason for suspicion and always smile sweetly when he looks in my direction.

Nan sees it too and is convinced the young man is my admirer. If only she knew that he thinks me divisive and dangerous.

I like it that way.

This year, Christmas is less festive than ever. Mother makes the best of it and insists we decorate the fireplace and window frames with sprigs of rosemary, and drape laurel and ivy from the cornices in the upper rooms.

'Who collected the holly and mistletoe?' I ask, admiring the dark glossy leaves interspersed with fat red berries on the fireplace, and the translucent white drops hanging from the ceiling.

'I did. From the wilderness garden of course,' Kate says with a withering look in my direction. 'I sneaked out there during the soldiers' drill practice.'

'And what would you have done, Mistress Kate, if one of them had seen you?' Cousin Henderson, her arms full of ribbons and holly branches, stares down her long nose at Kate.

'Parliament hasn't forbidden such things altogether, Cousin.' Kate tosses her head. 'Some of the soldiers did the same thing yesterday. I saw them'.

'It's like being in a forest!' Meg twirls in the centre of the room, her eyes lit with childish delight.

Her rapt face reminds me of the Christmases of my own childhood, when the house was filled with guests, food, wine and extravagant gift-giving. Memories Meg shall never have if this war goes against us and Parliament imposes its cheerless rules on the country.

Nan and Kate circle the dining table, laying bundles of dried herbs tied in muslin beside each plate; a family tradition to protect us from harm and disease.

'If Captain Fitton saw this,' Meg holds up her pouch tied with a bow of her favourite yellow ribbon, 'he would surely call us pagans and witches.'

'Hush, Meg!' Cousin Henderson snatches the offending object and thrusts it into Meg's pocket. 'Have a care, Missy. Such things are not to be said in jest.'

Meg sulks, her lips turned down. 'No one reveres the Lord as I do, Cousin. Besides, I do not believe in witches and demons.'

'Hang mistletoe about your neck,' Kate says with authority. 'And the witches can have no power over you.'

'Now that *is* a pagan superstition,' Mother says, taking her place at the head of the table, the other end left empty as a tribute to Father.

'Why do the Roundheads hate Christmas?' Meg asks, her innocent eyes wide.

'They say that Yuletide has no biblical justification,' Kate quotes in a sing-song voice. 'That it is a Pagan festival and a remnant of Papism.'

'Well, *I* think it extremely silly to forbid us to sing and dance in celebration of our Lord's birth.' Nan drags up a chair to the table in preparation to sit.

'To my mind,' Mother says. 'Christmas is a commemoration of a holy event, to be observed with cheerfulness as well as devotion.'

'And lots of good food.' Meg wrinkles her nose at the pheasant stew the footman places on the table. No steam rises from the surface, for all the heat has disappeared on its long journey from the kitchens and up an additional flight of stairs.

'Imagine this full to the brim with lobster and cream, Meg,' I indicate the silver tureen from which no steam arises. 'Followed by a fat goose instead of scrawny chicken that is more bone than flesh, and plum puddings afterwards.'

'I remember when a roasted boar's head with a lemon in his mouth was the first dish served at Christmas.' Nan cups her pointed chin in her hands, her bony elbows planted on the table. She is all angles and devoid of colour, like a painting of a Christian martyr. I tell myself the reason is our bland diet, but Nan has never experienced robust health.

Cousin Henderson folds her hands in front of her as a signal for saying grace. Once the prayer is said, a footman doles out portions of the weak stew that lies grey and unappetising in our bowls.

'Marchpane,' Kate says with longing. 'I miss marchpane.'

'Your teeth will not mourn the loss of such a rich delicacy,' Mother says.

Kate grimaces. 'When I reach my dotage I shall be able to thank Parliament for the retention of my teeth, if little else.' She sniffs, and pokes her spoon at her bowl of stew.

'We may not have dancing bands in the streets of Kingston, nor a special service for the Nativity,' Mother says. 'However, we shall have lambswool by the fire later.'

'We cannot sing,' Nan laments, pushing back her chair as the footmen arrive to remove the cloth. 'The soldiers taking supper in the hall will hear us.'

'Never mind, Nan.' Kate throws a comforting arm around her sister's waist as we troop into the salon next door. 'Reading poetry aloud will not offend the rebels.'

I trail after them, our meagre dinner over so soon, I am barely sated.

'I have my book of sermons,' Meg offers. 'What of you, Elizabeth, would you like to read Dean John Donne's sermon of Christmas in the year twenty-nine? It is quite soothing, listen.'

She reads aloud from the page in a high, clear voice. *'Let man be something; how poore, and inconsiderable a ragge of this world, is man!'*

'Very nice, Meg.' A thought springs to mind and I cut her off. 'You do not by chance read his poetry too?' I once earned a beating when caught reading *'The Flea'* when not much older than she.

Her head shakes from side to side, causing frizzy curls to dislodge and drop onto her forehead. 'Mother does not allow it. I do not know why.'

Nan discards her sewing and takes the empty place opposite Meg. 'Would you like to play a game of *Hazard*, Meg?' She withdraws the die from an ornamental box on the table. 'Perhaps Kate might care to join you?' I glance to where my second sister was only a few moments ago, but there is no sign of her.

Where would she be when the warmest place in the house is here in this room? Assuming she visits the close stool, I dismiss her, while conversation dies down and the only sounds in the room the turning of a page and the clatter of ivory cubes.

Restless, I wander to the window, where my eye catches a movement on the lawn that has me muttering a curse beneath my breath. Mother looks up startled, but ignoring her, I leave the room and tug the door shut behind me.

In the rear courtyard, a gardener leaps out of my way as I pass, then belatedly stoops into a low bow. I glare at him but keep going. He is not one of the athletic young men recruited from the village, for they have all been taken to fight. With no wish to waste my anger on him, I head for the object of my fury, a familiar figure at the gate.

'Captain!' My heart thumps in rhythm to my rapid footsteps as I walk, heating my cheeks. These soldiers take too many liberties on my family's property.

Captain Fitton arranges his face into a lazy smile. 'Is there something I can help you with, Mistress Murray?' The way he drags out my name reduces it to an insult. His casual gaze shifts to a group of four soldiers who manhandle a young heifer in the direction of the outbuildings.

No doubt, they intend to slaughter it there and roast the meat over a fire while they drink themselves insensible on the fruits of our stillroom.

I grit my teeth so hard my jaw clicks. 'If your men insist on stealing our cattle, can they have the good sense to pick one of the bullocks? Heifers give calves and provide milk.'

He plants his feet apart in front of me as if to consider my words. I suspect he revels in the havoc his men bring to Ham, knowing we are powerless to do anything about it. What a coward he is to flaunt his position over five helpless women.

'I fear it is too late for that beast.' He waves a careless arm at the retreating backs of his men. 'But I'll be sure to impart your sentiments at the next muster.'

'I suppose that is all I can ask.' I narrow my eyes at him, aware all he has to do to make his presence known is to shout an order. He doesn't. I hope the method of the animal's clumsy slaughter makes the meat tough. 'May I ask why your men ruined all the flower beds on the south front? Are not the kitchen and side gardens enough to feed you all?' My fists clench at my sides, the fabric of my skirt gripped hard enough to tear. 'There's nothing left there but brown earth and broken pavoirs. Is it some sort of sport you have devised, or does the sight of nature's beauty offend Puritan sensibilities?'

He leans a meaty shoulder against a tree, his face slack and eyes devoid of any emotion.

'Flowers serve no godly purpose on the land, but this is not simply wanton destruction. My men have orders from the garrison to plant every scrap of soil with vegetables, barley and wheat for food.'

'We have enough land between here and Richmond to grow food for the entire town.' My voice hisses with fury. 'Destroying our flowerbeds is pure malice.'

Goose bumps erupt on my exposed forearms, for the bone-chilling cold cuts viciously through my shawl. I need a heavy wool cloak with pelt lining to be out here in such weather.

'Malice, is it?' He folds his arms, grinning. 'Do you wish to address your grievance to Lord Fairfax himself?'

My fingers itch and I fight an urge to score my nails across his fleshy face. I could indeed send a complaint to Fairfax at Isleworth, but the fact the Captain suggests such an action indicates the result would disappoint.

'For all the good that would do me.' I summon contempt into my final glare and turn on my heel. His coarse laughter follows me all the way back to the house.

How I hate these invaders who tramp through our house as if they already own it.

In the hall, I narrow my eyes at the remains of the officer's dinner littering the long table. 'Get this cleared up!' I instruct a hovering footman, who jumps at my command.

It would be useless to take my grievance to Mother, for she would merely smile in her infuriating way that begs neither questions nor curiosity. 'You will not alter the nature of these men, so do not waste your anger on what you cannot change.'

How she maintains her composure is something I will never understand, much less emulate.

With my shawl clutched round me, I seek the relative privacy of a ground floor room set beside the staircase hall. Once our family salon, we abandoned it when the soldiers came, for Mother deemed it to be too close to the officers' accommodations. Most of the furniture was taken upstairs to a disused bedchamber, where we now spend our evenings.

The lock gives soundlessly and I step into a room twelve paces long and not much wider. Made gloomy by dark wooden panelling in need of a thorough waxing, the maroon brocade hangings outline a dusty window. Enraged by the captain's careless arrogance, I do not care for the gloomy surroundings. I simply wish to nurse my frustration in private.

I cross the threshold and freeze. The room is not empty.

A man in a common soldier's jerkin over buff beeches stands silhouetted by the window. He is bareheaded, revealing the hated shorn hair that betrays his allegiance like no other feature could.

Not an old man, but not very young either, his breeches are tied at the knee with strips of black ribbon, below which grey stockings drop into unadorned black shoes.

My gaze sweeps over his nondescript appearance and settles on the butterfly at his side. In a bright yellow gown with lace at the neckline and elbows, a girl stands pressed against his thighs. The skirt of her wide gown, flattened on one side, billows artistically on the other.

Her slim arms wind round his neck, her face lifted to receive his kiss. He wraps an arm round her waist, while his other hand cups her chin in a gesture so intimate, I know this is not the first time they have been together like this.

Inhaling, I slam the door hard enough to crack the frame.

They spring apart, identical expressions of guilt on their pale faces.

My tirade dies on my lips as I take in the girl's shocked face. 'Katherine!'

* * *

Kate casts the man at her side a long, pleading look before leaving his embrace. She takes a step toward me. 'Elizabeth, please allow me to explain. I-'

'Explain what?' I look from her dejected face to the equally dismayed one of the man beside her. 'That you choose to act the harlot in our own house with one of *them*?' I point a shaking hand at the soldier.

He does not speak, but the look in his eyes is of resignation.

'Don't speak of him like that!' Her face twists in anguish. 'He's a good man and an excellent soldier.'

'Indeed? And how many Royalists has this 'excellent soldier' run through with his sword?'

Kate opens her mouth to respond, but the rebel chooses this moment to step between us.

Not a handsome man, his eyes are too close together for beauty or trust, and his nose is over long. The look he gives my sister is of unmistakeable intimacy. No brief, impulsive liaison, this.

Kate's pale hand seeks his brown fingers and they entwine. Their shared look, full of such raw emotion, pierces my chest; a mixture of hope, regret and dismay that confuses me, until I cannot tell if I envy them, or am repulsed.

All my wonderings about her behaviour floods back. The unexplained absences, the distractions, the secret smiles. Of course. She has been meeting this blackguard in secret.

'Forgive me, Mistress Murray.' The soldier finds his voice, a weak, stammering thing that he may as well leave in his throat. 'I take full responsibility for the nature of this discovery. I harbour no

249

ill-intentions toward Mistress Katherine, I-'

'Ill-intentions?' My harsh, incredulous laugh echoes in the empty room. 'A clandestine assignation in a dark corner is not ill-intended?'

'It is not like that, Elizabeth, truly.' Kate's arm tightens on his.

He casts a fearful glance at the door over my shoulder, as if calculating his chances of escape, thus confirming my impression he is not willing to risk his ambitions for my sister.

I take a step sideways that puts me squarely in the line of his retreat and stare him down. In the chill silence, the wind that hisses down the empty chimney could be my enraged breathing.

'What do you have in mind for my sister, sir? A tumble on the floor and a hasty exchange of vows at St Peters Church?' My tongue lashes him with the depth of my disgust. At the same time, something inside me buckles at the way Kate searches his face. That intense look tells me that nothing I say will diminish him in her eyes. My anger will barely touch her.

If only I hadn't found them; but she must be made to see their love is doomed.

'I-I wish I could make you understand, Elizabeth.' Her eyes swim with tears that spill unheeded onto her cheeks and she steps between us as if to shield him.

'How long has this - friendship, been going on, Kate?' Though whatever answer she gives will make no difference. I must end this. Now.

'A few weeks, but long enough for me to know my heart.' She kneads her primrose silk skirt with the fingers of her free hand. How incongruous that fine fabric looks against this man's shabby uniform? The uniform of a rebel. An enemy of the Murrays and our beloved sovereign.

'Nothing can come of it, you know that don't you?' I keep my voice soft in an attempt to persuade her.

She hesitates, and I know then she does not possess the strength to defy me. Their love is a fine thing when it is theirs alone. Revealed to the world it will wither and die. Kate knows it.

'Men like him sent Father to prison, Kate.' Her face blanches, and I press my advantage. 'They are our enemies and would destroy all we believe in. Our home, our future, everything.'

The man at her side places a possessive hand on Kate's shoulder. He looks about to speak, but when I glare at his hand, he flushes and removes it. 'They could do the same to me, Kate,' I press on, desperate to break through her defiance. 'Could you bear being the cause of sending Mother and little Meg into a prison cell?'

'Please, Elizabeth,' she chokes back a sob, but I know she is weakening.

'What would Father say if he could see you? Do you expect his blessing?'

'He might understand. If I told him how much I love Bernard.' Her voice is strong, but defeat stands stark in her face.

The creature called Bernard juts his chin, such a jaw as he possesses in that ferret face. He looks about to challenge me, but whatever plea he summons dies on his lips.

'Do not grudge me a chance of happiness,' Kate's plea grates on my heart.

Forgive me, Kate. I have to be strong.

'We are Murrays. Royalists. Loyal servants of His Majesty King Charles. We don't choose our husbands. You cannot entertain an alliance with a man such as him.' I flick a hand at the man beside her, refusing to use his name or I would have to acknowledge his humanity. He is nothing to me.

'And you,' I glare at the man. 'You must know that I shall have to inform Captain Fitton of this illicit relationship?'

I almost wish he would stand up to me. Show a conviction that my Kate is worth fighting for. That he will allow no one to come between them. Much less me.

At the mention of his superior officer's name, his chin drops in defeat. It is not to be. Disappointment, not triumph fills me as I watch his resolve drain away and subservience take its place.

'I beg your indulgence, Mistress Murray.' A thin white mist erupts from his lips, but I do not feel the cold. My blood rushes through my veins and my hands twitch with the desire to strike him. 'I wish you to know my intentions towards your sister were ever honourable. I realise you are right, however, and I beg your forgiveness for my presumption.'

'Bernard!' Kate grips his arm tighter, her face lifted to his. 'You cannot weaken. Not after all you have said!'

Do not beg him, Kate, he is so far beneath you.

Her tears break my heart, as I hope they do his. Let him see how much he hurts her. What has he promised her? Or is his interest merely a way to pass the time between stealing our cattle and plundering the house? He releases Kate's hand and takes a step back. 'I shall accept whatever punishment my Captain sees fit, but I would ask you not to make Katherine suffer for her actions. She is blameless.'

'I know that, you fool.' I lower my voice to a snarl that makes Kate gasp. 'My sister is an innocent.'

He blinks, startled, then gives a slow, sage nod. 'I am at your mercy, my lady, and await your decision.'

Kate releases a long sigh and turns away, her narrow back to us both.

He brushes past me and in seconds he is gone.

The thump of the door in its frame acts on Kate like a blow, and she slumps against the wall with a tiny cry.

How I long to throw my arms around her; to tell her I understand and even sympathise, but I cannot. Nor can I tell her that if he really loved her, this creature would have put up more of a fight.

'You cannot ask me to give him up,' Kate whispers.

'It is the least I demand.' I do not tell her she doesn't need to, he has made the decision for them both. 'I shall see him whipped for his daring.'

Panic enters her face. 'No! Do not tell Captain Fitton. The punishment is severe for rebels who-' She cannot finish the thought, but the implication is clear. *Has he ruined her?*

She raises her head, her thin face ravaged by tears, her myopic eyes bloodshot. 'I will never love anyone else, you know that, don't you?' She dashes moisture from her face, hiccupping as she speaks.

I understand then why she did not watch him leave; because she couldn't bear him to see her poor looks ruined by misery. That he might remember her as she was, at her prettiest, because she was in love.

'You will marry one day, Kate.'

Her harsh, guttural sob comes as a shock. As does the hate-filled glare she throws me. 'Marriage is not the same thing. I will not love again, which is more important. Besides, who would want me?' She lifts both hands in mute appeal and lets them drop against her sides. 'This war may yet rob me of my dowry, and I have little else to attract a man.'

'Of course you do.' I take a step forward but her uncompromising stare halts me several feet away.

'Don't lie! I'm a plain, crippled thing and our allegiance to King Charles will beggar us. Who will want a wife with a twisted spine? I may even be barren. I'll be fortunate to receive an offer from a blacksmith.'

'What nonsense! My optimistic tone is reminiscent of Mother, and equally as unconvincing. 'One day we shall be at court with the king and all those who kept faith with him. Then you will have the pick of young men.'

She scrubs her cheeks with her hands and makes to march past, then pauses level with my shoulder and turns toward me.

'You deceive yourself! Bernard says the New Model Army grows larger every day. They are strong, disciplined fighting men who will decimate the Royalist soldiers, and force the king to comply. Then-'

'Be silent!' I grasp her upper arms and give her a shake. 'How could you listen to that rebel's lies? They will say anything to undermine us. Never let me hear you doubt our monarch again.'

She jerks away from me, her eyes glittering through unshed tears. 'He is a God-fearing, truthful man. And he told me something today which is important to us all.'

'Hah! And what could that be?' I fling the trailing end of my shawl over a shoulder. 'What can you know that I do not?'

'Just this. That the Scots are sick of the king's obduracy, and have declared they will not receive him in Scotland.'

'That rebel told you this?' I want to refute every vicious word, but Kate is no liar.

'The entire Kingston garrison knows.' She pulls a kerchief from a pocket in her skirt and blows her nose noisily. Once composed, she fixes me with a defiant look mixed with triumph and a quiet pride. 'They have agreed to hand Charles Stuart to the English, on certain conditions.'

'What conditions?' I ask, suspicious.

'That Parliament reimburses the Scots army for their involvement in the north with four hundred thousand pounds.'

'They want to *sell* the king back to us?'

'That is not all.' She tilts her head, lips parted as if she savours a rare moment. 'They demand certain personages must present themselves at York, where they will remain until the monies are paid. Then His Majesty will be surrendered to the English.'

'Hostages, you mean?' I gasp as a thought strikes me 'Not Father?' Her cold stare and shake of her head makes my blood run cold. She means someone else, someone important to us. 'Then who?'

'Sir Lionel Tollemache.' Kate's voice is icy, dull.

My stomach cramps. I fold my arms across my waist, my fingers clenched into the loose weave of my shawl. My knees give way and I have to lean against the wall for support. 'Are you sure?'

'The rebels talk of nothing else in Kingston. That the king-'

'Never mind the king. I mean about Sir Lionel?'

She gives a slow nod.

My deep, furious breaths are shortened by the grip of my stays. 'Is Parliament set on ruining my entire life?' I punch the panelling with a fist, sending pain lancing through my knuckles. 'First, Father, and now my future husband.' My eyes fill with hot, furious tears. 'Suppose Parliament will not pay? Maybe they cannot pay?'

Kate's face softens briefly. 'They only want to take possession of His Majesty. Once the money is paid, Sir Lionel will be freed.'

'How can you know?' I spit at her. 'The rebels and the Scots may decide to keep him incarcerated. Or they may hang him! Even if Parliament keeps its promise, he will never have me now!'

'Then we shall both have happiness unjustly snatched from us.'

Her barb finds its target. I bite my lip as my cheeks heat with my own shame. It is not the same, I did the right thing in sending her Puritan away. 'This might simply be a rumour put about to undermine the Royalist cause.'

'If it is, then you and Sir Lionel have nothing to fear.' Her scathing tone reminds me of Cousin Henderson. 'Although contrary to what you may believe, I doubt Lord Fairfax spends his days dreaming up ways to discompose Elizabeth Murray.' She folds her arms across her small breasts. 'I had no notion you had such strong feelings for the gentleman.'

'My situation is different to yours, Kate. If something happens to Sir Lionel, or he decides association with the Murrays is unwise, the search for a husband will have to begin again.'

'And there was I, imagining your heart was about to break.' Kate's scornful laugh fills the room. Her chin lifts in my direction, though with her head against the light I cannot see her features clearly, or what is in her eyes. 'As the heiress to Ham, a dozen eligible young men will take his place.'

'No one who has not already been slaughtered on the battlefield,' I snap, frustrated. 'And how many who still live are in possession of their estates?'

My anger dissolves into dismay, which only infuriates me more. Anger I can use, but despair simply leaves me helpless and unable to function. I would rather be known as a strong-minded woman with a fiery temper, than a weak female.

Kate turns to face me, a trace of defiance in her cynical smile. 'Perhaps the Lords would do better to take *you* as their hostage, Elizabeth. The negotiations would be completed with enviable expediency. The Scots need the money to pay off their soldiers. Many of them are in rags.'

'Did this - Bernard - tell you when this exchange is due to take place?'

'Yes. Sir Lionel must present himself at Newcastle on the fifteenth of January.'

Three weeks of sleepless nights, and stomach-churning dread. How will I bear it?

Kate's lower lip quivers. 'Elizabeth? Will you tell Mother? About Bernard, I mean?'

'I don't know.' But of course I do. I have never been able to keep a secret from Mother.

'Do what you must.' Katherine makes another move to sweep

past me, but I step between her and the door.

'Kate. You and Bernard, have you-?' I cannot complete the question.

Her eyes narrow with cunning and she inhales slowly. 'Do not fret, sister. No bastards will sully the name of Murray. He may be a rebel, but he is an honourable one.'

I can see she wants to pound me with her fists and scream that I have ruined her life, but she merely stomps past me without a backward look, pulling the door closed gently behind her.

I release a long breath, proud of her then, but can never tell her so. Why compound her misery? As the destroyer of her dreams, I can offer no comfort. She will have to bear her heartbreak during the long, quiet hours of endless night, when the pain is at its worst.

'My poor Kate,' I whisper to the closed door. 'He doesn't deserve your tears.'

Chapter 22

My fury at Kate's behaviour still burns within me, and I choose not to return to the salon for fear my anger will show and Mother insist I reveal its source. Instead, I head for my room, waylaying a servant on the way. 'Tell your mistress I have a headache and shall retire early.' Adding as an afterthought. 'And if there is any lambswool left, kindly bring me a goblet.' This Christmas night may as well end with some of its traditions intact.

If not for this dreadful war, the most danger my sister could attract would be to develop a preference for the son of an acquaintance. How innocent we were to believe our charmed lives would never change.

My comfortable world is where the royal court holds sway and every man knows his place. At one time, such men as Kate's Roundhead would remain in the town of their birth with no access to persons of quality. These days they tramp across the country gaining confidence and assuming liberties with every mile.

I want it back, that privileged life where farmers and artisans would not dare order their betters to bend to their will. The thought it may end is inconceivable.

Undressing quickly, I slide beneath the covers on my bed, grateful for the maid who has been there before me to insert a warming pan between the sheets and light a small fire.

The last half hour spent with Kate comes back with painful clarity, and pulling the cover up to my chin, I respond to the knock at the door, anticipating my lambswool. But it is not the maid who enters with a tray from which rise evocative aromas of roasted apple, beer, nutmeg, ginger and sugar, but Mother.

She sets the tray on a table beside the bed, and as she did when I was a child, pours a drink and hands me the cup. Then she tugs the bed curtains closed before joining me, spreading the heavy coverlet over our knees and folds her hands in her lap.

'You missed the messenger Master Isham sent, Betty. He has this moment left.'

'Justinian sends his greetings I assume,' I respond with sullen disinterest.

'He sent more than that, my dear. Do you not wish to know what his note said?'

I examine her hands but there is none in evidence. 'If you think it worth the repetition, Mama. Certainly.'

'Such an ill humour you are in tonight, but this will cheer you,' she lowers her voice, though there is no one to hear. 'He says His Majesty has created your father Earl of Dysart.'

I bolt upright, my black mood forgotten. 'As a reward for keeping his mouth shut, no doubt,' I say, allowing reign to my cynical tongue. But it does not matter. Father has another title to add to that of Lord Huntingtower. A rush of pleasure warms my cheeks, for if he was ever in doubt, surely Sir Lionel Tollemache will now see I am a suitable wife. Then Kate's words come flooding back and I realise it may all be for nothing if Sir Lionel has to spend the next few years as a prisoner of Parliament. Or worse, the Scots.

Then again, should the betrothal never materialise, perhaps the daughter of an earl may attract a wealthier suitor? The son of a duke perhaps?

'What are you thinking, dear?' Mother asks, frowning. 'Are you not pleased?'

'Of course. I am merely trying out my new name. Countess of Dysart,' I pronounce slowly, rolling the sound on my tongue.

'Tush, Betty!' She slaps my arm playfully. 'It is I who am Countess. You are the Lady Elizabeth.'

I choose not to point out that Scottish titles pass down the female line. I shall indeed be Countess Dysart. One day.

'Lady Elizabeth then. Do the girls know?' I ask, elated.

'Not yet. They may forget there are soldiers in the house and let it slip. Your father says we must keep this news to ourselves until things are more settled.'

'What does that mean?' My dreams dissolve into nothing and I slap the bedclothes. 'What is the use of a title if I cannot use it?

'The earldom is granted in principle,' Mother continues, ignoring my display of temper, 'however, the Privy Council has yet to pass the patent beneath the Great Seal.'

'There's no question it is legal, surely?' I search her face for uncertainty but see none. 'The king still has the power to grant titles?'

'Perhaps that is not his reasoning,' Mother says, thoughtful. 'Parliament may be simpletons enough to believe more money can be extracted from an earl.'

'I see. Yes I suppose that makes sense.' I sulk, aware it to be unworthy of me but I cannot help it. I want to flout my new status beneath Captain Fitton's nose.

'Now, Betty.' Mother shuffles closer. 'Are you going to tell me why you and Kate are at outs?'

I open my mouth with every intention of disabusing her, but her sharp look halts me. She will detect fabrications in an instant. 'How did you know, has Kate said something?'

'Nothing, but she disappeared into Nan's room, and when I passed the door just now I heard crying.

'Oh.' I sip the hot lambswool, the creamy sweetness and soft froth on my tongue evoking memories of happier Christmases. No doubt my sisters intend to share secrets beneath the covers, I wonder if Nan will also resent me by morning.

I have no choice then but to reveal everything. Not only Kate's liaison, but the threat that hangs over Sir Lionel which might destroy my future hope of being Lady Tollemache.

Mother listens in silence, the only sound in the room other than my voice, the spit and hiss of the fire as the wood becomes white ash and red embers.

'On the subject of Sir Lionel,' mother says finally, 'that is entirely out of our control; we shall simply have to wait and see.'

'A talent I do not possess,' I say sulkily.

'And as for Kate. I suspected it was something of the sort.'

'You suspected?' My mouth opens and closes in mute astonishment. 'Then why did you not put a stop to it sooner?' My tone is accusatory. Had Mother been the one to end the liaison, perhaps Kate would not hate me now.

'I was not sure, and could not act without proof.'

'You could have voiced your suspicions. She would never have dared flout you.'

Her laugh echoes in the darkening room. 'If you believe that, you do not yet know the power of young love. But we must be practical. I will ask Cousin Henderson to ensure her courses come as expected.'

'Kate assures me that-' Mother's plump hand closes over mine, silencing me.

'As I said, you do not yet understand love. It would not hurt to be sure.'

She is right, I know nothing about love. Nor may I ever do so, whether I marry or not. A thought that leaves me strangely envious of my heartbroken sister.

* * *

January 1647

January is every bit as difficult as I imagined. What with my worries over Sir Lionel Tollemache, which I lament at every opportunity, and Father's appearance before the Scots Lords, which I dare not mention at all, I risk wearing out the rug in my room to a thin thread.

Kate avoids my eye and when I try to speak with her, she rushes past me with red-rimmed eyes swollen from crying, her shoulders held stiff. I wish she would let me explain that all I do is for her, and that I have no desire to see her miserable. Or a spinster.

Nan stays close, a hand permanently on her shoulder, her face set in a sympathetic smile. She offers me wry shrugs to show she understands why I acted the way I did, but still I do not envy her being torn between us. Each time Nan smiles or acknowledges me, Kate scowls and shrugs off her comforting hand.

No one seems to acknowledge that I am as distressed as anyone, though my sisters have condemned me as the bringer of unhappiness.

To my relief, and to an even greater extent, Mother's, the Scots received their ransom and Sir Lionel Tollemache was returned unharmed to his estate in Suffolk after only a week.

King Charles was taken to somewhere called Holdenby House in Northamptonshire as a prisoner of Parliament. A strange captive he must have appeared, for church bells rang in greeting, and crowds lined the streets to see him, pressing forward with requests to be touched by the royal hands for luck.

'Not quite the welcome Parliament hoped for, I imagine,' Mother says from the bureau where she deciphers Father's latest letter.

March winds rattle the shutters and billow grey smoke down the chimneys making my eyes sting. I open the window nearest the fireplace to allow in some cooler air.

We seem to have spent the entire winter with coverlets as thick as rugs over our knees and hot stones at our feet. When I am mistress here, I resolve to have the larger chimneys properly capped. I rise to fetch a thicker shawl from a pile on a sofa and catch sight of Mother's stricken face.

'Mama, what is wrong. Not more bad news?'

She closes her eyes, and lifts a hand to massage her forehead. 'It appears the Commissioners suspect your father of persuading His Majesty against accepting their terms,' she tucks in her chin as she reads. 'Thus he and Sir Robert are to be permanently forbidden the royal presence.'

'Where is he to go if he cannot be with the king?' I try to read over her shoulder but cannot decipher the code. My outrage turns to fear. 'He is surely not a prisoner?'

Mother's ink-stained fingers run along a line of marks in her notebook which she compares with the letter.

'Apparently not.' She shakes her head and taps the page. 'He has secured passage on the first ship out of Hull and is on his way to the queen's court in Paris.'

'We must be thankful he is safe,' Cousin Henderson says.

'When King Charles returns to the throne, Father will surely be recalled,' Kate says confidently from the farthest window in the room. I try to catch her eye, but she stares at the garden as if I do not exist.

I turn a shoulder so I can no longer see Kate's frozen face, resolving to waste no more time feeling guilty. If anyone ought to keep silent, and her eyes cast down at mealtimes, it is my sister.

'The situation is more complicated than that.' Mother sighs. 'The king must make certain promises to Parliament before they will release him. Though I doubt he will compromise on anything. He believes himself to be an instrument of God, and refuses to acknowledge any authority but his own.'

'Colonel Cromwell believes he too is an instrument of God,' I say, cynically. 'Is it so unreasonable for the king to consider what his subjects want? He could work with Parliament rather than against them.'

'My goodness, you sound like an independent, Betty.' Mother's light laugh is unconvincing. 'You had better not let your father hear you speak like that.'

Bored with the piece of blackwork that has occupied me for part of the morning, I discard it onto a table. From the corner of my eye I catch Mother rolling her eyes at Cousin Henderson. I wish they wouldn't conspire like that, as if I were an irritation they have to tolerate in mutual and silent resignation.

I pretend not to notice their shared conspiracy, and turn my thoughts to other things.

Having heard so much about the beauty of Paris, the fact Father is there now makes me envious. Though I doubt he has an easy time of it, for the queen is a not a happy woman, and a strict taskmaster, who demands everyone around her pander to her slightest whim. What would she be like now she is forced to live on her brother's charity?'

'Maybe Parliament plans to dispense with the monarchy altogether?' Cousin Henderson suggests.

'What a dreadful thought, Cousin.' I swing round to face her, aware of Mother's equally surprised expression.

Cousin Henderson rarely offers her opinions on the state of the country, but evidently there is more going on behind that bland face I imagine. Is that how the lower orders feel? That we no longer need a king?

'Not that I advocate such a thing,' her face flushes as she looks from Mother to me. 'Simply that, if they cannot agree what kind of rule they desire, the next thing we hear will be that the army has removed the king from under Parliament's nose.'

'What a ridiculous notion,' Mother snorts.

I join in her tight smile, but my cousin talks sense. This man Cromwell has built a powerful army. An army under his total control. If Parliament's actions do not coincide with his demands, he may decide to negotiate directly with the king. What better way to do that, than march in and take possession of His Majesty himself?

The ensuing silence of our contemplation is broken by a discreet knock, and Ball enters with yet another letter. The thought strikes me that Father must have plenty of time on his hands to be so prolific with his correspondence. To my astonishment, Ball skirts Mother's chair and hands the packet to me.

'Thank you, Ball.' I keep my voice level, but my hand shakes. The seal is unfamiliar, and the parchment unblemished and clean. This letter hasn't spent hours on the road in the pocket of a terrified messenger.

'Well, open it, Betty!' Mother says, tucking her letters into her codebook and sliding both into a drawer. Like me, she always anticipates bad news.

'It is from Sir Lionel Tollemache,' I read the direction aloud, my heart thudding. My gaze frantically scans the page and my breathing settles. 'He says he was treated as an honoured guest at Newcastle and is now safely back at Hemlingham.'

'Yes, yes, never mind that. We heard it all from your father.' Mother slaps the bureau with the flat of her hand. 'What does he say about your betrothal?'

Her open-mouthed eagerness makes my lips twitch. I savour the moment and pause, but catch Cousin Henderson's you-don't-fool-me-for-a-moment-miss look.

'He reiterates the sentiments he expressed during his visit here and wishes to formalise our betrothal without further delay.'

A flurry of congratulations erupt, followed by hugs and kisses, all of which I accept with a relieved smile. Though Kate's brief, dry kiss and murmured good wishes leave me uncomfortable. She will thank me, one day.

When her turn comes, Mother enfolds me in a fragrant hug. 'My dear girl, I am so relieved.' Her hands slide down to my elbows and she takes a step back to scrutinise my face closely. 'You are pleased are you not? This is what you want?'

A spectre lifts from my mind and for the first time in months, I feel calm. At last, I am to become Lady Elizabeth Tollemache. 'Our estate will be safe from the Committee now. Or at least as safe as it can be if Sir Lionel is master. How can that not be what I want?'

Mother drops her arms from mine and steps back. 'That was not quite what I meant, my love.' Her eyes darken. 'But you are right, how could you not be happy with such an outcome?' She turns to encompass my sisters with outstretched arms. 'Sir Lionel will bring security for us all.'

A shadow I do not understand sits in her expression. Happiness is not something I have been taught to aspire to, so her question confuses me. 'A betrothal is all very well, Mama. I wish we may begin to arrange a wedding.'

'Weddings are complicated things, my dear, and must be prepared for with an eye to propriety. Besides, we have . . .'

I stop listening as my eye catches a scrawled note on the top of the next page of Sir Lionel's letter.

'...*Your esteemed father requests I assure you that the matter of the stolen watch has been entirely resolved.*'

The mirror above the mantle reflects my self-satisfied smile that Father has avoided tragedy, again.

'Betty, are you listening to me?'

'What? Oh, yes, Mama of course.' I re-fold the letter and slide it into my pocket.

* * *

August 1647, Petersham Lodge, Richmond

'You seem preoccupied, Elizabeth dear.' Joan Carlisle's tongue protrudes as she spreads the fibres of a fine brush in her fingers. 'Dare I suggest your thoughts are with a certain Suffolk gentleman?'

Her voice drags me back to the airy drawing room of Petersham Lodge, where summer has arrived bringing still, hot days and stifling nights. Joan uses this room as a studio, which is perfect with its floor-to-ceiling windows and double glass doors that flood the room with light. Not a breath of wind stirs the window hangings at the open casement onto Joan's garden, and only birdsong breaks the silence.

Meg moves around the room on silent feet, her head tilted to one side as she takes in the unfamiliar surroundings. With Nan and Kate always shut up in one or other of their rooms and Mother abed with another migraine, she insisted on accompanying me this afternoon. What commands her attention now appears to be Joan's collection of paintings arrayed across one wall.

'I am sorry, what did you say about Suffolk?' I say belatedly.

'No matter,' Joan says. 'I can see you were miles away. However, your pensive stillness serves my purpose.' She wipes a paint-encrusted thumb down the calico smock worn over her clothes.

My betrothal to Sir Lionel Tollemache is complete at last, though there is still no firm date set for the wedding. Mother's suggestion that I have an engagement portrait painted is, I am sure, her way to calm my fretful nerves at the slow negotiations.

In some ways, she is right, and this is my second sitting with Joan. Even so, I am restless again, for Joan has spent hours on the background and has not yet begun to draw me. Despite my protests that I wish to see what I look like, she will not work faster.

She repeats her question and I give her a wry smile. 'Maybe my thoughts dwell on the estate rather than the gentleman himself?'

'So cynical, my dear, and you so young.' Joan laughs. 'Now, I should like to paint you standing.' She balances the wide canvas on her easel and tilts her head to one side. 'As you are the most important subject, I shall place you in the centre.'

'Like this?' I face forward with my hips tilted slightly and one arm bent at my waist. 'Shall I look at you, or pretend to see something in the distance?'

'No, keep your chin tilted down a little. Like a demure young bride.' A smile hovers on her lips but I force myself to ignore it.

Demure? Me?

'Yes, that is perfect.' She nods and plucks a clean brush from a pile beside her and dabs it on a palette in her other hand. 'You look quite lovely. Young, fair and with an air of the ethereal.'

Resisting the urge to smooth down my silk skirt yet again, I keep as still as I am able. 'It was kind of you to let me come here for the sittings. Sometimes it is very pleasant to be away from all those soldiers.'

'I thought it more convenient. Besides, if I was seen arriving at Ham with a vast canvas and my painting box,' Joan says, laughing. 'They would all know exactly why I was there.'

'I care little for their opinion, though some things I wish to keep to myself.'

'Like your betrothal, for instance?' Joan peers at me through her abundant lashes.

'I do not see that it is any of the army's business,' I say sharply, though at the same time, a rush of pleasure makes me smile. 'There are still some details of the settlement to be finalised.'

'I suppose that must be awkward, what with your dear father in Paris and Sir Lionel in Suffolk. Messages and letters are often lost or intercepted and delayed.'

'I know. It is a matter of extreme frustration. And I am almost one-and-twenty years of age, and still unmarried.'

'Have patience, my dear.' Joan applies her brush with long, sweeping movements. 'Everything will turn out as you wish, your parents will make sure of that.'

'You have been talking to Mother,' I say, smiling.

'Perhaps,' she murmurs, obviously distracted. She blows air through a jutting lower lip and takes a step back, frowning.

I long to see what carves that deep scowl on her face, but the easel is turned away from me. 'You still do not look happy, Mistress Carlisle. Shall I adopt another pose?'

'What? Oh, no, I have chalked your outline and begun the gown. There is still something . . .' A sound from the other side of the room brings her head round and she points the end of her brush at my youngest sister.

'Will Margaret be content with so little to do?' Joan whispers.

'She prefers to travel in the carriage with me rather than stay and learn her catechism with Cousin Henderson, do you not, Meg?'

'I already know my catechism.' Meg flicks me a look of exasperation, and then wanders to Joan's side, her hands clasped behind her back. 'Where will you paint Sir Lionel?'

'He will occupy this spot here.' Joan waves her brush at the left side of the canvas. 'I have begun his outline, do you see?'

'That is simply a blob.' She sounds disappointed. 'Besides, how can you paint someone if you do not know what they look like?'

'Mistress Carlisle will make some sketches of the gentleman when he visits. Now come away and leave her to work,' I snap, envious that my sister is allowed to see Joan's work and I have been expressly forbidden. I shall question Meg about it on the way home with promises of sweetmeats.

'When will that be?' Meg rubs her cheek with grubby fingers, leaving a streak of pollen from a vase of flowers she has rearranged. The sheen of moisture on her forehead and an occasional sighs tell me she is hot and uncomfortable, but she is of such a patient nature and does not complain.

'Oh, the next time he is in London,' I say airily, recalling the disappointment that no actual arrangement has been made. Simply a polite note at the end of Sir Lionel's last letter, saying he hoped to call upon me at some time in the future.

Meg loses interest and wanders to the open casement, her face lifted to the sun.

'Come away, Meg, or your skin will turn brown.' She obeys me reluctantly and when she passes close to me, I grasp her by the shoulder. Pulling a kerchief from my pocket, I wet it with my tongue and scrub at her grubby cheek.

Joan puts down her brush with a firm click and an exhaled breath that is not quite a sigh. 'I cannot continue unless you keep still, Elizabeth.' She steps away from the canvas, her hands on her smocked hips. 'Besides, I am still unhappy with the right side of the painting. It is too empty. Perhaps another figure would balance the composition.' She bites her bottom lip. 'What do you think if I include one of your sisters?' She taps her bottom lip with the end of her brush, thoughtul. 'I have already painted Nan this year. What about Katherine?'

I hesitate, running viable excuses through my head. Since our confrontation at Christmas, Kate still avoids me. Or at least as much as she can without arousing comment. Whenever I try to talk to her, she finds something else she needs to do and contrives to leave the room.

Kate's hours spent by her window, her sad gaze on the Ham Road are all to no purpose. Since Cromwell came to the Kingston garrison, her Bernard must have been assigned other duties, for there is no sign of him in the locality.

It seems I have switched one unwelcome face for another, for with the presence of Cromwell so close to Ham, we are watched even more closely by our hostile protectors.

'Not Kate,' I say hurriedly, pushing unwelcome thoughts away. 'What about Meg here?'

Meg swings round with a wide smile. 'Oh, yes. I would love that.'

'Are you sure you have the patience, Meg?' I ask. 'This is a lengthy process and you would have to keep still for hours.'

'I cannot stand for very long.' She looks down at her slightly shortened leg, a subject rarely referred to. 'But I will try.'

'No need for that.' Joan puts down her palate and crosses the room. She returns with a chair and places it slightly behind me and to one side. 'One figure standing and one sitting will be perfect. Here.' She guides Meg into the seat and arranges her skirt before starting work on the bottom half of the canvas.

'Turn your shoe out a little, Elizabeth.' She indicates with her brush. 'And you, Meg. Extend your arm more. You have pretty arms and I would show them to their best advantage.'

The lazy afternoon stretches on, with nothing but Joan's occasional chatter to entertain us. The sunlight shifts across the window, throwing part of room into darkness and brightening up the other with white light in which dust motes bounce and flow.

'There! That is enough for today.' Joan drops her brush with a clatter onto her desk. 'It is tiring working in this heat. What say I call for some refreshment?'

'Oh good,' Meg sighs. 'I am so thirsty, but I dared say nothing in case you painted me with my mouth open.'

At Joan's summons, her housekeeper bustles in, a heavily laden tray in her fat arms.

'The elderflowers are scarce this year, Mistress.' The woman beams at Meg, whose frailty always elicits kindness in strangers. 'I hung the cask on a rope in the pond, to keep it cool, like.' She lays a feast of cake and wild strawberries on a low table.

A welcome breeze ruffles the curtains, carrying the scent of roses and honeysuckle into the room as we settle on chairs round the open casement. Richmond Park slopes away from us like a green blanket to a line of rooftops in the distance. Once, herds of deer ran between the trees and gathered round the pond like a red-brown carpet to drink, but these days I am fortunate to see one or two at a time.

Joan pours the clear liquid into goblets, while Meg sinks her teeth into a ripe strawberry, heedless of the juice that runs down her chin.

'What is that?' Meg points through the open doors to the shimmer of heat haze in the distance

'Those rooftops are London.' I absently hand her a napkin.

'No, not that. That.' She points again.

I turn to look as a blur of colour moves rapidly closer, then separates into the figures of horses and men approaching in double file over the knoll. Their hooves kick dust into a cloud around them so they seem to float above the grass.

Joan sets down her glass and hurries through the open doorway into the garden.

After a quick look at Meg's face, I know my command that she stay behind will go unheeded; but I am too curious to insist and lose no time in following Joan to the side gate that leads onto the road.

Joan, in her usual forthright and fearless way, has waylaid an officer to ask questions. If he was surprised, he shows no sign, though he regards Joan down his nose with mild contempt.

In a blue coat and black hat, he sits astride a massive bay gelding, one gauntleted hand resting on his thigh, and the reins in the other. Idly I imagine he must be uncomfortable in such thick clothes on this hot day.

'Where are they going?' Joan asks, nodding toward the column that moves steadily down the Petersham Road with a rattle of bits and scuffle of hooves.

The officer looks through me, but regards Joan with narrowed eyes. 'We are a special guard, Mistress Carlisle.'

'There are hundreds of soldiers hereabouts.' I push forward until my shoulder is in line with his boot. 'Why do we need more? Is something happening?'

'A guard of what?' Joan lays a hand on my forearm. I take the hint and fall silent, my gaze fixed on the blobs of blue paint on her knuckles.

'For Charles Stuart.' The man curls his lip as he speaks, his disgust clear.

I am about to correct him, but Joan's grip tightens and I swallow the barb.

The week before, we heard that Lieutenant General Cromwell sent a man named Cornet Joyce to Holdenby House with five hundred armed men, and persuaded the king to accept the protection of the army.

'The k-,' I say, then catch myself. 'Charles Stuart is to be brought here? To Richmond?' A fluttering starts in my chest and I cannot keep the smile from my face.

'To Hampton Court.' The officer's lip curls again, and I realise this is due to a puckered scar that runs down his upper lip and not a display of his feelings. 'Within the week.' He touches a hand to the brim of his hat and jerks the reins, causing the horse to swing its hindquarters in a wide arc.

At this dismissal, we back away from the massive hooves.

'He knew your name,' I say as we watch him catch up with his men.

'And I know his.' Joan slews her eyes sideways at me. 'Not all Roundheads are common peasants with a hatred of anyone who wears silk and lace.'

This bald statement makes me feel suddenly immature and foolish, and I store her words away for future contemplation.

'Will we be allowed to see the king?' Meg asks.

'Hush, Meg. Mistress Carlisle knows no more than we do.' I grasp Meg's hand and pull her into the house. 'Would you be so kind as to call our carriage, Mistress Carlisle?' An overwhelming need to return to Ham lends urgency to my voice. Mother must hear of this straight away, migraine or no. 'We must go home.'

'Of course, my dear.' Joan catches me up as I scoop my fan from a chair. 'I know what you hope for, but remember, your father is refused permission to be in His Majesty's presence. That edict may extend to his wife and daughters.'

'That will not matter to Mother.' I beckon Meg and hurry for the front door. 'She will find a way to achieve an audience with His Majesty, prisoner or not.'

Chapter 23

With shaking hands, I smooth down the skirt of my sapphire silk gown, the weft shot through with gold thread which shimmers in the soft evening light. The heavy jewel at my throat elicits a smile, my battle with Mother to wear it won.

'Is it wise to wear such an extravagant gown, Elizabeth?' Nan chews at a fingernail. 'He's a Puritan after all, and may scorn such finery.'

'Why should I not? Dark blue is my favourite colour.' I slap her hand away from her mouth, impatient that Mama cannot spare Molly to help me dress, so I have to make do with Nan. 'You will make your fingers bleed. And if you get blood on my lace you will ruin it.'

Nan sighs and tucks the offending hand behind her. 'I cannot understand why Mama invited him here in the first place.'

'We must be gracious and welcoming.' I tuck my bertha into the top of my bodice, then decide it hides too much and remove it again. 'We may have need of his influence if things don't go well with this infernal war.'

'But Oliver Cromwell, a guest in this house? Father would be mortified.'

My smile slips, but the purpose in my eyes remains. 'You deceive yourself. Father would applaud Mother's diplomacy. As do I.'

'It will seem as if we have lost faith in His Majesty.' Nan's lip quivers slightly, and I experience a rush of sympathy for her. I know how it looks for the Murrays to entertain Cromwell at Ham, but whatever happens, we must forge our own way with or without the king. If that means toadying to Parliament and the army, then that is what we shall do.

'Outwardly perhaps, to those who do not know us. But think about it, Nan. King Charles is a prisoner of the army. An army who will give no quarter, not when they have fought so hard to get this far. If we continue to resist them, we shall suffer the same fate.'

'What fate is that?' Nan's eyes widen in fear.

'Who knows, and it does not matter. We are better friends to the king with Cromwell as an ally rather than an enemy.' I conceal my nervousness beneath a brittle smile. 'Mama knows what she is doing. We must trust her.'

'I do, but it does not change the fact I feel we are betraying our sovereign lord.' She breaks off at my hard stare and opens the door. 'It is time we joined Mama. Some of the guests are already here.'

I precede her through the doorway and along the hall, where chatter and low male laughter reaches us from below like any other party Ham has been host to. Did I expect church-like silence and no smiles?

The voices grow louder as the distance closes and Nan plucks at my sleeve, her steps slowing. 'Are you not afraid? I know I am.'

'I am afraid of nothing!' I prise her fingers from the lace and move ahead of her. 'I know what is required.'

If Nan only knew how little I slept last night, afraid that when it came to facing *that* man, I would be unable to prevent my distaste from showing in my face.

When Mother told me she had invited the Lord General and his wife to dine at Ham, I thought she said so in jest, or some desperate measure to which she would only resort under threat of death. As it was, she took my fury as a mild irritant.

'There was a time I might have agreed,' she said, ignoring my protests. 'Things have taken a turn for the worst and we must consider our position.'

'Are there not enough Roundheads in this house already?' I had shouted, sweeping a porcelain figure from the mantle in my frustration.

With a frown of disappointment at the white shards scattered across our best rug, Mother drew me to one side. 'Have sense, Betty! The king has been at Hampton Court for near three weeks, and though I have written asking that we might visit, I have heard nothing. With Cromwell now at Kingston, he makes frequent visits to the king in his efforts to convince him to negotiate terms for peace.'

273

'Surely you do not intend to offer your services and add your persuasive tongue to theirs?'

'If that is the only way I can procure an audience with His Majesty, what is wrong with a little diplomacy?' She tugged the bell-pull to summon a servant to clear up the mess. 'I am an expert at dissembling, Betty. I can make them believe anything I wish.'

'I have no doubt, Mama. Do you intend to achieve this by feeding our enemy?' My anger turned to cynicism. 'Or do you intend to poison him?'

'Ridiculous girl.' Her expression turned thoughtful then, and I would swear she considered it, if only for a few seconds. 'No, of course not. Cromwell may give the impression he disapproves of elegance and beauty, but if I know anything about men who rise from the ranks, he is impressed by ancient lineage and good taste.' She had held my gaze, her expression bristling with warning. 'I shall rely on you to be charming to the man.'

'Me? Charm him?' I flung at her, searching for something else to destroy, but her hard glare told me she would not tolerate another display of temper. 'I would sooner slide a dagger between his ribs the moment he steps inside the house.'

'I expect you to be gracious and to make an effort to win him over.'

'Win him-?' What could I, who has barely stepped out of Richmond in my life have to offer to a world-weary soldier like him? Or did Mother expect-? I inhaled sharply, surely not!

'Don't look at me like that, Betty. I don't expect anything indiscreet. There must be something he likes which you can provide, a gentle voice to quote poetry, or-' Her eyes widen. 'What about Ancient Greek, maybe he would like to hear something from that book you are always reading?'

'Ovid? Do you really think Oliver Cromwell would read-'

She shushed me then, her chin cocked at the girl who sidled in with a dustpan.

The pause during which the maid completed her task gave me time to reconsider.

When my anger cooled, I realised Mother was right, and certain advantages were to be gained by dancing attendance on Cromwell and his band of self-righteous rebels.

The king has been a prisoner since winter, and yet nothing has been agreed. More soldiers flood the countryside and there are riots in London against Parliament's purging of those who resist the Puritans' austere form of worship.

Cromwell and Lord Fairfax entered the capital with eighteen thousand men to demand the army be paid. Now their headquarters at Putney makes them worrying neighbours.

And tonight, I have to fulfil my pledge to Mother.

I reach the bottom of the stairs to find Captain Fitton at the entrance to the main hall. Some ensign has evidently attacked his clothes with a brush; the effort mediocre at best. The fringed orange sash round his waist looks new, though it increases his girth alarmingly. His eyes widen when he sees me, and he shifts his feet, both fists clenched.

Seeing him so discomfited, an urge to goad the man is irresistible.

'Do not, Elizabeth,' Nan whispers at my shoulder.

Am I so predictable? 'Allow me to have some fun,' I murmur, coming to stand beside the Captain.

A tick appears at the side of his mouth and he avoids my eye, his uneasy gaze focused beyond the door to where a huddle of rebel uniforms crowd the hall.

'Eavesdropping, Captain?' I peer at him over the splayed spars of my fan. 'Or is it that you never imagined your Lord General would be a guest here?'

He coughs and swallows. 'I have to admit to a certain astonishment, Mistress Murray.'

'Mistress Murray is it now, I recall you referred to me as 'meddling wench' the other day.'

A trickle of sweat slides down his thick forehead. 'I-I was not aware you were still in earshot, Mistress. I hope you will accept my most profound apology.'

'Perhaps your Lord General would like to hear more about how you men treat their unwilling hosts?'

'I have done no more than obey orders.' His neck turns beet red and he bounces on his toes. 'You have no reason to complain.'

'What makes you think I need a reason to make your life as uncomfortable as you have made ours?' I say through clenched teeth, though my smile does not waver.

A few heads turn in our direction, but they quickly lose interest and go back to their conversations.

'If there is something I can do to make reparation for any inconvenience-' he stops and swallows as desperation lifts his voice an octave.

'I will give the matter some thought.' I hold his gaze for a slow heartbeat, then sweep away, dragging Nan with me.

'You do frighten me sometimes, Elizabeth,' she murmurs at my shoulder.

'Whereas I, Nan, do not tremble at all, see?' I hold my hand out straight to show her how steady it is.

The hall looks vast with the massive oak table pushed to one side. Pyramids of blood red roses, blue hyacinths and late tulips bring colour to the black and white space, the air thick with sweet fragrance. Ball must have set the gardeners to collect every remaining bloom not uprooted by the rebels, and, I suspect he stripped Petersham Lodge too.

I once saw a poor likeness worked by a talentless painter, but still I recognise the man with the sanguine complexion and far-seeing eyes as Oliver Cromwell. Attired in a plain coat and dark breeches, he stands with his head bent toward my mother, who smiles, dimples, flaps her hands and peers up at him through lowered lashes like a coy schoolgirl.

My cheeks warm with anger that she should not only have to accept this dreadful man in our home, but act the coquette with him as well. Until that moment, I imagined it would take courage to enter this room filled with the scions of the New Model Army. To have them know our faces must surely make us more vulnerable than we already are. Yet I do not flinch and walk forward with my head held high. Eyes widen as our guests' glances slide over Nan to linger on me, breaking off to exchange words with their companions. Others point and nod, but none ignore me.

Though I would never tell her, Nan makes a perfect foil for my healthy looks and upright carriage.

Before I reach Mother, Bishop Duppa breaks from a small group of soldiers and bows over my hand. 'I never thought to see you in such company, my dear.' His eyes crinkle with humour and his snow white hair glistens in the evening sunlight.

'No more than I did you, my lord bishop.'

'Dangerous times make for unexpected company,' he leans in to whisper before releasing my hand and stepping away to allow my onward progress toward the great man.

'And here is my eldest daughter.' Mother guides me forward with a firm hand to my lower back. Is my reluctance so obvious? 'Allow me to present my daughter, Elizabeth.'

Penetrating eyes that are almost black turn toward me, and immediately light with interest. A pleasant, if uneasy smile appears in the heavy jaw set beneath a long nose.

'I am honoured to meet you, my dear.' His kiss ends an inch above my upheld hand. 'I too have a child named Elizabeth, and she is the light of my life, thus I am predisposed to hold you in great affection.' His voice is low but not coarse as I had imagined. Did I expect him to roar like a beast?

I murmur a greeting that is probably not flattering enough if Mother's critical raised eyebrow is to be believed. 'Is your daughter present this evening?' I ask, my voice comes out as a croak and I have to clear my throat.

He massages my fingers and I withdraw my hand, ensuring my smile remains.

'Nay, but my other daughter Bridget is here.' He indicates a delicate-faced girl at the other end of the room. In a black, full-skirted gown, her deep collar and cuffs are plain white with not a scrap of lace anywhere; her only adornment a gold cross on a velvet chain that hangs from her slender waist.

No mention of his wife, I notice, who also shares my name.

A footman approaches Mother and whispers something, at which she excuses herself, taking her leave with a bright smile and a gentle hand on Cromwell's arm. 'Elizabeth will entertain you in my absence.' She darts me a hard look as she leaves. I swallow and glance round in search of Nan, but she is nowhere in sight.

Cromwell's broad chest fills my vision, his hands behind his back and a quizzical look in his eyes. I imagine this is the way he scrutinises Royalist prisoners, with that and-what-do-you-have-to-say-for-yourself air. He seems to be waiting for me to instigate some sort of conversation, but my mind has gone blank. No, not blank, but crammed with thoughts and images. So full, I cannot focus on one alone as they march through my head. Of friends dead, and others dispossessed. Blood spilled and a way of life lost, maybe forever. I try to summon a polite remark, but none comes.

All the usual subjects are forbidden; complaints against soldiers who ravage our farms and towns, the Sequestration Committee's repeated claims on our home. I cannot even lament at the closing of the playhouses. 'What do you think of my home, Lord Cromwell?' I ask at last, proud of the fact it still belongs to my family.

'A fine house, indeed, Mistress.' He indicates the ceiling with a thick finger. 'I see the influence of Joseph Kinsman in the cornices.' His half grimace of a smile settles on my face. 'I applaud Lord Fairfax's decision to allow this charming mansion to remain in the possession of such delightful ladies.' He cocks his chin at a man a few feet away with a pointed nose and a weak chin. I follow his gaze to a wiry looking man with soft, almost feminine features. and start with shock. *That* is Thomas Fairfax? The man the king calls a 'brutish general'?

'Take care, Mistress lest you cut him with the hatred in your eyes,' Cromwell whispers. 'He too has suffered in this war. He lost a son at Marston Moor.'

I look away. 'I-I regret the grounds are not as beautiful as they were before you men arrived, sir.' I may have stretched the rules of hospitality too soon, but have to finish the thought. 'What with tramping boots and horses kept on the lawns, for our stables are barely adequate for thirty extra mounts.'

His eyes bore into mine, but there is amusement in them. 'Soldiers need quarters, and I have twenty thousand to feed.' The heavy brows rise. 'However, I cannot imagine anyone being a match for you.' An uneasy smile tugs at the corners of his full mouth. 'Though let us not spoil this perfect evening with talk of soldiers.' He waves a broad hand at the lone harpist who seeks to make himself heard above the hubbub of chatter. 'Quite entertaining, but the harp is not my favourite instrument.'

'You have a favourite?' I speak so quickly, I must sound cynical.

'You think a Puritan cannot appreciate good music?' The grin appears again, and unnerved, I stare at my feet. Is he really amused by me, or simply waiting to pounce and denounce me as his enemy?

'I acknowledge the ability, sir. I merely question the wisdom of such a preference amongst those who advocate a silent and joyless world.' *Too curt!* I can almost hear Mother's voice chastising me.

I risk a glance to where Mother converses with a lady I assume is Mistress Cromwell. Mother's smile is open and honest, and even from here I can tell her responses are polite and she delivers compliments with ease.

Why cannot I be so sanguine?

'Mistress Murray,' Cromwell commands my attention again. 'You condemn me as a cold, heartless fellow with no soul for the finer things in life.' He presses a hand to his chest in mock surrender. 'When all I seek is to make the country better for all, not merely the rich and privileged. Music is one of my passions.'

I look at him askance, surprised at the word 'passion' on his lips.

'I see I shall have to convince you.' He cocks his elbow toward me and with his other hand, tucks mine inside his arm. A semi-circle of onlookers stand aside as he walks me round the room. 'Have you heard of Richard Dering?'

'Ah, no, I do not believe-' My cheeks warm as he parades me like a prize heifer. His assumption we occupy the same social status offends me.

'Of course not.' He presses my arm into his side. 'He died before you were born. His *Cantio Sacra* with its six part motets is reminiscent of Italian madrigals. He was once organist to the queen, and the king's musician for lutes and voices.'

I must look perturbed, for his voice drops to a whisper. 'You should not listen to all my detractors, Mistress Murray. Particularly those who say I harbour a hatred for everything that is beautiful.'

'Do you not?' I forget his broad, callused hand on my bare forearm, his brooding stare and the menacing timbre of a voice many must quiver to hear. His words interest me. 'Is it not true that you despise King Charles?'

'I despise nothing but vanity and abuse of my fellow man. I hold out the hope that I may negotiate with Charles Stuart and agree on terms which will bode well for us all.'

'Forgive me. I thought you abhorred his kingship.'

'Kingship is mere rhetoric. The man is admirable in many ways, would that he remembers he is a man.'

'I was told, his father, King James taught his children that they were gods, sent to rule us in the Almighty's name.'

'And what do you believe, Mistress Murray?'

We have reached the far end of the room where a door leads to the garden, left open to allow a breeze to pass through. A gust of wind sends a flurry of golden petals floating past the threshold, and my thoughts too take flight. I want every rebel back where they belong, running their minor estates and casting horseshoes, not ordering their betters how to live and deciding who will govern. These thoughts spring to my lips, but I choose discretion over precocity.

'My philosophy has been challenged often since the troubles began, sir. I fear I have become confused.' Can he see the lie in my eyes on so short an acquaintance?

The only guests close enough to hear are slab-faced men in uniform who form the Lord General's personal guard. They may look dull-witted, but I am sure their ears work tolerably well.

'Tell me, sir. What do you find admirable in our monarch?' I want him to admit, even if it is only to me, that he doesn't wish to destroy everything my family holds dear.

He strokes his chin and ponders. 'Charles Stuart has a fine collection of artwork, for all that it was bought with the sweat of his subjects.'

'A harsh condemnation.' His disrespectful use of that name grates on my nerves, but I swallow the rejoinder that springs to my lips.

One thick brow slides upwards. 'You think so? Then there is his love of gardens and his devotion to the Anglican Church, though his bishops are hostile to my army.' He nods towards Bishop

Duppa, but his eyes twinkle with humour.

'The Presbyterians think your army is a nest of heresy, and Parliament despises the expense of its upkeep and, uh- parvenu officers.' I catch his sharp look and laugh. 'Not that I fully understand the word.'

'Of course you do, my dear.' His tone tells me he is aware I refer to him, but that I got away with it. 'You have a keen intelligence, and if your mother has anything to do with your education, she has instilled in you the better aspects of sovereign rule.'

I hide a smile behind my fan. Would he be quite so indulgent if he knew what my mother has taught me of subterfuge and deceit?

'I have hopes that we will reach terms for a cessation of these troubles.' He gives a deep sigh. 'There has been enough bloodshed.'

'Amen to that,' I murmur.

'Perhaps, Mistress Murray, when you chance to visit Charles Stuart, you might mention that to him?'

'Chance? An interesting word, sir.' I fight for calm but my pulse quickens at the thought of what Mother would say if I succeeded where she has not. 'My Mother has made several applications, but thus far we have not received permission to call at the palace. I'm afraid I can be of no use to you.'

'And if I were to extend that small courtesy?'

We exchange a look, the intensity of which I cannot fathom. 'I am akin to a favourite niece, no more. What makes you think His Majesty would listen to anything I suggest?'

His grip on my arm tightens and his expression shows me my attempt at vacuity has failed. Again. 'I do not ask lightly, for Charles Stuart has spoken of you.'

'He-he has?'

'He refers to you as his 'Dear Little Will's pretty daughter'. He specifically asked that your mother and sisters may call upon him in what he calls his dark imprisonment.'

'Dark imprisonment? At Hampton?' I cannot help a laugh escaping.

Cromwell joins in, the sound low and guttural. The room falls silent and a sea of shocked and enquiring faces turn toward us.

In a glance, I meet Mother's eyes. When she nods and smiles, I relax and turn back to my companion.

'I make no promises, sir. What I can do, is impress upon His Majesty that you are eager to come to terms. I will not state what those terms are.'

The thick lips twitch. 'I see you are your father's daughter, Mistress Murray. Would tomorrow be convenient?'

A dozen questions fly through my head. I must secure the services of Master Blower, the Twickenham ferryman to row me to Hampton on the morrow. I could go on horseback, but that would take longer and I prefer to arrive less dishevelled when I appear before the king.

Warmth creeps into my cheeks at the thought I may actually see King Charles in a few hours.

'We are agreed, then.' Cromwell gives a satisfied nod, bowing. 'My son-in-law throws me pleading looks. I had better see what irks him.' He cuts his way through a knot of people who step smartly aside, then pauses to speak to a young man with a livid red scar on his cheek.

Kate appears at my side like a silent ghost, an annoying characteristic she has perfected of late. Our relationship is strained, but she now speaks to me without being prompted.

'Do you see that man?' She indicates the man to whom Cromwell now speaks, 'the one whose looks are quite spoiled by that awful mark on his face? He is Henry Ireton, Bridget Cromwell's husband. He got that wound at Naseby.' Kate lifts a hand to her mouth and whispers from behind it. 'They say he has a worse scar on his thigh.'

I swipe a glass of Rhenish from the tray of a passing servant, lifting it in line with my eyes. 'Here is to the Royalist who delivered each blow.'

'You are so wicked, Elizabeth.' Kate nudges me and giggles. A sound I have heard infrequently these last months, and one that brings a prickle to my throat. 'They say Cromwell is a saintly man.'

'Indeed.' I sip the cool liquid slowly. 'And is it not that mask of virtue which makes him all the more sinister?'

Kate frowns, uncomprehending and then stares at the door, alerted by the exuberant arrival of three soldiers who troop into the hall and greet their comrades as if they enter a tavern. My lip curls, but a look of such longing enters my sister's eyes, that I can barely swallow my wine.

I clear my throat and take a step closer, where the fragrance of rose petals clings to her hair. 'He will not come, Kate.'

'I know.' She stiffens and stares straight ahead, her lips clamped together.

I touch her shoulder in an attempt at a caress that becomes an awkward pat. She does not appear to notice, but does not shrug me off, her eyes still fixed on the door.

Mistress Cromwell catches my eye from the other side of the room, something she has done several times during the evening. As if she has something to say to me, but has yet to gird her courage to do so. Intrigued, I remain still as she weaves her way toward me through the throng of people, offering asides to each one she passes. With time to study her, I take in a strong face surrounded by pale golden hair and candid eyes that gaze steadily into mine. This is a woman who has seen both hardship and physical work. Her gown is dark and plain, over which she wears a crisp white bertha and a cap, but no one could mistake her for an ordinary goodwife.

We exchange curtseys and polite greetings before she compliments me on our lovely house and extensive grounds. I harden my jaw and have to resist telling her we had beautiful gardens, once. Before her husband's soldiers ruined them.

Amongst the low murmur of voices around me, I allow my thoughts to drift, still bolstered by the fact that Oliver Cromwell asked me, Elizabeth Murray, to speak to the king. The power of this request makes my spine tingle.

Kate nudges me, 'Elizabeth? Mistress Cromwell asked you a question.'

I drag my thoughts to where the lady's gaze is fixed expectantly on my face.

'I do apologise. What was that you said?'

'It is but a trifle, Mistress. I simply remarked that I believe your lady mother has visited France recently. I hear it's a beautiful country.'

283

'Er- indeed, I-' I search for Mother's face among those around me but cannot see her. Why would she tell this lady, of all people, such a thing? 'We have friends there.' Does her husband know of Mother's travels? A dull worm of dread tells me he does.

'I also heard,' Mistress Cromwell continues, seemingly oblivious to my unease, 'that you yourself are knowledgeable in the ways of remedies and medicines.' She drops her voice so low, I have to strain to hear her. 'An unusual knowledge in fact, which extends beyond these shores.' She snakes an arm through mine and draws me aside until we stand alone beside the empty cavern of the fireplace.

'On occasion I like to experiment with balms for sore throats and fevers.' I examine her face to discern whether she seeks to trap me. Since Ball's remark about my being taken for a witch, my skin crawls when such things are mentioned. 'Simple remedies only. Herbal infusions and ointments for wounds.'

Her round eyes widen and she gives a tiny gasp. 'I would never suggest anything else, my dear. I have certain interests in that direction myself, and I wondered. . .' Master Ireton strolls past and Mistress Cromwell drops her gaze until he is out of earshot. A strange reaction for the man married to her daughter. I would almost think she did not wish him to hear our conversation.

'I hope you will indulge me, Mistress Murray,' the lady continues, 'I too have a special interest in certain medicines.'

'How particular an interest?' The intense light in her eyes tells me this is not a casual enquiry. What did Mother say? Find out what Cromwell needs? Though in this case it appears the one in need is his wife.

'Well, perhaps you see through me.' She attempts a laugh but the pale skin on her cheeks flushes a mottled red. 'I am a simple Puritan woman and science is beyond my ken.' Her hand closes on mine, the gesture light, but the urgency in her eyes is unmistakeable. 'I have a reason for my enquiry, and your mother looks to be the kind of woman who might understand.'

'Then why do you not ask her yourself?'

'I would, but-' She licks her lips and looks to where Mother stands with Cromwell. 'She has not left my husband's side all evening. And when she is not with him, she is in the company of my son-in-law.'

'You need not fear my Mother would turn your husband's head, much less that of Master Ireton.'

'No - you misunderstand.' Panic flickers in her eyes. 'I simply do not want either of them to know I broached this subject with you.'

'It was but a jest, dear lady. However, you intrigue me.' *More than you know.*

I am playing with her, but the sensation is new and intoxicating. Any moment she will break, tell me what it is she really wants and why, though I am in no hurry to relinquish my power. 'How - exactly may I be of assistance?'

'I wish to obtain some of the substance they call quinine. It is a remedy for the ague, obtainable only from France. I wondered if you knew where... I mean how I might. . .'

'I see.' Now I understand. She is not trying to trap us, but use us. 'Do you suffer from the ague at times, Mistress Cromwell? I believe it to be a most distressing condition.'

Her face clears. 'Oh, no, not I - I.' Her gaze lingers on her husband before returning to me. 'Someone close to me suffers quite badly from the malady. His headaches and fevers are most distressing. I hate to see him suffer.'

As if he senses he is under discussion, Cromwell swings his head in our direction. I nod and smile in acknowledgment, but shift my stance so he is looking at my turned back. Hoping he is too far away to take this action as an insult, I concentrate on his wife, who is almost shaking with nerves. My compassion for a soul in need overrides my aversion to her beliefs. If briefly. 'I may be able to help you, Mistress.'

Her eyes widen and she gives a small gasp. 'If you could, the good Lord would regard you with especial attention, and indeed, I would be eternally grateful.'

My returning smile is brittle. I doubt this woman has the ear of God, no matter what the great Cromwell believes. 'I see it as no more than my Christian duty.'

Our gazes meet and the flash of understanding that passes

between us makes my blood rush. The conversation around us mutes to a low roar, but the birds in the trees beyond the open doors are sharp and sweet. A horse neighs in a field and the smell of roses fills my senses. I have never felt so alive, and on the edge of something momentous.

Oh, Father, I wish you were here right now.

The sound of our steward announcing dinner makes me jump. I gather myself and prepare to join the flurry of feet toward the upstairs dining salon, but Mistress Cromwell seems reluctant to leave my side.

'Mama, we must take our seats now.' The lady pointed out to me earlier as Mistress Bridget Ireton beckons her. 'Father becomes impatient.'

'Of course, dear.' Mistress Cromwell presses my arm again before leaving. 'You will not forget, Mistress Murray.' It is not a question.

In the gilt and cream apartment on the upper floor, rows of china and glass gleam and sparkle on an array of small tables. To give intimacy to the proceedings, the curtains remain drawn, with full-height silver candelabra set at intervals along both sides of the room. Smaller ones adorn each surface, and with one swift glance, I estimate we must have used up our entire year's supply of wax candles in one evening.

Winter will certainly be darker than usual this year with only tapers to light us to bed.

Rainbow coloured jewels sparkle on throats and fingers, each face made young and glowing again in a light that puts a glint in everyone's eye.

'You look quite flushed, Elizabeth dear,' Joan Carlisle says as she takes her place at my table. Lodowick and Bishop Duppa claim the remaining seats between two silent rebel soldiers and launch into a lively discussion on portraiture with Joan.

Flushed yes, Joan, with power.

I can hardly eat, a fact I shall regret later, for we have not had spiced fish and beef rump for a long time. Not only are my stays unusually tight, but my mounting excitement chases my appetite away and I merely pick at my food.

In the space of less than an hour, one of the most powerful men in the country has asked a favour, and then his wife has done the same. Though I respond to the remarks aimed at me, my thoughts are elsewhere as I nurse my growing sense of importance.

The dishes empty and the cloths are removed. The footmen bring fruit, nuts and more wine while the atmosphere softens to an easy camaraderie. The party adjourns to the next room to listen to the musicians, or sit and talk, though as if at a silent decree, no playing cards appear.

The music grows repetitive, as does the conversation. So many subjects are forbidden, I soon become restless, my cheeks aching from having to smile so much.

A little after ten of the clock, Cromwell announces that he has business in London the next day and must not stay up too late. At his silent signal, everyone troops down to the main hall where his honour guard form a double line.

'I must applaud your composure with Cromwell, Betty.' Mother clasps her hands beneath her chin like a young girl as the guests file past us and descend the stairs. 'He is positively entranced with you. He mentioned you several times during dinner. Your charm, your beauty and intelligence-'

'Later, Mama.' I hush her as Cromwell inclines his head toward me as he passes, his wife on his arm, the message in his eyes clear. Do not forget our bargain.

Mistress Cromwell glances back at me as she climbs the carriage step, her eyes bright with gratitude, though my view is quickly blocked by Bridget Ireton and her handsome, stern-looking husband.

She shall have my discretion, though not for her sake as much as my own. Has she any conception of the power she has just handed me?

When the last carriage rolls away and the door closes, Mother plants both feet in front of me, her head on one side. 'A successful evening would you not say, Betty?'

'Indeed, Mama. And I believe I have found a use for that powder you brought back from France.'

Chapter 24

While I await Mother's arrival at the jetty, I pay more than normal attention to the boatmen employed to row us to Hampton Court. Plainly uncomfortable in this heat, both sport damp patches on their backs, and sweat dampens the hair beneath their broad-brimmed hats. They look ordinary enough, though, that does not mean they are not Roundhead spies.

Then a thought occurs to me that hitches my breath. Perhaps I too am being watched? I arrange my skirts on the hard seat at the stern of the wherry, and sweep my gaze across the riverbank on both sides, but it remains sultry and deserted in the sunshine.

The idea of my actions being of interest to the rebels both excites and terrifies me. As Mother always says, let them watch. Cromwell's lackeys will find nothing to use against me. Like her, I relish keeping my enemies off balance. I only hope I am as successful at the task as she.

Finally, Mother bustles along the dirt path, a footman in her wake who hands her into the boat. She settles beneath the canvas awning, protective of her pale Scot's colouring which suffers beneath a hot sun.

'If the lady does not wish her husband to know she has the powder,' Mother says without preamble. 'How will she contrive to get him to take it?'

I shoot a quick look at the boatmen, but neither are within earshot. 'I had wondered the same myself, but it is not a problem I anticipate having to deal with, Mama.'

She wiggles her shoulders against the cushions. 'I cannot tell you how it delights me.'

'That Cromwell suffers from bouts of the ague?'

'Not exclusively. More that his wife came to us for help. Secrets are so delicious when they are useful, do you not think?' Her eyes flash with cunning. 'I hope you demand something in return? One does not grant favours to the enemy for no reward.'

'You have taught me better than that. I despatched a polite note to the lady this very morning.'

Mother leans forward on the seat, her eyes wide. 'You were discreet, I hope?'

'Of course, I am not your daughter for nothing. Besides, my request is small.'

Mother's head whips round to face me. 'How small?'

'That the rebels not take liberties with our food, firewood and livestock. It has always rankled that those soldiers keep warmer and eat better than we do on our own land.'

She wrinkles her pert nose. 'You undersell yourself, my dear. If it were me, I would insist on the removal of every soldier from the estate. Not to mention reinstatement of our tenants' rents. I am sick of penny-pinching and fighting for every crust to feed my children.'

I bite my lower lip to prevent a smile. 'I do not know how much influence Mistress Cr- the lady, has over her husband. She may not be able to obtain anything at all.'

'To my mind, it's a measure of her desperation that she approached you on your first meeting. She has power, do not doubt it.'

Is Mother right and I have made a poor bargain? We shall have to see.

The boatmen lean into their oars to guide the vessel around the s-shaped curve of the river ahead. I strain forward in my seat as the crimson Tudor facade peeks through the elms. This first sight of Hampton Court Palace fills me with nostalgic sadness. I half close my eyes and conjure a time from my childhood, when Father brought me here on a barge similar to this one.

In my childish confidence, I jumped from the boat into his arms, not doubting for a second he would catch me. I recall the pang of pure love that filled me when he shouted with laughter at my daring. The feel of his coat under my hands as he lowered me onto the barge walk; the sharp gravel that bit into the soles of my shoes. With my hand firmly grasped in his, he talked of the time when Katharine Howard was lady-in-waiting, and King Henry courted Anne Boleyn in the gardens. 'Look there, Elizabeth.' He crouched at my side to point out the intertwined lover's knot of 'H' and 'A' carved in the stone arch that led into the courtyard.

I can still feel his palm, warm against mine.

The wherry bumps against the jetty and jolts my thoughts back to the present. Another rough hand grasps mine and helps me out of the boat.

My heart quickens at the familiar red brick roundels above long lawns of the ornamental gardens, only to plummet again. No laughing royal children play amongst the trees today, and Queen Henrietta Maria will not appear on the terrace to beckon us into the ballroom because a masque is about to begin.

Rebel soldiers wander the grounds and stand sentry at intervals along the boundary wall. Their insolent gazes dog our every step, and at the door, a sentry roughly demands our names.

'Countess Dysart and her daughter, Lady Elizabeth Dysart,' Mother intones with her head held high. I raise my eyebrows at her use of our titles, for she never allows it at home. 'Come to see His Majesty.'

I smile and shake my head. Even if they placed a sword at her throat, she would never call him Charles Stuart.

The soldier cocks his head toward a corridor, at the end of which lies an open door.

Mother stiffens. 'Is he not going to escort us?' She makes no attempt to lower her voice.

'Shhh!' I pull her forward. 'There are more guards up ahead.'

She simply laughs. Sometimes I believe Mother is brazen for the sake of it.

Beneath the harsh gaze of another brace of soldiers, Mother and I pause on the threshold of a long room. Floor height windows run along one side overlooking the Privy Garden with its geometrical flowerbeds and crisply cut lawns.

This surprises me, for the hedges of the east front looked ragged, the flowerbeds empty and clogged with weeds. Yet the Privy Garden is neat and well-tended. Even the statuary looks clean. Halfway down the room, and facing this view stands a chair upholstered in red plush where sits King Charles. The sight of his familiar, narrow face with its sharply trimmed beard makes my throat prickle.

The high chair back extends two feet above his head. He looks like a child in his blue silk suit with frothy lace at his tiny wrists.

His hooded eyes are cast down and one delicate hand hovers beneath his chin. He might be on a throne in an audience chamber but for the presence of the guards.

Several men crowd the chair and in search of familiar faces, my gaze settles on a thin moustache that sticks out horizontal to its owner's top lip. Jack Ashburnham looks up and offers an uneasy smile.

I incline my head with cool reserve as indignation inflates my chest. Why is he allowed to remain at the king's side when my father is not?

On the other side of this throne-like chair stand two men in light cloaks. Both strangers. The third face I know, William Legge, the king's secretary.

There is no sign of Cromwell or his wife, despite the rumours that they scurry over from Kingston at every opportunity.

I can only speculate on what discourse has taken place before our arrival. The king taps his silver topped cane with a fingernail, his lips pursed like a petulant child. No one speaks in more than a murmur and gazes lock for mere seconds before being pulled away again.

'Everyone looks most uneasy, Mother,' I whisper. 'I hope we are welcome.'

'Cromwell has given his permission as an especial favour to you, Betty.' Mother places a firm hand on my back. 'I see Loudoun and Lanark are here.' She nods toward the men in cloaks.

'Who are they?' I whisper back.

'Loudoun is the one with the hawk-like nose. He's Lord Chancellor of Scotland.'

'A Covenanter?'

'Naturally. As is Hamilton, the Earl of Lanark.'

'The man Father tried to-?'

'The same.' Mother cuts me off with a hand on my arm. 'They urge the king to accept terms with the Covenanters.' She cocks her head on one side, thinking. 'It seems negotiations have faltered. In which case, you and I will bring some laughter into the royal presence.'

'I admire your confidence, Mama,' I murmur out of the corner of my mouth.

One of the two guards behind the king signals with a nod that we may approach. Do these rebels never use their hands? Or are they too firmly clutched onto their muskets?

The king looks up and sees us. His eyes twinkle and he flaps a hand, at which Ashburnham and the Scottish brothers step away from the chair and huddle in a corner.

'My dear Lady Dysart, and Lady Elizabeth!' The king waggles his fingers to signal me upright from my deep curtsey. 'What an age it has been since you last delighted my presence. I crave friendly faces after all these dour Presbyters.' He twists his hand in the air at eye level as if to condemn the entire room. 'I would dismiss them, but Jack and Will Legge pester me constantly with one document or another.'

'If they offend you, Your Majesty, then send them away.' Mother flaps her fan. 'They cannot make you do what is abhorrent to your inclination.'

I nudge her sharply with an elbow. According to Father, this sentiment is oft-repeated in the queen's letters to her husband, which is the main reason the king is forbidden to write to her. The last thing his gaolers want is my mother repeating them.

'It is so close in here, dear child.' His Majesty rises and offers me his arm. 'Would you care to take a walk in my garden?'

'You read my mind, Your Majesty.' A rush of triumph prompts my wide smile at the row of disgruntled faces behind his chair.

Mother remains talking to Jack Ashburnham, though two guards fall into line at our back as we approach the casement windows.

The king pauses to wave a lace handkerchief in their direction. 'I go but a short pace. Surely none of you imagine Lady Elizabeth intends to spirit me away?'

An uneasy laugh erupts from behind us, but the guards fall back, and in seconds I am alone with the king. He takes slow, dainty steps as we weave our way along the gravel paths, his arm frail and insubstantial beneath my hand.

'I think often of the days spent here, with the dear queen and my beloved children.' His sigh is heartfelt and sends a surge of anger into my breast that he is come to this - a prisoner in his own home.

'I remember them well, Your Majesty,' I say, and find I have to blink away sudden tears.

'Ah no, you must not call me that. My gaolers forbid it.' He casts a sardonic look over his shoulder, though our stern escort are too far away to hear.

'I recall,' he says, 'a particular masque my dear queen arranged in which you played a part, my dear.' He chatters on, pulling memories from his head like a jester's hat. Of happier times spent at Whitehall and Oatlands, of never-ending summer days my sisters and I spent there, with the royal children as our playmates amongst the trees by the river.

When his voice changes timbre, I am not ready for it. 'I hear Lord Cromwell took dinner at Ham last evening, Lady Elizabeth.'

'Ah - yes I- at my Mother's invitation, Your Majesty.' I say, unable to gauge whether he is affronted or not.

He turns to look at me, the hooded eyes sleepy but watchful. 'I admire your honesty, my dear. Many would have claimed duress.'

'No Murray would seek to deceive you.' I hold his gaze, aware of the soldiers and courtiers lined up behind the windows, watching us. 'You need not doubt our loyalty, even if our actions may appear - inexplicable.'

'I'm glad to hear it.' He gently swings his black-lacquered cane in his free hand. 'Was it a profitable evening?'

'I believe so. I learned a great deal.' I slip my free hand into my pocket and finger the parchment I prepared in readiness to send to Mistress Cromwell later.

'Whatever it is that puts such excitement into your eyes, Lady Elizabeth,' he presses my hand into his side, 'I trust you will use it to our best advantage.' His use of the word 'our' sends a shiver of excitement through me.

'You have my promise.' I turn to look at him then, my gaze steady, 'I would broach a subject you may find disagreeable.'

'Ah! Do I take it you have struck a bargain with our Lieutenant General?'

My lips twitch. Many accuse the king of being dull and stupid, but those who know him are often surprised by his perception. If only he would apply the same skill to his negotiations with Parliament.

'Your Majesty. I ask nothing that would compromise either of us,' I rush to reassure him. 'I merely promised to ask, that you have an open mind when it comes to the demands of Parliament.'

I sense him stiffen beside me. 'I assure you, my dear, that I always give their demands the attention they deserve,' he says, dismissive. 'Rumour has reached me that Master Cromwell's price for a swift settlement is an Earldom and the Garter.'

'What do you say to that, Your Majesty?' I find this hard to believe from my assessment of Cromwell, but keep my voice neutral.

'Huh!' He pokes a flowerbed with the cane and sniffs. 'The only garter that farmer will get from me is a hempen one.'

Our tour of the pathways is almost complete, and we are within yards of the doors. 'What answer shall I take back to him, Your Majesty?'

At first, I fear he will not answer, and protocol denies my asking the same question twice.

We mount the steps to the terrace, where he halts and turns toward me. 'I give you my word.'

I exhale slowly, my heart thumping. I have done what was asked of me, and can do no more.

'I hope I have not offended you, Your Majesty,' I say, sotto voce.

'It is not a question of offence, my dear. We must all make bargains and compromises in these times.' He plucks my hand from his arm and raises it to his lips. 'Promises are made to be broken, especially those made by a king.'

He places my hand back on his arm, and together we return to the room where he is immediately surrounded by attendants eager for his attention.

Dismissed, I back away, but he calls after me.

'Pray, do not leave, Lady Elizabeth. A hint of a smile twitches his thin lips. 'I find these Covenanting Scots a coarse, loud bunch. There is but one among them I would willingly spend time with.' He beckons to someone behind me. 'He is a man who can puncture men's egos with contemptuous ease.' The royal lips twitch with amusement. 'And here is the very man. Lauderdale!'

The name sparks my interest, but I do not dare show the king my back.

Prince Charles always said that neither of his parents would recognise their own children from the rear. The memory makes me smile.

'My lord,' he waves the newcomer forward. 'Have you the acquaintance of the wife and daughter of my dearest Will Murray? That same Murray whom you have twice helped avoid a protracted spell in the Tower.' The king cocks his head and whispers. 'I keep him with me in case I find myself in need of the same service.'

A shiver of foreboding runs down my spine, while Master Ashburnham gives a self-conscious cough.

Mother extends her hand. 'I have not the pleasure, my lord. However, you have my gratitude. My dear husband would be rotting in a prison cell were it not for your efforts.'

Intrigued to lay eyes on the stranger, I shift sideways. And freeze.

The face bent over Mother's hand is no courtier, more like a creature blown in by a mountain wind. A mane of thick, red hair falls to his shoulders in soft waves. Dark eyes within a tanned face peer from beneath heavy brows. A tightly fitting long coat strains over muscular shoulders, and my gaze slides to the full lips that press against Mother's hand.

He cannot be above thirty years, nor is he handsome in the accepted sense, but his is a compelling face nonetheless. I cannot help but stare in a mixture of fascination, and something like recognition.

My turn comes, and he raises my hand, the pressure of his mouth on my knuckles sending sparks into my wrist. His penetrating eyes rove slowly from my waist to forehead with such intensity, he may as well lay hands upon me.

My gaze shifts to those hands. Broad, strong palms and firm fingers with neat, square nails that hold mine. My pulse quickens as an image plants itself in my head. His face and mine close together, our bodies entwined. A prickling sensation rises on my skin, then a quickening of breath, a heat, a tightening deep in my belly.

'We meet at last, Lady Elizabeth.' Earl Lauderdale says. 'Your faither has spoken of ye often. He calls ye his jewel.'

'My lord earl.' I find my voice at last. 'I am honoured to make your acquaintance.'

Ann Harrison once told me Richard became the guardian of her heart at their first meeting. I laughed then and called her fanciful, only to be sobered by the hurt that appeared on her face. 'It will happen to you one day, Elizabeth,' she insisted. 'Then you'll believe me.'

I believe you now, Ann.

He examines every feature of my face in a slow, languorous look, and when our gazes meet, he gives a tiny start, his grasp on my hand still firm. 'Do I disappoint, my lord earl?' I say, surprising myself with my daring.

'Of course you do not, Betty dear,' Mother says at my shoulder, reminding me that we are not alone. 'My daughter is indeed a gem.'

'Forgive me, Lady Dysart.' The king pats Mother's arm. 'But I fear my Lords Lanark and Loudon command my attention.' He indicates the darting eyes and restless hands of the two Scots, then leans toward us conspiratorially. 'I command you to return in a half hour to rescue me, lest I die of tedium.'

'With Yer Majesty's permission,' Lauderdale says. 'May ah claim this lady's company whilst ye are occupied?' His hand grips my elbow with a force that makes me wince, but to avoid an unseemly tussle, make myself relax.

'Go along with you then, John,' His Majesty chuckles. 'Take care of my Will's girl. She is precious.' Charmed by his compliment, I dip into another deep curtsey, my thoughts swirling.

His name is John.

'Come, Jack.' Mother tucks her arm beneath Ashburnham's. 'While the young ones have their talk, you may keep me company. I have not seen you for an age.' She throws a quick look at the red-haired man and then back at me.

Earl Lauderdale guides me away from the royal presence, the space created instantly filled by the Scots lords and Master Legge.

Our exchange of trivial talk takes us half the length of the room. 'You do not wish to join their discussion?' I ask, pointing my closed fan at the huddle round the king's chair. 'I was under the impression you are one of them?'

I start to doubt the wisdom of a private conversation with this man, but cannot bring myself to break away, for something about him keeps me at his side.

A russet brow rises above one soft brown eye. 'By one o' them, do ye mean a Scot, or a Covenanter?'

'Both.'

He nods, and a smile crinkles his eyes at the corners.

I recall Mother's words at the time of Father's trial. 'Is not your ambition to make England Presbyterian?' I peer up at him through my lashes, unsure as to the wisdom of flirting with him. He looks the type who would not accept a woman's teasing. This man takes what he wants.

'In ma favour, I advocate His Majesty reject the proposals made by the Independents.'

'But you also approved the king's surrender to the Scots,' I say. 'What prompted you then to help my father?'

He doesn't answer; instead he resumes his stroll, giving me no choice but to half run to keep up as my arm is still imprisoned in his.

'When we were at Newcastle, Will Murray mentioned his estate is nae far from here.'

His swift change of subject disarms me. 'That is true, yes. We live at Ham, about five miles upriver.'

'You have access to the watter, or is the hoose situated some distance away?'

'Ham House is as close to the river as Hampton, sir.' I peer into his face. 'Is your interest in houses or rivers?'

'Both,' he says with a grin, halting in front of a picture of a child in a blue silk dress that hangs beside the fireplace. The Princess Mary looks out from the canvas with a haughty, yet sweet expression.

'This portrait is an especial favourite of His Majesty,' he says. 'Brought from Whitehall and hung in this room as a comfort during his incarceration.'

'She was six years old when that was painted,' I say, eager to display my own knowledge of the subject, yet mildly disturbed by the pressure of Earl Lauderdale's hand on my arm, and his hip against my side. 'My sister, Nan, became restless because we had to wait for the sitting to finish. She wanted to join the other Royal children for a game of Pell Mell.' I am gabbling, but cannot help it. 'Master Van Dyck chased us away with threats of a whipping, as I recall.'

'His Majesty looks at it often. He surely misses her.'

Something in his detached tone tells me he is impatient with emotions like regret. Is there no one in his own life this man would miss in similar circumstances? He exudes strength and self-reliance; someone who knows his place in the world and needs approval from none. Intrigued, I study his profile, my gaze lingering on the attractive creases beside his eyes and his full, but masculine mouth.

He turns abruptly to look at me, and my gaze shifts to the wave of bright russet hair that spreads over his shoulder, with copper highlights drawn there by the sun. Is it soft or coarse to the touch?

He catches me staring and I remove my smile.

'Does it distress you to see the king in this position, my lady?'

I frown, confused at his reason for such a question. Surely he knows where the Murray's allegiance lies? And if he doubts us, why did he risk speaking up for Father at his trial?

'I have happier memories of Hampton, my lord.' I choose vague politeness over confidence. 'I hate to see my sovereign with guards at his back.'

'Indeed, although it is Colonel Whalley who lives in a permanent state o' nerves.' He indicates a dark man who paces in front of the fireplace. 'To hae sole charge o' a Royal prisoner is nae an easy task.'

'Though this prisoner seems less eager than most to change his captivity.' I deliberately keep my gaze from the earl, watching as Colonel Whalley strays too close to the king, receives a hard glare for his impudence and retreats.

Lauderdale doesn't respond, merely stares at me for long, thoughtful seconds before giving a small nod.

'And surely terms will have to be agreed at some time?' I continue. 'The king cannot be kept a prisoner forever.' My unspoken hope is for the Royalists to break this impasse, take the king to Westminster and throw out the Puritans.

'Parliament think tae soften His Majesty's resolve by allowing friends and family tae visit.' He turns liquid brown eyes on me in enquiry. 'Is that no' why you and Countess Dysart are here?'

I bite my tongue, reluctant to concede Cromwell had a part in this audience. Or does Lauderdale think that one dinner makes the Murrays allies of the rebels? I still do not know what this man wants from me.'

'Cromwell's demands are no less galling than those of you and the Scots, who insist the king signs the Covenant? A document he cannot in all conscience agree to.'

The earl's contemplative gaze sweeps over my head to where the king is in deep conversation with the Scottish Lords. 'Mebbe, but I hae learned o' late there is nae dishonour in compromise.'

Everything he says confuses me, and simply looking at him makes me shake with desire. How can that be so? I am betrothed to another man. A man who does not affect me as this one does.

'No dishonour at all. Though an agreement of some sort must be reached, or I despair of His Majesty ever seeing his wife again.' I choose not to mention that Father regularly carries Henrietta Maria's letters across the Channel to her husband. Or do I deceive myself and Earl Lauderdale already knows?

'You and I, Lady Elizabeth, are more like-minded than ye may think,' he says, as if reading my thoughts. He flexes a wrist and casts a swift look at the watching guards. 'I fear you are right, and the king may ne'er see the queen again.' He leans closer, his wine-tinged breath warm on my cheek. 'Unless. His Majesty can be prevailed upon tae escape, and join her in Paris.'

Chapter 25

I stare at Earl Lauderdale's face in disbelief as the room tilts round me.

'You speak too rashly, my lord. And in *this* company?' I sweep the room with my gaze and prepare to stalk away. 'Such talk will put us both in danger.'

I do not get far. His fingers close on my upper arm none too gently.

I stiffen. What is he doing? And why do I allow it? I am a betrothed woman, not some tavern doxy with whom he can pass an idle hour. How dare he lay hands on me! I wince, but at the same time welcome the pain.

'Hush! Or it is ye who creates suspicion.' He steers me toward a casement window that stands open to the garden. 'I thought we were o' like mind?'

'I do not know *your* mind.' I shrug out of his hold and take a sideways step. But only one. Being near him is exhilarating.

'I dinna have time tae observe drawing room manners.' His 'r's roll off his tongue, with a fierce urgency. 'If I have offended ye, I crave yer pardon. But I must know. Are you with us, or agin us?' His glance drifts to the far end of the room, but no one stands out as a candidate for his attention.

Convinced he plays games, I snap my fan closed and rest it against my bottom lip, peering at him through my lashes. 'If you have something to say to me, my lord, say it. This verbal wrestling bores me.'

His eyes darken. 'Lady Elizabeth.' My name on his lips is like a caress. 'Admit it, ye want the king tae rid hisself o' his gaolers as much as me.'

'For what purpose? The Covenanters make as many demands on His Majesty as both Parliament and the army. You would merely change one prison for another?' I cock my chin at the figure of the king. 'Don't you know by now he will not compromise?'

He leans an arm on the window frame above my head, so close, his breath stirs the curls at my temple, his stance intimate as any embrace; and equally as effective, for I cannot walk away. 'Aye, that I do. So tell me, what should we do aboot that?'

'We?' I shrug, my fan trembling in my other hand. 'I have no idea.'

What is it about this man, who wears his expensive clothes with disdain. No tugging of lace cuffs or turning out of toes to show a muscled calf. Nor does he check his appearance in every mirror he passes. He thinks nothing of manhandling a lady either. No Prince Rupert this, or James Stuart. He has not even Prince Charles' charm, and him a mere boy of seventeen, but there is something I cannot define. An animal quality that appeals to a side of my nature I did not know existed. Until now.

'Do I see mistrust in those pretty blue eyes, ma lass?'

'I am not your lass. Now you *do* take liberties.' I lift my chin but remain within the circle of his arm. I cannot bring myself to walk away. Being close to him makes my skin prickle. He smells of wind and rain, touched with sweet wine and a tinge of male sweat.

Has Lauderdale really changed sides? Or is this talk of escape no more than a scheme to make me betray my fellow Royalists?

I do not know what to think, and like a small child threatened by a slavering dog, my gaze sweeps the room in search of Mother. She would know how to respond to his persuasive tongue.

I catch sight of her at the other end of the room, but she is too far away to read any signal from me. 'I believe you tease me, sir.' I attempt a flirtatious laugh. 'You have no such scheme to spirit away His Majesty.'

His gaze slides to my bosom and away again. A smile tugs at his mouth and he bends his head lower. 'Listen, and listen well. His Majesty went hunting, which is a pastime he is allowed here. Did ye ken that?'

I nod, and my lips part, but before I can speak, he continues.

'When our horses were far enough away from the guards so there was only Berkeley, Legge and myself. That is when I urged him tae go.'

'Go?'

'I called tae him. 'Run, Sire. Run, and do not stop for anything.' His upper arm grazes my bare shoulder, whether by accident or design I cannot tell. 'But he didnae run. He wouldnae.'

I glance across the room to where the king sits, flanked by two stone-faced armed guards; a constant reminder he is no longer free in his own home. I recall what Father said about his refusing to board the ship he and Sir Robert Moray had prepared for him at Tinmouth. It seems nothing has changed. 'If the king is not willing to escape, how can you make him?'

'Threats can appear from the most unlikely sources.'

'You think he is in danger?' I nod at guards. 'From them?'

Lauderdale laughs again. 'Nay, not them. But first, my lady,' he lowers his voice to a whisper more compelling than a shout. 'If there was a way ye could be of service to your king. Would ye do it?'

'How do I know this is not part of your seduction ploy of lady Royalists?'

He throws his head back and gives a full-throated laugh, a sound that creeps into my soul like warm spirit. 'I believe you have lately become acquainted with Lord Cromwell?'

'For expediency's sake only,' I say without thinking. His eyes widen and immediately I regret having revealed so much, though there is no triumph in his eyes, and no cunning either. Perhaps this is not a ploy after all.

His gaze goes to my parent, still in conversation with Master Ashburnham. She flaps her fan and waggles the fingers of one hand in the air, one shoulder hunched girlishly. As ever, she plays the coquette, but her mind is as shrewd as any man's.

'Will Murray told me his wife and daughter would help me if I asked,' Lauderdale says, his breath warm on my cheek.

Father told him that? I lift my splayed fan to hide my face, though no guard is close enough to hear us, nor does any show interest in our conversation. 'Did you not say the king has already refused to run away?'

His eyes close briefly. 'Aye, he listens and procrastinates, and when the time comes, he baulks.' His glance probes the room before returning to me. 'This time is different. Now he believes Agitators and Levellers plan to murder him.'

'And who led him to believe that?' My scepticism must show in

302

my face, for his full lips spread into a grin that tells me all I need to know. My stomach lurches, not in fear but excitement.

'Who am I tae discern real threat from rumour?' He pauses, and I wonder if he weighs the risks against my trustworthiness? 'Berkeley, Ashburnham and Legge are with me. I cannae tell ye all of it for ye own safety. My lady, I need you to let me know when Ham House is safe.'

'Safe?' I inhale slowly. 'You wish to bring the king to Ham?' At his slow nod my breath catches. 'How so? We have rebel soldiers quartered on us. Surely you know that?' Even as the words leave my lips, I discard them. We hid Father well enough when he came to see us in secret. The soldiers do not venture into the upper rooms. And Mother! Mother would be so proud.

'I hear Cromwell enjoyed his evening with the Murrays, and that he intends tae dine with ye again.'

'I had not heard that, but if it is true, I am sure my mother would happily issue an invitation whenever you wish.'

'Well. If the Lord General is at dinner with the Murrays when news arrives His Majesty has taken flight, would his first act be to search his hostess's house?'

'Why would he?' I cannot breathe at his daring. Have the king and Cromwell in the house at the same time? 'And when is this escape to take place?'

'Soon. There is much tae be arranged.' He flicks his thumb across my cheek, the contact so swift, as to be almost non-existent. 'May I rely on ye ?'

A rush of blood makes me light-headed. After all this time of hiding away at Ham, hoping things will change, this fascinating man presents me with an opportunity to alter the course of the failed war. Maybe even England's fate forever.

'You appear distracted, Lady Elizabeth.' Lauderdale commands my attention again. 'Do I ask too much?'

'When it comes to my king, nothing is too much, sir. Where do you intend to take him?'

'I shall urge him tae go to France and seek help from his relatives there. But first, I have tae spirit him away frae here.'

'And you expect me to keep Cromwell - distracted?' I peer up at

303

him through my lashes, convincing myself my flirtatiousness is for the benefit of the guard who strolls by. In truth I do so to see the gleam of admiration in Lauderdale's eyes.

'I do not ask you tae seduce the man, merely discover his movements.' He leans close, his breath warm on my ear. 'I have nae doubt you possess excellent skills of persuasion. If the fates allow, I hope there may be an opportunity for you tae practice them upon me.'

Fury tinged with excitement surges through me at his effrontery. Does he take me for a loose baggage who flirts with strangers? 'You are presumptuous, my lord.' Though my indignation is for the benefit of the guard, who now hovers nearby.

Stalking from rooms in a high dudgeon at implied insults is my speciality, though this time I am grateful the king's presence prevents me. I am not going anywhere, not when the heat from the earl's body makes me giddy.

'Secrets and conspiracy are an invigorating combination, my lady. Do you not agree?'

My gaze fixes on Lauderdale's fingers as he runs them along the inside of my forearm, and I have to suppress a gasp at the contact.

I nod, aware my cheeks burn and his rich, rolling laugh fills our private corner of the room. 'Dinna fear. I would ne'er put a jewel such as you in danger. That would hardly be the actions of a gentleman, or a prospective lover.'

'And what makes you think I would consent to be your lover?' My voice is unusually sharp, but had he asked, I would have thrown my entire fortune at his feet to gather up or trample at his whim.

'I am no' a man accustomed tae making advances tae betrothed ladies.' He makes no attempt to apologise. 'However, I am unusually affected by such a sharp mind coupled with an uncommon beauty.'

The flattery I accept, but mention of my forthcoming marriage disappoints me. I would wish to prolong our harmless fantasy a while longer.

'You are tae marry Sir Lionel Tollemache, I believe,' he goes on, throwing cold water on my mood. 'A good choice. Your parents are tae be congratulated.'

'He is *my* choice also, my lord.' I would not have him think I was sold like a yearling to the highest bidder.

His eyes darken. 'Ye are not wed yet, so I hope you will give my words due consideration.'

'I will give - your proposal - every attention.' Does he know I mean more than his plan to free the king? I squirm beneath his gaze, unable to tear my own from his mouth. Of course he does.

A flurry of activity at the far end of the room indicates the audience is at an end and the king is about to leave.

'I had better join my mother, sir.' I make movements to leave too, hoping he does not notice my reluctance.

He takes his cue and lifts my proffered hand. His kiss is soft and dry against my knuckles, but also firm and possessive. 'We shall certainly meet again, my lady. An occasion I anticipate with pleasure.'

His words challenge me, and yet I cannot summon a smart remark or a withering set down as I watch him leave, his stride confident and unhurried.

'You look flushed, my dear.' Mother says when I reach her. 'I trust Earl Lauderdale has been suitably entertaining?'

'Indeed he has.'

'Such a striking man, a shame his wife is a shy, mousy thing who eschews society.'

The room spins and I can barely take a breath. 'H-he is married?'

'Indeed.' She sighs. 'Since he was barely sixteen, and with only the one daughter to show for twelve years of marriage.' Her fan flaps lazily, but her gaze never leaves my face. 'And within a twelvemonth, I hope to see you safely married also.'

I swallow, but do not look at her. 'Yes, Mama. That would be for the best.'

Leaving Mother to take her farewells, I skirt the gardens and return to the barge walk, drawn by the line of pretty boats tied up on the bank in the afternoon sunshine.

Oarsmen sit idling on the grass, or sprawled beneath the trees. One whittles a piece of wood with a small knife, and another dangles a line into the river from the back of the barge. I wish him luck; these waters are virtually empty of fish, and have been so for a long time.

Thoughts of Earl Lauderdale fill my head, raising the hairs on my arms. An unsettling reaction, for I have always prided myself on having charge of my heart. In this dreamlike state, I am unprepared for the arrival of Bridget Ireton, whose feet skim the path in an unladylike run. Stranger still, she is alone, although the figure of a maid stands at the gate behind her.

Bridget halts before me, a hand on her bodice to catch her breath. 'I-I thought you might leave before I could speak to you, Mistress Murray. My mother told me you would be here today.'

'Your father was kind enough to arrange this audience with the king.'

'You have seen Charles Stuart?' Her lip curls with disdain.

'I have known His Majesty all my life.' I stiffen. *Charles Stuart indeed.* 'We talked of family matters.'

'I care nothing for what you discuss with the Stuart, my lady. He is held safe enough.' She indicates the row of guards lined up against the outer walls. 'I am here on behalf of my mother.' She lowers her voice, though neither the guards nor the ferrymen could possibly hear her at this distance. 'Mother says you would have a packet for her.'

My fingers close round the blue bottle that sits in my pocket, together with written instructions on how to dissolve the powder in laudanum. Can I trust this young woman? Or will my letter find its way to her husband? 'Did your mother tell you what the package contained?'

She lifts her chin, such as it is, and stares down her nose at me. 'I did not ask. I trust my mother implicitly. Do you have it?' She holds out her hand, palm upwards, the discussion at an end.

I comply, hoping that to any onlooker the gesture appears like a polite press of her hand.

She takes it without so much as a glance and turns to go.

'Do give my sincerest wishes to your mother,' I say, halting her. 'Tell her I am always at her service.' I bob a brief curtsey. 'Good day to you, Mistress Ireton.'

Her expression is unreadable as she turns and hurries away

without another word.

Mother is already seated in the stern when I reach the barge. 'Is all well, my dear?' she whispers as the boatman hands me in.

'I believe so.' I take the hard wooden bench beside her.

The barge pulls away from the bank and we head upriver toward Ham. Mother tucks her skirts clear of the spray while I relax against the cushions, allowing the gentle slap of the oars to soothe me.

I have done what I can. All that is left is for Mistress Cromwell to fulfil the rest of our bargain.

The five mile journey passes in virtual silence, apart from the thought that resounds in my head as loud as a thunderclap.

Earl Lauderdale is married.

Chapter 26

September 1647

Since that first call Mother and I made at Hampton Court to see the king, it has been twice repeated, although Earl Lauderdale did not appear on either occasion. Without even a note from him, I vacillate from fretful yearnings to chastising myself for a fool.

How can I think a man like that would pit himself against Cromwell on one side and the Presbyterians on the other? Does he realise the threat to his life and his fortune? Or is the draw of adventure too great?

And yet, the look in his eye when he asked for my help was not feigned. Throughout that entire interview at Hampton, he looked poised for flight, alert to every movement in the room and wary of who might be listening.

Then why has he not found a way to send me word?

A cacophony of sounds from the floor below breaks into my thoughts. Boots ring on the floor, while shouts and bangs contrive to shred my nerves.

I slam my hairbrush down on the dresser. 'Molly, what are those soldiers doing? Is drill practice being held in the hall?'

'I'll go and see, Mistress.' Molly makes one of her grotesque faces behind my back as she leaves. The girl must be dull-witted; doesn't she know what mirrors are for?

It is not Molly who enters the room a moment later, but Nan. 'Good, you have finished dressing. Now come downstairs and see what is happening. You will not believe it.'

'I do not need to see, Nan. I can hear every door slam and crash perfectly well from here.'

'You are so tetchy, Elizabeth. If only you would simply do what I ask instead of sniping at me. I promise what you see will make you smile.'

'Oh, very well.'

At the bottom of the stairs, the front door is flung wide and the main hall crowded with soldiers walking briskly from room to room. Officers signal and point to the enlisted men, whose arms are full of boxes, breast plates, books, hats, linen and boots.

A tiny light of hope grows and blooms in my chest. 'This looks very much as if they are leaving.'

'They are!' Nan bounces beside me, her hands clasped beneath her chin.

I step aside as two soldiers carrying an oak chest between them barge past us onto the drive, followed by several more with helmets and bits of armour.

I must find a way to let Earl Lauderdale know. 'This may change things with his plans for the king.'

'What plans?' Nan asks.

'I said nothing.' I grip her elbow hard. 'You did not hear that.'

'I understand, I-' She eases her arm from between my fingers. 'You do not have to pinch.'

I give the hall a sweeping glance to reassure myself no one else has heard. I need not worry. A cannon could go off and they would not notice it above the noise.

'Captain Fitton told Mother that more of Lord Fairfax's men have arrived in the district,' Nan says.

'If they are not coming here, where are they going?'

'Petersham Meadows, to make camp there for the rest of the summer.'

'The Meadows is our land. They will ruin it.'

'Better there than here in the house,' Nan says, laughing. She seems to have forgiven me for my small cruelty. 'You are never satisfied.'

'Nor will I be, until their army is disbanded and we return to normal.' *Whatever normal is with the king still captive.*

Packed trunks clutter the main hall. The door to the salon where the officers sleep stands open revealing scuffed and dusty floorboards, empty of truckle beds and boxes.

'See, I told you,' Nan says at my shoulder. 'Are you not delighted?'

'Of course I am.' I smile for the first time since rising. 'We shall have our home to ourselves again. And perhaps Kate may recover from her lovesickness. Bernard's permanent removal cannot be attributed to me.'

'Oh, Elizabeth, she no longer blames you for that.' Nan's sympathetic whisper is accompanied by a gentle hand on my arm. 'She knows what you did was for her sake.'

I am not so sure.

'Mistress Murray,' a familiar voice speaks and Sergeant Robin Carter approaches from the front door. 'I wish to inform you that we shall no longer trouble your family.'

'Thank you, Sergeant.' I will miss this young man, whose genteel manners and respectful nature helps dispel the rougher ways of his comrades. He seems to have forgiven me for threatening his reputation, our unfortunate encounter that summer night having faded into the past. 'Forgive me if I express no regret at your going.' Nan pokes me in the back, but I ignore her. 'And that you shall not be too uncomfortable in your tent on the meadows?'

'Not I.' A smile hovers on his handsome mouth. 'I'm to join the Levellers at the debate in Putney and state our case.'

'Your case, sir?' I frown at him, confused. What can he mean?

'Parliament,' he lowers his voice, although the hall is now empty, 'wants to cut our pay, as well as disband some of the stronger regiments.'

'If the war is over and all that is left is to sign an agreement with the king, why would there be a need of an army?' Nan asks.

His eyes widen in an astonishment that makes me smile. He is not the first to dismiss my sister as a simple soul, when a shrewd mind lurks behind that plain face. That she chooses not to display it at every opportunity is part of her charm.

'Many of us are afraid that with victory in sight, the army grandees, and the generals will betray us ordinary soldiers. We may have won the war for them, but we fear they have no further use for us. They have already refused to repair war damage and may even pack us off to Ireland.'

'I have no sympathy for the army, Sergeant, but that sounds to me like poor reward for good service.' I say.

'That is not the worst of it, Mistress.' His fervour shines from his eyes, making him quite an attractive man. Pity about the crude shorn hair and drab clothes for he would look good in satins. 'Most loathsome of all,' he goes on, 'is they also look set to betray our religious and political ideals.'

'Do I take it you feel there exists a way for you to put these issues to rights?' Nan asks, her expression as bewildered as my own must be.

'Indeed. We shall come together at Putney church, in October, to put forward our Agreement of the People, which argues the case for a transparent, democratic state free from the taint of Parliamentary or courtly corruption.' His sing-song delivery tells me this litany is not his own, but he has taken every word to heart.

'Who are these people who dare to make demands of their superior officers?' I ask, suppressing a laugh at such an outrageous notion.

'We call ourselves Levellers.' He kneads his gloves in both hands, his knuckles white. 'And yes, we demand that the law applies to all men, with no discrimination on grounds of estate, birth or place. We have a right to freedom of conscience, freedom from impressment into the armed forces, and no penalties for not going to church, or for those who wish to attend other acts of worship.'

'Even Quakers?' I expect him to see the joke, but his expression remains serious.

'Of course.'

'But, sir, men are not equal by birth.' I repeat the tenet Father taught me at his knee. 'We are placed here by God, our positions in society are thus decreed by Him.'

'That does not mean I, the son of a merchant, am not equal to you, the daughter of a courtier, Mistress.'

The protest that I am the daughter of an earl, and soon to be the wife of one hovers on my lips. Instead, I incline my head and smile. 'What does Captain Fitton think of these Leveller views?' I expect a shrivelling of confidence and a fearful sideways glance. I see neither.

'The Captain is one of us, Mistress. He will talk at Putney.'

I blink in surprise. 'I wish you luck with your aims, sir,' Hoping to bring the conversation to a swift end, I start to move away.

'With Colonel Chief Cromwell to speak up for the army, I will not need luck, merely God's will.'

A man like Robin Carter has much to gain, but the success of his ambitions means ruin to a king's man like Father. For the rank and file to have a vote on how things are run will surely mean anarchy and chaos, for how can a baker or a ferryman use such a thing wisely?

'In which church is this debate to be held?' Nan loiters, ignoring my signal to come away.

'At St Mary the Virgin that stands by Putney Bridge. There they will also decide what to do with the Stuart.'

I raise my chin, ready to challenge this disrespectful address, but have no time to ask him what he can mean as Captain Fitton's coarse shout comes from outside.

The Sergeant starts, then bows. 'I beg your pardon, I must go.' He takes a step back and then delves into his buff coat. 'I almost forgot.' He pulls out a piece of thin, poorly made parchment and hands it to me. 'I thought you might like to see this.'

'What is it?' My gaze goes to the foot of the page where Lord Fairfax's signature stands out.

'The reason for our departure.' I look up and catch his knowing gaze. 'It seems your family has friends in high places, Mistress Murray.'

I unfold the page, but am forced to break off and step aside, jostled by a line of soldiers who shove past me carrying bulky chests slung between them, their muskets strapped to their backs. Finally I am able to focus on the written words.

...are hereby ordered not to molest Mistress Murray either by plundering her house, or taking away her horses, sheepe or her cattel or goods whatsoever, or by offering any violence to her person or the persons of any of her familie, or to quarter private soldiers in her house.

I smile and look up, prepared to thank him, but he is no longer there.

'What is it, Elizabeth? What does it say?' Nan asks.

'It says, Nan, that Cromwell is not above granting favours to those Royalists whom he respects.'

And to whom he owes a debt of gratitude. Maybe Mother was right. I should have asked for more. Then my moment of triumph is tainted as I recall the sergeant's words about the king. 'At Putney, they would decide what to do with him.'

* * *

Relishing the silence, I wander through the lower floors to ensure every trace of the military occupation has been removed. Scuffed floors and skirting damaged by muskets are a small inconvenience compared to having Ham to ourselves again. My renewed sense of ownership alerts me to voices in the hall. For once, I do not dismiss them as having nothing to do with me and investigate, entering our reclaimed salon to find Mother ensconced with Mistress Cromwell.

'Do forgive my unannounced visit.' She advances on me and presses both my hands. 'We are about to quit our lodgings at *The Crane Inn* at Kingston to join the headquarters at Putney. I did not wish to leave without expressing my thanks for your help at our last meeting.'

'And I yours, Mistress Cromwell.' Mother closes the door and beckons our guest onto a sofa.

'I trust there was no mishap with the package Elizabeth gave to your daughter?' Mother says, wasting no time.

Mistress Cromwell runs her tongue over her lips. 'No, although my son-in-law did become suspicious after our visit here. He thought it strange we should have so much to say on so short an acquaintance.' The lady's light eyes flick to me and away again.

'Mistress Ireton was most discreet when we met at Hampton Court,' I say, hoping to establish whom the lady has made party to our arrangement.

Her gaze drops to her clasped hands in her lap. 'When girls marry, their allegiance transfers to their husbands. Which is of course as it should be. Everything Bridget hears naturally finds its way back to him.'

'So Master Ireton knows-' I begin, my heart thumping in my

313

chest.

She holds up a hand and I fall silent. 'Bridget adores her father. When I told her our arrangement was for his benefit, she agreed to say nothing. I can trust her.'

I exchange a look with Mother over her head. 'And Master Cromwell? Did he find the powder efficacious against the ague?'

A slow blush colours her face, but the eyes that lift to meet mine are clear. 'I tried the powder as you instructed, dissolved in the laudanum. He slept well that night, and the three following, which alone has convinced me of its powers.'

'I take it you require more?' Mother asks, cutting to the crux of the matter.

'Am I so transparent?' She splits a look between us, one slender hand pressed to her throat where a crisp white collar flattens the bodice of her black gown. 'I hesitate to ask, but I would be most grateful.'

'Your request will not be a simple one to execute.' Mother adopts a martyred look. She rises slowly and skirts the sofa, a ploy I know well, designed to increase the tension before giving her answer. 'I will have to send word to my husband in France. Not an easy task, as we are constantly watched and my dear Will lives in almost penniless exile.'

Mistress Cromwell's expression hardens. 'William Murray's conspiratorial nature has proved to be his enemy. I am sorry for his fate, but it is not of my husband's doing.'

'Well.' Mother eases back onto a sofa, putting our guest between her and myself. 'I admire your honesty, despite that what you ask is fraught with danger. For both my daughter and myself.'

'My husband's health is my most pressing concern.' Her gaze drops to her lap and her lips move as if she debates with herself. Or maybe she is praying. 'If what you require is in my power to grant, consider it done.'

Mother flicks me a glance and I mime weighing a purse in one hand.

'I shall need money,' she says, not missing a beat.

Mistress Cromwell's gaze sweeps the room to scrutinise the paintings, and then the rich carpeting. 'You speak of need, Mistress

314

Murray.' She raises one brow. 'I would have you see my farmhouse in Huntingdon.'

'Let not our grand surroundings deceive you.' A nerve in Mother's cheek twitches. 'I have had to sell many possessions to keep up with Parliament's demands.'

'My mother merely wishes to emphasise,' I interrupt, determined the conversation does not descend into a comparison of sacrifice, 'that messengers willing to cross the Channel in these dangerous times are exceeding expensive.'

Our visitor's light eyes turn to me. 'I understand.'

'The powder is also highly prized and difficult to obtain.' Mother resumes control of the situation with a benevolent smile. 'I have no idea how long it will take to acquire the quantity you need, or how much it will cost.'

'You shall have everything you need, Mistress Murray.' The lady's calm tone is contradicted by her pinched mouth. How she must hate to be at the mercy of her husband's enemies. Too bad, does she imagine we are friends?

'The messenger himself requires special qualities, also,' Mother goes on.

I frown, unsure of where this is going.

'In what way?' our visitor says, equally wary.

'He must appear to be a rebel officer, and thus unlikely to attract suspicion and questioning by the army.' Mistress Cromwell flinches at the word 'rebel' but remains silent. 'Also,' Mother continues, 'the documents he carries must not be subject to the scrutiny of anyone I do not wish to see them. For my own sake as well as yours, Mistress.'

'That may be more difficult to arrange,' Mistress Cromwell murmurs, while her long fingers pluck at her sleeve. 'I cannot condone passing information to enemies of the army.'

'Mistress Cromwell,' Mother's tone turns ingratiating. 'It is necessary for me to mention the powder in writing, and where to deliver it, even if the name of the recipient need not be mentioned.'

'I see, of course. I had not thought of that.' She bites her lip and I know she wishes to be anywhere but here.

'How difficult can it be to obtain a New Model Army uniform?'

Mother tilts her head, evidently pleased with herself. 'Appearances are everything. Besides, once the messenger reaches France, he will need to change his costume. I doubt he would be well received at the Queen's Court in a red coat and lobster-tail helmet.' Her light laugh elicits a weak smile from our guest.

I realise then that Mother intends to write to Father that Earl Lauderdale and Jack Ashburnham plan for the king's escape. She couldn't possibly commit such things to paper and entrust them to a real Model Army soldier. Clever Mama.

Our bargain is soon forged, and arrangements concluded, I stand with Mother at the door to wave Mistress Cromwell goodbye.

'I think that went rather well, Betty,' she says, her smile directed at the retreating carriage. 'Although I had to hold my tongue when she told us how comfortable the people of Kingston made them during their stay. As if her hosts had a choice.'

Leaving her at her post, I withdraw to my room seconds after the carriage has cleared the gates, and unearth the letter to Earl Lauderdale concealed in my bureau. I contemplate adding a few words about Mistress Cromwell's visit, but decide against it.

I owe the lady some discretion after the risk she has agreed to take. I re-fold the page into a thick square and seal it clumsily, burning my finger on the hot wax in my haste, and summon a footman.

Chapter 27

November 1647, Ham House

The wind rattles the window frames and howls through the trees outside my window. With a blanket and shawl wrapped round my shoulders against icy draughts, I leave my bed hangings open, afraid I will miss the sound of footsteps on the gravel terrace below.

It must be well after midnight, for my candle, marked with the hours, burned down some time ago, though sleep is a long way off. I could not be more excited if I awaited a lover.

He must come soon.

My door creaks open and Mother stands in a shaft of moonlight, fully dressed and a burning candle held aloft in one hand.

'Douse the light, Mama! The signal that Ham is safe must be total darkness.' I quote Earl Lauderdale's instructions.

'I doubt it can be seen beyond the river,' she says, but obeys.

After weeks of no word, I believed Lauderdale's scheme was no more than a figment of his imagination. And mine. Then three days ago, a letter arrived by messenger, its unfamiliar writing conjuring nothing but mild curiosity.

In seconds, my pulse raced at the sight of his name scrawled at the bottom of the page. With a shaking hand, I read his apology for the protracted silence, followed by a stream of flowery compliments. These gave way to an assertion that there was no need for us to entice Cromwell to Ham, for while the grandees argued with the Levellers in Putney, Lauderdale would take his opportunity to facilitate the king's escape from Hampton and smuggle him abroad.

'Is there any sign?' Mother checks both the hallway and then the window before closing the door to join me on the bed.

'Not yet. It cannot be long now, unless things have gone awry.'

'Do not think it.' Her voice comes out as a hiss. 'We are in enough danger as it is.'

The feather mattress sinks beneath her weight and she gives a tut of annoyance. 'I must get the maids to tighten these bed ropes, or you shall be sleeping on the floor.' She folds her hands in her lap as if this was a cosy chat.

'If Ashburnham and Berkeley have been dismissed,' Mother plucks nervously at the lace at her elbow, 'is Lauderdale sure they can organise the horses?'

'Mama, we have already discussed this. Everything is arranged.' My thoughts go to the letter hidden in my bureau, the page soft from repeated reading.

'Suppose the earl is wrong and there is no secret passage in the palace?'

'I doubt he would act without checking the veracity of his information first,' I snap, my already taut nerves pulled tighter. 'The king will retire, with the excuse he has letters to write and lock his room. He will slip out of a private door and down the back stairs to an underground passage to the river.' I repeat Lauderdale's words again like a litany, conscious Mother is not really listening.

Suppose His Majesty is followed to his meeting with Earl Lauderdale, and in turn tracked here? I rub my clammy palms together, dismissing the thought. I must not be a coward now.

'How long do you think the king must remain here in hiding?' Mama rocks gently back and forth, her tension palpable.

'Until the initial panic of the escape has died down, I suppose. The soldiers will be set on false trails, then the earl will escort the king to Gravesend, and from there to France. Please, Mama, no more questions. I know as much as you do.'

A rattle sounds above us and Mother stiffens. 'What is that?'

I have heard this sound a dozen times during my silent vigil. 'It is nothing. The wind shifting slates on the roof.'

She exhales slowly. 'Are you sure you have not mentioned any of this to the girls?'

'Of course not. Have you?'

She shakes her head. 'I cannot help but-'

A light tapping brings my head round. 'Shhh!' I grip her arm. 'Do you hear that?' Without waiting for a response, I rise. 'Stay here, Mama. I'll go and investigate.'

318

Moonlight floods through the landing window, raindrops clinging to the glass. When did it start to rain? I shrug the thought aside and descend quickly, my feet skimming the treads. In the contrasting blackness of the staircase hall my steps slow and I feel my way to the front door.

With no footman to assist me, I have to manage the massive door by myself. The knob is too large for my small hands and precious seconds are wasted when I cannot get a proper grip. At last the chink between the door and the frame widens into a shaft of pearly light and the welcome sight of Lauderdale's face appears in the gap.

He is little more than a dark outline silhouetted by the moon. The face beneath the wide-brimmed hat thrown into deep shadow, but I know it is him.

He is alone.

Frowning I beckon him inside and he helps me close the door.

'Has something gone wrong?' I ask.

'I dinna knaw,' he gasps, breathless from either running or a hard ride. He whips off his hat and slaps it against his thigh, scattering raindrops on the tiled floor. His face is drained of colour and that startling red hair is muddy grey. We stand no more than a foot apart in the weak moonlight, his breath on my cheek sending shivers of pleasure down my spine.

He draws me toward the bottom of the stairs where there is more light. 'I waited at the meeting place but nae one came.' His touch on my arm makes me dizzy; or is it the sheer terror of this, the most dangerous moment in my life?

'What do you think happened? Was the plot discovered and the king is still at Hampton Court?'

'Either that, or his absence has nae yet been noticed.'

'What of Ashburnham and Legge?'

'Nae sign of them either.'

I exhale slowly, thinking hard. It is too early to panic. 'If the king got away, surely he would have joined you?'

'That is what concerns me, although. . .'

'What?'

'I hae a feeling Ashburnham convinced His Majesty tae remain

319

in England.'

'Why would he do such a thing? Is that not more dangerous than going abroad?'

'*I* believe it is, yes.' He shrugs. 'Ashburnham is o' the opinion that once His Majesty leaves the country, he may ne'er find a way back.'

A stair creaks and a shadow enters my line of vision. Mother leans over the balustrade with a candle held high. 'My lord, is His Majesty not with you?' Disappointment dulls her voice.

'No, Mother. We don't know where he is.'

She nods and pulls back her shoulders, accepting this new information, glides down the stairs like a ghost towards us, beckons us into the hall and closes the door. 'Tell me, my lord. What do you think has happened?'

Ignoring the etiquette of a man not sitting before a lady, Lauderdale perches on a wooden bench drawn up to the long table, his forearms braced on his knees. 'If the king escaped, I fear he has been persuaded not to leave England.'

'Where would he go?' Mother sets the candle on the massive oak table where weeks ago, army officers took their meals.

'I dinna knaw.' He stares at the floor, knees spread. 'I dare nae return tae Hampton Court.'

'That is exactly where you must go.' I slide onto the bench beside him. My knee touches his thigh and despite the layers of fabric between us, his touch burns me. 'You must arrive as normal and request an audience with the king. If he is still there, you must hope no one denounces you and everyone behaves normally. If he got away, you must be as surprised and shocked as anyone. You know nothing.'

'Elizabeth is right,' Mother says. 'If the king has gone and you disappear, you are bound to be implicated. He may not have escaped at all, in which case you can devise another plan.'

'Hah!' His throaty laugh makes my stomach knot. 'If the plan has failed, they will either double the guard or remove him tae a more secure prison. You know all his attendants hae been removed?'

'We do. Either way.' My fingers slide onto his arm. 'If you

320

return to Hampton, you will be able to find out for certain.'

'Aye, yer right.'

With difficulty, I drag my gaze from his face. I must not stare. Mother will notice and take me to task for such foolishness in mooning over a man I can never have. Yet I cannot help it, with Lauderdale in the room I cannot look at anything else.

'Well.' Mother gathers up her candle and curls a hand round the flame. 'If I am not to be granted the honour of entertaining His Majesty, I may as well retire.' She pauses at the door to the staircase hall. 'I trust you to keep us informed, my lord.'

Lauderdale leaps to his feet like a courtier and makes an elegant leg, murmuring assent.

Mother turns a look on me that probes the gloom. 'Lock the front door before you come up, Betty.'

Left alone again with the earl, I can think of nothing to say. My tongue sticks to the roof of my mouth, conscious of my plain gown and undressed hair.

Not so my rakish earl. 'You are a canny young woman, Elizabeth. I wish you were mine.'

'An easy wish, sir, and one you know can never be fulfilled.'

'Never?' He looms above me.

His belt buckle is in line with my eyes, his hand brushes my cheek and I sway lightly, longing to lean into him, smell the wind and rain on his coat and his arm round me. I hold my breath and my eyes close.

'What is that?' His hand presses down on my shoulder, and freezes.

I blink and listen. Above the wind in the trees, there is only deep silence. Then from a long way off, something else.

Hoof beats. Lots of them. 'Soldiers?'

Lauderdale laughs; he bends and grasps my waist with both hands, and lifts me from the bench as if I weigh nothing. He swings me round in a circle, my feet inches from the floor. 'Do you nae see wha' this means, Elizabeth?' My name on his tongue is a caress. 'He got awa'. Or why would there be patrols on the roads before dawn?

A muffled laugh escapes my lips and the grip of his hands make me giddy. I feel light-headed and never want him to let go.

Then the faint sound becomes a rhythmic pounding, and I grasp both his arms. 'They are coming here!'

He sets me down, his hands still on my waist. 'Oh Jesu, I must nae be found here.'

'They cannot know why you are at Ham. You could simply be a guest.' The last thing I want is for him to go.

'It's the middle o' the night. We canna be sure what they ken. Betrayal is a possibility.'

The jingle of bit and bridle is followed by a command to halt and a scuffling of feet.

I must think, but my mind is a fog of indecision. 'I-I could hide you.' I sift through the likely places in the house where a man may be concealed. Places we had planned for the king

He shakes his head. 'Too dangerous. Is there a back way oot o' here?'

'Through the kitchen garden.'

A candle glow appears signalling Mother has returned. 'There are soldiers in the courtyard!' She waves us toward the rear offices, her shawl flapping like the wings of a giant bird. 'The time it takes them to rouse the servants will allow you to get away, my lord.'

Cold leaches through my slippers as I drag John with me across the flagstones toward the rear door. Snapping the thumb latch, I throw it open where a blast of chill rain whips my face; whorls of storm clouds in midnight blue, grey and white churn in the sky above us. The shower is rapidly turning into a gale. I step aside as Lauderdale slides past me, plants his hat on his head and dips his face level with mine.

'I hate tae leave ye like this. With them.' He nods to where shouts and banging echo along the narrow passage.

'It is not the first time. Besides, Mother will deal with them, she is a strong woman.'

He runs a hand down the side of my wet cheek. 'I have ne'er met a lass like you, Elizabeth.' He grasps my chin in his hand and drops a kiss on my lips.

He steps back and the amusement in his eyes turns to something else. His pupils widen and his smile dissolves. His hand slides from my chin to the back of my neck and with a tug, he draws me into another kiss. This one is slow, tender, demanding and far too short. When he pulls away, I lean with him, reluctant to break contact.

The soldiers have gained the house. By the treatment meted out to our front door and their barked orders, they make no pretence of friendliness. Their voices are joined by others, bewildered footmen roused from sleep and frightened maids pleading for explanations.

Belatedly a thought strikes me. 'Where did you leave your horse?'

'I brought a groom wi' me, he knows to keep well hidden.'

His gaze shifts to a point above my head, and I shove him toward the door. 'You-you must go,' I whisper, while in my head I want him to argue. A silly, feminine desire to which he cannot possibly respond, and my eyes slide closed in a silent prayer he will get away.

When I open them again, I am faced with an empty doorway and the steady rain lashing the trees, their branches crashing together in a rising wind.

He is gone.

My stomach lurches with loss as I creep back the way I came, duck behind the hidden door and up the servants' stairs to the upper landing. Fighting down nausea borne of fear and yet exhilarated with the danger of the moment, I reach my room and haul off my plain skirt. The bodice is harder to discard without help; I am too hasty with the pins and rip the fabric. Molly will tut over me in the morning when I give it to her for repair.

Throwing a loose robe over my shift, I am about to saunter onto the landing, when I realise my hair is damp. Grabbing a cloth from a chair I rub my head with vigour, hoping I look as if I have that moment risen from my bed.

As I leave my room, the doors on either side open. Nan and Kate appear and together, we pause at the head of the stairs to peer over the balustrade.

'Where is Mother?' I ask, feigning a yawn.

'She is down there with them.' Nan pokes a finger beneath her nightcap, and scratches her scalp.

'What do they want?' Kate chews a thumbnail, her eyes wide with fear.

Cousin Henderson appears further along the hallway from Meg's room holding my sister's hand. Awakened from a deep sleep, the child blinks and rubs her eyes.

Alarm clouds my cousin's features, and suspecting Mother has confided in her, I whisper, 'He did not come.'

A growling male voice drifts toward me as I descend the stairs for the second time that night, the sound magnified by the enclosed hall.

'In the name of the New Model Army, I demand to know if you have any knowledge of the whereabouts of Charles Stuart.'

Halfway down, I pause and clench my fist against my mouth to prevent the laugh that rises in my throat.

Lauderdale was right. The king has escaped.

The question as to where he went and with whom is yet to be answered, but for the moment excitement fills me and I push my way through a brace of guards at the bottom of the staircase.

At the edge of a group of six or so men in red uniforms and black helmets, their faces eerily similar, stand three sleepy footmen carrying lit candles.

Ball stands at the door to the salon while the housekeeper peers from behind his shoulder, her hair awry and eyes wide and terrified.

Surely this picture of rudely disturbed sleep must convince these soldiers?

Copying Meg's expression of sleepy innocence, I focus on their officer, a man I do not recognise, though he is of the same mould as the rest of them. Surly faced, over-fed and lacking in either compassion or sensitivity. 'What is going on here?'

Mother stands like a tiny child in the centre of the hall, hands gripped at the edges of her shawl pulled tight round her shoulders. 'These men say the king has escaped from Hampton Court, my dear.' If I did not know better, I would attribute her rapid breathing and wide eyes to genuine shock.

'With all those men guarding him? How could such a thing happen?' I hope my acting is as good as Mother's.

'Charles Stuart did not attend Evensong last night,' the officer says in a monotone. 'Nor did he take supper afterwards. Master

Whalley found the prisoner's room locked. By the time he investigated through the back way, he had gone.'

'I do not envy Master Whalley when Lord Fairfax learns his bird has flown,' I say, unable to resist the barb.

Mother's hard look renders me silent. '*We* were all abed, sir,' she says, craning her neck to meet his gaze, for he is very tall. 'Kindly allow us to dress, and I shall be happy to co-operate with you.' She pulls me behind her toward the stairs. 'I trust you will wait until my family and I have completed our toilette. We will not keep you long.'

'Do as you please, Madam.' His harsh laugh reverberates round the hall. 'However, dressed or not, your chambers are the first place we will look.' His lip curls as he gives a silent signal and four soldiers jostle us aside and climb the stairs.

'I assure you, sir, His Majesty is not within these walls.' Mother appears to change her mind about leaving.

Heavy footfalls resound on the floorboards, but no indignant squeals or scuffling come from above my head, indicating Cousin Henderson has got the girls out of the way.

In the hall, a soldier throws open the lid of a large chest and proceeds to haul items onto the floor. A rough blanket and leather bucket is piled atop a pair of boots of unknown ownership.

'Really, sir.' My gaze sweeps the officer with contempt. 'Do your men imagine the king would hide in a wooden box?'

His skin flushes above his neck, evident even in this low light. He snarls and orders the men away.

Ball bounces on his toes beside the disarray on the tiles, his fists clench in what I imagine is eagerness to restore order to the mess.

The search of the upper floor is of short duration, but thorough. As footsteps resonate across the boards, I avoid Mother's eye, lest our triumph show in our faces.

The soldiers clatter down the stairs, and one approaches his officer and whispers in his ear.

'Are you sure?' he barks. 'No sign at all?' He utters an oath under his breath.

'I think you should be aware,' Mother says, 'that we entertain Lord Cromwell and his family here quite regularly.'

'I am indeed, Mistress Murray.' The officer slaps his gloves against the palm of his hand. 'I am also informed you are Royalists and friends of Charles Stuart, which is why this was the first house we thought of.'

'Surely not the first,' I say, emboldened. 'There are many to choose from between here and Hampton. It is five miles.' Mother glares at me but I refuse to be silenced. The longer we keep them here the further away Lauderdale will get. 'You could always try the attics,' I say sweetly to the last man in line. 'I doubt you found them as they are well concealed.' I take a step toward him. 'I could show you if you wish.'

The man blinks in surprise, tucks in his chin and stares down his nose. 'Aye, if ye would, Mistress.'

'Fool!' The officer growls. 'If he was there, do ye think this chit would volunteer his hiding place?' He glares at me before hustling the rest of the line outside.

Chit! A rebel soldier referred to me, Lady Elizabeth Murray, as a chit!

'Have they gone?' Mother whispers at my shoulder.

I resist the urge to snap that she can see as well as I, but merely nod. 'Jack Ashburnham must have got his way and taken the king somewhere close.' I keep my voice low. 'I wonder where?'

'Wherever it is, I hope he does not live to regret not going to the continent.'

I am about to agree with her, but at that moment, my sisters appear and line up on the other side of the long table, their expressions full of questions. Somehow, Cousin Henderson has managed to get them dressed, despite the invasion of our chambers.

'The soldiers aren't coming back to live here, are they?' Meg's bottom lip quivers.

'No, pet.' Cousin Henderson reassures her.

'Is it true the king has escaped?' Katherine's eyes are bright and her cheeks so deeply flushed, she looks almost pretty.

'Apparently so.' Mother claps her hands. 'Summon a girl to lay the fires, would you, Ball. And tell cook we may as well break our fast early this morning. I doubt any of us will get more sleep this night.'

'Yes, my lady.' His mouth curls into a knowing smile as he withdraws.

'Not for me, Mother. I am not hungry.' I head toward the stairs before she can question me further. How can I eat? All I want to do is lie on my bed and conjure the feel of Earl Lauderdale's kiss, which I fervently hope will not be our last.

Chapter 28

The neighbourhood seethes with rebels who search every outbuilding and even the boats on the river for the runaway monarch. Each hour have I spent in a fever of anxiety, for both Lauderdale and the king.

On the second day, chance takes me past the upper landing window at the same time as a horseman canters through the gates. I speed down to meet him, convinced he carries a letter from the earl.

'Give that to me!' I thrust a hand at Ball as he closes the door on the messenger.

Beneath my hasty fingers, the seal breaks into speckles of red wax that litter the floor. The first lines contain no personal word for me, only bland statements about the king's escape.

'You are over eager, my dear,' Mother says from behind me.

Startled, I swing round, peeved at the interruption for I have not finished reading. 'I-I hoped it was news of His Majesty.'

She ignores the letter and continues to stare at me. 'You do not deceive me, Betty. Your eagerness is entirely for the sender, not his message.' Her gaze settles on the footmen on either side of the door and a maid who cleans ash from the fireplace. With a finger held up for silence, she beckons me into the salon.

'You are mistaken, Mama,' I insist when she closes the door. 'Lauderdale says-'

'Lauderdale could say the queen arrives for dinner this evening and you would believe him.'

My face grows hot. 'You do not trust the earl?'

'He has proved himself. My concerns are for you.'

'What do you mean?'

'I merely offer you a warning. Do not fall in love with that man.'

I attempt a light laugh, but my hands shake. 'How can you think such a thing? We owe him a debt of gratitude. Not only for his help in keeping Father out of prison, but his efforts the other evening.'

'Gratitude would not put such sparkle into your eyes.' She nods at the paper in my hand. 'What does he say?'

'That the king has reached the Isle of Wight.'

'Let me see.' She takes it from me and scans the page, one thumb pressed to her lower teeth. 'Lauderdale is a clever man. He writes as if shocked at the king's escape. That the governor of the island, Colonel Robert Hammond, has taken His Majesty to Carisbrooke Castle.'

'You make it sound as if he's a prisoner again.'

'Exactly.' Her chin lifts and her eyes flash. 'Ashburnham and Berkeley must have imagined Hammond was a sympathiser.' Her anger shifts to the paper that she shoves toward me. 'It seems they miscalculated.'

I take the letter back. 'It says here Hammond invited the king as his guest. You think that was a ploy?' At her nod, I slump onto a sofa by the window, one elbow propped on the wooden arm to massage my temple. 'Then it was all for nothing?'

'Not nothing.' She comes to stand beside me, a hand resting on my back. 'The army have been spared the task of transferring their captive to a more secure prison.'

'Such cynicism, Mama.' My voice rises at her easy acceptance of what to me is a disaster. 'The king was supposed to gather his supporters and march to London, take control of the capital and dismiss those rogues in Parliament.'

'There will always be rogues in Parliament.' She gives a weary sigh and massages the tense space between my shoulders. 'I must send word to your father and tell him the plan failed.

'You are giving up on King Charles?'

'Not at all. There remains hope for the negotiations with Parliament, and failing that, the Scots.'

'Huh! As if either Parliament or the army will trust the king now. By running away he has shown he has no intention of giving in to their demands.'

Mother sighs. 'We all have disappointment in our lives, Betty. We must endure them with fortitude.'

'You're no longer speaking about the king, are you?' I blink back tears, conscious of the crumpled page in my hand that bears *his* name.

'I can see why Earl Lauderdale fascinates you,' she whispers. 'He is strong, brave and fearless in his pursuit of a noble cause that touches your heart.'

'Like Father.' Now I realise why I admire him. Because he is exactly how I imagine my father must have been as a young man. Vigorous and determined with a wicked gleam in his eye. Though as far as I know, Father's hair was never red.

'In some ways, yes.' She stares off into the distance as if conjuring a memory of younger days. Then she drops onto the sofa next to me, the warmth of her thigh against mine comforting. 'Lauderdale is admirable, ambitious and manly, but he is dangerous, my dear. You must not see him again.'

I whip my head up to face her, shocked. 'My association with Earl Lauderdale is entirely innocent.'

Her expression softens. '*Now* it is. That he is out of your reach due to the fact he has a wife is some consolation. However, he may make you dissatisfied with what God grants you.' She smoothes back a curl on my temple. 'There are few fates worse for a woman than to be an unhappy wife.'

Is that what Mother sees for me? That I shall be wife to one man but spend my life yearning for another? Such a fate had not occurred to me. I did not seek John's admiration, but even the sound of his name makes my heart jump wildly in anticipation. To hear his voice again, and have him smile and make jokes about being my lover are enough to sustain me through whatever fate awaits me. Are those not innocent flirtations? Or is Mother right, and I tempt danger?

I am not like my friend Ann Fanshawe. To follow a man through the worst privations life offers yet remain devoted. Self-sacrifice is not part of my nature. I will take my place in society as the wife of a great man, not the mistress of a disgraced one.

I swallow the lump in my throat and inhale slowly. 'I understand, Mama. Sir Lionel Tollemache will never have reason to feel I am not wholly devoted to him.'

Mother pats my hand and rises. 'I knew you would see sense. I will ensure Lauderdale does not come to Ham again until after your wedding.'

The click of the door closing behind her makes me wince. The sound so loud in the silent room, I liken it to the seal I must put on my heart if I am ever to know contentment.

* * *

May 1648

Spring has not yet come to Richmond, though bluebells struggle through wet earth beneath the trees on the riverbank. A blustery wind and frequent showers chase away any warmth this May brings, but the house is wonderfully warm for the first time since the war began. As a special concession to our guest, Mother ordered every fire in the house lit to banish the musty damp of a long winter.

Sir Lionel Tollemache arrived three days ago, bringing with him no fewer than six servants, not to mention his coachman, two lackeys, four footmen and six armed outriders.

Mother's initial dismay at having to provide board for so many is tempered by the fact Sir Lionel included in his luggage enough beef, mutton, chickens, wine and cheese from his Suffolk estate to feed us all for a year.

'I would not have you put to extra hardship on my account, my dear lady.' He grasped Mother's hand in both of his and planted a slow, almost amorous kiss on her hand.

Blushing furiously, Mother threw me a look, which clearly said she hoped I would value the prize I have in this paragon.

She is right. Sir Lionel is a most charming, unaffected young man with an even temperament and a desire to please. He traverses the gardens from one end to the other at a frustratingly slow pace I have never been able to master, whilst teasing my sisters and listening to their girlish chatter as if their every word holds divine inspiration. All this, without a second's display of impatience for their infirmities.

He sat for an entire afternoon to enable Joan Carlisle to complete our engagement portrait. I say sat, but she painted him standing at my left, his unruly sandy hair slightly awry and a boyish line of bristles gracing his top lip.

It is indeed a charming portrait, with little Meg seated to my

331

right, like a tiny version of me.

Sir Lionel even consulted with Mother as to where the picture should be hung to best advantage.

His attentions to me cannot be faulted, although a more gullible soul than I could easily be led to believe they were the most beautiful, clever and animated young woman he has ever met. He tells me daily that my eyes and hair are perfection, and that even my walk and tiny waist have him dreaming of me every night.

Had anyone told me I would attract such a devoted suitor, I would have dismissed them, convinced I would find such overblown compliments tedious beyond measure.

I do not. Lionel is like a puppy eager to please, and I am more than happy to cast him a careless favour or a kind remark here and there. The fact he is impressively rich enhances his attractiveness, and I cannot help hoping his infatuation does not diminish with time.

Only one shadow mars my anticipation of our wedding. The press of his lips, on my hand, or the feel of an arm around my waist when he thinks no one is looking; even a stolen kiss in the hallway sends a tiny pang of regret into my chest that he is not John.

John. Either he has no desire to see me again, or Mother was true to her promise that day in November. He has not been near, although I have received three letters from him over the course of these last months. Discreet but formal missives that contain news of the king's continuing talks with the Scots. One came from Carisbrooke Castle, to assure me His Majesty is in good health and that he and his fellow Scots are granted audiences to discuss their terms.

His letters are welcome, but at the same time disappointing, for his correspondence is bland. Apart from a few kind remarks for my loyalty and assistance, a reference to my bravery and a compliment or two for my mother, I may show them to anyone I choose without fear of misinterpretation.

I keep them wrapped in linen and read them once a day; a secret cache that takes on more self reproach now my betrothed is in the house. A childish spite tempts me to write to John and extol the virtues of the man who is to be my husband, but common sense prevents me, and once written, I consign them to the fire.

The door flies open and I shove the parcel of letters into the back of a drawer and slide it closed.

'Why are you sitting here alone, Elizabeth?' Cousin Henderson enters with a pile of clean and folded linen shifts that she arranges on shelves in the press. Even my cousin has to help with the laundry since Sir Lionel arrived, for our servants are run ragged with all the extra work.

'I am granted a respite from my bridegroom's adoration.' I push aside thoughts of John and offer the bright smile expected of a bride. 'Sir Lionel insisted on calling on the Carlisles this morning.'

'Ah, yes. The portrait. I believe it is finally finished?'

'He claimed the right to fetch it, though I suspect he judged it a good opportunity to take a ride out in Richmond Park. He is a great hunter, and takes pleasure in exercising his own horses.'

'You must be looking forward to being the mistress of Helmingham.' She perches on the end of my bed. 'From Sir Lionel's description last night at dinner, anyone would envy you such a luxurious home.'

'I long to see it,' I say truthfully. 'Though I shall miss Ham dreadfully.' My gaze sweeps the room where I have spent most of my childhood. 'It will be strange to live anywhere else.'

'I doubt you will stay away long.' She regards me with knowing eyes.

'What choice do I have?' A bitterness I was unaware of until now creeps into my voice. 'As Lady Tollemache, it is my duty to reside at my husband's family estate.'

'Noble words, Elizabeth.' She folds her hands before her and regards me with the same expression I have seen often on Mother's face. 'I'm willing to wager you will be back here within a twelvemonth.' I have no time to contradict this assertion before she speaks again. 'And it will be a relief to see you married at last.'

'Why so, Cousin?' Does she mean for myself, or the future of Ham?

Her restless fingers pleat and then straighten her skirt. 'This last winter has been difficult for you. I fear you have been unsettled, preoccupied.'

'You fear, Cousin?' I raise a brow and she appears to regret her presumption.

Her complexion reddens. 'Your Mother has been concerned for you, since. . .'

'Since what?' Though I know to what she refers. Since I last saw Earl Lauderdale.

I hold her gaze, daring her to mention his name.

She does not.

'Well.' She avoids my eye and turns to leave, only to hesitate at the door. I anticipate she is about to say more, but something distracts her and she cocks her head. 'I think I hear a carriage outside.'

'It is probably Sir Lionel returning.' I rise and brush past her, grateful for a reason to quit her company. It is all I can do not to snap that she broaches a subject which does not concern her, but she would carry such an outburst straight back to Mother.

I reach the bottom of the stairs at the same moment Ball admits our returning guest. Aware of Cousin Henderson close behind me, I arrange my face into a bright smile of welcome.

The figure who enters the staircase hall is not Sir Lionel.

His cloak flaps as he strides in and hands his cane and gloves to Ball, his wide brimmed hat with its swooping black feather effectively hiding his face.

I know that walk, and have imagined that voice often as he laughs and stamps his boots on the floor. 'Good day to ye, Ball. And a terrible dreadful journey tae get here.'

I rush forward and throw myself into his arms. 'Father!'

Any second now, word will travel through the house like fire and I will have to share him with my mother and sisters; so I savour this moment when he is entirely mine. I bury my chin in his cloak that smells musty and sour from the road. His chin sports a day-old beard and he is in need of a hot bath. I do not care. Father is home.

His arms close round me and he chuckles deep in his throat. 'And how is ma little bride?'

'We thought you were in Paris!' I pull back and stare at him. 'How did you get here? Is it safe? Are you not being hunted by-'

334

'Enough, enough. I shall answer all your questions in due time.' He twists his cloak from around his shoulders and throws it carelessly into a beaming Ball's arms. His hat goes the same way and as the steward bears them off, Father looks past me to where Cousin Henderson stands.

'Ah! My dear, Anne. You do look well.'

She bobs a shy curtsey. 'I am so glad to see you safe, sir. I will go and tell the Mistress immediately.' She turns and disappears back up the stairs.

'She looks as she always does,' I whisper, 'like a red squirrel.' I repeat the family joke Father devised when she arrived from Scotland with her indelicate colouring and small round eyes.

Father slings a muscular arm round my shoulders and draws me into the front salon.

'What's this?' He takes up a stance before the fireplace, warming his rear. 'Fires in May? What is yer mither thinking of?'

'They are for the comfort of our guest.' I perch on a sofa arm, drinking in the sight of him, from the grubby linen at his throat, to his frayed cuffs.

'Aye, of course. Tollemache is here, then? And when is the wedding?'

'You do not know?' I tease. 'When you have spent months handling the settlement?'

'Aye, well. I left the final arrangements tae your mither.'

'It is in three days.' A thought occurs to me that wipes away my pleasure at his unexpected arrival. 'Will you be able to stay that long?'

He nods, smiling. 'Not come tae see ma Betty wed? How could ye think it of me?'

'And Ham will be safe.'

'Aye, there is that.'

'Is it dangerous for you to be here, Father? Are they looking for you?' A knot forms in my stomach at the thought this visit would be as brief as all the others.

'Nay, Ahm safe enough. I cannae be implicated in the king's escape frae Hampton, and no one can prove I hae been in contact wi' him since then.'

335

'If it wasn't for that awful man, Hammond, His Majesty may be free even now.'

'Ah, he's nae so bad. Hammond's an honourable soul. He does his best to keep the king safe from both Parliament and the army, and treats him more as a guest than a prisoner.'

I tuck in my chin, surprised. 'How do you know such things, if you have had no correspondence with them?'

His slow wink tells me all I need to know. 'Keep this tae yer'self, my dear. But I hae joined Lauderdale and the Engagers.'

The earl's name on his lips makes my pulse race. I dip my head so he cannot see my flushed cheeks. 'What exactly is this *Engagement*, Father?' I ask, though I know full well the details from John's letters. I also know the original document was buried in a lead casket in Carisbrooke Castle garden to keep it away from prying Roundhead eyes.

He slides onto the wooden bench, my hand in his. 'It means King Charles has agreed tae enforce Presbyterianism in England for the next three years, in return for a military alliance with the Covenanters.'

'You are no Covenanter!'

He shrugs. 'Semantics, Betty. I'll do whatever it takes tae get the king back on his throne.'

'And you think the Scots will achieve this, after everything?' He hesitates and I press on. 'Has he not already refused similar terms when they formed part of the *Newcastle Proposals*?'

'Another day, another agreement.' Father shrugs. 'What else will bring an end to all this infighting? We may not have Lord Leven or David Leslie, but the Duke of Hamilton will make a more than adequate commander.'

'Commander of what? Another invasion?' The thought makes my stomach lurch. And how long this time will Father stay friends with Hamilton, a man he was happy to see killed? 'Hasn't there been enough bloodshed?'

'I am no more eager than you fer more fighting,' he says wearily. 'But how else are we tae restore the king? The Engagement guarantees Scotsmen greater influence in government and they undertake to bring the king to London to negotiate a personal

336

treaty with the Westminster Parliament.'

'Negotiate,' I cannot help a snort escaping. 'King Charles won't negotiate, and he's steadfastly refused to take the Covenant. He will never accept he is not the head of the kirk, so what chance is there he'll honour this agreement?'

His gaze shifts from mine and his shoulders slump, but he is prevented from answering when the door opens and Mother sails across the room to embrace him. 'I knew you would not miss the wedding, but I dared not hope.'

I mouth 'later' to him over her shoulder and back out of the room, just in time for my sisters to arrive in a flurry of coloured silk and squeals of delight.

In the hall, Sir Lionel Tollemache hands his cloak and hat to Ball.

'Ah, Elizabeth, there you are.' He beckons to two footmen who manhandle Joan's painting through the door. 'Careful there, it's a precious thing.' He whips the hessian covering from the canvas with a flourish. 'Is it not a fine piece of work?'

'It is indeed.' His enraptured face indicates his belief in what he says. 'You look very handsome in it.'

He takes my hand in both of his. 'It is only the first of many I hope to commission during our marriage, Elizabeth.'

'Perhaps Master Peter Lely may be willing to paint me again.' I say, delighted that I no longer have to worry about the fee that gentleman will charge.

Chapter 29

New shoots struggle through wet brown earth, and wildflowers dapple the meadows and woods with points of colour as spring comes out of hiding for my wedding day.

I dress in a white silk gown with a slashed skirt, Honiton lace at the neckline and sleeves held back by white silk ribbons tied above the elbows. Parted in the middle, my hair hangs loose with a crescent of intertwined thyme, rosemary and parsley flowers on my head, tiny pearls attached to the edges.

'You look beautiful, my dear, and quite virginal. Exactly as a bride should be,' Mother says, making me wince.

A virginal bride is not an image I relish, nor any others that consign me to being a weak, malleable female. As the new Lady Tollemache, I intend to be a woman in charge of her own destiny, a sentiment I convey to Anne Henderson, who hushes me with a sharp hiss. 'You must not say your new name aloud before the vows are said. It tempts the spirits who may then ensure it never happens.'

I dismiss her foreboding with disdain, though remain silent, unwilling to upset her today, of all days.

My sisters burst through the door, all flying hair and flushed cheeks. Mother urges quiet, but nothing dampens their noisy enthusiasm. Mother must have bought an entire mile of white ribbons from the haberdasher, as it is in evidence everywhere in the house. No one dare pause for too long in case she ties another strand around a waist or to a sleeve.

They have never attended a wedding before, and today all three look the prettiest I have ever seen them. In white silk with sprigs of rosemary and wildflowers in their curls, they each carry tussie mussies of thyme, bluebells, rosemary and feverfew.

'What a shame it is too early for lavender,' Mother laments, pouncing on Meg and winding another yellow flower into her hair.

Kate is less melancholy these days, and endures Mother's

ministrations with patience. With her counsel and Nan's sympathy, I hope Kate has come to realise her rebel lover's interest was merely a diversion and not true love at all.

'Is my Elizabeth ready?' Father appears at my door, eliciting another wave of giggling from the girls. 'The Carlisles have been here an hour and Bishop Duppa is restless.'

'My lord Bishop will wait a little longer.' I take Father's outstretched arm. 'It is but a small price to pay for his supper.'

'I am so relieved the soldiers have gone from the house.' Mother ushers the girls into place behind me. 'They would insist the wedding take place in St Peters Church during Sunday service, where the entire congregation could gawp at my Betty.'

I enter the gilt-and-gold state apartment on Father's arm, where Lionel fidgets beside the fireplace in a pale blue silk suit. He tugs down his jacket points, coughs and shifts his feet. Is it nerves, or do his new heeled shoes with the jewelled buckles pinch?

The wedding party stands at one end of the long room, while a long table sits at the other in preparation for our wedding breakfast.

We exchange our vows; Lionel in a hesitant, low tone while my responses are clear and unfaltering. The lengthy sermon on which Bishop Duppa then embarks has me suppressing a yawn. My mind wanders and I make plans for the salon beside the staircase hall. When Ham is entirely mine, I will have panelling installed and turn it into a chapel.

'Elizabeth,' Father hisses, nudging me. 'It is time to complete the signing of the contract.' He gathers the three stone-faced strangers at the back of the room to the signing table. The two lawyers, and an executor produce a daunting pile of documents from a leather bag.

Father hands me a goose quill pen, and I add my signature to Lionel's at the bottom of each page. When I feel we must surely be finished, the lawyer produces yet another.

'You are content, Elizabeth?' Father asks, pouring sand on the damp ink that effectively hands Ham and its lands over to Lionel and me.

'I am indeed, Father,' I reply, aware he does not refer solely to my new husband.

The formalities complete, we withdraw to the table where a raised wooden block covered with linen runs down the centre to give height to the gathered dishes. Platters of sliced roasted beef, pork and lamb jostle with dishes of braised onions, carrots, sallets with tiny crystallised mimosa and crocus flowers for decoration. Tureens of soup, pyramids of fruits, puddings and pies vie for attention between dishes of caudle, spiced fruits, nuts and the finest white bread.

In the centre stands a white sugar subtlety fashioned in the shape of Ham House, complete with chimneys and bow windows at both front and back.

Bunches of herbs tied with more white ribbon lay scattered at intervals along the cloth, while others hang on strings from the windows.

'One would not know the war is over.' Lodowick Carlisle's fingers flex, ready to grapple with the food. 'There are still soldiers in Kingston and Richmond. Though I have to admit they appear less self-assured and are not so arrogant as they once were.'

'They have a fight of their own on their hands.' Father flicks up the back of his coat before sitting. 'Royalists are the least of their problems at the moment.'

'What are these problems, Father?' Nan asks, surprising me with her enthusiasm. I was not aware she took more than a passing interest in the war.

'Lodowick refers to the recent debates at Putney church,' Father replies.

'I do not feel talk of John Lilburne and his Levellers are appropriate for my wedding breakfast,' I say, glaring at Father, who ignores me and pours himself another glass of wine.

'The debates settled little,' Father goes on. 'Apart from establishing man suffrage.'

'Not every man.' Nan deliberately avoids my eye. 'Those without property are excluded, as are servants, apprentices, foreigners and beggars.'

'You forgot women,' I add. Despite my wish this discussion be abandoned, I refuse to be left out. 'Women cannot vote either.'

'Well, naturally.' Lionel looks up from his plate with mild surprise. 'Even the Levellers would never give such power to the female sex.'

His patronising tone makes me sit straighter. Does he take us women for weak, pliable creatures with no will of our own? If so, he is in for a shock.

'The grandees have a disturbing solution for their problem with the king,' Lodowick says through a full mouth.

Father nods sagely. 'Aye, Cromwell and Ireton want tae put him on trial for treason.'

'They wouldn't dare!' Kate gasps, her knife held in mid-air.

'What a ridiculous notion.' Mother signals to the footmen to clear the empty plates and bring the full ones into our guests' reach. 'What sort of court would set itself high enough to impeach a sovereign? It cannot happen.' She holds out a plate to Lionel. 'Have you tried this beef, my lord? It is simmered in red wine for richness.'

'You serve an excellent table, Mistress Murray,' Lionel says, eyeing the plate hungrily. 'I appreciate well-reared meat cooked in a wholesome manner.'

'Has he forgotten this meat was reared at Helmingham?' Kate whispers at me across the table. 'He is eating his own food.'

'Hush!' I glare at her before directing an insistent look toward Father. 'Do you know how King Charles fares?'

'Carisbrooke Castle is a poor comparison to Hampton.' Father hacks a slice of pork from a joint with his knife. 'He plays bowls on the green on the barbican, takes Rogue his spaniel, and Gypsy his greyhound, for walks round the castle walls. He is also gracious to those with scrofula who beg to be touched for the King's Evil. So Earl Lauderdale tells me in his letters.'

Startled at the unexpectedness of John's name, I fumble my knife. It clatters onto the table bringing the conversation to an abrupt end. All eyes remain on me as a footman wipes the implement on a cloth and hands it back to me.

'We met the earl last year.' Mother breaks the silence, casting me a swift warning look. 'Did I not mention it in my correspondence?'

'You did, my dear.' Father beams at her across the long table.

'Lauderdale sends me frequent and detailed reports of his meetings with His Majesty.'

Lionel reaches for his own knife, and his hand brushes my arm. His touch and smiling face remind me John is the last person I should be thinking of today. I smile back and push Lauderdale into the recess of my mind.

'When will the army free the king?' Katherine asks.

'As to that.' Father sighs, twirling his glass between his fingers. 'His rejection of the Four Bills, and his secret negotiations with the Engagers have tested Parliament's temper. They have decreed no more approaches are to be made to the king.'

'The negotiations are at an end?' Like a child denied a treat, Joan Carlisle's mouth turns down in comical dejection.

'In that case, the king is likely to abide by this treaty with the Scots. Is he not?' I speak for Lauderdale's sake, worried that if the Engagers' agreement fails, the army may decide the earl is another foreign enemy. He could be arrested, or worse, put on trial for treason.

'We can only hope,' Father says. His faraway gaze does not inspire confidence. 'What say you, Sir Lionel?' He sits back in his chair to regard Lionel steadily. 'Do you think the king will honour his agreement with the Engagers?'

'I have no opinion on the matter, sir.' Sir Lionel plucks my hand from my lap and tucks it beneath his elbow. 'I have a more agreeable future to look forward to.'

Aware his soft gaze is levelled on my profile, I stare straight ahead. Our wedding feast is not the time to display my contempt at his blatant disinterest.

'You do not care if the king does not return to his throne?' Kate voices my own silent question, her wide blue eyes fixed on her new brother-in-law.

I spot Mother's well-aimed elbow and Kate's wince.

Sir Lionel shrugs. 'I am no courtier, merely a country gentleman, content to hunt my woods and attend church unhindered. The rest can be decided by greater men than I.'

An uneasy silence accentuates the sound of clinking glass and scraping of spoons on plates.

Father nods, wipes the grease from his fingers and flings the napkin over his shoulder with a flourish. 'I think we understand yer position, ma lord.' He lifts the wine jug to shoulder height. 'More wine, Sir Lionel?'

'I would like some too, please.' I use the act of reaching for my goblet as an excuse to remove my arm from Lionel's. Somehow a distance has opened between us that disappoints me.

John would never have answered in such a casual, self-interested way. He would bring his fist down upon the table and declare his belief with uncompromising directness, that His Majesty must be king; once he agrees to more liberty for other faiths.

A shiver of trepidation runs through me. What kind of man have I married? Then the Devil on my shoulder whispers in my ear that his detachment from politics is exactly why my parents chose him.

I cannot have everything.

The bedding ceremony is over, garters thrown, possets drunk and giggling sisters ushered away. Lionel and I sit like bookends beneath the covers as footsteps recede along the corridor.

The hallway falls quiet and he leans back against the pillows, one arm flung carelessly above his head, his shirt open at the neck to reveal pale, flawless skin.

'Have you any idea how long I have awaited this moment?' he says on an expelled breath. He invites me closer with his eyes, but I do not move, pinned to the bed by the heavy coverlet over my knees and an unaccustomed shyness.

'Since your arrival at Ham? Or before?'

'Since we first met.'

'That long?' I pat the mattress with a surreptitious hand, hoping the maids obeyed instructions to tighten the ropes. With both of us in here we could well sag onto the floor.

With one brow raised, and a smile on his lips, Lionel slips an arm beneath me and with surprising strength, pulls me onto his side of the bed.

There is nothing boyish or hesitant about the lips that crush mine in a kiss so firm, so possessive and demanding, my breath leaves me in a rush of desire. Arms I imagined as slender and girlish prove muscular and wrap tightly round me. My tongue explores his mouth where a tantalising, yet elusive taste of wine lingers.

Having cast my new husband as a sweet, gentle boy, this ardour comes as a startling, yet welcome surprise. Am I expected to return my husband's touch? Or should I resist a little lest he regard me wanton?

The question is answered at the touch of his strong fingers, tentative, yet urgent, as they tug my cambric nightgown from my shoulders.

Gently, I push him away, one finger pressed to his lips in a promise. 'You will tear the fabric. Allow me to remove it.' After the hours my sisters spent embroidering the tiny blue flowers on the neck and hem I will not have it spoiled.

He assents with a smile and leans back against the pillows again, propped on one elbow with a hand beneath his head. I slide from beneath the covers, twisting to look at him over one shoulder; while he watches me through half closed lids.

My fingers shake as I fumble with the ribbons, anticipation making me clumsy. I have seen such admiration before on the faces of young men when they look at me, but none have been half dressed and in my bed.

The knot loosens, and the fabric slides down my body to form a soft puddle around my bare feet. Naked now, but not at all shy, I scoop the robe from the floor and discard it carelessly on a chair where it will come to no harm.

He smiles, lifts a languorous hand and pulls aside the coverlet, beckoning me into the pristine whiteness of the bed.

Now he is all urgency and grasping hands as he covers my mouth with his, one leg slung protectively across my hips. I can barely breathe and pull away, but he seems not to notice and buries his face in my neck. His firm lips explore my shoulders and move down to my breasts with kittenish mewling that turns into throaty groans.

'You are so beautiful, Bess,' he says, then straddles me and leans up on his elbows. 'I have never loved any woman more than I love you. And that is not a bad thing in a marriage do you not think?' His passion turns to breathless gabbling and I have to bite my lip to prevent a laugh. Why should I care how many girls he has tumbled before? At least then one of us would know what we are about.

'It depends upon how many women you have loved, Lionel.'

His face hovers inches above mine, his unruly sandy hair loose on his shoulders. 'Hardly any at all, I mean, only-'

'I do not really wish to know, husband. What is important, is that you married me.'

His face relaxes, relieved. 'Yes, yes of course. That is what matters.'

A wave of tenderness uncurls to send sparks into my blood. I snuggle closer, my lips brushing the hollow of his throat. I doubt I am in love with this man, but I am determined this marriage will be a success. I will be the only one who will own his heart. In time, perhaps he will also own mine.

I grip his shirt with urgent fingers and tear the seam.

He throws back his head with a laugh, hauls the ruined garment over his head and hurls it into a corner. His arms close round me and I tuck my body beneath his.

Lionel is not a heavy man, but his weight atop me makes my blood fizz with longing. Now I understand why my hound bitch's tongue lolls when the dog mounts her; his weight on her hindquarters is a primal signal of what is to come.

I grit my teeth in anticipation, but Lionel balances on his hands on either side of my head, his gaze roving my face with a pleased smile on his full lips.

Why does he wait?

His scrutiny makes me nervous. Have I missed part of this ritual between a man and a woman? If so, how can Lionel expect me to understand, for he knows me to be a virgin, despite my advanced age?

He exhales gently, and his lips come down on mine, releasing his full weight upon me, one knee prising my legs apart.

His hand moves between my thighs and I release a gasp of shock at the unfamiliar, yet pleasing sensation. A small moan

345

escapes my lips as my teeth scrape the soft, white flesh between his neck and shoulder. In response to his probing fingers, something happens within me, unfamiliar but urgent. Lionel's soft words and gentle touch make my nerves jump. My temper shortens. I no longer require admiration or love, only the sating of this strange burning that creeps into my belly. Or is it not my belly, but somewhere deeper? Whatever the truth of it, there grows a need that I need him to fulfil.

If only he would stop talking. I grasp his head in my hands and stare into his eyes. 'Yes, my Lionel. I hear your words of love.' I wind my hands into his soft hair and tug sharply. 'But it is past time for talk, I need you, now.'

My breathing quickens and I dig my fingernails into his clammy skin, inhaling the animal, male smell of him.

'What a lioness you are, my Bess,' he whispers beside my ear.

'And you, my lord, torture me.' I force the words through gritted teeth, seeking release for this urgent burn within.

He chuckles, and at last, fills that aching space inside me. A sharp pain makes me tense and bite my bottom lip. I suppress a cry for fear he takes it for anguish and stops.

Slowly he begins to move, building to a strong rhythm, while I grip his taut buttocks in both hands in a bid to prolong the waves of rushing blood that makes my head spin. Before I can raise my hips to meet his rapid thrusts, he groans and holds still.

Confused, I wriggle beneath him in search for that elusive, tingling jab that lasted but a few seconds.

Lionel raises himself on his hands and plants a brief kiss on my nose, before rolling away. He collapses onto his back, arms raised and gives a deep sigh.

I brush hair from my face and turn on my side, giving Lionel the same scrutiny he gave me moments earlier. Is the consummation complete? Am I a wife now? If so, I am a nervy, trembling one.

Lionel sighs again and pushes a hand through his sandy hair. He reaches for my hand and brings my fingertips to his lips. 'My own Bess. My wife,' he whispers, answering one of my questions.

In seconds, he snuffles in his sleep and emits a tiny snore.

Wakeful, I lay staring at the canopy above my childhood bed

and recall my talk with Mother the night before.

If that was an example of a *'woman's exquisite destiny'*, either I have a great deal to learn, or Mother left something out.

Chapter 30

Our boxes are loaded onto Sir Lionel's carriage which stands on the drive in readiness for our journey to Suffolk. Farewells to my family comprise tears shed, lingering hugs and promises to write, repeated endlessly during a protracted leave-taking. Finally, the Tollemache carriage rolls down the drive and I lean back against the upholstery with a sigh.

Lionel sprawls beside me, his arm draped across the back of the seat and his knees apart. His pose so masculine, I cannot help but smile. No lady could defy her stays in such a way.

I ease further into the corner and he scrambles upright, instantly apologetic.

'I am unused to travelling with a lady,' he indicates the empty seat opposite. 'Do you wish me to move?'

'Please, no. I like to have you beside me,' I say, and mean it. 'I adore the way everyone stops to watch us go by in the knowledge I am your wife. For a while I wondered if this day would ever come, but now it has . . .' I leave the thought hanging in the hopes he will take it up and give it due consideration. I intend to be appreciated.

'Do you recall,' he says, 'that day when my passionate heart prompted me to call upon you at Ham House. What year was it? Forty-five, forty-six?'

'Forty-five.'

His benign smile endears him to me. Like a boy pretending to be a man. And yet he is a man. He is a baronet and my husband.

'I imagined we were doomed never to see this day,' Lionel continues, reassuring me I was not the only one who railed against the obstacles that kept us apart, 'we have all been forced to make sacrifices during the war.'

'Indeed. Some more than most.'

He frowns, but as yet I am unwilling to explain Mother's constant fight with Parliament's Sequestors. In due time I shall expect him to unburden her of that particular debt. His life, spent far from the machinations of the war, has continued, comfortable and uninterrupted. How can he appreciate the terrors that have beset those who choose to remain loyal to our king?

'We make good time to Helmingham.' Lionel's fingers gently stroke the bare skin at the back of my neck. 'One night we will spend at Chelmsford and another in Ipswich. The rest will give us a chance to repeat the pleasures of our first night together.'

I wondered when he would broach the subject. 'As to that, Lionel.' I ease closer and press my bodice into his upper arm. 'I wish to talk about my role as a wife.'

He clears his throat. 'I know little of how women pass their day. My sisters-'

'Are not my concern at this moment. I refer to my duties in your bed.'

Lionel flushes and tugs his collar away from his throat. 'What can you mean, my love?' He has difficulty meeting my eye, but I am determined he will not brush me aside.

I snuggle closer, my fingers stroking his thigh. If his squirming is anything to go by, the fabric of his breeches proves no impediment to the sensation.

'I wish to know what pleases you, Lionel.' My voice takes on a wheedling quality I despise, but needs must in such a delicate situation. 'And in return, I expect you to explore what pleasures me.'

'Did-did I not please you last night, Bess?'

'Very much.' The lie slips easily from my tongue. 'But I cannot help feel that for a truly accomplished lover there is more. Much more. And if I am content in that particular area, then you will be too.'

The pale skin above his nose puckers, an indication I am learning to recognise of his confusion. 'I am quite satisfied with-'

'Trust me, Lionel.' I press a finger to his lips to silence him. 'You do not yet know what satisfaction means. I promise you.' I tuck my shoulder beneath his and rest my head on his chest, hoping I can fulfil my extravagant promise

While Mother assisted me in dressing for my journey this morning, I challenged her on the unremarkable night I had spent.

'A pleasant enough pastime, but hardly worth all the fuss,' I remarked, upon which she flushed and patted the coverlet and bid

349

me to sit.

Tentative at first, when she realised I was an eager pupil unlikely to fall into a horrified faint, she quickly fell into the role of sharer of secrets of the marriage bed. 'There is as much pleasure to be gained by both promise and anticipation as there is in fulfilment between a man and woman.'

'I am intrigued as to what a gently brought up lady like you may teach *me*, Bess,' Lionel says, mildly affronted.

'You shall see.' I am not certain myself, but as Mother said, I must pay attention to what his body tells me.

Unbidden, an image of John Lauderdale floats into my head. I doubt his women would need to explain how they wish to be taken by him. His touch would be neither tentative nor apologetic in his possession of a lover. He could stir a female heart with a mere look or a firm touch. He stirs mine. Something tells me John has the power to reduce a woman to a shivering, compliant vessel for his pleasure. And theirs.

I wrestle with the Devil on my shoulder who would have me judge my husband. If he lacks the skill to be masterful in our bed, I will teach him myself rather than pine for what he is not. That way lies only discontent.

'Besides, John already has a wife,' I murmur beneath my breath.

'What was that, my love?'

'Nothing, Lionel.'

* * *

'There!'

I jump at Lionel's explosive shout and haul myself upright, blinking sleep from my eyes. After three days on the road, my temper is short.

I yawn, peering through the window to the glimpse of a roof above a copse of trees, and then it disappears.

He clasps my hand tighter in both his and bounces on the seat beside me, one arm pointing out of the window. 'You will see in a moment, when we turn this corner. Look, Bess, look now or you will miss your first view of your new home.'

Fatigue holds me in its grip, but I summon a smile and obey, in order to please him for his beatific expression is that of a boy seeking approval.

At the end of a bridge, a moat surrounds the substantial half-timbered house built on a square that hints of an enclosed inner courtyard, set on its own island and surrounded by parkland.

Despite my silent vow to be unimpressed, I gasp at the scene before me. 'It is indeed a fine house, Lionel. And a moat, how wonderful!'

The carriage sways gently as we pound down the drive, the horses moving as one now they are on familiar ground.

'Of course we shall not live here.'

Instantly awake, I stiffen. 'Why ever not?' My demand dissolves into a muffling cough to cover the harshness of my voice. 'Is this house not your ancestral home?'

'Oh yes. The house has been here for three hundred years.' He appears not to notice my shock and keeps his gaze directed through the window. 'The Tollemaches are Normans, and for the first four hundred years lived near Ipswich. Their name then was Talemache.' He spells out the letters in slow, measured tones as if explaining to a child. 'It means 'purse bearer'. Hugh Talemache was Purse Bearer to the first King Henry.'

'My ancestors fought for both Henry the Second against the Welsh and Edward the First against the Scots,' Lionel prattles on, blithely unaware of my cramped muscles and painful hips. These seats are punishingly hard.

'You have not answered my question!' I snap, irritated at his talk of service to kings. We Murrays too are well thought of by royalty. The fact this king's position is discredited is, to my mind, merely temporary.

'Two Talemache knights fought at the Battle of Crécy in thirteen-forty-six.'

'Very interesting, my dear, but what about-?'

'Then in fourteen-eighty-seven, John Talemache married Elizabeth Joyce, the heiress of Helmingham, and his son Lionel also married a Joyce. So they moved to Helmingham.' He raises both hands in theatrical conclusion of his story.

'And Helmingham is where the Tollemache heirs have always lived?' I prime my mental musket and take aim.

'Why yes, of course.'

'Then surely it is just and right that the present earl should reside here?'

'Mother has arranged for the house at Fakenham to be opened and aired.' He looks hurt, as if his mother has gone to some monumental effort. 'It is but two miles from here.'

'Am I not Lady Tollemache now, Lionel? The mistress of Helmingham?' I keep my tone light and teasing, but inside I am furious. 'Aren't dowagers supposed to take the smaller estate house once their son and heir marries?' My hackles rise at the idea his mother, a woman I have never set eyes on, has banished us to an inferior property.

Lionel gives a self-conscious cough, and tugs at his cravat at his throat. My fingers itch to rip it away and hurl the cambric through the window, or tighten it further. Before I have decided which, Lionel grabs my hand.

'Indeed you are, my Bess,' he wheedles. 'But I couldn't expect Mama to quit the home she has known all her life.'

I snatch my hand away and lean back in my seat, unable to summon a single reason why he shouldn't insist she do exactly that. Had I been given some prior warning, I could formulate a plan, but this news leaves me floundering. If Lionel thinks I have left Ham to come and live in a merchant's house in the middle of a flat, featureless country miles from London, he suffers delusions.

My husband's gaze slews to mine and away again, his hands closed fists on his knees. This reaction makes me think this decision has caused some dispute between him and his mother, and at heart, I have no wish to make things worse.

Certainly not for myself.

'Dearest.' I run a hand up his sleeve and across his flushed cheek. 'If Fakenham is half as nice as the Hall, I shall like it very much.' At the same time I silently resolve this will be my last concession for some time.

'We shall spend a few days here at Helmingham first,' Lionel says as if offering me a consolation. 'My sisters have a wealth of advice to offer and Mother will teach you how to run a household.'

'I already know how to run a household, Lionel.' Are my cheeks as red as they feel? 'I have been doing that for years, with my mother often away and no man in residence at Ham.'

'I do not mean to insult your abilities, my dear,' Lionel stammers, the endearment false on his lips. He reaches for my hand again, but I slide it away before he can make contact. 'You need to be made aware of the traditions of Helmingham so you might introduce them at Fakenham.'

'Really?' I toss my head and stare out of the far window as the coach rumbles across the drawbridge and through the red brick arch into a square interior courtyard. 'Ham traditions will be more than good enough for this Fakenham place,' I say, my teeth clenched so tight, my jaw hurts.

Lionel stiffens in his seat. 'Oh, look! Mama has summoned the servants to greet us. Isn't that kind of her?'

'Not kind, Lionel, dear. It is exactly what I expect as the new Lady Tollemache.' *Has he forgotten he is an earl?*

He looks about to deliver another apology, or a rebuke. Whichever it is, he changes his mind at the last second and nods. 'Of course.'

A liveried footman strides forward and tugs open the door. Lionel hands me down from the carriage onto a gravel drive. Before he can step away from me, I tuck my arm through his and pull him tightly to my side.

Even this early in my marriage, I am aware of the importance of showing my husband's family who takes first place in his life.

It appears a small army is gathered outside the wide expanse of the house, old and young faces all turn to me as I approach. Aware this spectacle is contrived to ensure my humility, I lift my chin and take steady, unhurried steps toward the unremarkable-looking fair-haired woman I have singled out as my mother-in-law.

Elizabeth Tollemache has the bearing of a duchess, but without the beauty. Expensively attired in an embroidered gown that must have kept six seamstresses busy for months, her thin face and short-sighted eyes peer at me down an unremarkable nose. And is that a nervous tick beside her left eye? Good.

353

'Bess?' Lionel bends to whisper while we are still out of earshot. 'I would ask you not to contradict anything Mother says. For your peace of mind as well as mine.'

A sharp rejoinder hovers on my lips, but is swallowed and stored away for another time. I smile and press his arm harder against my bodice, delighted to see him redden.

'I will be no less than an exemplary wife, my dear Lionel.' *While it suits me.*

He exhales in relief, apparently unaware I have not acquiesced to his request. 'I'm so glad. If you comply with Mama in everything, you'll have no reason to be discontent.'

'Welcome to my home, Elizabeth.' I accept the outstretched hands of my new adversary. 'I hope you will be very happy here.' Her clipped words hold both challenge and condescension. 'I will instruct a servant to show you to your room.' Dismissing me, she takes Lionel's face between both her hands and presses papery lips to each cheek before snaking an arm round his waist. 'I have missed you so, my dear one.'

'I am sorry you chose not to attend our wedding, my lady,' I say loudly. 'You were more than welcome.' *And invited.*

Her hands fall to her sides and a sneer curls her pale lips. 'I am sure I do not need to tell you how restricted travel is in these times, dear girl.'

'Do call me Elizabeth, Lady Tollemache.'

'Very well, Elizabeth.' She spits the word between yellowing and uneven teeth, as if the fact we share a name is a slight. 'Besides,' a hand flutters to her throat, 'I doubt my constitution would stand a journey to the great stink.'

'Richmond is several miles from London.' I refuse to endure the insult. 'A beautiful country town, and quite fragrant.'

'Indeed?' She hesitates, as if trying to summon a suitable rejoinder. And fails.

Turning, I scan the faces of the assembled servants, from which an odd cough and mutter erupt, while some shuffle their feet. I raise a hand and address the sea of awestruck faces. 'I thank you for your welcome. Now you may all go.' I hold the gaze of several as they file past me, a silent threat directed at them that if any dare

354

show impatience before me again, they will feel the birch on their backs.

My mother-in-law gasps and a deep flush mottles her face and neck into near ugliness.

I resist a strong urge to laugh as the servants disperse, murmuring their thanks.

At least they recognise *I* am Mistress here. Or should be. And those who do not, soon will.

'Bess!' Lionel hisses in rebuke, as his mother latches onto his free arm.

I smile sweetly as the three of us enter a vast hall that glitters with glass and gilt.

'Lionel, this is quite magnificent!' I clutch his arm with both hands, having already learned the effect even the slightest physical contact has upon him. A mixture of bubbling desire and embarrassment he cannot hide or resist.

He glances down at an uninterrupted view of my décolleté, blinks and bites his bottom lip.

'Elizabeth,' my mother-in-law's voice shakes as she commands my attention, her gaze never leaving Lionel. 'Drake here will show you to your chamber.' She indicates a liveried footman, who bows.

Have a servant show me up? I think not.

'I cannot wait to see this wonderful bed you told me about, Lionel.' I peer adoringly into his face.

True to my promise, our two nights at roadside inns have proved more than educational. I think Lionel quite likes my taking the lead in our lovemaking. He obeys directions perfectly and seems to enjoy doing so.

'Did I?' Lionel blinks again. 'I cannot recall. But it is this way.' He slides his hand down my arm and grasps my hand, guiding me toward the stairs. We move too fast for his mother, who is left at the bottom clutching the newel post.

At the gallery, Lionel halts. 'We shall see you at dinner, Mother,' he calls down to the stiff-backed figure, alone in the hall, her face stony.

The metaphorical glove hits the flagstones with an inaudible slap.

'Our ancestors came to England from Avranches at the time of the Conquest.' My mother-in-law sweeps out of the dining hall after dinner and takes up the family history Lionel began in the carriage. 'That's in Normandy, you know. We have a history of serving kings.' She sniffs as she speaks, avoiding my eyes as if to convey I am barely tolerated.

'My father serves the present king, my lady,' I remind her. I may be the granddaughter of a clergyman, but my royal connections are as good as the Tollemaches. How many times will I need to remind her of that during our stay?

Fresh anger surges through me that this is only a visit. I should, by rights, be making my home here, and should banish the dowager to this Fakenham place.

Lionel steps closer as if about to take his mother's arm, but I slip mine through on his other side and hold him back. His gaze flicks between us for a second, then he takes the line of least resistance and remains at my side, putting us two steps behind his mother.

She drops back, tucks her hand through Lionel's other arm, and the three of us traverse the wide corridor. A lamb between two lionesses. Every few steps, Lady Tollemache rakes me behind Lionel's back with a withering stare. Giving thanks for the fact I do not blush easily, I turn my attention to the family portraits lining the walls.

She pauses beside a cabinet, where behind bevelled glass doors lies a handsome viol on a velvet cushion.

'Are you acquainted with John Rose, the viol maker, Elizabeth?' she says, peering at me down her nose. I hesitate, and her eyes darken with amusement. 'He made this instrument for Queen Elizabeth.' I suspect there is more and paste on a smile to accept her inflated pride. 'Her Majesty presented the instrument to our family for their service.'

Lionel snorts behind me. 'I fear great-grandfather got the worst of the bargain.'

She turns on him with a swish of her skirts. 'What can you

mean, Lionel? It was a gift, there was no bargain.'

'Of course there was, Mother.' Lionel winks at me, and a warm glow runs through me that he is not above making a joke at the expense of her pride. 'Queen Bess brought an entire entourage to Helmingham one summer, and all at the expense of her hosts. They ate and drank the storerooms dry in three weeks; rowed and wrecked boats in the moat and trampled the flowerbeds with the courtiers' drunken games.' He chuckles as we continue our stroll along the long hall - our company of three that threatens to become a habit. 'Father was glad to see the back of them. Took him months to put the house to rights again. And all he got for his trouble and expense was a viol.'

My mother-in-law pats her chest as if warding off an attack of something, most likely hysteria. 'I am sure your version is inaccurate, but I won't contradict you in front of your wife.' She puts unpleasant emphasis on the final word.

A rush of sympathy rises in my chest at the way she constantly berates my husband. Her affection for her only son seems to swing between casual contempt and cloying devotion. Her gaze lingers on him relentlessly, and yet at any dismissive remark, she bridles like a she-cat protecting her litter and lashes out with vinegar and vitriol.

'Wait until tomorrow,' Lionel says as we make our way to bed. It is still light and too early for me, but my mother-in-law insists they keep 'country hours'.

'Then you will meet my sisters. Well, the youngest two anyway, the others are at their own estates with their families.'

I offer a thin smile that I hope he mistakes for fatigue.

* * *

When I open my eyes the next morning, the space beside me in the massive bed lies empty, and a fluttering of panic enters my chest. Nothing is familiar in the room and it takes a moment for me to realise that I am not at home.

Well, not my home, not Ham.

I ease into a sitting position and freeze.

357

At the bottom of the bed stands a boy.

Not an ordinary boy, but one with a completely black face and shorn hair that sits in tiny curls all over his head. The object of my incredulous stare is dressed in the house livery, with a long coat of deep green and a lace cravat tied round his neck.

The figure moves, and I emit a sharp scream.

At that second, Lionel strides into the room from the direction of his dressing room.

'Screaming at this hour?' He gives a lascivious wink that reminds me our nocturnal lessons continue in earnest. His open enthusiasm stirs an excitement in my belly for the previous night, and this coming one.

'I have brought you a wedding gift.' He comes to stand behind the strange looking boy, both hands resting on his shoulders.

'Wh-where does he come from?' I clutch the covers over my exposed breasts.

'Barbados,' Lionel says with relish. 'I have an interest in a new venture there growing sugar cane. I expect it to be very profitable.' He pats the boy's tight black curls. 'Nero here is the son of one of my workers.'

I ease up onto my knees, arranging the coverlet around me to hide as much of my naked body as possible. 'His father did not mind that you brought him all this way to England?'

'Mind?' Lionel pours ale from a pitcher that sits on a side table, his boyish face lit by an incredulous laugh. 'The man is a slave. His children also belong to me.' He hands the ale to the boy and gives him a none-too-gentle shove. 'Give this to your Mistress, boy.'

The child Nero approaches me with slow, nervous steps.

'Th-thank you.' Gingerly, I take it from him. His hands are the same colour as his face, but the palms and fingernails are paler, almost pink. Intrigued, I study his features. I have never seen such dark, glowing skin. Is it warm to the touch?

Nero smiles for the first time and I jerk backward, startled by the combination of gleaming white teeth and the whites of his eyes visible around dark centres. He is less a child than I first thought, possibly about fourteen or so, with the beginning of muscles on his adolescent shoulders.

'When you say he is a gift to me, Lionel.' I drag my eyes away from Nero, who resumes a bland expression that betrays nothing. 'What exactly do you mean?'

'Quite simple, my dear. In Paris, Queen Henrietta has a negro page. She dresses him in silk robes and a turban. He follows behind her wherever she goes, to fetch things, and so on.'

'Is that so?' If Her Majesty has one, perhaps it would not appear strange for Lady Tollemache. 'Can he read?'

'Of course not, my dear.' Lionel guffaws, one hand balanced on a slim hip. 'Read indeed, he can barely speak.'

I take a sip from the ale and place it on the dresser beside me. 'Is that your home, Nero?' I enunciate every syllable. 'In Bar-ba-dos?'

'Oh, no,' Lionel answers for him. 'He and his parents were taken there from West Africa. On a slave ship.'

'I see.' I retrieve the goblet, burying my nose in its yeasty fragrance, unsure what to think.

Nero stands silent, his hands clasped in front of him, his gaze on the floor.

'How strange, and terrifying. To be dragged thousands of miles from everything you have known twice in such a young life.'

'Hmm?' Evidently bored, Lionel looks up from his examination of the items on my dresser and heads for the door. 'When he's full grown, I'll send him back to the plantation.'

The boy's head lifts at this, and something in those black pools shifts, revealing something beyond silent passivity.

There is nothing wrong with his ears.

Chapter 31

As I suspect, Fakenham is small, ancient and draughty. A half-timbered black and white house built in the last century set behind thick hedges with a neglected garden at the rear that resembles a meadow. The fires smoke, and the hangings and rugs are dust-filled and well past their best.

My mother-in-law claims a dozen servants were sent to make it ready for us, but I find that hard to believe. Either that, or her staff are lazy and as unimpressed by the house as I am.

I commanded them to begin again, and by mid-afternoon, every floorboard is covered with wet sand and orders issued that they be scrubbed until at least three shades lighter.

'I am sorry there are only eight bedchambers, Elizabeth,' Lionel laments from the doorway to the first-floor drawing room.

'Not to mention the poky kitchens and the lack of dressing rooms.' I sigh and slump down on a brocade sofa that has seen better days. 'How do you expect me to entertain in such a small house? The dining room will hold no more than eight people.'

'You are disappointed,' Lionel says with hurt surprise.

I cannot bring myself to castigate him further. He does not need a nagging wife, but a clever one. I force a smile onto my face and glide toward him. 'Oh, my dear, I am sorry to be fretful. This house-' I wave a hand at the room while with the other I stroke his cheek. 'I simply did not expect to begin my married life here.'

His blush and sharp intake of breath at my touch is more than gratifying.

'I do not know what I can do.' He shrugs, bewildered. 'We own no other properties larger than this one.'

My fingers drift to his neck. 'Helmingham is larger.'

He stiffens, disengages my hand and eases away. 'I have explained, my dear. I cannot oust Mother from the home she has known all her married life.

'I see. Although I have been removed from mine.'

'That is different, you are married now and . . . ' I do not linger to hear what else he has to say, and retreat to the room he laughingly calls our bedchamber.

The room faces the front of the house, a wide narrow window above waist height looks onto nothing more agreeable than a hedge. Its panes are uneven, the leading thin and the glass pitted and cracked in places.

The bed too is old and heavy; the ropes that hold the mattress in place need replacing. The hangings are new, for which I assume I have my mother-in-law to thank, but the chairs are mismatched and the dresser looks like something my own mother would have consigned to the outbuildings for firewood.

I sigh again in self-pity, my rear resting on the ugly dresser to survey the room. It is then I realise I am not alone. The boy Nero stands at the door, his unwavering gaze levelled at me.

'Have you nothing to do?' I snap, uneasy at his silent scrutiny.

Nero shrugs his thin shoulders, but does not utter a word. I have yet to hear him speak.

How I regret not bringing a maid of my own with me to Suffolk, but Mother could not spare Molly and no one else was suitable. Lionel has promised to provide a local girl, but the prospect is not a welcome one, for she too would be a stranger.

I push away from the dresser and balance both hands on my hips. 'You may as well do something useful as stand there gawping.' I wave at a box full of my gowns. 'Put these away in that trunk over there. Fold them gently, mind, as the silk is easily snagged. And wrap each in a length of muslin.'

Leaving him to his task, I wander the halls with a sense of purpose I do not feel. The kitchens are in chaos with pots and sacks of flour strewn everywhere. Chairs sit on benches and the floors are an inch deep with wet, cloying sand. My presence is viewed with surly resentment by the sweating maids, and I return to my bedchamber and the silent Nero.

Except Nero is no longer silent. He prances the room wearing my best blue sapphire gown, a bonnet on his head and one hand balanced on a hip. The other he waves in the air and chants, 'Get you gone. I will have the boards shining.'

Furious, I halt on the threshold, and wait for him to notice my presence. Then watching him, my anger abates and a smile twitches my lips. He is indeed a good mimic, and so comical with my skirt trailing on the floor behind him. I need something to amuse me in this dismal place. Why not him? Besides, the dress is three years old and Lionel has promised me as many new gowns as I wish.

His gaze finally alights on me and though he freezes to the spot, no fear enters his face. Lips pursed, he hunches his thin shoulders in a theatrical shrug and the gown puddles onto the floor on a whoosh of silk.

'Will I be whipped, Missus?' he asks, more resigned than afraid.

Like me, he is totally alone in this strange world.

'On this occasion, no.' An idea springs into my head, and this time when I emerge onto the landing I have a specific purpose in mind. 'You there!' I address a female servant carrying a mop and bucket. 'Send for a seamstress. I have a gown I wish to have cut down.'

* * *

August 1648

August is stiflingly hot and barely a breeze ruffles the trees as our carriage hits every bump in the parched roads. Lionel keeps up a stream of animated chatter, but I hardly listen. It is bound to be about how I ought to behave in the presence of his mother, who, he insists, is always unfailingly gracious and indulgent toward me.

Not generous enough to allow me my rightful place at Helmingham. I am tired of accepting scraps from her table as if I were a poor relation. Lionel's indolence is a constant burr beneath my saddle. All he cares for are cards and hunting, his conversation peppered with anticipation for the forthcoming season.

I understand his mistrust where his mother is concerned. Our last visit was an unmitigated disaster because I insisted on taking Nero with me; my intention to show him off in his new silk jacket and turban, and thus display my sophistication. How was I to know it would all turn out badly?

The Dowager Tollemache's servants had never seen a blackamoor before. When Nero entered the kitchen on an errand for me, his arrival was greeted with a good deal of hysteria. A footman suffered an attack of apoplexy and two maids fainted.

Dinner was delayed while Lionel mollified the servants and assured them no Devil was going to rob them of their souls.

My mother-in-law chose to level the entire blame upon me, but to my everlasting pride, Lionel took my side.

'God's blood, Mama!' He actually shouted at her. 'My wife's page cannot possibly cause so much disruption in a properly disciplined household. In this case, I refer you to Elizabeth's management of our own staff. They are Suffolk born too and not one of them would run screaming from the house on encountering a small black-skinned boy.'

Thus rebuked, the Dowager Tollemache reverted to simpering apologies and pleas for her darling boy's forgiveness. A most satisfying sight. I even exchanged a wink with Nero, whom I installed on a stool beside my chair. I suspect he too enjoyed himself.

I have only been here in Suffolk a few weeks, and already I am restless and long to return to Ham House and my family. I did not anticipate missing them all so much. Father has returned to Paris, and therefore Mother's letters always end with how much she misses me.

'Did you not hear me, Bess?' Lionel's mouth turns down. 'I asked what is in that letter you have carried in your pocket these last three days.'

Ah yes, the letter.

'It is from Nan.' I lick my lips and try to remain impassive. 'She says my kinswoman, Lady Anne Murray, helped the Duke of York escape from St James Palace.'

'How did she contrive to do that?' Lionel snorts, betraying his scepticism.

'It is quite true.' My hackles rise. 'She provided him with a female disguise, and-'

'Hah! I imagine that soft-faced boy looked very pretty in it,' Lionel interrupts.

'As I was saying,' I continue, my temper close to the surface. 'The duke was smuggled onto a ship at Gravesend, and is now with the Prince and Princess of Orange in a place called Sluys.'

Lionel waves a pomander beneath his nose and sniffs. 'A reckless act which could have ended in disaster. I hope you do not admire her?'

'Of course I admire her! Better that, than have him rot in prison.' In truth, I envy her. Where I failed to help the king escape Hampton Court, she will always be known as a heroine who ensured the young prince's freedom.

'Your cousin may have been caught, my dear, and then she would be the one imprisoned.'

'She would regard it worth the sacrifice.'

'Why are you so contrary?' Lionel is genuinely puzzled. 'You have no close kinship with this lady.'

'That hardly matters. She is still kin and a Murray has been attributed heroine status among the Royalists.' *And it is not me.*

'Then you shall have to be content to be a heroine by association.' Lionel laughs.

I grimace and turn away, sulking.

Lionel's ambivalence towards the Royalist cause frustrates me, while at the same time, I know it is the reason I am safe and Ham is not in Parliament hands. How easily the Murrays could have suffered the same fate as the Harrisons and all those others who pledged their fortunes to the king.

Still surly, I do not reveal the rest of Nan's letter, instead I open out the page and read it again in silence as the carriage bumps and rumbles over the uneven road.

...and so Earl Holland persuaded the Duke of Buckingham, and his brother Lord Francis Villiers, to join him in an attempt to demand the release of the king from Carisbrooke.

After an aborted attempt to seize Reigate castle, they assembled at Kingston with six hundred horsemen, though Mother forbade Kate and me to venture out to see them.

Though the earl's intent was to ensure peace, Parliament sent out soldiers from Windsor to intercept them.

They clashed on ground near Surbiton Common, and although Earl Holland's men were quickly defeated and he fled, he was soon afterwards taken prisoner and will most likely face a traitor's death.

Buckingham escaped; but, and I hate to impart this news to you in such a curt, impersonal manner, my dear Elizabeth, but his younger brother, Lord Francis Villiers, was killed. Such a beautiful young man and him only in his twenty-first year. He fought with such courage they say, but was pinned against a tree and set upon by several soldiers. He stood no chance. The poor young man has gone.

Some brave soul crept out in the night to carve his initials on the tree under which he was slain. Rumour says that they will remain there until it is cut down.

Mother is distraught at the loss of the pride of the Villiers. It is said Lady Mary has not stopped crying for her brother...

I re-fold the page and return it to my pocket with a deep sigh, my thoughts on Lady Isabella. Does she look back on those days when she and Ann Harrison danced on the college lawn for Doctor Kettle with nostalgia, or regret? Did she ever think then that her father would face an executioner's axe? The thought makes me shiver for my own father

'I trust your mother is well?' Lionel asks, apparently attacked by a belated sense of guilt at my melancholy. 'The news from Ham has not upset you?'

Of course it has upset me!

'Mama mourns my departure and her headaches grow worse.' I choose not to mention Nan's account, or risk more scorn about the futility of the Royalists. I lick my lips, gathering courage for the task ahead. 'Lionel? Might we return to Ham soon?'

His mouth forms a silent 'o' and I rush in to placate him. 'I don't mean now, but perhaps at the end of the summer? But certainly before Christmas.'

'I am at a loss my dear. The grouse season is exceedingly good in Suffolk. I was looking forward to taking out my new hunters for the first time.'

'I want to go home.' A whine enters my voice for which I silently despise myself.

'But you *are* home? Fakenham is where we live. Are you not content, my love?'

'I-I am homesick, and worried for my mother.'

'She has your three sisters and your kinswoman, Anne Henderson for company and help. Is that not enough for her?'

He will never understand. How I long to see the river that winds past our garden into Richmond town, sometimes brown mud, but at others, a silver ribbon that sparkles in the sunlight. I miss the willows that dip into the water on the bank, the fields I walked in as a child and the cobbled streets of Kingston on market day.

My resolve hardens and this time I will not plead with him. 'My sisters need me too, Lionel. Mother is a woman alone with much to concern her. Although Ham is safe for the time being, Nan tells me the New Model Army makes frequent demands for money. She laments I am not nearby to appeal to Cromwell for some respite.'

His eyes darken and I know he considers my request. 'There is good hunting in Richmond Park at the New Year?'

'Excellent, the best in all Surrey.' I relax and hide a smile.

'Hmmm. Then perhaps we might return in December.'

'Thank you, Lionel.' I run a finger down his thigh, aware that I shall have to leave my chamber door open this evening. It is but a small price to pay for a compliant husband.

The carriage rolls across the drawbridge into Helmingham Hall and I brace myself for another afternoon of playing cat-and-mouse with my mother-in-law.

The morning after our visit to Helmingham, I take Nero to gather feverfew and wild strawberries in the woods outside the village. The boy is my constant companion these days. At social evenings and dinners, he walks at my side attired in the blue silk coat and a pair of heeled and buckled shoes made especially. Lionel says I spoil him and make him unsuited for plantation life, but I cannot think of that now.

Nero's favourite turban is in saffron yellow and I instructed the bemused seamstress to sew a glass jewel and a peacock feather to the front. An ugly pair of pearl earrings left me by a long-dead great-grandmother I never met serve as ornaments for his ears.

The locals think I am an odd sort of mistress for their lord. I have seen them step back off the road with fearful expressions when I pass by in the carriage, Nero's head poking out of the window. I do not care. Nero has proved my main source of entertainment since coming to this cheerless backwater. There is little else to amuse me.

He has grown since he came to Fakenham, probably because I insist he eats as well as we do, much to cook's annoyance. A few inches shorter than I, he hovers at my side and has learned to adopt an adoring expression.

I say adopt, because when he thinks I am not looking, he mimics me. At times, I have no choice but to have him whipped for his impudence, else the other servants would not respect me, and Nero's life would become more unbearable than it is already. I cannot help but admire the quiet resignation with which he takes his punishment. It makes me wonder what he had to endure in Barbados.

On our way back through the fields, I espy Lionel in dun coloured jacket and buff breeches striding toward me along the country road. The sight of his smile when he sees me lifts my heart and I hitch my skirt and hurry to meet him, leaving Nero to follow behind with the basket of herbs and plants.

His smile dismantles and I immediately anticipate bad news.

'What has happened, my love?' I ask, taking his arm.

'The minister called upon me this morning.' I match his pace, the high grass on the verge swishing against my skirt and intermittent birdsong the only sounds as we retrace our steps on the lane. We might be a country farmer and his wife.

The silence stretches too long and always impatient, I shake his arm. 'Well, what did the minister want?' I suspect he imagines his cautious speech gives him gravitas, but I have come to believe he thinks and speaks at half the speed of most people.

'The constable has similar concerns, even the magistrate has broached the subject more than once. I fear some of the villagers also have doubts.'

I wait for him to reach the end of his rambling thoughts, aware he will not be rushed. Except in bed, of course, but I think we shall solve that problem to our mutual satisfaction soon.

'The minister is concerned about consorting with a blackamoor.

He demands my reassurance that my wife does not practice the black arts.'

I halt and turn to face him, dragging him with me. One glance at his face tells me he does not jest. 'You cannot take such an accusation seriously, Lionel. Nero was a gift from you.'

'It is not simply the presence of the boy that worries the minister. He says you were seen with him, chanting while gathering wild flowers.'

I am about to refute this, but cannot. Nero and I do indeed sing, but with none of the sinister intent Lionel imbues in our behaviour.

'Do not look at me like that, my dear.' Lionel winces. 'I do not believe you commune with the Devil.'

'That is some consolation.'

My sarcasm is evidently lost on him as he continues. 'However, I must insist you behave in a more circumspect manner, Bess.'

'Circumspect?'

'It seems odd, I know. But folk round here are simple, country people who have strange notions about the unusual.'

'Is it I who is unusual, or Nero?'

'I cannot say, but to take him gathering plants in the woods is hardly wise. Can you not take one of the maids with you instead?'

We have reached the house and I stride away from him and fling open the side door, preparing for a theatrical show of temper, but change my mind. It is not Lionel's fault I am viewed with suspicion; I am a newcomer after all. 'I will do as you wish,' I say, allowing the door to swing back into the frame behind me, leaving him standing on the step.

Lionel's relieved sigh as he opens the door again and steps inside is pathetic, but I have other thoughts swirling in my head.

Nero is discreet, the maids are not. The last thing I want is for them to know I gather raspberry leaves to infuse in hot water to drink each morning.

Married only four months, and already I exhibit signs of being with child.

Chapter 32

September 1648

Lionel attributes my blossoming figure to a diet of good food and an idle life. I do not disabuse him in case he rescinds his promise to return with me to Ham. And yet, with each day that passes, I know it is foolish to perpetuate the charade, for the maids already whisper in corners and soon my condition will be clear to all. Once the imminent arrival of a new Tollemache heir is known, Lionel is bound to insist we remain in Suffolk.

The transformation of the house at Fakenham, from an unloved building to a sumptuous home is complete: my desire for beauty and colour allowed full reign with no regard to cost. Glass, silk and silver abound, and there is no limit to the number of candles we leave burning in rooms to which we have no intention of returning in the course of an evening.

Lionel and I share a chamber, which I have come to love and Mother-in-law declares unnatural. We do not care, this is where we lie beneath the coverlet to whisper like children and make plans for when the king comes home. In this private place, Lionel lets me believe the royal cause will one day prevail.

Through the long days of a cold, wet summer, nature already plays her tricks on both my body and my temper. I have neither the inclination nor the energy to bestir myself to do more than sit with a book in my lap and let the hours slip by.

Nero shares my secret, and brings me elderflower water, cushions for my back and titbits from the kitchens to satisfy my new hunger. When he can think of nothing more to offer, he weaves sparse flowers from the sodden garden into garlands, crooning softly in a soothing tongue I cannot understand.

The rains abate at last and in the quiet of a late summer afternoon, I imagine my entire life continuing in this way, with no thought of the fate of King Charles or the accursed rebels. The first tremors of the quickening child make me smile, and I wonder if perhaps it is not such a trial to pass my days instructing servants and laying aside fruit preserves for the winter. Then I grow restless again and decide brewing ale and sewing shirts for the poor may occupy my enforced laziness, but in my heart, I will never stop praying for the Royalists to succeed.

Then there is my poor mother, left to cope alone at Ham. Not only does she struggle to send money to Paris for Father's upkeep, but the fines to Parliament grow more demanding each quarter. Lionel has been more than generous thus far, but I feel his mother is aware of every penny he sends to Ham.

In preparation for a visit to Helmingham, I entreat my maid to tighten my corset to hide my burgeoning belly. Her pursed lips and sideways glance make her disapproval clear, but I pay her no heed and stalk to join Lionel in the waiting carriage. My smile remains fixed as I have to endure a jolting ride to the manor in a near faint.

Once we are ensconced in the vast sitting room, Lionel launches into the failure of the recent uprising in the north, which ended with a Royalist defeat at Preston. With no emotional or financial investment in the outcome, he tends to be scathing about the fact the Engager plan was badly co-ordinated.

'The Royalist leaders were unable to raise much support in such an unusually cold and wet summer. The English didn't want to leave their hearths, and many of the Scots deserted and returned home.' He shakes his head in bemusement, as if he were reporting on no more than a disappointing horse race.

This very morning in bed, he promised to buy me the grandest court dress for King Charles' return to the throne. I cannot believe he did so simply to humour me. Or is he more like me than I imagine, and can play both sides of the game?

'You declare you hate the rebels, Bess, yet make a great show of flattering Oliver Cromwell,' he threw at me when I challenged him on his hypocrisy. 'To great effect I might add, for the man is charmed by you.'

'The Engager army should not have lost at Preston,' I say, earning a scowl from my mother-in-law. 'Their army was twice the size of Cromwell's.'

'But not so well organised,' Lionel says, annoyingly smug. 'It did not help that Monro's veterans were left behind in reserve, while the Engagers marched south and became notorious for plundering and lawlessness.'

Lionel pauses to light a pipe from a taper he plunges into the fire. I abhor this newly acquired habit of his, but he seems mellower with a pipe in his hand, so I do not protest.

Instead, I revert to silence, my fingers twisting in my lap. Will Lionel mention Earl Lauderdale? Does he know how John fares? And if the news is bad, will I be able to conceal my feelings from him, and more importantly, his mother?

I fidget on my seat, my stays biting. How casually he discards the stout hearts of the Royalists, who have been defeated again and yet always come back fighting.

Lionel chatters on, goaded by his mother's enraptured face.

'Lionel, dear,' she interrupts. 'Elizabeth and I do not need to hear every detail, only how it ended.' She bestows a smile upon me which smacks of an intimacy I doubt she feels.

'Ah, well, as you wish.' Lionel waves his pipe stem in the air. 'It seems the whole affair faltered at the two bridges over the Ribble and Darwen rivers. They held hard for some time, but finally, the Scots were driven back by Parliamentarian pike men.'

'An exceedingly tedious story,' Mother-in-law says on a long sigh. 'Do we not have more interesting things to discuss?' She gives me a penetrating sidelong look that makes me uneasy.

'I have not begun to tell you of the Battle of Winwick Pass,' Lionel says, despondent.

'Another Royalist defeat, I take it?' Mother-in-Law's attention diverts from me to her son and I breathe more easily.

'Well, yes.' Lionel sniffs. 'Baillie surrendered to Cromwell after a chase across the north and gave up their colours and weapons.'

'What happened to the Scots commanders?' I ask, my thoughts squarely on John, whom I know joined forces with the Duke of Hamilton, though I dare not mention his name. Most of the time he is a long ago memory I bring out in melancholy moments, but at times like this, when he could be in real danger, my stomach knots at the thought he might be harmed.

'Middleton was captured in Cheshire after his horse fell on him.' Lionel gives a bark of laughter as if telling a joke. 'Sir Marmaduke

371

Langdale reached Nottingham but was captured in an alehouse. Callendar and Monro escaped, one to the Netherlands and the other back to Scotland, while Hamilton surrendered to Lambert at Uttoxeter.' He puffs on his pipe and blows smoke into the room which irritates my throat. 'Hamilton is to be tried for treason. They'll have his head, of course.'

My heartbeat quickens. Did John escape? Or did he not take part in the battle? If he lives, where is he now?

'Whatever the results, the Engager army is destroyed.' Lionel taps his pipe on the fender and lays it aside. 'Only Pontefract Castle holds out for the king, but it is a futile resistance that will not last long. Cromwell will strike terms with the Marquis of Argyll, but those who approved the Engagement will be removed from their posts.'

'Enough!' Mother-in-law instructs, though I suspect from boredom rather than sensitivity to my feelings. 'Were it not for the Scot's obstinacy, the war would be well and truly over and our lives returned to normal again.'

'Only normal as far as Parliament is concerned, my lady,' I remind her. 'Which is not what everyone wants.'

'Hmmm...yes, I forgot, your family is Scottish,' she says, rising.

I follow meekly, aware that my allegiance is tolerated, but not encouraged. Sometimes I wonder if they would feel the same should these defeats become victories?

She leads the way into the lofty dining hall, where the three of us occupy a long table that stretches down the room, two footmen to each diner.

'What pretention she employs for an intimate family meal,' I whisper to Lionel. 'Why can we not take supper in a smaller room?'

'Does it not occur to you, my dear?' Lionel's hand in the small of my back makes my nipples peak in reflex. 'Mother feels she needs to keep standards high to impress you.'

'Impress me?' I blink and take the chair a footman holds for me. 'She does everything she can to remind me my family is not as important as yours.'

'Perhaps; but if King Charles were to appear in this room tonight, which of you would he recognise and call by their given name?' He flicks up the back of his coat to take the chair opposite.

His caramel eyes glint in the candlelight and my throat prickles with emotion. More goes on behind that benign gaze than I give him credit for. He takes my side often lately, dismissing his mother's petulance with a casual wave of his hand. At times I believe his indulgence toward her is purely to keep the peace.

'You look fatigued tonight, my dear.' Lionel presides over a dinner I cannot eat, his gaze on my untouched plate. 'Are you unwell?'

Mother-in-law's eyes fill with cunning, and I know my attempt at subterfuge has failed.

'Surely you are not such an innocent, Lionel that you cannot see your wife is breeding?' She sucks her wine through her teeth, a habit that has gained special irritation for me lately.

'Is this true, Elizabeth?' Lionel leaps to his feet and crosses to my place in long strides. 'My love, why did you not say?'

His enthusiasm thrills me, as does the concern on his face. I realise then I was unwise to allow the situation to go this far. I should have told him when we were alone and savoured his pride without his mother watching.

'I was not sure,' I whisper through a wave of nausea. 'I have never been er- enceinte before, and, well - I did not want to raise your hopes for nothing.'

'Not sure?' The harridan's voice rises a painful octave. 'I'll wager you have missed your last five courses.'

Lionel frowns at his mother, then turns a softer look at me. 'When do you expect to be confined?'

Confined! How I hate that term. It makes me feel I am to enter a prison.

'The New Year, most likely,' his mother forestalls me. 'The child must of course be born at Helmingham.'

'Why?' I split a look between them. 'If his father cannot live in the family seat, what does it matter if the heir is nursed elsewhere?'

'Not now, my dear.' Lionel deflects this oft-repeated argument with a pat of my hand, his touch more paternal than lover-like.

'It is tradition the Tollemache heirs are born in this house. You will have the best of care.' Mother-in-law's tone turns conciliatory, as if she realises that in this matter, if in no other, I have the upper hand.

I sip weak ale and sit in enigmatic silence as they squabble. At last I have something they both want.

'I shall engage a midwife for you,' Lionel says. 'The Dutch are the best qualified and there are plenty in London.'

I squirm at the mention of midwives. The thought I will need one in several weeks brings my coming ordeal home to me in sharp focus.

'If I agree to come to Helmingham for the confinement,' I pause to take in Lionel's beaming grin and Mother-in-law's triumphant smirk, 'there will be certain conditions.' I grip Lionel's hand hard to make it clear I am serious.

He glances at her before he answers. 'Um-anything.'

I dig my nails into the fleshy part of his palm to bring his gaze back to my face.

'I want you to write to my mother and ask her to send Nan to me for the birthing.'

'A reasonable request.' Mother-in-law relaxes back in her chair, both hands folded in her lap. 'However is not your sister unmarried?'

My teeth clench. I do not require approval, only their promise. 'That is not all. As soon as the child is born, you and I, Lionel, will return to Ham.'

'In the spring, perhaps, my dear, certainly,' Lionel says. 'We may even stay for a few months.'

'No! We go when the baby comes.' Once back in Richmond, I am determined nothing will dislodge me again.

'If Elizabeth insists.' Mother-in-law bites into a peach, unheeding of the juice that runs down her chin. 'We can engage nursery maids to care for the child while you are gone.'

'The baby comes with us,' I say, my gaze on Lionel.

'Outrageous!' Mother-in-law drops the mangled fruit onto her plate and half rises. 'Such a journey would damage you and prove hazardous for the child. You cannot drag a babe not yet weaned across the country!'

Ignoring her, I twist in my chair to block Lionel's view of his mother so he has to look at me. 'Promise me, Lionel. Or I fear homesickness may be more hazardous to this child than a journey.'

His eyes widen and I know he believes me. 'If that is what you really want, my love.'

'It is.'

He flicks a look over my shoulder at his mother, whose jowls wobble with indignation. Objections race across both their faces, but neither dare deny me. Strange how a quickening woman takes on qualities that unnerve the strongest character.

My husband squeezes my hand, his eyes soft as he exhales a long breath. 'I promise.'

The babe kicks beneath the stretched mound of my skirt. Lionel looks down in shock and gasps.

By these small things are men captured and then bound.

I am going home.

* * *

January 1649

Christmas is over and a bitter January arrives to drape an already featureless landscape with a layer of hoar frost. The days are intolerably long and empty, for I am forbidden to leave the house or attend church service until after the babe is born. It seems Helmingham has gone into mourning, not preparation for a new life.

The arrival of Nan proves the only light that penetrates the gloomy sky, bringing with her a letter from Ann Fanshawe.

'This is a wonderful house, Elizabeth!' Nan pivots in a lop-sided circle. 'Much larger and more elegant than Ham.' She catches my glare and flushes. 'But it is not home.'

A massive bed dominates the room draped with brocade hangings in rich shades of amber, brown and gold. At one end stands a full height bay window onto the moat, and another on the opposite side looks out on the inner courtyard. The same brown and gold hangings are draped in deep swathes over lead paned glass that I insist are opened wide to bring light into an otherwise dark and masculine space.

'Indeed,' I say absently, my nose in the letter Ann sent from Paris, her elegant scrawl expounding on her grand lodgings at the Palais Royal, where she was welcomed cordially by Queen Henrietta Maria, and *all those gentle friends we knew at Oxford including your dear father*'.

A sudden, unreasonable burst of jealousy makes me hurl the page into the fire.

'Elizabeth!' Nan springs forward and whips the object back again, slapping the sparks from the curled brown edges. 'I trust you have read it, for it is scorched beyond repair.' She discards the damaged parchment on a table with a sniff. 'Breeding has not improved your temper, I see.'

I regret my impulse immediately, but refuse to apologise. 'Mistress Fanshawe enjoys Father's company in Paris.'

'Paris,' Nan says dreamily, then catches my expression and sinks onto the bed. 'Margaret Harrison wrote to me saying Ann is on her way to Calais now.' I show scant interest and she pouts in sympathy. 'My poor sister. Are you very uncomfortable?'

'What do you think? I lift both hands to indicate the mound under the bedclothes that turns my once slender body into a travesty. Tears well and I dash them away with impatience. This constant blubbing I seem to do lately angers me beyond measure. 'I hope this is not indicative of how much the babe will cry when he gets here.' I sniff and dab at my face with a kerchief.

A female housemaid I have never seen before enters without so much as a cursory knock. She hurries to the far end of the room to perform some task in which I have no interest. As yet I am unfamiliar with the routines of Helmingham, or the faces of servants that appear at intervals.

'I think the Dowager sends them in every half-hour to spy on me,' I whisper, while Nan and I follow the maid's progress across the room.

'Surely not.' Nan rises and closes the door. 'Lady Tollemache gives every appearance of being concerned for your welfare. She told me this room was her late husband's sanctuary, and therefore a fitting place for the birth of Lionel's first child.'

'Hmm, most likely he died in here too,' I mutter through clenched teeth. 'I can only hope the sheets have been changed since then.'

The double doors swing wide again with a noisy rattle of the catch and a swirl of cold air.

I narrow my eyes as Mother-in-law sweeps in. The woman never knocks. Judging by the twitch at the corner of her mouth, I suspect she heard my last remark, and Nan's loud giggle; thus earning further disapproval for the Murrays.

Behind her troop three liveried footmen, their shapely calves encased in white silk and identical embroidered coats; their arms filled with firewood they add to an already impressive pile beside the fireplace. The tang of cut wood mingles immediately with smoke, old dust and dried flowers.

'Goodness!' I shift my bulk as a swift kick in my belly takes me by surprise. 'Am I to be imprisoned here for the rest of the winter?'

'You disappoint me, Elizabeth.' Mother-in-law peers at me down her nose. 'Surely you are aware a confinement chamber must have a fire burning at all times to banish draughts. Bad air can be fatal to both mother and child. Besides,' her lips curl into a sneer, 'this room is bitter at night. You will be glad of it.'

She retreats, taking the footmen with her.

I exchange a look of martyr-like suffering with Nan that threatens to become a habit. 'She will not even allow Nero to come and see me.'

'You cannot have a young boy in a confinement room.' Nan attempts to placate me by offering a dish of marchpane fashioned into tiny hearts Lionel sent to cheer me. 'Nero spends most of his time these days in the stables. The head ostler has quite taken to him.'

'I don't care!' The notion Nero prefers someone else's company to mine adds to my discontent. 'With my time so close, even Lionel has stopped visiting. His mother says it is not seemly.'

My swollen belly has taken on proportions that Lionel no longer finds inviting. On the rare occasions when he visits, he stares at me with an expression of abject horror. 'It is as if he cannot believe anyone could grow so large from natural causes.'

'Oh, Elizabeth, you have such fancies. Mother warned me that women tend to odd dreams and strange ideas at this time. It is to be expected.'

'I despise being what people expect.' I ease myself out of the chair, and with both arms slung below my belly, approach the window seat. 'Do summon a maid to open this window. I can hardly breathe it's so hot and stuffy in here.'

'You heard what-' My glare silences her and with a long, meaningful sigh, she approaches the bell-pull by the door. 'Oh, very well.'

'Now,' I say, as Nan returns to lift my puffy feet onto a stool, 'Tell me what is happening in the wider world. No one here talks of anything interesting in my presence.' I ease backward on the cushion and smile as crisp air tinged with snowflakes cools my face. 'Does the king remain a prisoner at Carisbrooke?'

'Oh, no, he is no longer-' Nan breaks off and busies herself tucking the coverlet around my swollen body.

A trickle of alarm creeps up my spine and I straighten. 'He is no longer what, Nan? Has something happened to him?'

She flushes and starts to back away. 'Lady Tollemache said-'

'*I* am Lady Tollemache!' I grasp her wrist and pull so she faces me. 'Is there something you are keeping from me? You know I abhor secrets.'

'Unless they are of your own making.' Nan flicks a sideways look at the door before easing onto the seat beside me. 'I was told not to bother you, but I suppose you will find out soon enough. Everyone is talking about it.'

'Talking about what.' I grunt and try to shift into a position that eases my aching back, but fail.

'I see you will not be diverted.' She arranges her face into a look of soulful resignation. 'The king has been taken to London and an ordinance passed by the House of Commons.'

'Is that all?' I release my grip on her wrist, my fingers leaving red marks on her skin. 'The king cares nothing for Parliament's ordinances. He never has and he never will.'

'I fear he will have to care about this one.' She swallows and avoids my eye. 'They have appointed a special court to put King

378

Charles on trial for treason.'

'What?' I jerk upright, causing a giant hand to grab at my lower back. 'The king is not answerable to any court!' I examine her face for reassurance that it is all nonsense. The gripe in my back comes again and I ease forward in search of a more comfortable position. 'Parliament has no authority to try the king!'

'You are partly right.' Nan places a finger on her lower lip, and stares at the ceiling in a pose that means she recalls a lesson carefully learned. 'No law could be found to try a monarch, so the order to set up the court was scribed by a Dutch lawyer named Isaac Dorislaus.'

'Nan, will you stop gabbling about lawyers and tell me what is happening?' A low pulling sensation in my belly makes me squirm.

'I'm trying to explain!' Nan snaps. 'The order is based upon an ancient Roman law which states the government can legally overthrow a tyrant.'

'Tyrant? They are calling King Charles a tyrant?' Nan does not reply and my hand closes on her wrist again, this time in response to a deep twinge that lances through my belly.

She gasps and leaps to her feet. 'Are you in pain? Has the baby started?'

'I-I do not know. I have never done this before.' I conduct a silent inventory of my discomfort. Of the various aches and pains I endure on a daily basis, perhaps this is different. Sharper and more urgent.

'You must allow me to fetch someone, Elizabeth.' Nan strains against my grip on her arm, but I hang on.

'Tell me about the king first!' I snarl through gritted teeth.

First horror, then indecision chases across her features. 'They are putting the king on trial at St James Palace the day after tomorrow.'

A scream erupts from between my lips, though I cannot tell if it is the vice on my spine that causes it, or fury at being kept in deliberate ignorance of the king's fate.

Hot tears of pain and frustration wet my face and agony turns my belly rigid and twists my back. I turn pleading eyes on Nan but I cannot speak.

She breaks away from me, and ignoring the bell-pull, rushes to open the doors, at the same time yelling at the top of her voice.

I squeeze my eyes shut and bend double as waves of pain sweep over me, and wish my mother were here.

Chapter 33

I never doubted my firstborn would be a son, or that the Tollemaches would stand firm and insist he bear the name Lionel. Triumphant and exhausted, I am too weak to argue with his gaggle of sisters and a domineering mother-in-law. There have been too few male children born in the family for them not to view this one with special attention.

No matter; I am young and strong and there will be more babes whose given names shall be my choice.

Waking from a doze in a lumpy bed musty from infrequent use, I smile and stare at the ceiling, savouring the constant clatter of carriages and the cries of costermongers from The Strand. This entire house holds a pervading stench from the river Thames, but I love it here, triumphant that a mere few days after the ordeal of childbirth, and despite the Dowager's impotent anger, I am here.

As it transpired, I did not need to resort to womanly pleadings from my childbed that my husband keep his promise. News of the king's trial changed everything and Lionel could not get to the city fast enough.

'In the event I am called upon to attend as one of the king's judges,' Lionel said. 'It may be prudent to be in town at this time.'

'Then you must refuse!' Mother-in-law voiced my own terror that he might be expected to speak out against King Charles.

'If it comes to it, I may well do so,' Lionel said, flapping an impatient hand against her whining voice. 'I wager half who are summoned intend to do the same. However, I have a mind to discover what Parliament will finally do with His Majesty.'

I had no intention of his leaving me behind, and so here we are, comfortably ensconced in his late grandfather's house. Ham can wait a little longer for my return. I am eager as anyone to know the outcome of the king's trial.

Sloughing off the remnants of my afternoon doze, I ease up onto an elbow and wince at the persistent soreness of my nether regions.

Nan looks up from the crib where my sleeping son lies. 'Ah, you are awake. The babe took a good feed from the wet nurse and I swaddled him again.' She tips the cradle gently with a foot and sighs. 'All he seems to want to do is eat and sleep.'

'Help me to dress would you, Nan?' I push my dishevelled hair away from my face, throw back the covers and swing my legs onto the floor. 'Lionel will be home soon and I want to know how the trial went today.'

'Elizabeth! You have not even asked about your beautiful son.'

'I do not need to.' I keep my gaze on the ribbons of my shift as I untie them. 'You give me reports every few moments, whether I ask for them or not.'

Sometimes I feel he is more my rival than my child. When I carried him, *I* was the focus of everyone's attention. All my whims and cravings immediately met, and my slightest discomfort enough to send everyone into a fluster.

Now when visitors arrive, the cradle is their first call and the boy-child's health their only enquiry. Perhaps they feel he is not as easily replaced as a wife?

'I will fetch your gown, Elizabeth.' Nan says, signalling to the nursery maid to take her place at the cradle.

I try not to sigh or roll my eyes, but it proves difficult. These two and the wet nurse are of the opinion that the child will stop breathing if he is not kept under constant watch. He is certainly not sickly, though not pretty either, with an egg-shaped head and no hair. Ah well, he is only a few days old and will likely change as he grows. His grip on my finger is strong, and his piercing cry can be heard throughout the house. Like me, he refuses to be ignored.

'You need to become accustomed to being his mother.' Nan sniffs and fusses with my hair, though not in an effective way.

'What do you know of being a mother?' I brush her hand aside and she backs away, pouting.

If truth be told, I am still troubled by the unflagging discomfort that remains of the birthing process. Though my labour was pronounced by the midiwfe as being mercifully short and easy, my memories of the unrelenting agony that lasted several hours left me with scant emotion for its cause.

And how can such a prolonged assault not cause permanent damage? When alone, which is not often, I examine myself closely, amazed that the bruising already heals. Even my flabby stomach contracts a little more each day.

I pull my linen shift over my head and climb into the petticoats, while Nan holds out the skirt of my green worsted gown. I stand compliant while she pins the bodice across my tender breasts and fastens my stays, but my mind wanders. Today is the last day of the king's trial.

To our combined gratitude, Lionel was not called to act as a judge, and his prophecy proved right in that only sixty-eight of the one-hundred-and-thirty-five men summoned put in an appearance. I believe he was disappointed, for he thought he would present an impartial and credible witness.

I agreed with him, how could I not, but relief filled me that Lionel will not be associated with what goes on inside that hall. Something tells me those who stand witness against our monarch will forever be tainted, no matter what the outcome.

Cromwell forbade entry to any who objected to putting King Charles on trial and formed what they call a 'Rump Parliament' of forty-six men. He also packed the court with soldiers to protect the judges against a restless crowd that gathers daily outside St James Palace.

In response to my pestering, Lionel recounts the trial's progress over subdued family dinners. His Majesty refuses to accept the authority of a court that accuses him of overthrowing the rights and liberties of the people of England. How could he respond to such an accusation, when such things come through him as our sovereign?

'If you are hungry,' Nan offers, bringing me back to the present. 'I could send for some bread and cold meat.'

I glance out of the window at the lowering sky. 'No thank you, dinner cannot be far off and-' I pause at the sound of the front door opening and closing. 'Is that Lionel returning?'

Without waiting for an answer I rush from the room and down the stairs, with Nan limping at my heels.

Lionel stands in the hall, but does not look up as I approach.

Preoccupied, he shrugs out of his cloak and hands it absently to the footman. He drops his cane into the rack by the door with an ominous click. When he looks up and catches sight of me, his arms lift in welcome and I run into them, my chin against the cold, slightly damp, fabric of his coat where I inhale familiar dust and the smell of tobacco.

'You have been in *The Mitre*,' I say into his shoulder, but without accusation, knowing it to be one of the best inns in Fleet Street from which to obtain the latest gossip.

'How are you today, my dear?' he whispers into my hair without releasing me.

I experience a rush of pleasure that it is me he is concerned for, that his first words were not about the child. 'I am quite well, if tired.' A tremor of unease creeps up my spine and I push away from him, both hands flat against his chest to search his face. 'Did the trial go badly today?'

He sighs and closes his eyes briefly before answering. 'The king refuses to acknowledge the legality of the High Court. He will not even remove his hat.'

'How else do you expect him to react? I imagine he sees the entire spectacle as an impertinence.'

Lionel grasps both my elbows and pulls me to him again, more firmly this time. 'Bess, listen to me. They have lost patience. The judges see the king's arrogance as a sign he cannot recognise his own faults. Thus he is a danger to others.'

'Hah! They should worry more that he is a danger to them. When the Prince of Wales is told-'

His grip increases, cutting me off. 'He has been found guilty of all charges.'

Behind me Nan gives a sharp cry and a muttering starts up from a line of footmen and servants who have appeared from nowhere.

'He did not accept that surely?' I say, unable to process what he can mean. Guilty? The king?

Lionel shakes his head. 'His Majesty tried to talk at the end, perhaps to defend himself. However, Bradshaw announced the accused is not permitted to speak once sentence is passed.'

'They wouldn't allow the king to speak?' My mouth falls open, aghast.

Releasing me, Lionel pushes a hand through his hair. 'No. He was bundled from the court by the guards.'

'Wh-what does that mean? That sentence has been passed?' In my heart I know, but I need him to say the words aloud to make them real.

'King Charles has been condemned to death.'

'No!' I thump my clenched fists against Lionel's chest.

He grabs my upper arms, murmuring endearments I do not hear above the roaring in my ears.

Behind me, Nan begins to cry. Faces appear round doors as rumour spreads and more servants creep closer to listen, voicing their own dismay.

I want to shout at Nan, at all of them, that Lionel is wrong. It is all nonsense. No one has the right to kill a king.

'They cannot do this!' I pound Lionel's chest, harder this time. He winces, but there is no recrimination in his face. 'I will go to Cromwell,' I shout into his face. 'Beg him if I have to, as a friend and a Christian soul. He cannot in all conscience take the king's life.'

Lionel gives me a firm shake which halts my frantic voice and forces me to look at him. 'It is not Cromwell's decision alone. He cannot change the verdict of the High Court, even should he wish to. You will obey me in this, Bess and not involve yourself.' I open my mouth to protest but he forestalls me. 'Thus far my family has kept out of this war. To stand against Parliament now would bring their wrath down upon the Tollemaches. I have sisters too.' He shakes me again. 'We have a son.'

Something inside me buckles and I slump against him. The face of Nan and the servants blur with the walls that swirls and recedes. Had Lionel not held me, I would surely crumple to the floor. Then Lionel's voice comes to me as if from the end of a dark tunnel.

'Nan, she is in a faint. We must get her upstairs.'

* * *

30th January, 1649

My eyes sting from the sharp, fine snow carried on a brisk wind that cuts through my clothes, though a vizard envelopes my face from chin to nose. The cold mutes the kennel stench, but the sweet, fetid smells of mildewed clothes, sweat and bodies is as bad as any London day.

The broad thoroughfare of The Strand remains relatively quiet, but through the Gate to Scotland Yard, a mass of hurrying people spill onto the cobbles from side streets and alleys, filling the open area in front of the Banqueting Hall. They press so close, I am overwhelmed by a giddiness that makes me stumble on the slick cobbles.

'We should not have come,' Nan says, hauling me upright, her breath a stream of white through the breathing hole in her mask.

'It is too late for complaints!' I snap, instantly regretting my sharp temper.

Nan could have refused to accompany me, or even run to Lionel with stories of what I intended. She did neither, and would not allow me to venture out alone.

'This is no quiet walk to visit the 'Change, and you know it.' Nan presses against a shop window as a man in a billowing cloak shoves past without stopping. 'I cannot fathom why you would want to witness such a thing? To see a thief hanged for stealing a coin is one thing, but King Charles? It is almost blasphemy.' Her limp is slightly more pronounced today in her effort to keep pace with me.

'Go home if you wish. I have to be here, or how will I ever believe it could happen.'

'You should not be out of the house,' she hisses beside my ear. 'You have not yet been churched.'

I brush her objections aside, my anger reflected in every back I shove and ribs I have to elbow to force my way through the melee. 'I'm perfectly well,' I lie, fighting dizziness. 'Look! There's the Whitehall Gate. It's not far now.'

A black-draped wooden platform has sprung up overnight outside the Banqueting Hall, where companies of foot, and troops of horse line up on one side of the scaffold leading to King Street, with Charing Cross on the other.

Do they expect a last minute rescue? Or are the Rebels out in force to stop the crowd tearing the lords to pieces? I know which I suspect.

The grassed areas between the pathways heave with well-dressed gentleman and ladies who mingle with Quakers and Puritans, many of whom are women. Some even gossip and laugh with their neighbours as if they are attending the Bartholomew Fair.

'There must be thousands of people here,' Nan says. 'Stay close, I am afraid if I lose my footing, we shall both be trampled like stalks of straw.'

'If we can reach the rail there,' I point to the wooden platform, grimacing as someone steps on my foot. 'We may find some shelter.' I pull her behind me and sidle between elbows and carelessly handled canes that threaten to poke out my eye.

The platform is higher than I imagine, and I have to strain on tiptoe to see over the rim. Even then, my view is limited to that of the booted feet of foot guards who line up across a black cloth laid on the boards. I am about to suggest we step back apace for a better view, when my gaze alights on the executioner's block and my throat fills with bile.

They are really going to do this. They are going to kill the king!

'Elizabeth!' Nan whispers fiercely in my ear. 'What is it? You cried out.'

'Did I?' I fight down nausea, and panicked, tug my vizard away from my face. Cold air bathes my skin, but offers no relief. 'This crowd smells bad.'

'Lack of soap and a surfeit of ale most likely.' Nan wrinkles her nose in distaste.

I sway slightly, and a burly man jostles me and sniggers. 'No time ta faint now, Mistress. Waits until they cut the 'ead off the awld sot.'

My fists clench in fury, but I can summon neither the courage nor the energy to demand he show proper respect. If the rest of this crowd feel as he does, I could be torn apart by a hostile mob.

Nan and I huddle together in the shadow of the platform in the bitter cold, while crowds press into the square. My toes and fingers turn numb until I can barely stamp my feet to keep the blood moving.

At a little after two of the clock, a casement window opens in the Banqueting Hall and the murmurs are cut off as a troop of musketeers march onto the platform; drums beating and colours flying like a parade, they form a line in front of the scaffold. They hold muskets like shields before them to force the crowd back, Nan and I amongst them, though we maintain our position at the front.

A figure I recognise as being Doctor Juxton, the Bishop of London appears, followed by two others who are unfamiliar.

'There be Colonels Hacker and Thomlinson,' a man behind me growls. 'Those whoreson prats who are His Majesty's guards.'

My question answered, I watch the small, slight figure who follows behind, draped in a black cloak that looks too large for him. The king.

The drumming stops and a sigh of sympathy moves through the assembled crowd. Someone shouts, 'Shame!' but is quickly smothered. The musketeers jostle those closest to the platform and demand silence in rough voices. Some people are crying, while others croon in premature grief, comforted by their companions.

A figure in a black hood and jerkin moves to the front of the platform and leans down to retrieve a curved bladed axe from the floor beside the block.

'Elizabeth, is that the-?' Nan breaks off with a sigh as if she cannot bring herself to finish the thought. 'Why does he wear a hood?'

'Lionel told me, the customary executioner refused to do the deed. This man agreed only if he was guaranteed anonymity as he fears reprisals.'

'And so he should,' Nan says, on an anguished sob. 'How could anyone do this?'

I clutch my cloak around me and focus on the tiny man in the centre of the platform, apparently fascinated by the wooden block at his feet. How can he bear to look at it?

King Charles has changed since we met at Hampton Court last

summer. His once lustrous jet black hair is grey at the temples, his cheeks sunken beneath pouched and shadowed eyes. His grizzled beard is badly cut and too heavy for his thin face, making him look old and dreadfully worn. Did they not allow him a decent barber in his gaol?

His expression is one of calm detachment, as if the vast sea of faces does not exist. Then he steps forward, hands outstretched and chin lifted. His hooded eyes sweep the front of the crowd where Nan and I stand.

I shrink back, fumbling to replace my vizard in case he catches sight of me and imagines I am here to revel in his final humiliation.

A hush falls as he begins to speak in his clear, Scots accented voice.

'I cannot hear very well,' Nan whispers.

'The king said that by not speaking, we may think he is guilty. Now hush, Nan, I am trying to listen.'

His next words are muffled by the flapping of the drapes on the scaffold, and others are lost to the wind. Though the words, 'I am the martyr of the people,' come to me clearly.

A martyr. Is that what he has become?

I lean a hand against one of the makeshift uprights of the platform, where the rough wood scratches my palm. I may be sick to my stomach, but I must keep watching. When more rational times return, and surely they must, I want to be able to say I was there. Witness to the depravity of Parliament and what their hatred and fear brought them to. They must never be allowed to forget their crime.

With an effort, I look to where Doctor Juxton assists His Majesty in securing his hair beneath a cap.

'I go from a corruptible to an incorruptible crown.' The king addresses the Bishop. 'Where no disturbance can be, no disturbance in the world.'

'You exchange a temporal for an eternal crown,' Doctor Juxton's response is softened by sympathy. 'A good exchange.'

My eyes burn and I long to scream at the king to run, leave this dreadful place and the barbarous intentions of these cruel men. I open my mouth, but only a strangled sob escapes my throat. Waves of dizziness threaten to overwhelm me, and my legs shake. It is all I can do to remain upright. I must not faint. Not now.

Nan presses closer and gently strokes my cheek. 'He will be in Paradise soon, Elizabeth.' She has removed her glove, and as her hand lifts away from my face, a tear glistens on her fingertips.

With his hair now secured out of sight, His Majesty turns to his executioner.

'I shall say but very short prayers, and when I thrust out my hands, so.' He holds his child-sized hands toward the man in the hood who nods, the long-handled axe cradled in his meaty hands.

The king removes his George, the jewelled badge he wears to represent his Order of the Garter. He reaches behind him to hand it to Doctor Juxton, and as he does so, he utters the word, 'Remember.'

Remember? Remember what? Has he promised the medal to someone and he wishes the bishop to carry out his instruction? Prince Charles perhaps, or maybe the queen?

Then the king raises a delicate hand and speaks.

'Wass 'e say?' A man behind me asks, pressing forward. His companion shrugs and grumbles he cannot hear either.

'Can you hear, Elizabeth?' Nan rasps in my ear.

'He asks to have the block set higher.' I raise a hand to quiet her as I strain to listen. 'So his death may be seen by his people.'

'Ugh!' Nan's grip on my arm tightens and her breathing quickens.

'Be still, Nan. Should you faint, this crowd will trample you, and I have not the strength to carry you home.' I am less sure about myself, but do not say so.

'I will not fall.' She slips her other hand beneath my arm, and leans against me.

The king kneels and with hands clasped, offers a silent prayer, his eyes cast Heavenward in supplication.

Then his prayer ends and in the same breath, his head dips to rest on the block.

The hooded man lifts the axe and holds it aloft. I follow the movement with my eyes, my blood thrumming in my head as I fix my gaze on the shining blade in horrified fascination.

It is happening too fast. I have not said goodbye. I am not ready.

The kneeling figure raises both hands and a singing noise cuts through the air.

The blade falls, swift and straight followed by a wet, dull thump as it meets its target.

The king's head in its white cap tilts forward and tumbles onto the platform. A streak of blood quickly becomes a torrent and spurts from the inert body slumped against the block.

A loud, low groan erupts from the crowd, held for a long second and then dies away to dismayed silence. A woman screams and another faints, caught before she hits the ground by those who stand nearby.

'Sweet Jesu!' Nan says beside me.

A metallic tang reaches my nostrils. *Blood.* I fight down nausea at the smell that drags me back to the birthing room I have so recently left.

The executioner plucks the severed head from the platform and holds it up to the crowd. 'Here be the head of a traitor!'

I look away, but not quick enough. The man's hand is twisted into the cap, from which strands of bloodied hair escape. It doesn't look real, more like a paper mask with closed eyes and no expression. No life.

No answering applause or encouragement greets the executioner's words; instead the groan changes to uneasy murmuring, followed by gentle sobbing.

The soldiers shoulder their muskets and glare with menace ʳ the throng, who step closer to the platform. Had they hoped foʳ more enthusiastic audience? It seems so.

Let them see how the people feel; let them know the hostiˡ these same Englishmen whom they proclaim to represent.

I drag my gaze away, staggering as faces and buildingsˊ recede before me. Voices boom in my ears, addiʳ disorientation. I push away from the rail, step bacˡ collide with a matron, who glares at me and shoves ʳ

I stumble against Nan, who cries out, 'I have losˊ

'Never mind,' I snap, aware that we are not mˊ the platform, but are trapped against it by the wᵉ crowd. I wrap an arm around Nan's shoulders and grasp the support to stop us being swept beneath the scaffold. My vision of the upper side of the platform is obscured, though the pounding of footsteps on wood reverberates in my head as the crowd surges onto the platform.

'What are they doing, can you see?' I release my hold on Nan, who cranes her neck to look through the wooden slats above us.

'They have taken the-the body away, but now there are dozens of people stamping on the black cloth, they-'

'What? What are they doing?'

Nan turns to me, ashen-faced. 'They are dipping kerchiefs and pieces of cloth torn from their clothing in the king's blood.' She narrows her eyes. 'The soldiers are making them pay first!'

A wave of dizziness threatens to overwhelm me, but I grasp her hand hard enough to make her wince. 'Nan, do you have a coin?'

'What?'

I rummage in a pocket of my skirt and find a neatly folded square of linen edged in lace. 'Take this and do the same.'

'But-I.'

'Nan, do as I ask. Please.' I squeeze the words through a thickening tongue as nausea and dizziness rob my legs of the strength to hold me.

She snatches the kerchief from my hand and slips through the crowd. In a second, I can no longer see her, aware only of the smell of sweaty, greasy bodies in foul clothing and the underlying stench of blood.

'I have it.' Nan's voice beside my ear makes me jump. She thrusts the now red-stained square into my pocket with a grimace of distaste. 'Now can we go home?'

I nod, then cast a lingering glance at the place where my king vas murdered, obscured now by the flapping hands of human ultures in their eagerness for his blood.

Am I not a vulture too? A voice inside my head demands. No, intentions are honourable. I will not sell the kerchief or pretend as the power to cure illness. I shall keep it as a talisman. A hol of how even righteous men stoop to savagery when it suits

An icy wind slices along The Strand and cuts through my bodice, while I count the buildings on our seemingly never-ending walk home.

'You look pale unto death.' Nan chastises me gently, an arm thrust beneath mine to keep me upright. 'You are still weak. Lionel will be furious if he finds out.'

I cannot summon the energy to respond, though Lionel's arms, angry or sympathetic, are all I long for.

Still uttering mild reproofs, Nan assists me into the deserted hall. 'Where is everyone?' Her voice echoes up the stairs as she props me against the newel post. 'Probably gossiping somewhere about the execution.' Her tone tells me she is furious they have left their posts, but I am too exhausted to care. 'Wait here,' she says, darting into a side hall.

She is back in an instant.

'Lionel is not at home,' she whispers. 'We must get you to bed before he discovers you are gone.'

She is so anxious to get this deed done, she seems not to notice I have not spoken a word, too focused am I on putting one foot in front of the other as we negotiate the wide stairs. As soon as the door to my chamber is closed, I collapse onto my bed and squeeze my eyes shut to banish the images that float into my head.

Nan rolls me over to unpin my gown, uttering endearments and stroking my hair.

'You need comfort too, Nan,' I say as tears squeeze out from the corners of my eyes. 'You loved him too.'

'I was thinking more about Father.' Nan lifts the bodice away and I can breathe again. 'He will be destroyed when he hears what they did.'

'Of course. Father,' I sob, ashamed of my own selfishness. He is the king's man. What does he have left now?

Then I remember something and reach out to grab back the skirt, fumbling in the pocket. 'The kerchief.' The fabric is stained bright red and feels damp, though the ragged edges of the mark are turning brown. I hand it to her. 'Put this somewhere safe.'

My lip quivers and hot tears flow down my face. I sniff and swipe them away, impatient. I rarely cry and being unable to control my feelings is unfamiliar. 'It must be the birth,' I offer Nan in explanation. 'I am never this weak.'

'I told you we should not go,' Nan admonishes gently. 'Look at you. How can you travel across the country so soon after leaving childbed, and then put yourself through such a dreadful sight?'

'Did you see how old and melancholy he looked, Nan?' Exhausted and dizzy, I allow her to settle me between blissfully comforting sheets.

'It does not matter now.' She rises and pats my covered hip. 'Try to sleep. I will go and see how the baby is.'

The baby. I had given him no thought.

'No, nothing matters. He is gone.' I am cold. My teeth chatter and I clasp my hands together. I thrust my hands between my knees, bent at the waist in an effort to drag warmth into my body. Behind my eyelids all I can see is blood. So much thick, gouting blood that spurts from the king's butchered neck onto the black cloth in a scarlet river.

I turn my face into the pillow to muffle my sobs until darkness overwhelms me.

Chapter 34

September 1649, Ham House

The soft knock at the door of my chamber prompts me to slide the letter I am writing into the top drawer of my bureau. 'Come in.'

Cousin Henderson, garbed in a worsted mourning gown that does nothing for her ruddy complexion, sidles into the room to take up a subservient stance before me. 'May I speak with you, Elizabeth?'

A dozen possible complaints she may have race through my head as I return the goose quill to the inkpot. 'I am always available to you, Cousin.' *Do I sound too much like Mother, or not enough?*

'I have not had an opportunity to speak with you very much since - since Mistress Murray-' She swallows and tears spring to her eyes.

I wait, giving her a moment to compose herself, whilst at the same time pushing down the sadness that clamps my chest.

It is six months since the king's murder and my return home to Ham. When we first arrived on a stormy February night, I attributed the purple shadows beneath Mother's eyes to her deep grief for the outrage perpetrated on King Charles. An emotional homecoming, combined with the disruption of the household in order to accommodate my husband's servants and the establishment of a nursery, meant I paid Mother scant attention.

Sunk in self pity and using my premature rise from childbed as an excuse to hide away in my room and mourn the king, it became easy to shut out my sisters, the baby, even Lionel.

'Elizabeth is exhausted.' Lionel would respond in answer to requests for my company. 'She will recover her strength soon.'

A more charitable excuse than I deserved.

Then one spring morning, Nan invaded my room with fire in her eyes and lashed me with her anger. 'Mother has been ill for months, Elizabeth. Desperately ill. And if you could but look beyond your own concerns, you would see it for yourself.'

Taken aback at this uncharacteristic outburst, I stood mute as she railed at me. 'Cannot you see how thin she is? She hardly eats and the medicine the chirurgeons give her does not help at all.'

Like a naughty child beneath her onslaught, I knew it was all true, and that I had simply chosen not to face it.

'Why did you not tell me when you came to Suffolk?' I threw a half-hearted accusation at her as a sop to my conscience.

'Mother forbade me to say anything when I came to Helmingham for Lionel's birthing,' Nan said. 'However, you have been here over a month, and yet you have not deigned to notice she worsens daily.'

Her tirade over, she stood biting her lower lip until she split the skin. The tiny bead of blood that appeared told me what this interview cost her. At twenty, Nan is no longer a child, but long custom prevented her castigating me before that day. No one in the family had ever dared. Guilt surged through me then that my sister had borne the burden alone.

'We shall summon another chirurgeon. There must be something that can be done.' Instead of comforting her, I chose action over emotion, and in my selfish way, imagined that by refusing to acknowledge how sick Mother was, I could keep the inevitable at bay.

'Do you think I have not done that already?' Nan slapped her skirt with both fists and paced the room, her restless steps hampered by her twisted hip. 'I have had three separate opinions on her condition. They will not give whatever ails her a name, and their opinions range from old age, which is a ridiculous pronouncement for a woman of forty-three years, to melancholy and a tumour of the stomach. None of them could offer a specific cure.'

I made my peace with Nan after that, both of us taking turns with Cousin Henderson to tend Mother, who spent the remainder of that spring and the entire summer in bed or resting on a chaise in the salon. Despite our care, she wasted away before our eyes, though we tempted her with the best food and kept a fire burning at all times. It was never enough, and she complained constantly of the cold.

Now she is eternally cold. Catherine Bruce Murray lies in the vault of St Peters Church beside the river at Petersham. We gave her the honour she deserved at the end. The brass plaque affixed to her coffin declares her Countess Dysart, the title she used only once during her lifetime: on the day we visited King Charles at Hampton in the summer of forty-seven.

That interview with Nan solidified a decision I had made months before. No matter what excuse Lionel used to return to Fakenham, my place was here where I was most needed, at my beloved Ham.

Strangely, Lionel did not object, and now my days are spent supervising the kitchens, the bakehouse, storerooms, laundry, and dairy. The servants come under my complete control, the duties they perform, where they sleep, what they wear and even whom they marry. All are now my domain.

It is all I have ever wanted, and yet a shadow hangs over Ham.

Since the war, more ragged people than ever before come to the gates for alms. Many of them maimed soldiers with little chance of finding work. I do what I can, and with Lionel's largesse, I can ensure my tenants are fed. Lionel has filled the stables, but it will take years yet before we can build up the livestock that once filled the Petersham Meadows.

Soldiers still occupy Kingston town. Idle for the most part, they strut about and demand entry into houses to ensure everyone attends church services, or pounce on anything that resembles a ball game or the most innocent of celebrations. It seems all feast days that brought some laughter and colour to hard working people's lives must now go unobserved.

Bright colours and flamboyant clothes are also discouraged, which affects us little as we went into mourning for the king, and will remain so until next summer for my mother. All the lovely gowns Lionel bought me for my trousseau, together with his embroidered satin suits, now lie locked away in chests lined with box leaves and sprigs of lavender.

Cousin Henderson's cough brings my gaze to her face. 'Where is my husband, Cousin?' I ask, giving her time to muster her thoughts, knowing she will come to the point when she is ready.

I suspect I am in for a lecture, for I have not been to see my baby today. My neglect is not deliberate, for every day I revel in his growing strength and the way his mouth widens in the semblance of a grin when he sees me. Young Lionel thrives, thank the Lord, and with two efficient nursery maids and a wet nurse to see to his needs, I feel ill-equipped to make decisions about him. Perhaps my pride will not allow me to appear ignorant before such well qualified carers, but I rarely contradict them. Sometimes I do not know what questions to ask.

'Lord Tollemache has gone to the horse sale.' She twists her hands in front of her. 'He said you were asleep when he left and did not wish to wake you.'

Lionel and Lodowick Carlisle formed an immediate bond on their first meeting and they spend hours in Richmond Park together exercising horses, or at Petersham Lodge playing cards.

'I sat up with Ball most of last night,' I say quickly, though I owe her no explanation. Should I wish to spend my entire day abed I will do so. 'His stomach troubles him again.' Our poor steward grows old, and Mother's death affected him badly.

'I wanted to ask, now that my mistress, I mean your lady mother-' Cousin Henderson swallows, her hands twisting in front of her. 'Will you require my services further?'

I am nonplussed at her words. What can she mean? Then it comes to me with a small shock. 'You wish to leave us, Cousin?'

She came to us as little more than a child from her native Fife, and was devoted to Mother. So much so I experienced acute jealousy of their closeness. Sometimes I harboured a feeling of not being needed that made me mischievous on occasion, even cruel. I could not imagine Ham without Anne Henderson.

Does she think me so heartless, I can cast out a young woman who has lived beneath our roof for as long as I can remember? If so, perhaps she is right and she should go, for she does not know me at all.

'I have not given the matter any thought.' Hurt tinges my voice with ice. 'I will have to broach the matter with Sir Lionel.'

'I understand.' She bobs a curtsey and turns to leave.

I half rise and call her back. 'I would not keep you here if you have a mind to leave, nor would I ever reproach you.' Somehow I cannot summon the words to ask her to stay, though I cannot recall whether she has family in Scotland she might return to.

Anne turns back, despair in her mud-coloured eyes that reminds me she is a young woman still. 'I assumed, that as Lady Tollemache, you would have no need of a simple country lass like me.'

Her compliment finds its mark and I soften. 'My mother was a grand lady, a countess, yet you served her well.'

She creeps forward but halts several feet away, her heavy features twist in hope mixed with despair. 'I would serve you with the same devotion. Or perhaps I could serve your sisters? Nan and Kate are young women now, and you will likely seek husbands for them soon. But Meg is not yet thirteen, she needs me.'

All remnants of my cruelty leave me in the face of her distress. How can I dangle the prospect of an unknown future in front of her, she, who has been so loyal? Mother would never forgive me, and Father would not countenance my turning her out.

'I would be honoured to have you as my waiting woman.' Her lips part, but I hold a hand up to silence her. 'I will henceforth call you, Anne. Cousin Henderson is something a child uses for her governess.'

'Then I might stay? Or do you wish to wait upon word from the earl, your father?'

Ah yes, Father.

We have heard nothing from him since before the king's trial. After the execution, we assumed he had gone into hiding in case the wrath of Parliament extended itself to Charles Stuart's followers. In the spring, I wrote to Sir Robert Moray in Edinburgh asking that if he saw Father, he might inform him of Mother's demise. I did not dare write to the queen's court in Paris, lest a rebel spy took the opportunity to arrest him. As yet, no word has reached us as to his whereabouts. Or even if he lives.

A look of panic crosses my cousin's face, and I realise I have not responded to her appeal.

'I do not need to ask Earl Dysart. I would like you to stay.' Relief floods her features and I rush on. 'However, I shall demand complete loyalty from you, Anne. Despite recent events, I am a

Royalist to my bones. My allegiance is now firmly set on the new king, Charles the Second. I expect the same discretion you showed my mother.' I hold her gaze, about to test our future relationship. 'By that, I mean there may be certain things that Sir Lionel does not need to know.'

'I never imagined it would be any other way, Mistress,' she says, faltering slightly on the unfamiliar address.

Like most people, Sir Lionel expressed horror at what they did to the king, but while Parliament bickers about how the country will be run, and the army complains at being disregarded, my husband advocates we exercise discretion. I, however have no intention of crumbling beneath a regime that feels they do not need a monarch.

'I understand perfectly.' She bows, but still lingers, while my fingers itch toward a corner of the parchment visible in the open drawer.

Earl Lauderdale's letter came last month, lifting my spirits more than I dare admit. In his irascible way, he made me laugh at his account of having fallen foul of the kirk. All those involved in the Engagement against England at Preston were to be deprived of their office for the rest of their life.

I was forced to grovel on my knees before the Lords and vowed to obey them henceforth. What a shaming thing it was and how glad I am ye did not have to see it. What the English have forgotten, Elizabeth, is that Charles Stuart was their king too, and no one asked us Scots if we wanted him dead.

John understands my anger at the king's murder better than anyone. An emotion my husband will not discuss. Instead, I pour out my feelings on paper to John, who holds out hope that even if the English have surrendered, the Scots never will. *Trust me, Elizabeth,* he writes in his confident scrawl. *We have not finished yet.*

'You may go now, Anne,' I prompt her, hoping to return to my letter.

She bobs a curtsey, her shoulders relax and her features soften in repose.

With such a simple gesture I have the ability to lighten my kinswoman's life. A woman with little to offer the world other than her steadfast heart.

Would my own task is so straightforward. Great lady I may be, but my life is not free from trouble. Even though Mother is no longer here, the Sequestration Committee performs its duties with new diligence. Whether they wish to take revenge on Father, or are desperate for money to fund their new regime, I cannot tell. Perhaps they are furious Father handed Ham to Lionel and me, or regard us as a threat? Whatever their reasons, their demands persist.

My hand hovers above the drawer. 'Is there anything else, Anne?' This time I am brusque, but she doesn't flinch.

'Yes - I wanted to ask you about the boy.'

I look up sharply, the letter forgotten. 'The nursery maids have expressed no concerns. They say he is a sturdy, lusty child.'

'Young Lionel is, Mistress. I meant Nero.'

'What about him? I thought he had settled in well. Does he cause trouble?' Nero's sunny nature won my sisters' hearts within days of his arrival. Especially Meg, who treats him like an exotic playmate. The servants were less easily won over, but as far as I know, none have expressed discord at his presence.

Anne's face flushes again. 'I confess, I showed little charity toward him at first.' Her eyes round in awe. 'I have never seen a - well.'

'Yes, I know. He comes as a surprise to most people. I think you will find he has a kind heart, if a somewhat mischievous one.' I smile in remembrance. 'I hear cook cannot keep him away from the pantry, but then he does seem to have an insatiable appetite for cake.'

'Mistress Nan tells me,' Anne pauses, staring at the floor. 'Well, she says Sir Lionel intends to return him to the plantation in the spring.'

'Oh, yes. I had forgot. He will be too old soon to act as a personal attendant.'

'He-he is a strange lad, I admit. However the maids like him and he's clean,' she says, as if this is unexpected. 'He is also strong and turns his hand to whatever needs doing.'

'Poor Nero. I have neglected him of late.' I hold out my hands palms upwards to indicate the papers on my desk. 'There has been so much to do on the estate. Mother became too weak to-'

'He cannot send him back!' She leans both palms on the desk and looms over me. 'England is his home now. It would be too cruel!'

'But Sir Lionel-'

'He would not miss one blackamoor labourer. There are plenty more. Please, Mistress Elizabeth, do not let him send Nero back to Barbados. He is only fourteen and would not survive in one of those dreadful slave camps.'

'What do you know about slave camps, Anne?'

'We sit round the kitchen fire in the evenings and he recounts stories to the servants.' She shrugs and flushes. 'I do not believe everything he says, for he has a fanciful nature. Yet some of it rings true. Those camps are terrible places. And him such a gentle lad to whom God has given a kind soul.'

'Hmm…there would be no silk tunics and turbans for him in Barbados.' I give her words some thought. Nero has a unique way of wheedling his way into most hearts. I steeple my fingers and rest them against my lower lip. 'For a dour Scot, you possess a surprising compassion, Anne. I will talk to my husband.'

'Talk to your husband about what, my love?' Lionel strides into the room, bringing with him the smell of the stable. He resembles a true countryman in a dun jacket, his sandy hair gathered in a queue at his neck, and his breeches splattered with dried mud.

Anne flushes, as she often does in Lionel's company, reminding me again what a handsome man he is.

'About allowing Nero to remain in England,' I say, turning the key in the lock of the drawer where John's letter lies. I have not yet summoned the courage to tell him that Earl Lauderdale and I are in regular correspondence. Not that there is anything that would shame either of us in our banter. I justify my secrecy with the excuse its political content might offend my husband and he may

402

try to forbid our letters. It is a contact I have come to anticipate with joy these last weeks, and to rely on.

'Nero can hardly remain your page, Bess. In another year or two, he will overtop you by inches.' Lionel throws his lithe body into a chair and reaches for a decanter and glass on a side table. 'I shall obtain another, a younger child this time, of about six or seven. He may take longer to train, but-'

I catch sight of the horror on Anne's face, though she makes no attempt to interrupt.

'Lionel,' I say gently. 'Please allow Nero to stay. He has made himself useful here, and perhaps he could train the new page when he arrives. Accustom him to our ways.'

'If that is what you wish, Bess. So be it.' Lionel tosses back the watered wine and gives a bored shrug, the subject closed.

I dismiss Anne, who mouths a thank you, at the door before leaving.

Lionel leaps to his feet again as the door closes on Anne and claps his hands together. 'Do you not wish to know about the horses I bought today?'

I cast a longing look at the drawer where my unfinished letter lies before turning a bright smile upon my husband. 'Of course, my love, I wish to know everything.'

Chapter 35

September 1650, Ham House

Entering Mother's room is a simple enough task, so why then do I freeze two steps inside the door, where dust sheets blur the furniture into unrecognisable shapes, and sunlight sidles through chinks in the drawn curtains?

I catch my breath, as through half-closed eyes I see her in the corner, one hand on a drape as she stares out onto the garden. The illusion fades and I blink it away, forcing myself into the room whose smell evokes childhood days and a faint sound of her laughter.

The lid of the chest where Mother's gowns lie gives a tiny creak and a waft of rose-scented air rushes to meet me. I am ten years old again and caught rifling between sheets of soft muslin, holding up the soft fabrics against my cheek.

Her voice resonates in my head as she tried to be stern with me, but a chuckle would always rise in her throat for she never really minded my being there.

Anne gives a gentle cough at my shoulder. 'Would you prefer to wait until another day?'

I shake my head, loosening the curls on my cheeks. 'I have left it too long already, and cannot postpone the inevitable forever.' I reach into the chest and run my fingers over a sage green gown. Is it really a whole year since her death?

A sigh turns to a sob as I clutch the fabric to my chest, inhaling the slightly stale scent of the rose petals scattered into the folds.

'I know.' Anne gently prises the silk from my stiff fingers. 'Sometimes I too find it difficult to accept I will never hear her voice again.'

Even as we laid her in the church vault, I did not suffer this ache beneath my breastbone. I had no time then for melancholy, nor did I sit crying for hours like my sisters. There was far too much to do, what with the funeral to arrange and death notices to be sent out. Ordering mourning clothes for the family and servants was not the simple task I had imagined. Ball scoured the whole of Richmond and Kingston for enough black cloth to hang over the mirrors and every reflective surface in the house so Mother's spirit would not remain earthbound.

Too numb to cry, I took comfort in the familiar rituals of death, which could explain why I am doubly lost now.

'What was I thinking?' I hold out my arms, palms upwards. 'To make a shrine of this room with all her things in place, and yet not one of you objected.'

'Who dares tell Lady Tollemache what to do?' Anne's smile is wary, but when I don't correct her she relaxes. 'Most of these things can be sold, apart from the items you and your sisters wish to keep as mementos.'

'I have Mother's jewels, and a few keepsakes. I need nothing else to remember her by. Apart from this, of course.' I stroke the black lacquer of the Chinese cabinet I have already claimed as my own. 'When we have finished here, please instruct the footmen to move it to my own rooms.'

'This is the largest bedchamber in the house. Do not you and Sir Lionel plan to use it?' Anne asks.

'No, we are content where we are. Perhaps, when Mother's possessions are removed and the lingering smell of roses is gone. Maybe then.'

She nods in acquiescence and I watch her fold gowns and shifts, arrange gloves in neat lines and empty drawers with swift, economical movements.

'Anne?' I say softly. 'Is there something of Mother's you would like?'

'Me?' Her ruddy complexion darkens even more and a hand flutters at her bodice. 'I never thought - I.' She glances round the room until her gaze falls upon the table where lies a leather-bound bible. She runs a hand over the cover, the corners curved upwards and softened by much use. 'If I may, I would like this. I used to read aloud to her from it when she couldn't sleep.'

'It is yours,' I say, though I cannot think of more enervating night time reading. But then I know that isn't why she wants it. The Bruce emblem is inscribed in the flyleaf and Mother had recorded each of our births there, including Mary's, the babe Mother lost many years ago. Did Anne remember her? I do not know and I am too sad to ask today. Maybe that is a subject for another time.

Suddenly nauseous from the cloying scent of the clothes press, I squeeze my growing bulk between the bed and a chair, causing a sharp rustle from the pocket in my gown where a letter from Earl Lauderdale sits.

'You look fatigued today, my lady.' Her brow puckers with concern. 'Does the child bother you?'

I slide a hand beneath my burgeoning belly. 'No. This one is quieter than Lionel. Perhaps it is a girl.' I pretend to crave another son, but a daughter would thrill me, and perhaps with her, I may recreate the closeness Mother and I shared.

Anne goes back to her folding and stacking. 'May God grant you a healthy child, whether it is a son or daughter. And may He also preserve their mother.'

She speaks as if in prayer, and yet I am not one to be disturbed by the dangers women face in childbirth. I refused to order a winding sheet amongst the childbed linens, despite my cousin's gentle reproach that every woman who enters a confinement chamber also faces death. I am young and strong enough to birth a dozen lusty babes with little trouble. Childbirth holds no fears for me, for there is still enough danger in our everyday lives to keep us alert.

The Puritans continue to watch and vex us, but we are not the only ones to suffer under their autocratic rule. Horse racing and cockfights are banned among the alleyways of Richmond and Kingston, while playacting of even the most innocent sort is prohibited, with maypoles being cut down and burned. I grieve less for the closing of gambling dens and brothels, but drunkenness and blasphemy are too harshly dealt with.

Poor Justinian Isham, caged at Richmond Lodge all year with the Carlisles, makes regular pleas to the Sequestration Committee, his life made miserable by their persistent claims on his home, Lamport Hall.

We 'Richmond Royalists' are forbidden to travel to London anymore, nor even to go beyond five miles from home without permission. We ignore them all as best we can and gather together to gossip and complain, to discuss John Donne with Bishop Duppa and the Carlisles, and pretend we are not surrounded by rebel troopers. I do not care that Dolly Long writes her catty letters to Justinian Isham, where she makes Shakespearean references to me as 'Dame Quickly' and Lionel as 'Sir Cautelus in the Chimney Corner'. I am more than an intellectual match for her, and others.

The child inside me kicks and I pause, wincing.

'My lady, why do you not sit down?' Anne urges. 'You should rest more being so close to your confinement.'

I shake my head. 'Rest is for old women. I prefer to walk, it eases the ache in my hips that plagues me at this stage of pregnancy.'

This time I have delayed as long as I dare, though the confinement room has been prepared these four weeks. How can I explain my reluctance to shut myself away. Imprisonment, even at Ham, fills me with more dread than the anticipated ordeal to come.

For the tenth time that day my thoughts drift to John's letter, where he laments the dreadful failure of yet another Scottish invasion three weeks before; a defeat that signifies an end to months of plans and hopes of the Royalist cause.

Sir Thomas Fairfax objected to taking arms against the Scots on their own land, and resigned from command of the New Model Army, replaced by Oliver Cromwell. This time, Cromwell did not wait for the Scots to invade England like he did in forty-eight. Instead, he sent messengers across the border to proclaim the righteousness of the Commonwealth cause before attacking them on their own soil.

The Scots outnumbered the English, but being dominated by the Kirk Party meant their ranks were purged of all but strict Covenanters. Eighty veteran officers and three thousand experienced soldiers were judged unfit to serve and were replaced by raw recruits.

The Earl of Leven brought his covenanting army close on Cromwell's troops at Dunbar, but while they slept in rain-soaked fields, the English launched a surprise dawn attack.

Two servants enter and remove the boxes Anne has packed, I

assume at her instruction, though I did not notice her summon them. My mind drifts so easily these days and time passes unevenly, at times dragging interminably, and at others flashing past on wings. Perhaps it is the babe.

'I will show the maids where to stack these boxes and return directly,' Anne says.

Alone, I settle in a brocade chair beside Mother's bed and re-read part of John's letter.

... and Cromwell is now the hero of Parliament, John writes, his bitterness stark on the page, *and as if ten thousand prisoners were not enough, a Dunbar Medal is to be struck and presented to all ranks who fought there. How they rub our noses in our disgrace.*

Combined with John's disappointment is the belief that even with thousands dead, he clings to his conviction that the cause of the second King Charles may prevail. The young king hangs on his every word they say, which cannot be a bad thing for John, despite the whispers he holds undue influence over his new royal master.

My russet-haired Scots adventurer; a bold, brash, impulsive man who will never capitulate or betray his ambitions. I love his enthusiasm, and his passion though both are aimed at his own advancement. Most could not claim otherwise.

How I envy him, though have to accept I am no longer the same as he. I am a wife and mother with an eye to the future of my children and responsibility for three unmarried sisters. In some ways I sympathise with Lady Anne Lauderdale; being married to this eternal adventurer must frustrate her with his constant quest for glory. Or is she his rock, his unquestioning island in the storm of his life, and I am the one who lacks faith in the cause?

In him?

'Elizabeth, my dear.' Lionel's voice breaks into my reverie. 'What are you doing here all alone?'

'Thinking.' I stuff the letter into my pocket and adopt a welcoming, if distracted smile.

'You look fatigued.' He searches my face with his gaze, his boyish features puckered with concern. 'I know you said you were not ready, but surely it is time for you to be confined?'

'All in good time.' I drag my thoughts back to the present. 'Was there something you wished to say to me?'

'Um. . . perhaps it can wait.'

Alert, I grip his hand tighter. 'You searched me out, now tell me what you came to say.'

'As you wish,' he says on an exhaled breath that is like an exorcism. How lightly he unburdens his concerns onto me. Fortunate then that I possess the spirit to accept them. 'I have received a communication from the Sequestration Committee.'

My stomach lurches. 'Surely not, they cannot put us through this again?'

'It appears they can. They claim that due to your father's continued dealings with the exiled queen and the Scots Engagers, they claim Ham and all its estates forfeit to Parliament.'

'They cannot have it.' I bring my fist down on the arm of the chair. 'Ham belongs to both of us, and you are not, and have never been a Royalist.'

'I fear it is not so simple. We might have no choice but to concede.'

'Concede! You want me to relinquish Ham to those Roundhead dolts after everything my mother did to keep it in the family? A struggle that sent her to an early grave? How can you even think it?'

A nerve in my leg spasms and I shift in an effort to relieve the pain.

The thought of some canting Puritan and his hatchet-faced wife with their brood of plain children in my house makes my bile rise.

'I know you have been brought up here, my love, but-'

'It is my home and my inheritance,' I growl through gritted teeth, my voice trembling with rage. 'How can you think I would give it up so easily? And what of my sisters?'

'I have given the matter some thought.' He pats my hand consolingly, but it is all I can do not slap it away. 'There is plenty of room for all of us at Helmingham.' He speaks as if he offers me some sort of prize. 'We will close up the Fakenham property and move in with my mother. Your sisters will want for nothing.'

'And they will *have* nothing that is rightfully theirs. And how will they marry while they live on the charity of the Tollemache name and - and your mother?'

'I will grant the girls sufficient dowries.' He shrugs as if I make difficulties to an easily solved problem.

'They *have* dowries, Lionel. Set aside by my parents.'

'Not if Parliament forces us out, Bess.'

'You can prevent that. We could compound!'

His eyes widen. 'Have you any notion how much that would cost?'

'You are wealthy enough!' I snatch my fingers from his, and cannot find it in me to regret the hurt that clouds his eyes. What a fool he is at times. I married him to keep Ham, I won't give it up now due to his apathy.

'I am indeed, my love. But not so rich I can throw good money after bad.'

'Bad? To employ some of your fortune to keep a valuable property like this?' I wave an arm to encompass the room. It may not be as grand as Helmingham, or as ancient, but contains treasures of its own in the silver and ebony framed mirror in our bedchamber, the Italian marble figures that flank the fireplace in the main hall. The gilt trimmed friezes in the dining room and the magnificent oak staircase admired by everyone who sees it.

'Bess.' Lionel's tone is one he might use to an intractable child, which sends a fury into my chest. 'Even if we do exactly what they want and pay this extortionate amount, who is to say they won't make yet another demand? Then another, until my own estate is drained, and we are all paupers? This way, I can guarantee there will be nothing left for them to confiscate.'

'Parliament will not take this house from me.' I stare around the room that echoes my mother's soul. 'I shall never, never give it up. Nor will I betray my father.' I exhale slowly, confident Mother watches from wherever she is and approves.

'I fear you are not listening to me.' He adopts his little-boy-thwarted face and gives a chagrined huffing noise that infuriates me even more. 'It is only a house and some land. I cannot fathom another way for us to remain unscathed by Parliament.

They appear to hold a particular grudge against the Murrays.'

'You are convinced this latest demand is due to my father?'

'Why else would they believe they have a case? What with his secret visits to Edinburgh and Paris, they regard him as a dangerous spy.' Lionel pauses and coughs. 'If you could persuade Will Murray to agree not to scheme against Parliament. Maybe even supply certain information they may deem valuable, they may let him return home and-' I narrow my eyes at him and he backs away. 'But I see that is not possible.'

Does Lionel actually expect my father to betray everything he believes? Or does he voice this because he feels he signed a poor bargain with my parents in our marriage settlement? I want to lash him with my tongue, but know the only way I will win him round is by being his loving Bess.

I push myself up from the chair and slip an arm round his neck, my bodice pressed tight against his chest, though at this moment his touch makes me recoil. 'Make no hasty decisions, Lionel. Consider a while, and I am sure a solution will present itself.'

'As your husband I have quite decided, my dear.' He pulls away from me, runs a finger across a table and peers at it, bored with the subject. 'We shall pack up everything and retire to Helmingham.' He plants a distracted kiss on the tip of my nose, his gaze already on the door. 'I advise you not to spend too much time in this gloomy room, full of a dead woman's possessions.'

His casual dismissal makes my fingers itch to slap him.

How dare he dismiss my courageous mother, when his own has been feted and indulged her entire life, first by her husband and now by a doting only son. He has no idea what Catherine Murray had to do to keep us fed and this roof over our heads. How casually he imparts this latest threat and his decision to surrender, for no better reason than he cares too little to expend the effort.

What would Mother do?

Summoning patience, I slip my arms round his waist and smile up at him. 'Please think about it, Lionel, if only for the sake of my health. I miss Mother dreadfully and even after all these months, I have no way of knowing if Father is aware of her death.' I tuck my head beneath his chin. 'My greatest fear is he might walk through that door, calling her name and I have to tell him she has been gone a year.' I snuffle and wipe away a non-existent tear.

'He would never blame you.' His voice resonates through me as he strokes my cheek with one hand. 'Your mother held duty above her personal feelings. He always did the same.'

I wince at his use of the past tense to describe Father. If I am sure of anything, it is that he lives.

'A quality you admire it seems, and yet you discourage it in me?' I peer up at him through my lashes, relishing the light blush on his skin. It seems there are compensations to the way nature inflates a woman's body in pregnancy. My husband revels in my voluptuous curves more than he ever did my girlish figure.

'I do so to keep you safe, my love.' He runs a lazy finger across my décolleté, a smile tugging at the corner of his mouth. 'You spend too much time in your room writing letters to Lord knows who. I suspect you involve yourself in intrigue which may come to the attention of the wrong people.'

'Or the right ones.' I pull back to look into his face. 'Were you aware, that when Ball went into Kingston the other day, he was pointed at and accused of being the servant of a traitor?'

'Whatever has Ball done to attract such derision?' Lionel blinks in total incomprehension.

'Not him, Lionel. Me. They say his mistress has abandoned the cause now the king is dead and now grovels to Cromwell.'

'Ah, I see. And Lord Fairfax removed the soldiers from the house at your request. No wonder they are confused.'

'The fact Cromwell dined here frequently during the Putney Debates did not go unnoticed. My point is, that even the locals are no longer sure if the Murrays are for king or Parliament. I am content to let it remain so if I can work in secret to help restore the new monarch to his throne.'

'I wish you would not involve yourself, my love. Playing both sides of the coin is dangerous.' He rests a hand on my swollen belly. 'To you and this new little one.'

'You wish for another son?' I say, trying to distract him. 'With so many girls in both our families, the odds are against us.'

'I have no preference. The Tollemaches have a healthy heir in

412

young Lionel. You may fill the house with daughters if you so wish.'

Which house does he mean? Ham, or Helmingham?

My thoughts drift and I wonder how many times my husband and I will have this same argument? At which point will my persuasion not be enough, so he finally loses patience and refuses to pour more money into Ham? There must be a way to keep my inheritance, and I am determined to find it.

Restless, I fidget in his embrace and give a small groan as an unseen hand grips my back. Then a deep-seated drag in my lower belly brings forgotten sensations rushing back with dreadful clarity.

'Lionel?' I growl through clenched teeth as the breath is forced from my lungs. 'Summon Anne for me.'

'Of course. Are you unwell? Or is it-?' His face whitens with shock and he drops his hands as if burned and backs away.

'No! Never mind the bell-pull,' I gasp. 'Go. Run and call her. She will be nearby.'

I brace a hand on the bedpost as yet another grinding pain bends me double. It is happening much faster this time, with little respite between each onslaught.

Out in the hallway, Lionel's voice carries high and nervous as he does my bidding.

Grinding pain bends me over again and when I look up again, Anne is at my side, all brisk efficiency and tutting with annoyance.

'How could you leave it so long?' Her wiry but strong arms close round me and she half drags me along the hall, from which Lionel has long gone.

'If this one is a boy,' I spit out the words between the pain, 'he is to be called Thomas, after my uncle, who was tutor to King Charles.'

'Never mind that now.' Anne's scowl is as powerful as any Mother aimed at me. 'By the look of you, we will be hard pressed to make it to the birthing chamber in time.'

Chapter 36

The trouble the maids are put to heaving buckets of hot water into my closet without ruining the Turkey carpet is well worth the effort, as is the messy process of removing the dirty water after my bath.

My skin is so clean it glows, and I dress in a loose gown with no petticoats, a gossamer light manteau draped over the top that I leave unfastened to reveal my low-cut bodice. As the mother of two healthy sons, both of whom lie sleeping at the end of the hall, my confidence has never been higher.

Lionel struts the house like a peacock since his second son was born, an achievement for which he claims sole credit.

This last sennight before my upsitting has given me adequate time to apply to how best I might secure Ham, not only for the immediate future, but forever. By the time the maids came to remove the birthing linens, I was insistent one of my first visitors was a lawyer from Richmond.

Disarmed at first by being shown into a confinement room by a wet nurse, the man soon settled into business, and when I explained our difficulty, he suggested we engage an agent.

'What sort of agent? I asked.

'A Parliament man, who, in return for a small pension, will buy the estate in its entirety on your behalf. Once the deeds are put into his name, he relinquishes his interest, so Ham and its lands and chattels will become yours again.'

Intrigued, and with a growing excitement, I pressed for details.

'For legal reasons,' the lawyer said, peering at me down his long nose. 'We retain the bill of sale in case the Surrey Committee makes enquiries. But, Lady Tollemache, to all intents and purposes, in law, Ham House becomes yours again.'

All I have left to do is convince Lionel to sign the papers, which is the reason behind my careful preparations and the prolonged bath. There is the little matter of my husband having to part with over thirteen hundred pounds, but I intend to soften that particular blow for him.

'Is Sir Lionel downstairs, Anne?' I address her reflection in my dresser mirror as I gather my loose curls on top of my head. 'If so, would you inform him I wish to see him?' If Lionel knew how much rosewater I used to scent the rinse for my hair, I doubt Helen of Troy would be enough to distract him.

Anne brushes a loose strand of hair from her face with a forearm. The bucket episode has left her flustered and red-faced. Her gaze skims my neckline and roves over my casual hairstyle. 'Isn't it too soon for you and the earl to resume-?' She pauses, embarrassed, but makes no attempt to hide her disapproval at the fact I appear to want him back in my bed with such unseemly haste.

'Time is something I do not have, Anne. A Committee member will call on us tomorrow, and if we do not have the documents signed and the money ready-' I break off and return to my toilette. I refuse to admit, even to myself, what might happen if Lionel does not agree.

'I thought he was set on giving up the Ham estate. Has that situation changed?'

I hold her gaze in the mirror to convey her presumption borders on insolence. 'It is about to. Now kindly do as I say. And while you are downstairs, have some wine and cakes sent up.'

I ignore her long-suffering sigh as she bows and leaves.

Moments later, movement in the corridor alerts me to Lionel's arrival, giving me only enough time to remove my stockings. I might have saved myself the bother of donning them in the first place, but my unmarried cousin is shocked enough at my behaviour.

Lionel pauses at the door as if unsure of his welcome, but once glance at my attire has him flushing like a schoolboy.

'My dear, I had no idea you were well enough for a visit from me.'

'Forgive my impatience, my love.' I twirl a pale ringlet round my index finger. 'I have missed you these two weeks.'

He blinks, surprised though he should not be. He must be aware by now that it is I who am the instigator of our intimate life, which ensures he will never find me unwilling.

Thus encouraged, he takes a step toward me, but I skirt a chair to keep a distance between us. I need his co-operation before I remove any of this carefully arranged clothing.

A scrawny maid scurries into the room and rattles a tray in a clumsy attempt to pour wine into our best crystal glasses. Impatient with her cringing apologies I dismiss her and see to the task myself.

I shall be glad to have Nero back. He not only moves like a ghost, but he performs such duties with efficiency and never breaks anything.

'Did your day in London prove a profitable excursion?' With a finger, I remove a drip of red wine from the side of the glass and transfer it to Lionel's bottom lip, then hand him the glass.

He runs his tongue across the drop, his gaze never leaving mine. 'Indeed. I went to Lloyds Coffee House where the lists said three sloops arrived in Woolwich yesterday. All with full and intact cargoes, and no storm damage to the vessels. A most satisfactory result.'

'I am so glad, Lionel.' Three ships. That should be more than enough to pay for Ham. I choose not to question the nature of this cargo, suspecting part of it will be slaves from the Gambia. Lionel cannot understand my aversion to what is, after all, a respectable trade. I cannot bear to see them, sullen faced, chained and naked on pedestals while overfed, leering men bid for their futures. The young girls I find especially distressing.

'If you are well enough, Bess. We might return to Helmingham at the end of the week.' He says this to please me, but my heart sinks at his timing.

'If you will allow, I wish to remain here a little longer. Thomas is but three weeks old and I do not want to leave him in the sole charge of nursery maids.'

Lionel does not remark on the fact I spend less than a few minutes a day in the nursery. Not that I have no affection for my babies, but I find them so dull at this stage.

I take up a position in front of the window, aware that despite the autumn chill, weak sunlight floods the room and renders my gown almost transparent.

Lionel's start of pleased surprise tells me my ploy is effective. His eyes darken and he places his glass on the table with exaggerated care. 'I am disappointed, Bess, that still you do not view Helmingham as your home. I agree that Ham is charming, but would such a small and unimportant mansion be such a loss?' He holds his hands out to indicate the room. 'It has only a quarter of the accommodation we have at Helmingham.'

My hand shakes as I pour my own wine. 'If you recall, I was eager to enlarge the house last year when we returned here, but you were unwilling, when all I wished to do was make Ham into a house fit for you.' My glass clinks against the pitcher as I set it down hard on the tray, mainly to stop myself lobbing it at his head. His disinterest already makes me nervous I may yet fail.

'Then I count myself fortunate I have not wasted yet more money if Parliament shall be the one to benefit.' His dismissive laugh grates on my nerves. 'Besides Helmingham, there is the White House in The Strand, and others in Suffolk. Are they not enough for you to queen it over our friends and acquaintances?'

I come to stand beside him, my skirt brushing his knee. 'You are indeed a noble man and an impressive landowner, Lionel. So surely my little estate is worth adding to your assets? You know how much it means to me so why will you not save it?'

He pouts at me like a spoiled child denied a treat, waves a dismissive hand, and glances at the door. 'I am weary of this subject and insist we cease such talk.'

Panic rises in my chest at his implied threat, that if I do not comply, he will leave and all my careful preparations will be wasted.

'I wish I could make you understand how my heart would break if I lost Ham.' I press a hand to my breast, dislodging the lace almost as far as a swollen nipple.

His gaze flicks down and back up again to my face. He places his glass on the tray without looking at it, and stands.

Before he can close the space between us, I fling away from him with a sob, at the same time keeping a close watch on his reflection over my shoulder in the gilt mirror above the mantle.

A cloud passes across his face and I know he is torn. He comes to stand behind me, both hands on my shoulders in a firm grip.

I lean my chin on his arm and stroke my lips across the inside of his wrist, aware of the tremor that runs through his arm.

Despite my irritation, I cannot prevent the blood pulsing in my veins. My body says yes with every quickening breath, yet my chin juts angrily at his reflection. Why does he have to be so stubborn? He could afford it, and must know it is all I want in the world. Almost.

I nuzzle his arm and he drops his head, sliding his mouth across the exposed flesh on my shoulder. 'I only seek to protect you, and at Helmingham you are less likely to be treated with suspicion.'

'That is a poor excuse. Lord Cromwell visits us at Helmingham as easily as he does here. No troopers dare bother us knowing of his patronage.' Frustrated, I pull away from him though Lionel follows like a puppy, plucks a pale curl of my hair from my neck and twists it in his fingers.

'Captain Fitton does not trust you,' he whispers into my hair. 'I am sure he spies on the house when we are here.' His hands drift to the back of my neck and I close my eyes and lean into him. 'You do understand my concern?' Lionel's voice drips like silk. 'Your friendship with Cromwell protects us both to a point, but your father's activities-'

His hands massage my shoulders and his breath on my neck makes it hard to concentrate.

I swing round to face him, aware I must break his contact so I can focus. My body betrays me at the most inconvenient times. 'You are overly cautious, my love. Cromwell is regarded as a friend of the Tollemaches. How many tedious dinners and lectures on the rights of man have we endured in our own dining room this last two years?'

'I cannot deny that.' Lionel shrugs. 'And maybe you are right, I am over cautious.'

'Indeed you are.' I straddle the stool at my dresser, the surface strewn with feminine combs, creams and perfumes that fill my senses, hoping they affect his too. Then I watch him close his eyes briefly and inhale, and I know I am halfway there.

418

'Let us not argue, my dear,' he whispers, his voice thick. 'Nor waste this precious time alone.' His fingers wrestle with the fastenings on his breeches, and I watch, my arms pressed together to push my breasts higher.

A smile tugs at his mouth as he enjoys the display, then he kicks off his shoes and the breeches join them on the floor. His fingers are shaking now as he grapples with the cords on his linen shirt, which falls open to reveal a surprisingly muscular chest for such an athletic man.

He does not remove the shirt, a task he always leaves to me, the naked need in his eyes as eloquent as his firm, almost hairless body. Lionel enjoys the chase as much as I and is content to move slowly in our game of wills.

Without meaning to, my mind drifts and I wonder if Lauderdale's chest is as smooth and boyish as Lionel's. I think not, for once I glimpsed a tuft of coarse red hair below his throat. My blood heats at the thought of that russet fuzz pressing against my breasts.

With an effort, I banish John and paste on a flirtatious smile to which Lionel never fails to respond. My loose robe slides from my naked thighs and I run a light finger across his chest, my tongue protruding slightly through my cochineal-stained lips.

He eases forward until he stands between my splayed knees, his hands massaging my shoulders in wide, firm strokes, eyes darkened, he bites his bottom lip.

Briefly, I wonder if the day will come when my husband's predictable and easy capitulation bores me. But not yet, not while my seduction is as satisfying for me as it is for him.

'You do wish me to be happy, don't you, Lionel?' I flick an upward look at his face, content to see he is lost in the sensations. 'If you sign the papers, our marriage will always be in accord.' My fingers snake a trail down his belly toward the light hairs of his groin, and then pause, circling a finger into the soft, red-blond hairs. 'Could you accept us never being together again. Like this?' I ask, sharper this time and abruptly remove my hand.

He releases a short, disappointed breath and his eyes snap open. 'Is that a threat, Bess? Without Ham, will our life together become empty and stale?' A smile tugs at his mouth but there is doubt in his eyes.

'No indeed.' I slide his hand from my shoulder and bring it down to cup one of my breasts. 'I do not wish us to become strangers with separate lives who no longer share these intimacies.' My nipple peaks to meet his fingertip and he sways, his weight pressing down on my shoulders.

Smiling, I wrap both arms around his waist beneath the shirt, and flick the tip of my tongue against the sweet, unblemished skin of his belly. I kiss my way down his soft stomach, much slower than I know he wishes it, pausing between each touch until he bucks against me as a hint to resume. I am in no hurry and enjoy the sweet, herby scent on his skin.

Lionel's short, sharp breaths become more frequent, though I resist the urgent pressure of his hand on the back of my neck.

Not yet, Lionel. I may have to defer to this boy-man in front of his family, and mine, but in this chamber, I am queen.

Lionel gives a whimper and I run my hands across his boyish hips, memorising the planes of his body in my head, and which touch draws the most delight. My nails furrow his lean thighs, the muscles beneath the skin tense and flex. A slow ache throbs and snakes its way through my belly, born of both my own desire and the heady thrill of my power over him.

'I love you, Bess,' he moans huskily as his stomach tightens.

My hands trace slow, winding circles ever upward. 'Do I please you, my love?' I murmur against his taught skin. Sharp flicks of my tongue, and not-so-gentle nips replace those feathery kisses.

He sighs and moans that I am his only love, his delight.

I force my voice to a low, husky whisper. 'Then fulfil this one wish of mine, and I will submit to all of yours.'

'Anything,' he gasps, his knees bent and one hand on the dresser as if he would tumble to the floor without its support. 'I would do anything for you, my Bess.' His sharp intake of breath accompanies a grip of his hand on my shoulder that is almost painful. I am tempted to bite him in return, but resist. Pain is not the way to fuel my husband's ardour, and I intend a seduction, not punishment.

420

'Let's go to the bed,' Lionel whispers, hoarse. 'I have to have you. Now.'

I can barely speak for laughing. What a heady thing it is to control a man so easily. Pity I am only permitted to lead one man by a rein, when there are others who might serve my purpose and ambitions as well.

No matter, I will have to confine my seduction of men like John, my Scottish earl, and Mrs Cromwell's husband, to sweet words, compliments and promises; Lady Elizabeth Tollemache is no whore.

Knowing that to hold out longer would cool Lionel's ardour, I choose with care the second when I bend to run my tongue along the length of him, taking him into my mouth with a light, flickering touch that ends almost before it begins.

I pull away and lift my face to his, immune to his gasp of disappointment. Did he blink and pout like that when his nurse forbade him a sweetmeat? I imagine so.

'Why do you laugh, my Bess?' His smoky eyes plead. 'Is your passion not as great as mine?'

'How can you doubt it? You are everything to me.' The sweet, half lie slips easily from my tongue. 'Will you sign the papers and pay the Committee what they demand?' I run a finger round the exposed head of his manhood, aware of his stomach tightening again as he trembles against me.

Stroking down to the shaft, my grip slackens, purposefully. Eyes wide, lips parted, panting, hesitation, and longing war within him. He wants to deny me, but cannot.

Closing my fingers around him, my hands glide upward again, whisper soft, then back to where they began in firm, caressing movements.

He quivers, eyelids fluttering. 'Yes, yes, I will sign the papers. Whatever you wish, my Bess, I can deny you nothing.' His hand tightens on my neck. 'Don't leave me like this.'

I would thank him, but my mouth is full.

Chapter 37

July 1651, Ham House

The door to the salon opens to reveal my steward, Ball in profile, his face set in an expression he uses for impertinent footmen and unwelcome visitors. I throw a quick look at Nan before rising from the untidy pile of letters and papers on the bureau, praying nothing amongst them is likely to arouse suspicion.

Captain Fitton barges into the room. I give him a weak smile I hope hides my satisfaction, that after six years of enduring his particular brand of persecution, he has yet to be promoted.

Ball's eyes widen in affront and he reaches my side at a run. 'He brought six men with him, my lady,' he whispers behind a hand. 'They are now searching the house and outbuildings.'

'We've survived such indignities before, Ball. No doubt we shall do so again.' My throat dries and I swallow with difficulty, but hope my voice sounds normal.

'As you say, my lady.' Dismissed, Ball casts a last withering look at the intruder before backing out of the room.

'Good morrow, Captain,' Nan says from the window seat. She barely looks up from her book, much less rises. 'My sister and I thought we recognised your heavy tread. Although I was more inclined to believe someone had allowed a horse into the hall.'

I have to force my mouth closed, stunned by her courage. When did Nan become so pert? At that moment she resembles Mother so keenly, I have blink away sudden tears.

'Horsemen have been spotted in the district, Miss-Lady Tollemache.' The Captain cuts his belated bow short, his narrowed eyes scanning the room.

'Horsemen? Not such an unusual occurrence, surely?' I take a step forward, intent on discouraging his further entry into the room. The man was always impertinent, how dare he barge into my private salon uninvited?

'Never mind your milksop innocence, ladies.' He skirts round me to peer into corners and twitch the window hangings aside.

'These riders took pains to avoid our patrols. We suspect they are Royalist spies.' He opens the door to a cupboard in the corner of the room, closing it again with an impatient oath when he finds it empty.

'And you imagined you would find them amongst us ladies?' Nan asks, languorously relaxing against the padded window seat.

'My orders are to keep a constant watch on this house.' His lips curl and he pauses in front of the hearth. With a contemptuous stare at the bowl of dried flowers on the tiles, he inserts his bulk into the empty chimney. His pale, over tight breeches and high cavalryman's boots remain visible below the mantle shelf, while a fringe of orange bandeau swings like a horsetail from his waist.

Nan giggles and despite my clammy palms, mirth erupts from my lips in a poorly suppressed snort.

Captain Fitton ducks back into the room and strides toward me.

'Laugh at an officer of the New Model Army, would you?' He jabs a finger at my face. 'I know you scheming Royalists. If anyone is helping these spies, it will be you.'

'You aren't even sure they *are* spies, Captain.' Nan spreads her skirts across the window seat, cocks her head and smiles. 'Or has persecution of lone ladies become your main purpose in the district?'

'Sir Lionel Tollemache is now master here, is he not?' He clasps his hands behind his back in a stance he must think intimidating, though he looks less certain of his ground than he did a moment ago.

'As you very well know, Captain.' I decide not to challenge the premise as to who is master here. I wield more power than this man would understand. 'My husband is in Richmond. He returns this evening.'

A scuffling on the gravel outside the window precedes the appearance of a soldier's helmet above the sill. I hold my breath, but within seconds its owner moves on.

'And I suppose you know nothing of any riders in the area?' The captain's face looms in front of mine.

With an effort, I drag my attention back to him. 'My sister and I received no one this morning and do not expect to.' I step back, putting a side table between us. I do not fear this man, but he has a distant relationship with soap and water I refuse to suffer for longer than necessary.

A scuffle comes from outside the door. My breath catches, and I glance again at Nan. She loses her grip on the book that slips from her lap and hits the floor with a dull thud. She closes her eyes briefly and inhales, but does not bend to retrieve it.

A soldier appears in the door, and Captain Fitton excuses himself to conduct a one-sided conversation with the arrival.

A muffled knock has me gritting my teeth. I glare at Nan, who shrugs in apology.

Captain Fitton returns to my side, his stance altered from supreme confidence to a reddening neck and shifting feet. 'My men are content the house is empty but for your family and servants.'

'Which I would happily have volunteered had you simply asked.' I march past him and fling the door wider, indicating the interview is at an end. My other hand trembles and I thrust it behind my skirt, or simpleton that he is, he would notice.

Fitton halts as he draws level with me, his shoulder in line with my forehead.

I hold my breath against the sharp tang of sweat and stale ale that emanates from the man.

'If I discover at a later date, that you,' he raises a finger at me and then flicks it toward Nan, 'or you, Mistress, knew these spies, or had knowledge of their business here, I will be back to-' Without finishing his threat, he snorts and leaves.

I slam the door on his retreating back, turn and lean against it. Relief sends nausea into my throat as the sound of rhythmic footsteps recedes along the hall, followed by shouted orders and far off hoof beats.

'Have they gone, do you think?' Nan leaps to her feet, one shoe planted on her forgotten book, creasing the page.

'Wait,' I say gently, my hand raised as I count to twenty, during which a reprimand flits through my head as to how Master Donne's poems should not be treated, but goes unspoken. 'I think it is safe now.'

The lid of the window seat flies open with a crash, and a

dishevelled male figure emerges.

'I thought I would suffocate in there. Could you nae find a more comfortable hiding place?' he says, ignoring me with mild rebuke, but there is laughter in his voice.

'Fortunate then Mama had holes drilled into the base.' I regard my father with fondness mixed with irritation. 'The Captain arrived moments after you did. There was no time to get you upstairs.'

'Thank the Lord he believed you.' He throws his cloak carelessly over a shoulder, and his boots connect with the wooden sides as he clambers awkwardly from the deep cavity.

I cast a fearful glance back at the door. 'He didn't believe us. He had the house searched!'

Nan helps him upright and pats his jacket, releasing puffs of dust. He flexes his knees and slaps dried mud from his breeches.

'He says you were seen!' I take Father's proffered cloak and bundle it into the window seat to avoid casual eyes. Our servants give us no reason to mistrust them, but I will not take chances. 'Why did you not wait until after nightfall to come to the house?'

Closing the lid, I rearrange the cushions, calming my nerves by the performance of trivial tasks.

'It is July, Elizabeth.' Father slides his fingers into his hair and roughly pushes it behind his ears. 'Darkness comes late and I could not wait to see my girls. Besides, what would you have me do? Skulk in the bushes for hours?'

'Why such impatience?' I pick a ball of fluff from his sleeve. 'We last saw you all of two years ago. At my wedding, if you recall.'

'And I can see how fruitful your marriage has proved. A coming grandchild, no less.' He delivers an affectionate pat to my swelling stomach.

'This is her third, Father, as well you know.' Nan laughs, sliding his hat brim between nervous hands. 'There are two boy babies upstairs in the nursery.'

His hands drop to his sides and his mouth turns down. 'You are angry with me.' It is not a question.

'We have certainly missed you.' Though I do not disabuse him. 'You've been gone so long, and without a word.'

'Ah sent several letters.' He looks from Nan to me, and back

425

again, his face a picture of affronted innocence.

'We never received them,' Nan whispers.

'Ach! I might hae known, the messengers most likely kept the sovereign I paid them but had no conscience about nae finishin' the task.'

'Or the messages were seized by the New Model Army,' I say.

'Aye, I didnae think of that,' he says with a self deprecating shrug.

It strikes me then that he still regards me as a young girl who needs protection from the worst aspects of the times. I am both irritated and touched. Of course he knew.

Restless, I make a quick check of the window to ensure no soldier lingers in the grounds. 'We would have written, had we any notion of where you were.'

His face softens, and with one arm round Nan, he lightly traces my jaw with his fingers. 'Moray passed on your message about your mother.'

A lump forms at the back of my throat. Is that all he can bring himself to say? That his wife of over twenty years died without him at her side, but that he is merely aware?

'Dinna fret, lass. It cannae be helped.' He eases onto a sofa as if every bone in his body aches. 'Her last letter arrived at my Edinburgh lodgings while I was still in Paris. Ah finally got tae read it when I returned there. It held something o' what she suffered.'

My head jerks up. 'She told you she was ill?'

'Nay, Catherine would ne'er complain tae me. She said she had appealed tae Lord Elgin to see tae her will. She was tired and worried about you being in London at the time of the execution when you were still weak from childbed.'

'And you did not gather from that she was setting her affairs in order?' I want to hug him to me to reassure myself he is well, but at the same time my hand clenches ready to pound him with a fist. Why wasn't he here? A man should be at his wife's deathbed. It was the least he owed her.

'Elizabeth!' Nan pleads with her eyes. 'Please don't be angry. Father has risked much to come here.'

426

'Nay, lass, your sister is right.' He makes a weary gesture at Nan and then strides to stare into the empty grate where Captain Fitton stood moments before. 'Ah sensed an inevitability aboot that letter, but ah could do nothing.'

'Mother also had another fine to pay and was frantic about where to get it.' I ignore Nan's frantic gestures for me to be silent. 'Lionel helped.' I say, hoping to engender some guilt in that cold Scots heart of his. Or am I being unjust, and losing Mother is as hard for him as it was for all of us?

'Aye, Ah'm glad. Because I couldnae help her.' His features relax into sadness and he looks suddenly old. My resentment subsides as the strain of these last months flows out of me. He is home, even if it is only for an impossibly short time.

'Oh, Father.' Nan limps toward him and takes his hand in hers.

'Where?' He says gently, that one word loaded with a dozen questions.

'St Peters Church vault,' I say with difficulty. 'We had her full title inscribed on her coffin. We did not shame her.'

His silent nod is slow and filled with regret. 'I see your hand in that, Elizabeth. Catherine was always happy bein' Mistress Murray.'

I remain silent, though I always believed Mother deserved the title, whether she could enjoy it or not. Perhaps Father is right and she never did care for it. Not the same way I did. Never mind, it is done now and I am content she will always be a noble lady.

'You were in Paris, you say?' Nan says, hovering at his elbow as if to remind him of her presence. 'How did the queen take the news of the king's execution?'

'Worse than you could imagine.' He gazes at his hands as if recalling the scene. 'I thought she would die o' grief. Screamed and greeted fer hours she did, like a lost soul. Even little Minette couldnae comfort her.'

'Is that what they call Princess Henrietta?' Nan asks.

He nods. 'Aye, a funny little thing she is, but a comfort tae her mither. Then the queen's grief turned to an almost insane fury,' Father goes on. 'She knows all their names ye know.' He looks at me and gives a slow nod. 'All those who signed the death warrant.

427

May God save them if she ever returns to England.'

'How can she?' I say, sceptical. 'Parliament will never allow her back, and why would she wish to come?'

'The queen always believed that if the king refused tae give in, Parliament would have to relent. Facing the fact she had given him bad advice all this time was what broke her.'

'No one believed they would kill him,' I say as once again tears threaten.

His frown darkens his face, ageing him. 'Cromwell made a grave mistake. Scotland will never forgive the English fer such arrogance.'

I am about to tell him Earl Lauderdale told me the same thing, but decide against it. Nan gives me a knowing look, and I wonder if she is aware the earl and I correspond? I dismiss the notion immediately. I can easily explain his letters away should the need arise.

Father slaps his thighs with both hands, turns and heads for a dresser where a tray laden with glasses sits. He pours a glass from a pitcher and downs it in one before pouring another. 'I hae messages to deliver to those whom we hope will join the new campaign.'

'Not another invasion, Father?' Nan says, a resigned whine I echo in my own head.

'Aye, though this one is different. Charles the Second was crowned King of Scots by the Marquis of Argyll at Scone, and he has taken command of the Scottish army.' He gulps a draught from the glass and smacks his lips, waving it in the air.

I try not to sigh as I make a note to summon Ball and order more wine. Lionel will not be pleased, for he commented only yesterday that stocks were low and obtaining more will not be easy. French wine is subject to exorbitant taxes and the French privateers plunder English shipping with impunity.

'Why must there be more fighting, Father?' Nan asks, still clutching his hat like some sort of talisman.

I cannot blame her. After Dunbar, we are all weary of war that goes nowhere but to waste Royalist lives. With each defeat, Parliament seems more determined than ever to punish families like us.

Father wipes away the red stream that dribbles down his chin. 'This one is different. O'er twelve thousand men are recruited already and King Charles is in Edinburgh.' He holds a finger to his lips to warn us this is a secret.

I pace the floor, trying not to let my scepticism show, but I doubt this new plan will be any different from the last. 'Father? Hasn't Robert Blake broken up the Royalist stronghold on the Scilly Isles? And Sir Edward Hyde was ordered to leave Madrid by King Philip, who prefers to remain on friendly terms with the Commonwealth?'

'Och who cares aboot the Spaniards. The Irish are negotiating for aid from the Duke of Lorraine.'

'And is not William Penn's squadron chasing Prince Rupert around the Mediterranean?'

'That is simply a rumour, Elizabeth. Rupert is nowhere near the Mediterranean. He's playing the pirate off the coast of Madeira.' Father laughs and slaps his thigh.

I open my mouth to offer more arguments, but Nan shoots me a warning look and I revert to silence. I dare not even mention the new Confiscation Act. Seventy Royalist estates are to be sold for the benefit of the Commonwealth. How long before Sir Lionel Tollemache joins that list, targeted due to the continuing rebellion of his father-in-law?

'Father,' I say carefully. 'I want the king back more than anyone, but realistically, what chances does this invasion have?'

'Wheesht, girl, have ye no faith?' He halts with the glass halfway to his mouth. 'Our new King Charles believes the Scots will turn awa' from the Kirk Party and look tae the Royalists to drive Cromwell out of Scotland. Those Puritans are a hard bunch to deal with, ye knaw. The clans dinna like 'em.' He strides to a sofa and sprawls inelegantly across the squab. 'Our agents have been recruiting a Royalist army in the Highlands fer months now.'

'Can you stay a little while?' My tone is hopeful, but at the same time brittle. I expected more emotion from him about Mother, but his mind is so full of the Scots invasion plans he has no room for her. Or perhaps two years is long enough for a man to mourn a wife and the mother of his children?

'Fer the night. But I must be awa' by the morning.'

'I shall set cook to make a family dinner and you can tell us all about your adventures.' Nan bounces at his elbow, his hat finally discarded on the sofa as she limps to the door. 'I think I hear Cousin Anne returning from Kingston with Kate and Meg. They will be so thrilled to see you, Father.'

The door closes and his eyes soften as he takes in my swollen figure. 'How goes it, Betty?'

'I am very well.' The lie slips out easily. What good would it do to tell him the nausea has not abated this time and I am plagued with stomach pains and intermittent bleeding? I pray all might be well, if I am careful.

'Ah wonder what yer husband will say when his fugitive father-in-law joins you for dinner.' He nudges my shoulder playfully, chuckling as I join him on the sofa.

'Lionel is very tolerant of our scheming family. He would never criticise us for our allegiance, though it frustrates him sometimes.' I bridle at his making jokes about the man he chose for me and to whom I have pledged my loyalty and respect.

'I heard Parliament tried to take the estate again?'

'We found a way to manoeuvre our way out of that predicament. The compound fee and the fines were harsh, but we have survived thus far.'

'Ah'm glad.' He leans both forearms on his knees and looks sideways. 'Then what worries ma lovely girl? I know ye well, and there is something. . .'

I glance at the door which remains firmly closed, rise and slide open the drawer of my bureau. I retrieve a letter lying there and hand it to him.

'The Cromwells dined here frequently right up to the time he was sent to Ireland. We had not seen them for some time when I received this letter from Mistress Cromwell.'

Father opens out the parchment with a slow nod. 'Your mother wrote and told me how delighted she was wi' Cromwell's visits. She says it kept the neighbours guessing and the troopers at bay.'

'A certain Captain is not so easily fooled. But never mind him, read the letter.'

. . . I am sore worried for the fever is great this time, and he has sunk into a deep melancholy. I appeal to you as a Christian soul, to send some of that which is the only thing I believe will soothe his malaise.

He looks up after a few seconds, as if too impatient to read the whole page, so I jump in to explain.

'Cromwell's ague gets worse, the episodes increase in frequency.'

'We wondered why he had handed over command of the army to Generals Monck and Lambert.' He waves the letter in the air before handing it back to me. 'This is dated two months since. Have ye acted upon it?'

I nod, ashamed at the eagerness with which I reacted to the request, so I might appear benevolent to someone I secretly view as an enemy. Who could resist being of consequence to the Lord Chief?

'I expect your supply has run low by now.' Father takes a wrapped packet from his pocket and hands it to me. No tiny blue glass bottle this, but a square of canvas and oilskin not easily concealed in one hand. 'Fortunate then I brought you more.'

'You carried this with you all the way from France?' I slowly turn the package over in my hand. A firm square like a small brick tied with rough string and sealed with wax.

'Aye, where else can quinine be obtained? Those Jesuit monks can always be persuaded tae part wi' it too. For a price.' He sniffs, cynicism etched on his features.

'Were you not afraid of being searched?'

'Huh, I was more afraid o' being recognised by some ambitious Puritan who decides ma arrest might further his career.'

'You don't think I did the wrong thing in helping Mistress Cromwell?'

A light of understanding enters his gaze. 'Is that what carves those lines beside your pretty eyes, my love?'

'If Cromwell defeats the Royalists again, it will be my doing.' The doubts that have plagued me in the small hours rise to the surface. Up until now I have remained strong, resolute in that what I do is for the family. Now under my father's gaze I am a child again, begging for approval.

'His victories cannae be placed at your door, Betty. Whether Cromwell lives or dies has little effect on the next Scots invasion.'

'How can you be sure? Maybe if he is not their leader, they will not fight so well. The New Model Army is Cromwell's achievement after all.'

'It is nae so simple as that. Besides, who is tae say he woulda died without the quinine in any case? They say he is a tough ould bird and has shrugged off the fever before.' He wraps a comforting arm around my shoulder. 'You cannae take on tha' responsibility. Your mither and I promoted your friendship wi' Cromwell. It keeps yer enemies off guard.'

'Not yours. The entire Parliament army would applaud your capture.' I nudge him playfully. 'Though Lord Cromwell believes I have come to see the error of my Royalist ways. I expound on the rights of the common man with deep conviction.' I execute a mock bow to make him smile, while my fingers pick at the wax seal on the parcel string. 'If this new invasion fails, it will be partly my fault.'

'Whatever happens is God's will.' He inhales and licks his lips, thoughtful. 'Cromwell is a great leader, and talk says he will be offered the crown.'

'He would never accept it.' An image of his rough hewn face enters my head. 'He hasn't worked so hard to rid us of the last king simply to step into his shoes.'

'Mebbe so. But is it not a good thing for Lady Tollemache to have a friend in high places? Especially if that friend is Cromwell?'

'You make it sound as if we are already doomed.'

'Nay, lass, Lord Leven knows what he is about. He says there is a chance at victory, an' I believe him. I simply like tae play Devil's advocate and prepare for all outcomes.' His grip tightens and he leans toward me until my cheek brushes the light stubble on his face. 'Saving Cromwell's life is a Christian mercy to a sick man. You have nothing to feel guilty about.'

'And if Lord Leven brings about this Royalist victory? Suppose it becomes known I helped keep Cromwell alive? It would put me at risk of being branded a traitor.' My nerves stretch tight and I drop the parcel onto a low table, glad to be rid of it.

'Who knows you sent the quinine to Mistress Cromwell?' His eyes narrow and he strokes his chin with one hand.

'Mother, of course, but she can tell no one now. Cousin Anne, who is fiercely loyal and would never betray us. Then there was Mistress Bridget Ireton.' His face clouds and I rush on. 'Her mother swore her to secrecy, both of them too afraid of discovery in case it came out that Cromwell took 'Devil's Dust'.'

'That is all to the good. And Lionel?'

I shake my head. 'No. Nor would I ever expose him to such a risk. Besides, he may have tried to stop me.'

Father chuckles softly. 'I doubt it. He has more diplomacy in his boyish head than you or I could imagine. It wouldnae surprise me if he knew everything, but pretends otherwise so it cannae be held agin him. You could learn much frae that husband o' yours.'

'Sometimes I regret deceiving him. He is so devoted to me.'

'Do ye love him?' The question comes as a surprise, especially from this source.

'I do, very much.' John's face floats into my head but not in a disturbing way. I love them both, one gently and quietly, the other with an overwhelming passion I cannot ignore, but am in no position to do anything about. Perhaps it is better that way.

'Have you heard from Earl Lauderdale of late?' The question startles me, as if Father reads my mind.

I frown. 'You know he writes to me?'

'Aye, ah encourage it. If you are tae be of any use to the cause, ye must be aware o' what is happenin'.'

'He hasn't said much, other than I am to hide any weapons we keep in the house. The Trained Bands have orders to confiscate anything suspicious and are watching known Royalists. Captain Fitton said the same himself not an hour ago.'

'Aye, my journeys to France become more hazardous. Ah suspect ah'm being followed by one o' Thurloe's lackeys to see what ah'm up tae. Twice now I hae been spotted and yet nae one tried tae stop me.'

'Tell me truthfully, will this new invasion be so different from Preston and Dunbar?'

433

'Of course it will.' His hand comes down on my shoulder. 'Then I may be able tae return home fer good. How ah hate being a man in hiding, unable tae stay in any one place for lang. Nor do ah wish tae end ma life on the end of a rope.'

My smile is weak, for we both know a traitor's death is far worse than that.

'Cromwell is not a vengeful man, Father. I have learned that much about him during our acquaintance. He may grant you a pardon if you-'

'Renounce ma king and swear fealty tae Parliament?' His lip curls. 'Nay, ah'm nae willin' tae take such a risk, ma girl.'

My cheeks grow hot as I realise the absurdity of what I am saying. Of course he can do no such thing. He is a king's man and his life is inextricably linked with the royal court. He has nothing else.

'Leslie argues we should make a stand in Scotland.' His enthusiasm lightens the room as his soft voice flows over me. 'Support for the Royalist cause is strongest there. Whereas, the young king wants to march the Scots south down the western side of the Pennines and gain support from Wales before his march on London. We should be able to gather sixteen thousand men by the time he nears the capital.'

If he gets that far.

'We, Father? You surely don't intend to join the fight?' Panic grips me as I recall the Royalist army is led by a twenty-one-year-old youth who seeks revenge for the murder of his father; his adversary a veteran soldier with five years' experience, and a well-honed army to command.

'Nay, ah'm too old to pick up a sword. Diplomacy has always been ma greatest weapon, not soldiery.' He slaps his knee with one hand and laughs, but there is regret in his eyes.

'And Cromwell? How many men can he summon to oppose the king?'

Father's sheepish shrug is the only response he gives. 'Now.' He encircles my shoulder with an arm. 'I think it's time ah met ma grandsons.'

434

Chapter 38

October 1651, White House, The Strand

This house is the least restful place I can think of to recuperate from any illness, much less the loss of a child. Carriages rumble past at all hours and costermongers call from in The Strand on one side and on the other, the river is crowded with boats and catcalling rivermen, all of whom contrive to mock my enforced idleness.

I insist my sisters stay with us in London, hoping their company may help distract me from brooding on my loss; a stillborn daughter come too soon. Conversely, after ten long days confined to bed, their sad expressions and over-soft voices grate on my nerves.

Lionel too eschews the sickroom, though he sends me sweetmeats, flowers and small gifts to cheer me. On the occasions when he spares me a half hour, he parrots the chirurgeon's pronouncement; that no damage was done. I am young, so there will be other babes.

What does he know? What can any man know? I carried a living child within me for six months. She had a face I imagined to be a feminine version of my pretty Thomas, but without the strength of her brother. I wonder if her laugh was also like angel wings.

Now she is gone, and I am bereft, empty in a way that the removal of a collection of flesh and blood from my womb cannot adequately describe.

'Is there anything I can fetch for you, Elizabeth?' Kate hovers. She cannot bear to leave me since it happened, though I long for some solitude and time to think.

Bring my baby back.

I blink away welling tears that flow too easily these days. 'No, dearest. There is nothing I need. Except perhaps the news-sheet. I would read the report again.'

'Is that wise?' Kate adopts her matronly face. 'Such melancholy news might sap your strength further. Besides, Lionel says you must not be bothered by any talk of the battle.'

'Nonsense! I would read the casualty notice. I may recognise some names.' She is about to forbid me, but I tap a finger lightly against her cheek. 'If I become upset I will stop reading. I promise.'

Kate hands me the latest soiled copy of the *Mercurius Politicus* with an apologetic sigh. 'This is weeks old, but all I could find I'm afraid. A woman in The Strand was handing out copies for three pence.'

'I do miss the *Mercurius Aulicus.*' I take it from her with a grimace, wary of the suspicious stain on the top right corner of the front page. 'Though what proportion of this is rebel propaganda, and what is truth, who can say.' I read the gloating tone of the page with dismay.

During Father's visit last July, he failed to tell me the campaign had already begun with Cromwell having crossed the river Forth to dislodge General Leslie from Stirling. Unable to break the English line, the Highlanders withdrew, but were surrounded and pursued for miles. Two thousand Scots were killed and another fourteen hundred taken prisoner at Inverkeithing. Even while we sat with Father that precious summer evening, all those men already lay dead.

Driven south by David Leslie's troops, King Charles occupied Worcester in late August, but it was no use. The Earl of Derby and Sir Thomas Tyldesley were soundly defeated by Colonel Robert Lilburne at Wigan.

'It seems, Kate,' I lower the page, thoughtful. 'Father's belief in support for the young king was misplaced.'

Did memories of the violent plunder after the Engager invasion of forty-eight remain fresh in their minds? Whatever the reason, anti-Scottish feeling ran high.

'Don't think about it, Elizabeth. It's bad for your humours.' Kate offers me a steaming bowl, the smell of which makes my nose wrinkle. 'It's calves' foot jelly,' she says, interpreting my look. 'To build up your strength.'

I roll my eyes and return to the news-sheet, though there is nothing in the report I do not already know. King Charles' route to London was cut off, leaving him trapped on three sides in Worcester, with his men bombarded by Parliamentarian artillery.

I skip the details of the final battle, unwilling to torture myself when I know too well the outcome. One snippet cheers me a little. 'The Duke of Buckingham, Lord Wilmot and King Charles must have escaped, for a reward is offered here for their capture.' Silently I hope that they may continue to elude their searchers.

At the bottom of the page, a jumble of letters leaps out at me, then settles again to form words, and a groan escapes my lips.

'Elizabeth?' Kate sets the bowl of brown sludge on the dresser. 'You've gone pale, what is it?'

'Earl Derby was court martialed in Chester, condemned as a traitor, and executed.'

I recall with a pang the bravery of his wife, Lady Charlotte, who refused to surrender Lathom House to the Roundheads. The fact that when she was away from home two years later, her servants relinquished the house she had fought so hard for, reminds me why I must not leave Ham unprotected for long. Could a similar fate befall us if I allowed Lionel to whisk me away to Helmingham?

About to crumple the news-sheet, a name catches my eye, and a gasp is forced through my lips. How could I have missed this? 'Earl Lauderdale was captured at Worcester,' I read aloud. 'He has been taken to the Tower of London.'

'I knew that news-sheet would upset you.' Kate flaps round me, makes a grab for the page, but misses. 'There is nothing written about Father is there?'

'What? No, no, he is not mentioned.' I wave her away, impatient.

My hopes for Father are that he keeps his head low in Edinburgh, or that he has escaped to Paris and hides amongst the exiled court. 'Don't you see what this means? Earl Derby paid the ultimate price, so what will they do to Lauderdale?' My hands shake and a roaring starts up in my ears.

'Earl Lauderdale you say.' Kate drapes an arm round the bedpost behind my head. 'The name is familiar. Is he a friend of Father's?'

'Er-yes, yes he is.' Images arise of John's smile at Ham on the night the king escaped, when he kissed me before he left. How many times have I relived that kiss since then? A hundred? Two?

The door opens again and Nan enters, Cousin Anne hard on her heels, their cheeks and noses red from the crisp autumn cold. Kate leaves my side with a swish of skirts to gabble the fate of the Earl of Derby with accompanying hand gestures.

'Enough, Kate, that is dreadful news.' Nan winces as she pulls off her gloves. 'But I have worse.'

How can that be so? Unless . . . I haul myself higher in the bed. 'You have heard something of Earl Lauderdale? He has been sentenced?'

Nan's mouth opens and closes again. 'Lauderdale? No, I-' She frowns, glances at Kate and then back at me. 'Our news is of another sort. Cousin Anne and I have this moment returned from the New Exchange, at Charing Cross. More soldiers are gathered there even than yesterday.'

I struggle to remain interested, wishing them all away. All I can think about is John, shackled and incarcerated with nothing in his future but a traitor's death.

'How these survivors of Worcester manage to reach the city I will never know.' Nan takes Kate's place on the side of the bed, her face close to mine. 'Each time I see them on the streets, my heart twists all over again. You would think I would be accustomed to the sight of them by now.'

Cousin Anne fluffs out her springy hair flattened by her cloak. 'How can one become used to a sight of such tragedy?' Her distress seems excessive, until I recall that most of them are Scotsmen.

'Many of them are in rags,' Nan says. 'Too desperate to hide, they beg openly on the streets where they risk being handed over to the army, or simply dying of exposure in filthy alleys.' Her voice catches. 'Such brave men, and many of them officers. Their property is forfeit and they have families to feed.' She looks to Cousin Anne for confirmation. 'We gave them all the coins we had, but it was not nearly enough.'

I am proud of Nan, but at the same time frantic with worry. She and Cousin Anne issued notices to the churches and alehouses that alms were being given out at our rear door to any who ask.

'Ball says thirty poor souls arrived last night,' Nan says proudly. 'He allowed some to sleep in the coach house and sent them upriver by barge this morning. I only wish I could find more clothes so they could discard those ragged uniforms. It makes them too easily identified.'

'There are hundreds of destitute souls in London, Nan.' I ease backwards to relieve the pressure on my back, then wince as the soreness in my nether regions peaks, bringing the horror of my recent ordeal back to me. 'We cannot feed them all,' I snap. 'Besides, nothing gets past those Parliament spies. You must be careful.'

Mother would have been proud of Nan. I hope she remains discreet in front of Lionel, but I hesitate to remind her. I do not wish to see her silent scorn for my husband, who chooses to avoid trouble at all costs.

Nan turns back at the door. 'It is hardly a secret we are Royalists, but I will take care.' She grabs Kate's arm as she passes. 'Come and help me, Kate, I must see what we have spare in the kitchens for this evening's visitors.'

The abandoned calves' foot jelly sits cooling on the dresser as their uneven footsteps recede along the hall.

'Nan has taken to her mission of charity with enthusiasm.' I address Cousin Anne, who bends over the press folding fresh linens.

'Indeed she has. And before you ask, I have tried to dissuade her, but she is adamant. The girl treats her new task like a calling.'

'Perhaps there is a young man who has engendered these merciful feelings in my sister?' Nan's bright eyes and breathless enthusiasm are reminiscent of Katherine's in the presence of her Roundhead. The thought I may have to face such a situation a second time makes me uneasy.

'I doubt you have to look in that direction.' Anne snorts and straightens, one hand pressed to her lower back. 'Did you think you were the only one in the house who holds the Royalist cause close to their heart? She is as brave as you are, that one.'

'Her courage is admirable, but still causes me anxiety. These days no one of rank is above being arrested.'

A discreet knock comes at the door, and leaving Anne to deal with the intrusion, I relax back on my pillows and allow my thoughts to drift. Could one of those ragged soldiers who had marched through rain and dangerous roads for days without food have been John before his capture?

A shadow passes over my closed eyelids and I look up into Anne's worried face. 'My lady, you have a visitor.'

I frown, confused. 'Lionel? Surely he knows not to stand on ceremony? He always-'

'It is not Sir Lionel.' Her sharp tone silences me. 'Master Cromwell is downstairs and requests an interview with you.'

I glance down with dismay at my creased nightshirt, the rumpled bed covered with news-sheets, and the remains of a late breakfast on a tray I have not bothered to have removed. 'I cannot receive him here.'

'Shall I tell him you are indisposed?' Anne asks.

'No! Instruct Ball to ask him to wait. Give him wine, or something.' I hurl back the covers and ease my legs over the side of the bed.

'What are you doing, Elizabeth?' Anne tries to restrain me. 'The chirurgeon said-'

'That charlatan!' I throw off her hand. 'He errs on the side of caution to secure his fee.' My legs shake as blood surges through my veins. 'The bleeding is staunched and the pain almost gone. I refuse to lie here like an invalid when I could be-' My hand grips hers in panic. 'Nan! She must be warned. Cromwell doesn't travel alone, and if his men suspect her, they will show no mercy.'

'Be easy now, I will see to it.'

While she is gone, I pull clothes from the closet at random, my head full of questions. Why has Cromwell come here? To tell me Father has been arrested for his part in the invasion? Or has he news of John? No, he has no idea Earl Lauderdale and I are... What are we? Not lovers, but there is something between us I can neither identify nor explain.

By the time Anne returns, I have a pile of clothes gathered in an untidy heap on the coverlet.

'Look at the mess you have made,' she chides me gently and wrests a petticoat from my shaking hands.

'What can he want?' I step into a petticoat and almost trip. 'How

440

does he seem? Are there many men with him?'

'I do not know.' Her deft fingers fasten the ribbons of my gown. 'Ball showed him into the Master's office. I have not seen him.'

'Lionel always leaves everything such a mess in there. It is not the best room. Will Cromwell feel slighted?'

Anne ties my sleeves and fluffs out my hair. 'You will find out soon enough.'

'No, Anne, not those slippers. The heeled ones make me taller.' I chew a fingernail, thinking. 'If he is not here to deliver bad news, maybe I can ask a favour.'

'Trust you to turn every situation to your own advantage, Elizabeth.' She laughs but it is a sad sound. Anne is never easy with Cromwell in the house. 'What favour do you wish of him now?'

'Hand me some milk, would you. My throat is so dry.' I take the glass from her and drain it. 'The news-sheet said Cromwell supported Earl Derby's appeal, although it failed. If he was prepared to save one earl, he might be willing to do the same for another.'

Anne's eyes widen in the only display of disapproval she dares, her fingers gripped on the metal catches beneath my bodice. 'Hold still. These stays are difficult to fasten.'

* * *

I cannot fully describe my shock on entering the room where Oliver Cromwell stands beside the window that looks onto the river.

Without waiting for his master to acknowledge my presence, the uniformed officer who let me in bows and retreats. The door clicks shut and I am alone with a man I barely recognise.

Cromwell stands on the far side of Lionel's desk, his hands clasped behind his back and his full attention on something beyond the window. Or does he see nothing except his inner thoughts? Sunlight floods his coarse, fleshy features and I have to prevent a gasp escaping at the grey pallor of his skin. Never an attractive man, now he looks the figure of vengeance before whom so many have trembled.

441

His brown jerkin is no better made than any common soldier's attire, and his boots are worn and scuffed at the toes.

Since our last dinner at Ham, he has spent over a year conquering the Irish and then the Scots. How many men has he killed since we last spoke? Ten thousand? Twenty?

I do not tremble. And even if I do, it is from weakness at leaving my sick bed so soon, not from fear.

'Welcome to the White House, sir,' I say to remind him he is here uninvited.

His head turns slowly, as if mildly curious as to who dares to intrude on his moment of contemplation. 'Is this printed silk I see on these walls?' His slow, ponderous gaze sweeps the room.

The remark takes me by surprise but I refuse to let him discompose me. 'Indeed, yes. This house belonged to my husband's grandfather and he had the silk imported, I believe. What think you of these bold colours?'

'Frivolity and extravagance are vices akin to vanity.' His voice is a snarl, rougher even than I remember. 'I think I will have the draping of walls with coloured paper banned.'

My mouth opens but nothing comes out. Is this the same man who expounded on the music of Richard Derham at Ham when he came to dinner?

'I see by your expression you are disturbed by my countenance, Lady Tollemache.' His fleshy lips stretch into a travesty of a smile. 'You are, I believe, familiar with the state of my health?'

'There are always rumours.' I toy with denial, but a blatant lie will only engender his distrust. 'I was told you made a complete recovery.'

'Another rumour, and one that is somewhat embellished.' The smile returns. 'Are you aware I reside now at Hampton Court, my lady? Though the palace is more my sick room than a prize for my triumphs.'

I choose not to respond, hating the very idea that this man occupies my beloved king's home. My murdered king.

'The fever subsided,' he continues, 'but there are days when the black spirit plagues me.' He leans his weight against the desk and sighs as if glad of its support. 'I'm relieved to see infirmity does not haunt you, my dear Elizabeth. As usual, you look in rude health.'

I bridle at this careless disregard all men have for the ordeals of women. 'I have recently birthed a stillborn child, sir. An event that caused me both physical and mental pain, though melancholy is not part of my nature.'

A glint of sympathy enters his eyes and he nods his large head. 'Forgive me, but there is colour in your cheeks and your eyes are bright, whereas, I-' he closes his eyes briefly, 'am under no illusion how time and sickness treats me.'

'Is not all our suffering God's will, sir?' My sharp tongue proves stronger than my pity.

He turns from the window, hands still clasped behind his back. 'Now you mock me, Lady Tollemache.' He rakes me with his cynical gaze. 'I have come to a difficult place, and can only wait upon the good Lord to tell me what to do next.'

'Did the fight at Worcester not prove a satisfactory victory?' My stomach churns with distress at the thought of over eight thousand prisoners who face being sent to the colonies.

'There are those who would say so, and others who wonder why I cannot inspire total devotion in the people.' He brings a fist down on the desktop with such violence, it makes me jump. 'Whenever I feel we have established order, another rabble of malcontents rise against me in support of a king who offers them nothing but vanity and his own form of slavery.'

'The young King Charles is not like his father.' I hesitate, wondering how much to reveal. 'Those who know him well say he is more willing to compromise.'

'Hah! He has his father's cunning and took the Solemn League and Covenant to keep the Scots on his side. I doubt Presbyterianism in England will last long. The Anglican Bishops would not allow it.'

'You make it sound as if you might accept his kingship on certain terms.'

Has the great Oliver Cromwell had enough of fighting? Will the king be permitted home? The thought makes my pulse race. With an ally in both camps, I may achieve what I have always wanted. A place at court.

'Those Stuarts will never negotiate,' he snarls. 'And you surprise me, Lady Tollemache. To advocate a new king, when I thought I had played a part in your education?'

With Mother's encouragement and her whisper in my ear, I pretended to take this man's rhetoric and treat it like Holy Scripture, my mouth pulled into a tight smile as he condemned all I loved to oblivion. I fawned and charmed to the best of my ability, when what I wanted more than anything was to claw my nails down that flabby cheek and call him a bloody, hard-hearted murderer.

'I still read the *Mercurius Politicus*, as you suggested so I may understand how things are being altered for all our good.' I choose my words carefully. 'Does not the power of the sword give title to Government, who, though unlawfully invested, must be obeyed.'

His shrewd gaze settles on me and then slides to the chair beside the empty fireplace. 'Forgive me, my lady. Please sit.' He waves a hand in my general direction. 'And yet I wonder if you really believe, as I do, that all men should decide their own destiny, with laws designed to protect them?'

'Perhaps.' I stand firm, unwilling to sit in his presence, though I am surprised to find I am shaking. 'But we still need a king to lead us. Men of lesser origins lack the weight of authority, or the wisdom of a sovereign.'

'And do you think your late king possessed such wisdom? Does the new one?'

He sighs, as if he grows weary of forcing his beliefs on a reluctant audience. Not at all like the man who paced the ballroom at Ham making informed and lively comments on architecture to an enraptured audience; albeit of his own peers and obsequious followers. Within recent memory, this man pontificated upon the beauty of Hampton Court, and the sonorous verses of Donne.

Rumour has it, that after Naseby, he revelled in his victory and laughed like a drunkard, eyes shining, and his coat splattered with blood. Now he looks spent, shrunken somehow with vagueness in his eyes. Is he in pain, or as he said himself, troubled by the unfathomable hearts of a nation he believed he had finally conquered?

'I lost my own son to the war, did you know that, Elizabeth?' his eyes take on a faraway look as if remembering. 'My Oliver.'

The names of other men's lost sons spring to my tongue, but a silent nod is my only response.

He lifts a hand to waist level and stares at it. 'Do you know how much blood I carry on this hand? To surrender what I have sacrificed to a despotic ruler would be a betrayal of everything I, and indeed the common man, has fought for.'

Disappointment burns my throat. He is as intransigent as the man he destroyed.

I can summon no sympathy for him now as he wallows in his uncertainty, and rails against the ingratitude of those he dominates. Well, let him doubt himself, it is fitting.

He sighs and massages his brow with his fingers. 'I apologise. The time for regret is long gone. I swear Worcester was the end of Royalist aggression. I hope you welcome that, Lady Tollemache?'

'I do, sir.'

'Are you aware, my dear Elizabeth, that gossip has made us lovers?'

My chin jerks upward to meet his burning gaze. 'Surely not, sir?'

A lump forms in my throat, but before I can reply, he speaks again.

'Does that scandalise or disgust you?' A cynical, almost proud smile curls his thick mouth, showing he is neither.

'I feel it dishonours us both.' And he, twice my age!

'A clever answer, but it will not stop the gossip which threatens to harm my reputation as a man of God. I am appointed by Him to do His work, and as such, I must be above reproach.'

'His Majesty King Charles said the same thing.'

His eyes darken and he takes a long stride forward, taking my chin in his calloused hand. 'Still my headstrong and reckless Elizabeth, though I admire your honesty.'

I want to pull away, but instead grit my teeth and endure, unwilling to give him the satisfaction of giving in first.

His harsh laugh fills the room, and, as if he senses my revulsion, he drops his hand.

'Are you saying that our association, innocent though it is, must end, sir?' I step away from him and re-arrange a pile of books on a table, using the action to put space between us.

'Why? Would you miss me, Elizabeth?' His voice is unbearably soft.

I compose a pretty lie which dies on my lips when I realise it is not a lie. I will indeed miss him. His quick mind and our discussions sometimes remind me of my father; though without the divine inspiration. At the risk of sounding insincere, I merely nod.

'Aye, I too.' His eyes close briefly. 'Though I hold our friendship in high regard, and will not bow to cheap talk. However in future, our meetings must take place in a more public forum. No private dinners with no one present but your husband and my wife.'

'Of course, sir.' I wonder when this caution will begin, for we are alone now and my husband is from home. Did I really think he was about to ask me to become his mistress? Surely not. He is too conscious of his position as a guardian of men's morals to succumb to base behaviour. And how would I refuse him without offending the great man? Because God knows that is what I would do.

'I came here to ask a favour of you, my dear.'

He seems unable to meet my eye and then it comes to me and my pulse quickens. There is only one thing that it is in my power to give. The reason he risks these rumours that could ruin his standing as God's instrument. Nor could he request Lionel to quit the room in his own house so he might be alone with his wife.

'Allow me to make this interview easier for you. You require more quinine.'

He releases a slow, relieved breath. 'You never were one to play games, Elizabeth. For that I applaud you.'

You don't know me at all. I do that very thing all the time.

'I do not ask too much?' His heavy brow rises and there is uncertainty in his face. The great Lord Cromwell is not sure of my answer.

His wife must have revealed her source, which doesn't surprise me for she is a good woman and would find such a secret a dreadful burden to bear. Then why did he come himself? Is it his pride that prevents him using his wife to plead for him? Whatever his reasons, I have to admire him.

'You do not.' I savour this moment of superiority; one I doubt

446

will last long.

He gives a low chuckle, relaxed now. Did he expect the ceiling to fall in on us? 'I trust you not to fail me. And that you will keep my secret.'

'Is it a shameful thing that you succumb to bouts of the marsh fever? Or. that you take quinine? Why should you suffer condemnation for making use of an effective medicine?'

'Do not toy with me.' A glint of amusement lights his eyes. 'You are no ignorant lass without knowledge of the world. Everyone knows the 'Devil's Dust' is brought from the southern Americas by Jesuit monks, a Popish concoction designed to undermine the church.'

'No matter how many times I hear those words, I can never make sense of them. This is a cure for a deadly fever? What fools could reject a natural remedy?'

His shrug tells me he too is at a loss. 'What I know, is that when the ague takes me, it lasts longer and saps more of my strength each time. After Dunbar I thought I would die. Indeed it will kill me one day.'

'Something will kill us all,' I retort with a calmness I do not feel. This conversation takes a sinister tone that makes me uneasy. I do not wish to hear of his struggles. His fears. I have enough of my own. If only Lionel would return, for I have had enough of this game.

'Hah! You always were a forward wench.' He leans his rear against the desk and folds his arms. 'What would a lovely young woman like you know of the shadow of death that hangs over a sick old man.'

A sick old man who has killed thousands. Perhaps they come back to haunt you.

'I will send to the queen's court in Paris for what you need on the morrow.' I still have the packet Father gave me, safely locked away at Ham, but I prefer to let him believe the dowager Queen Henrietta Maria holds the key to his health. The irony appeals to me. 'In return, I would ask something of you.'

His eyes narrow and he leans back to regard me down his nose. 'You would bargain with me, Elizabeth? The leader of the best fighting force the country has ever known?'

'I would ask a favour of a friend, knowing it to be in his power.'

'And what is this favour?' He lifts a brow.

'Several prisoners were captured at Worcester and are being held in the Tower of London.'

'You glorify that rout by calling it a battle?' He plays for time, which makes me think he weighs his request against mine.

'Call it what you wish. There is one whose life is important to me. I would ask you to spare it.'

'*All* those incarcerated are guilty of treason against the English people.'

'I'm aware of that. I do not ask for this man's release. Only clemency. Spare him from a traitor's death.'

'And who is this man who brings the colour to your cheeks, my lady?'

'The Earl of Lauderdale.'

'That Scots bastard.' He snorts and turns away. 'The blackguard who urged Charles Stuart to escape from Hampton Court, though the dithering fool wouldn't trust his plan.' He turns back to me, chin jutted forward inches from my face. 'He's not even a pretty fellow one might expect a fine lady to plead for. His hair is as red as a fox and his voice so distorted with that Scots speech, I cannot make out a word he says.'

'A slight exaggeration, sir.' My hands clench as I stop myself springing to John's defence. I will not weaken my position by revealing how much this means to me. 'The earl has been of service to my family. He saved my father from certain execution twice. I-we owe him a great deal.'

Narrowed eyes regard me steadily and I pray he is not about to ask if his capitulation hinges on my obtaining the quinine. To turn a gentleman's agreement into an unseemly tussle would be the final indignity.

His shoulders slump and he dry washes his face with both hands. 'Lauderdale, eh?' he says after a moment.

'Yes, sir.'

He stares off into the distance, though I doubt he sees anything other than what is in his own head. 'If I let that Scots braggart live, he'll remain in the Tower for as long as it pleases me to keep him there.'

I clasp my hands together to stop them trembling. 'I understand. The earl will be eternally grateful for your mercy.'

'The Tower of London offers little in the way of mercy, my lady.'

'Perhaps not, but he will have his life.'

He pushes upright away from the desk, leans back to grasp a pair of gloves from behind him and makes for the door. The creak of his leather jerkin grates on my nerves and I try to think of a way to keep him here a little longer. There is something I must know. His hand grasps the handle but halts, and his head swings toward me.

'I see something else in your face.'

I clamp my lips together, unable to form the words.

He straightens and smiles. 'Ask me the question that tightens your gut, Lady Tollemache, lest it poison you.'

I lick my lips and inhale. 'Why did King Charles have to die?'

His hand falls to his side and he sighs, his gaze sliding to the window again. 'How could I know what demons I would unleash? That by a single act, my name will be cursed for an eternity.' His fleshy lips tighten into a straight line. 'They call him 'Martyr' now, can you believe that? Though I ask no one's forgiveness. Not even yours, Elizabeth.'

'Good.' Anger surges through me that even now, he can summon no compassion for what he did to the king. 'You shall not have it. I ask only your reasons.'

A shadow passes across his face. 'I killed him, because I had no choice.'

'There is always a choice.'

'Not so. He betrayed his own people through his overweening pride, and refusal to concede to any terms I offered him. He deserved to die.'

'King Charles' belief he was appointed by God was not rhetoric, nor was it a shield he chose to hide behind. For him to betray that would be to betray God and imperil his own soul. He was the one with no choice.'

'Then what was I to do?' His voice drops to a whisper. 'His own stubborn arrogance was his downfall. If he still lived, we would be fighting this war forever.'

'You think it is over? Even after Worcester?'

'I lost good men at Worcester. The Royalists lost far more. It *must* be over.'

This time it is my laugh that rings harsh. 'How can it be? If you capture Charles the Second and-'

He slams a fist into the panelling beside the doorframe. 'And I will find the dog and he will suffer the fate of his father for bringing foreigners into the country.'

I wince, praying the king is far away, and safe. 'Even so, Prince James comes after him and then Prince Henry, who is just a child. Will you kill them too?'

'Who but God knows how far a man will go when he has to.'

I swallow and back away, appalled at the weight of his fury and my own precocity.

Can he not see his pride comes from assumed arrogance? The king had grounds for his aloof superiority. Who is this man but a jumped-up farmer with a penchant for power? And yet, I do not want to alienate him forever. I may still have need of him.

'Forgive me. I can only attribute my quick tongue to my recent loss.'

His smile returns. 'I have always admired that same quick tongue, Elizabeth. Do not change on my account.'

'I am grateful for your indulgence to Earl Lauderdale, and will send the powder to you when I am able.'

'Before I go, Mistress, I would give you a warning.'

'What sort of warning?'

'It has come to my notice that Anne Murray supplies shelter and money to fugitive officers of Worcester who have found their way into the district.'

My stomach twists and I feel slightly sick. I knew this would happen. 'My sister is mindful of her Christian charity to those less fortunate. She does not seek to insult you, only to help those in need.' He does not react and I step closer. 'What-what will you do to her?'

450

'I have no wish to punish her, simply alert you to the fact her activities are noted. She should be aware that my officers would not baulk at rounding up her lame dogs. I have ships waiting to take them to the colonies. Tell her to take care.'

Dizzy with relief, I smile. 'I shall. And thank you.'

'I hope you now regard my debt paid in full. Do we understand one another?'

'We do, although I would also remind you, sir. Anne is a Murray. I can guarantee nothing.'

His low chuckle trickles down my spine as he tugs open the door and waves me through. 'Now how did I know that would be your answer?'

Chapter 39

November 1651

My fur-lined cloak billows behind me as I descend the stairs, its weight oppressively welcome against the chill wind that blows upriver. It will be even colder on the barge that waits to take me to the Tower, but my heart is light and I would happily endure a blizzard today.

'Bess!' Lionel's growl halts me on the half landing. 'Did you misconstrue my meaning? I do not wish you to go.'

Anne looks up from the floor below, takes one look at Lionel's face and ducks out of sight.

I take a deep breath and summon my most appealing smile before I turn to my husband. 'I did not think you serious, my love. We return to Ham on the morrow, so I thought I would take the opportunity to pay a visit to a poor soul in prison. How can you object?'

His knuckles on the balustrade whiten. 'It is not your place to visit - that man!'

I inhale slowly, weary of this changeless argument. I wish now I had not told him about Cromwell's visit and my pride at having secured his mercy. Serve me right for my own vanity. 'Tis the least I can do for Earl Lauderdale. He deserves our gratitude for his help when my father stood trial.'

'Then write him a letter expressing your thanks.' Lionel's pleading turns to fury. 'How will it be viewed for my wife to enter a man's prison cell alone?'

'I am not alone. Anne accompanies me.' I pull on a kid glove, mainly to keep from looking at him. 'Or you could come with me,' I say sweetly, praying he will refuse.

'I have nothing to say to him.' He pushes away from the balustrade and follows me down the stairs.

On the front step, Lionel grasps both my upper arms and forces me to face him. 'I know what he is to you, Bess.'

How can he know? I never mention his name and John's letters reside in a place Lionel would never violate. Or would he?

'What a strange thing to say.' I feign surprise. 'I have not seen the earl since before our marriage.'

'You think so? And yet you used his name just then with a tone I doubt you ever employ for me.'

'You doubt me, Lionel?' I instil appeal into my face, hurt he seems not to know how much I love him. Then in the same heartbeat I realise I do not tell him nearly enough. Silently, I resolve to be more attentive in the future, though at the moment, I wish he would simply let me go.

His face twists in anguish and he drops his hands. 'Not your faithfulness, I would never doubt that. What I fear is his influence over you.'

'My dear.' I reach my arms round his neck and press my lips against his cheek. 'I never took you for a jealous husband. What influence can a man wield from a prison cell? He could be incarcerated for years.'

'Until you are an old woman, I hope.' Lionel twists one of my ringlets round his finger. 'When your charms are unlikely to interest him.'

'Indeed?' I tighten my embrace. 'Will I not make a handsome matron then?'

'I will want you when you are forty.' He rests his lips against my forehead. 'Lauderdale lives with no thought for tomorrow. Cavaliers like him seduce women as a game. I will not have you treated with disrespect.' He leans back and blinks me into focus through moist eyes. 'Let his own wife visit him, not mine.'

A rush of remorse almost changes my mind. I turn my face into the wind so he will not see how I wrestle with my conscience. If only he had gone out riding as he promised, then he would not have been present to witness my departure. With a silent vow never to defy him again, I pull away from his embrace and lightly tap his cheek. 'I will be back before you know I'm gone.' I call over my shoulder, running to where Cousin Anne awaits at the jetty with the bargemen.

'Bess!' His anguished voice cuts into me, but I dare not look back.

453

The warden by the Byward Postern glares at my handwritten pass for so long, I doubt the man can read at all. With ill-concealed reluctance he allows me entry, while eyeing my wide skirts and voluminous cloak with suspicion.

Ignoring his blatant stare, I slip a coin into his grubby hand while looking straight ahead. It is a trick I learned from Father, not to expect gratitude from those you bribe, or you attract only their resentment.

The guard's face remains impassive as he leads me up a twisting staircase so steep, I have to watch my feet or risk turning an ankle. Anne labours behind me, muttering to herself as our footsteps drum a discordant beat on the stone. I do not recognise the entrance hall, or the corridors the warder leads me into. This is a different part of the tower to where Father was kept back in forty-six.

The man halts beside a low door, beside which is set a wooden bench.

'Wait for me here, Anne,' I say without looking at her.

She releases a noisy breath, but obeys. Her stiff shoulders and resentful stare bore into my back as the guard gestures me into a square lobby. Three doors are set at right angles, behind which I imagine are the dungeons where the prisoners reside.

My wait is mercifully short and the same gaoler returns with a bunch of keys. Barely acknowledging me, he rattles the lock and pushes open a door that swings on a surprisingly well-oiled hinge. 'Lauderdale's quarters, Mistress,' he growls low in his throat.

What greets me is not a dank, dark cell too small to stand up in, but a large chamber with mullioned windows giving on to a manicured green. A pot-bellied stove in a corner belts out welcoming warmth into a pleasant room with a plain but scrubbed and clean-boarded floor, part of which is covered by a brightly-coloured turkey rug.

The tester bed has deep blue brocade hangings over a mattress as thick as those I possess at home. An oak desk occupies the space below the window, piled with books, maps, papers and a half written letter cast to one side.

I smile and tell myself I should not be surprised. My father secured similar lodgings during his incarceration, no doubt John has friends who purchase the same for him.

My breath catches at the sight of John, not from shock or dismay, but because he looks exactly as he did when I last saw him. He occupies a low chair beside the stove; both forearms balanced on his thighs and his head bent forward over his clasped hands. Beneath a dark woollen waistcoat, his white linen shirt stretches over muscular shoulders, undone at the neck to reveal a triangle of red-gold hairs covering lightly tanned skin. His abundant red hair is longer than I recall, falling in waves over his shoulders. Memories flood back with painful intensity. If I couldn't be his wife, why then did I not at least have the courage to become his lover?

'Have ye come tae berate me agin for yer impoverished state?' He doesn't look up, but addresses his hands.

'And why do you think I would do that?'

He lifts his head and gives a start. A wide grin appears on his face and rising, he sweeps a hand through his loose hair. 'Elizabeth! I cannae believe it's you.'

My eyes smart and blur with tears as he takes a step toward me but halts a few feet away. 'Forgive me, I thought-' he purses his lips in embarrassment and grins again. 'Would ye be insulted if I said I thought ye were my wife?'

'Dreadfully!' I conceal my self-consciousness in mock indignation. 'When I have defied my own husband's wishes to come here.'

'Defied him, eh?' He plants a hand on one hip above buff coloured breeches and flicks his foxy hair over his shoulder. 'I hope ah'm worth the trouble.'

What strikes me then is its cleanliness. In fact everything about him is clean. His beard is trimmed and his skin glows with health, his long fingers are expertly manicured.

'I came to offer you comfort in your sparse prison cell, my lord Earl.' I ignore his question. 'However it appears you have everything you require.' His gaze bores into me as embarrassed, I wander the room, running my fingers over the desktop with its pile of papers obscuring the surface. 'I see you even have sealing wax for your letters.'

He leans against a bedpost, arms folded and one ankle crossed over the other. 'Did ye expect tae find me shackled to a wall wi' rats running over ma feet?'

Fine lines crease the skin beside his eyes; the eyes of an adventurer not yet cowed and beaten. What would it take to wipe the animation from that face? I hope I will never know.

'I certainly did not expect this of a man convicted of treason.' Suddenly warm, I remove my gloves and tuck them inside my muff. Tempted to remove my cloak, I make do with untying the ribbon and let if fall loose to reveal my gown.

His teasing smile dissolves. 'It's still a prison. And one no one expects me tae leave.' He lifts his chin, and a glimpse of defiance enters his eyes. 'On ma way here under escort, a man poked his head into the carriage and said he gave not a fig for ma life.'

At my shocked gasp, his boyish grin appears.

'Dinna worry, I laughed in the sot's face. I'll face what 'ere is to become o' me.'

'Perhaps Cromwell believes the people will think better of him if he shows mercy to the defeated of Worcester?'

'Hah! Tell that to Lord Derby'. He pushes away from the bedpost and stands before me. I hold my breath in anticipation as his hands close on my elbows. 'Forgive my surly manners. I didnae expect the lovely Lady Tollemache tae visit me here.'

My arms burn at his touch and I sway into him, keenly aware of what desire is. He is the only man I have ever met who can make me feel this vulnerable. It's as if all I am waiting for is that one word that will make me willingly surrender to him. With Lionel I am in control, the calm, calculating one. With John my nerves quiver as I silently will him not to let me go.

'And I am more welcome then than Lady Lauderdale?' My jealousy tinges my voice with malice, but I cannot help it.

'My puir, Anne.' He releases a sigh. 'It is nae her fault she has tae hire a hackney tae come and see me. But I wish she wouldnae rage at me the way she does.'

Enough. I don't wish to hear about her.

I reach a trembling hand and slip my fingers beneath the collar of his shirt. The skin is soft but the muscle beneath is hard, sinewy, and warm. 'Cromwell came to see me.'

He catches my fingers and holds them there, his gaze fixed steadily on mine. 'And?'

'He asked for a small favour and I demanded one in return.'

'So it is true then? Ma sentence has been commuted? And I have you to thank for my life being spared?'

I purse my lips in mild disappointment. 'I see rumour has already reached you, when I hoped to be the one to tell you the news.'

'Ah care naught for that.' His hands close round my waist and he lifts me into his arms the same way he did four years before when he learned the king had escaped. I giggle like a virgin as he swings me round in a circle as if I weigh nothing. Every emotion I felt on that day then comes rushing back, this time tinged with a worldly sadness that tells me I will never be that young and innocent again.

He sets me down again, but holds me close. 'Thank ye,' he whispers beside my ear. 'I will ne'er forget this.' He links his hands behind me and leans backward to look into my eyes. 'Tell me now. Did ye crawl on your knees before the Colonel Chief and beg for ma life in exchange for your virtue?'

'Do not joke. His name and mine are already linked. Rumour has it that I am his mistress.'

His laugh is raucous, disbelieving. 'Then rumour is a liar. I know where yer heart lies, wi' King Charles, and hopefully wi' me. My vanity demands that you humbled yerself afore that Puritan dog for the man ye love.'

'You cannot be my love.' My voice chokes and I lower my chin, burying my face in his coat that smells of mildew and wood smoke. 'Oh, John, how different everything might have been.'

'I know. But if we could, would ye be mine?' he whispers into my hair.

'You know I would, but it cannot be.'

'Hae a little faith in the future, Elizabeth. Our future.'

'Now you tease me.' I pummel his chest lightly with a fist. 'I have a husband and you have a wife. We have no future.' I close my eyes and inhale, memorising the feel and smell of him to conjure in my solitary hours.

He puts me gently away from him, his grip still firm on my upper arms and looks into my face. 'I hae something tae ask of ye. Will you join us, Elizabeth?'

I frown. 'Join whom? What do you mean?'

A gaoler steps into view, staring at us through the grille in the door and John pulls me close again. The guard leers and nods knowingly, but continues to watch.

'We are tae form a society of loyalists.' John's low murmur into my hair makes my pulse race. 'King Charles the second will nae let his fither's murder go unavenged.'

I lift my face to his. 'The king managed to get out of the country? You are sure?'

He nods, dislodging a strand of red hair from his brow. 'He is safe, trust me. Buckingham too.'

I do trust him, more than I have trusted anyone. I will our silent observer not to move away and allow me to relish the feel of John's arms about me a little longer; my hands gripping his coat so hard my knuckles whiten. 'Say there will be no more fighting, John, please.'

'Dinna fret, lass. We have a new weapon now. Information. The more we know about the plans and activities of Cromwell and his ministers, the better prepared we shall be for another onslaught on the usurpers.'

I cannot believe what he is saying. 'John, you must face your life as it is. You are in prison, your future is uncertain and yet you talk of more plots?'

His laugh ripples through me and my desire to reason with him, to see sense, dissolves. I lean into him, knowing I will have to go soon and maybe never see him again. I will not spend what brief time we have together in discord. 'What do you hope to do?'

'Supply the king with the names of those on whom he can rely, and those who plead loyalty, but co-operate with the Puritans.'

'Are my father and Sir Robert Moray involved?' I wonder why I did not think of it before. Father may have hidden himself away in Edinburgh afraid of arrest, but he would not remain idle.

'Hush, mention nae names.' He nods toward the door and the eavesdropping gaoler.

'I cannot bear the thought these Puritans have beaten us.' I clench my fist against his doublet, savouring the feel of his muscled chest beneath.

'Then join us in *The Sealed Knot* and help restore the monarchy.'

Even in this grey and gloomy place where the hopes of so many have been cruelly extinguished, John fights. He has lost everything, his castle at Thirlestane, his house in Highgate, his wife and daughter reduced to virtual penury, and yet, he believes the cause will triumph.

At last the gaoler moves away, but John makes no move to release me.

'What must I do?' I can hardly breathe.

'Thass ma girl.' He drops a kiss on my forehead. 'Keep in touch wi' our members, collect whatever money ye can. Dinna entrust it tae messengers, but take it personally tae the king if ye are able. Trust few and believe no one except your own eyes.'

'Travel to the continent? Lionel would never allow it.'

'I dinna believe ye cannot manage Sir Lionel.' He chuckles and steps away, grabs a tightly folded packet from beneath a pile of papers and without even so much as a glance at it, tucks it inside my cloak. 'Keep this close. It is a list of our members. Take it tae the king.'

'And if by some miracle I manage that, how will I contact you to say it is done?'

'Send me word through the third name on the list. He has a hoose in Covent Garden he uses as a drop. Never write names into your correspondence, identify them by their numbers or marks. I am two sevens, you are four and a nought.'

'I am part of your code?' The thought sends a bubble of excitement into my chest. *He trusts me.* 'Mother taught me her code, this cannot be so different.' I am no longer nervous, but anxious to begin this momentous task.

The guard's face reappears at the door and with a gesture of his hand indicates the visit is over.

The thought we must part brings a soft cry to my lips, but before I can speak, John's mouth is pressed hard on mine. His hands on my back crush me to him so the muscles of his chest are taut against my breasts. The tip of his tongue flicks lightly along the inside of my upper lip, the spark it ignites so intense, I have to squeeze my eyes shut to prevent tears from spilling down my cheeks.

How can I bear to leave him? This man who has stirred in me with one kiss what three years of an amiable marriage have not?

His kiss ends, but he seems reluctant to break contact and runs his warm lips along my jaw line and into my neck. 'Carry me in your heart, Elizabeth, for as long as it takes.'

What can he mean? For as long as what takes? We are both married, him with a daughter and I with two sons. My loyalty should lie, must lie, with Lionel and our children, with my dependent sisters and the retention of Ham House and all that means to me. There can be nothing between us; no promise or hope for an unknown future.

'Will ye come and see me agin?' he says when I do not speak.

'Lionel would not allow it a second time,' I say through a tightened throat.

'If ye can, I will live for the day. But letters may have tae do.' His hands slide down my arms and he turns away. 'I'll nae watch ye go.'

My heart is a stone in my chest as the grinning guard pockets another coin before escorting me back to where Anne sits patiently on the bench.

I stumble through gloomy halls, windswept pathways and the cobbled walkway that leads to the river steps. She questions me at each step, but I can only shake my head, numb with grief.

When I pause on the jetty, she holds out a linen kerchief. I frown at it uncomprehending until she runs a finger down my cheek that comes away wet with my tears.

The oarsman hands me into the barge, where I take the seat far in the stern that faces backward: my gaze on the grey stone fortress where my John is kept.

He said this time our war will be different; our weapons are information, knowledge and patience. The hardest of these will be patience, for neither of us knows how long he will be kept a prisoner, or if we shall ever be alone together again. Despite gossip, I intend to continue my friendship with the Cromwells; an open association from which I can glean knowledge with charm and discretion to pass to my fellow conspirators.

With such devices, the Murrays may take their revenge on those who humbled us and shortened my mother's life.

The barge pulls into the current and I narrow my eyes against the icy spray that whips my cheeks. Though my heart is heavy, I am filled with a new sense of purpose, that of continuing the noble task Catherine Bruce Murray began.

Destiny may keep John and I apart forever, but one day, the king will come home again.

Epilogue

My sore leg pains me more than usual today, though I am content to sit and while away this warm evening in the window seat of this room. Portraits of past Murrays, Tollemaches and the Stuart kings line the walls, their sightless eyes staring down at me in reproach or understanding; who can tell which. Through this window lies my favourite view of my father's garden, a sight I loved as a child. Sometimes, I pretend that it is young Elizabeth who sits here, not this old carcase with its aches and pains that mar my every waking hour.

Death has not stalked me, as it has both my husbands and all my sisters. How I have contrived to live so long is either malice or bile, for I refuse to accept it is God's will. Perhaps I live to spite those who have wished me dead over the years, God rot them. Even now, my servants bow at the waist until I pass by. I stopped turning to watch them a long time ago, but they dare not rise until I am out of sight. Becoming a duchess was no birthright, I had to fight for my rank and no one was allowed to deny me my due honour.

Despite that gossip once made me Cromwell's mistress, I never wavered from my devotion to my sovereign. I was there beside Lionel when King Charles returned to the throne in the spring of the year sixty. Not the diminutive, vacillating man we all loved, and whose stubborn heart we sighed over; but his dark giant of a son, a man of thirty by then. His years of hardship had changed him. Even with these old eyes that have seen so much, still I remember the fourteen-year-old prince who flirted with me at the Oxford court so long ago. At least he proved a wiser man than his father, if a more manipulative and sensual one.

Three years after the king's execution, my father crept out of hiding long enough to make a brief visit home to Ham, though he scurried back to Edinburgh within days in case someone felt it would be in their interests to betray him. I thank God we had that time together, for within another two years he was gone: his last days passed in an Edinburgh lodging, not his beloved Ham.

I hope they were peaceful, and not filled with bitter regret.

Of my sisters, only little Margaret married: another John, a kindly man whom we all loved. After her husband's death, she returned home to spend the rest of her days here with Anne and Kate, indulgent aunts and loyal sisters. Kate never reproached me for her spinster state, though had I been in her place, I would certainly have done.

My beloved Ham is like an old lady now. Her skin sallow and dried by the weather, the neglected gardens gathered around her like a faded, tattered skirt. I fulfilled my wish to build a cherry garden where I could see it from my apartments. Neither my children, nor even my sisters dared to touch the fruit without my permission, which I rarely gave. Those trees are no longer pruned, they have become overgrown and succumbed to disease, while now only wasps gorge themselves on the fruit.

I can no longer afford to fill the kitchens, and it becomes harder each year to persuade the lowest creature to work at Ham. Not that I need them. My crippled limbs keep me from the upper floor, where so many elegant rooms lay neglected and unused. The furniture I have not been forced to sell is covered with dustsheets and the blinds kept drawn.

A dying house for a dying woman.

It wasn't always like this. My twenty years as Lady Tollemache and Countess Dysart were spent here in security and comfort with Lionel, though I could never persuade him to spend more of his money on improving the house. I had to be grateful he at least agreed to save it from the Parliamentarians during the long years of the Commonwealth. Sweet, devoted Lionel to whom I gave five live children, and six dead ones. He always believed my frequent travels to the continent to further the Royalist cause weakened me, and in turn, the babes I carried. I scorned him for a fool then, but on reflection, perhaps he was right. He often was.

My firstborn son, Lionel, visits rarely, and only when I request money, which he is reluctant to give. How I managed to birth such a tight-purse I cannot imagine, not even Lionel was quite so parsimonious, and he had less money at his disposal than my son.

My other sons, Thomas and William were so different. One became a gallant soldier whose reputation rivalled that of Marlborough. While my baby, my sweet William was ever a trial. Always fighting and duelling, causing scandals. I was forced to buy him a commission in the navy in the end, only for him to die on a Caribbean island of some native fever. Neither son married or gave me grandchildren, but I loved them both to distraction.

My eldest, Lionel gave me five grandchildren. My girls too, Elizabeth and Catherine, both good wives and mothers, provided another five bairns between them. Poor Betty soon became estranged from her Scottish duke. That marriage was a mistake, though I will not take all the blame. Young people know little of duty. Both daughters have inherited my sharp temper and wilfulness. Not that I would have it any other way.

It must be near thirty years since my first husband, Lionel died. In Paris. Of all the strange places to meet his maker, without me near to offer nursing or comfort. Though I must not dwell on that. He would never reproach me, he never did.

Then there was my John, Duke of Lauderdale. My brave, red-headed warrior; hero of the Royalist cause who risked everything for the king - and lost. His seven years in prison dulled his fervour not at all, and he was by the side of Charles the Second when he brought the monarchy back to England.

How proud I was that day, some say too proud, for our names were linked for years in whispers and rumour. Not all of it true.

That I loved John and he loved me was never in doubt, though we never acted on that love. The fact that Anne Lauderdale took herself off to France in disgust is immaterial. That she chose to die there and release John was something I will always thank her for. Many urged John to find a young wife, one who could provide him with heirs to the dukedom. I did not fear for a second he would listen, for fate or God had decided years before that we should be together.

How we scandalised London by our marriage, just weeks after his wife's death. I was forty-four, and still, thank God, beautiful. The doubters soon regretted their scurrilous gossip, for John and I became a force to be reckoned with.

I spent a fortune on my beloved Ham, my own and John's. We doubled the number of rooms and filled them with gilt and silk from the continent fit to entertain the royal court that gathered here. How we were gossiped about in every drawing room from Edinburgh to London, and revelled in the fact we engendered both jealousy and spite, tinged with admiration.

As His Majesty's closest advisor, John, and I with him, rose to the stations we always saw for ourselves; until, that is, my John and the king quarrelled. Then he closed the gates he had built especially for the king on the South Front, never to open them again.

When John died, my life became a hollow shell. Crippled by debts, I sold so many of the prized treasures he and I had collected. My palace is now my prison with so many memories rolling in my head. Memories so real, I imagine I see them sometimes, on days when the sun shines through the closed shutters in a certain way. As I tap my way from one room to another, Lionel looks up at me and smiles from the chimney corner while puffing away at his pipe.

On my better days, I summon the strength to wander into John's apartments opposite mine. A task I mostly avoid, for it causes such regret and heartache. My foggy eyes pick out a tall shadow at my shoulder, or a wisp of red hair disappearing round a corner, followed by a growl of affection, or anger. Echoes of the past rising to taunt me, or are they the ghosts of Ham who have seen such tragedy and even more joy?

No one cares now what regrets an old woman harbours, no one but my faithful Anne Henderson. She treats me with her enigmatic smile, which rebukes me more than her impudence ever could. I should not treat her so ill, for she has more years than even my seventy-two and bears her own discomforts with fortitude.

She approaches now with her halting gait, a posset to help me sleep clutched in her gnarled, arthritic hands. Her once glowing red hair is wispy and thin above coarse skin and a narrow nose. Never a beauty was Anne. Not like me. Yet I have never told her how much she means to me. Perhaps I should do so now before it is too late.

She chides me for sitting too long in the draught and holds out the potion for me to take.

I wave her away. I have no need of her concoctions, for this night I will rest.

I am ready, and my John awaits.

Author's Note

Whilst writing this novel, I have tried to keep as close to the known facts as possible, though according to Elizabeth's biographer, Doreen Kripps, little is known about her early life and details were not faithfully recorded. I have no proof that Elizabeth and John Maitland, Earl Lauderdale, met in 1647 during King Charles' house arrest at Hampton Court, but it could certainly have been possible, even likely.

The Earl's capture after the Battle of Worcester and his imprisonment are fact, but speculation exists as to whether it was Elizabeth's influence with Cromwell that prevented Lauderdale's execution. Earl Lauderdale certainly believed Elizabeth had saved his life, and said as much when he mentioned her in his will.

That Oliver Cromwell took quinine for his malaria is also disputed, and the connection with Elizabeth tenuous; but from my own interpretation of Elizabeth's character and Cromwell's, I doubt they were lovers, so their relationship is based on something more prosaic than the attraction of an older man for a pretty young girl.

I have tried to remain true to the attitudes and actions of a tragic and confusing time in England's history, and hope Elizabeth would have approved of my interpretation of her story.

Anita Seymour

Bibliography

Elizabeth of the Sealed Knot: A Biography of Elizabeth Murray, Countess of Dysart by Doreen Cripps (ISBN: 978-0900093432)

God's Fury, England's Fire: A New History of the English Civil Wars by Michael Braddick (ISBN: 978-0141008974)

The English Civil Wars: 1640-1660 by Blair Worden (ISBN: 978-0753826911)

Rupert Prince Palatine by Eva Scott (ISBN: 978-1104450700)

The Memoirs of Lady Ann Fanshawe by Ann Fanshawe (ISBN: 978-1417906277)

Ham House: Surrey (National Trust Guidebooks) by Christopher Rowell (ISBN: 978-1843591726)

Hampton Court Palace by Matthew Sturgis (ISBN: 978-0752213194)

ALSO AVAILABLE FROM
CLAYMORE PRESS...

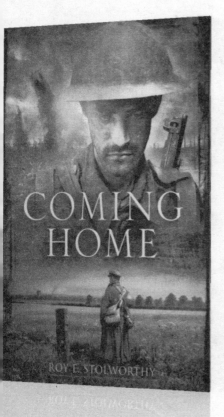

9781781590713 •
368 pages • £7.99

A brutally honest portrayal of the realities of war, this novel relays the story of fifteen-year-old Thomas Elkin as he engages in the First World War. A tale of conflict, both global and personal, and of redemption, this is a novel that has the potential to rank alongside the best of retrospective First World War literature. Accepting the blame for the accidental death of his recently conscripted brother, Elkin switches identity with his dead sibling and enters into the fray of the conflict. His burning ambition is to die a glorious death in his brother's name.

Believing that in fully submitting to the reality of war he is atoning for his sins, he faces all the attendant horrors with a steel will and a poignant resignation.

His personal conflict sees itself mirrored in the wider events and soon the two are inextricably linked raising issues of mortality, morality, guilt and faith. This novel enacts the kind of existential crises experienced on the battlefield with the constant threat of the imminent and fatal danger a companion.

Written with deft skill and sensitivity for the subject matter at hand, this is a piece of stylish work that places the reader at the heart of the action. Featuring nuanced characters and vivid action scenes, it works to evoke a real sense of the times as the story unfolds.

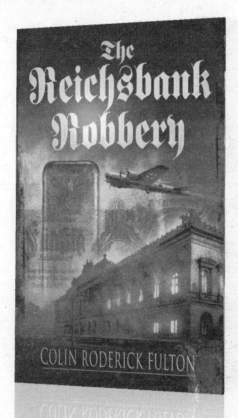

9781781590782 •
336 pages • £8.99

In February 1945 the US Air Force launched the largest day time bombing offensive against Berlin, dropping over 2,250 tons of bombs on the German capital.

The Reichsbank, Germany's state bank, received 21 direct hits. This left the building badly damaged, its vaults unsafe and meant that most of its contents were at risk.

The German authorities made the decision to take most of the Reichsbank's treasure away and hide it for safekeeping. Some $200 million US in gold bars, weighing around 100 tons, plus much of the paper currency reserves, as well as a great deal of foreign currency (approximately $4 million in US currency alone) was sent in trains from Berlin.

All this loot was placed in a salt mine at a place called Merkers. This was captured intact by the US Army. After this disaster, the Germans spent the next six weeks transferring their remaining bullion and currency reserves around what remained of the Reich in armoured trains, an area that included parts of northern Italy, Czechoslovakia, Austria and Germany, looking for somewhere safe.

Much of the treasure actually either ended up back in Berlin, was stolen, disappeared or, was captured, mainly by American troops and the SS.

This novel, by Colin Roderick Fulton, imagines one plot which could have been enacted around this time. The mystery surrounding the locations and ultimate destiny of the liberated treasures provides fertile ground on which to impose such a fiction. Secrecy, intrigue, and fast paced action combine to create a well paced novel, sure to appeal to fans of wartime fiction.

9781781590843 •
208 pages • £8.99

This enthralling piece of work by first-time novelist Robert Southworth explores the avenue history could have run down if Spartacus had survived the slave rebellion in 73BC, an uprising whose aftermath didn't deliver the remains of the famous slave leader. The brute force of this famous figure of Roman history is relayed, and the events of the period re-imagined to great effect. The work is sure to appeal to fans of Roman history, as well as those enamored by stories of action and adventure. Whilst the figure of Spartacus continues to hold massive appeal for contemporary audiences, this work offers a fresh vision of the Roman era; a dark and brutal reenactment of high gladiatorial drama.

9781781590645 •
320 pages • £9.99

It is 1861. Tom Wells is in pursuit of a girl from North Carolina. He accepts an offer from his employer to leave the quiet obscurity of his job as an office boy in a London shipping firm to cross the Atlantic to Nassau in the Bahamas. Now he must face the hazards of the Union blockade of the Confederate ports in the American Civil War. Tom's bravado may help him with the dangers of running the blockade, but how will he cope with the conflicting issues of love, loyalty and morality as he becomes entangled with a lady of easy virtue in Nassau?

Tom's adventures take him through the perilous triangle between Nassau, Charleston and Wilmington NC, where he must smuggle arms and munitions through a gauntlet of Union warships to the Southern ports, bringing cotton and tobacco back to Nassau.

David Kent-Lemon presents us here with a fast paced and dynamic narrative, exploring a fascinating, dramatic and less well known corner of that extraordinary conflict – the American Civil War. The characters are finely drawn, with the balance between deceit and morality offset by courage and humour. The realism and historical accuracy of the background complete the picture.

As the Civil War reaches its climax, so does the drama in Tom's life, heightened by the historical events within which he is embroiled.

9781781591741 •
272 pages • £9.99

In 1804, Liverpool was the largest slave trading port in Great Britain, yet her influential traders felt threatened by the success, in Parliament, of the anti-slavery movement. Few, in Liverpool, condemned the 'Trade'. William King, son of a Liverpool slave trader, sickened by what he experienced aboard a Spanish slaver, was one of the few who did speak out. This epic, set during the dying days of this despicable practice, weaves themes of generational change, moral wickedness, greed, romance, and the fortunes of war as they impact upon the lives of a father and son caught up in the turmoil that preceded the implementation of the British Trade Act of 1807, which would end Britain's involvement in the slave trade.

The city of Liverpool is one still scarred by its past involvement with the morally contemptible Triangle Trade. Indeed, the cities prosperity was built on the profits of slavery, and the reverberations of this inheritance continue to impact on the city today. This novel roots the reader firmly in a city on the brink of change, evoking a real sense of the struggles at play, and informing our understanding of the realities of slavery, those who fueled its continuation and those who brought about its eventual cessation, as well as the legacy inherited by the City of Liverpool and the wider world.

9781781592403 •
320 pages • £9.99

When Germany's leading tank ace meets the Steppe Fox it's a fight to the death. Faced with overwhelming odds Kampfgruppe von Schroif needs a better tank and fast; but the new Tiger tank is still on the drawing board and von Schroif must overcome bureaucracy, espionage and relentless Allied bombing to get the Tiger into battle in time to meet the ultimate challenge.

Based on a true story of combat on the Russian Front, this powerful new novel is written by Emmy™ Award winning writer Bob Carruthers and newcomer Sinclair McLay. It tells the gripping saga of how the Tiger tank was born and a legend was forged in the heat of combat. Gritty, intense and breath-taking in its detail, this sprawling epic captures the reality of the lives and deaths of the tank crews fighting for survival on the Eastern Front, a remarkable novel worthy of comparison with 'Das Boot'.

THREADS OF TREASON

MARY BALE

9781781591000 •
272 pages • £9.99

When two of the nuns creating the Bayeux Tapestry fall from the tower of the Priory of St Thomas the Apostle, Abbess Eleanor and her protégé, Therese, are sent to investigate. As the adventures unfold, the intrigue created between the Norman Princes and Bishops, as well as the tensions between the conquerors and the native Britons, deepen to great and dramatic effect. Mary Bale has captured the spirit and feel of the times which she evokes in this, her first novel. The sense of intrigue is heightened by the writing style which is taut, fast-paced, and heavy with a sense of mystery. This extensively researched novel is sure to appeal to those looking for an evocative tale of adventure and intrigue, made vivid by fascinating period details.

9781781591734 •
256 pages • £9.99

Peenemünde: windswept corner of the Third Reich and birthplace of the space age. Otto Fischer, a severely wounded Luftwaffe officer and former criminal investigator, is summoned to solve a seemingly incomprehensible case: the murder of a leading rocket engineer during a devastating air-raid. With only days until the SS assume control of the production of a remarkable new weapon, Fischer must find a motive and perpetrator from among several thousand scientists, technicians, soldiers and forced labourers. As he struggles to get the measure of a secretive, brilliant world in which imagination moves far beyond the limits of technology, what at first appears to be a solitary crime draws him into a labyrinth of conspiracy, betrayal and treason.

McDermott brings skills previously honed whilst producing well-researched history books to the discipline of writing fiction, creating work that is both historically accurate and evocative as well as stylish in a literary sense.

If you would like to read some of these fantastic new fiction titles you can order your copies direct from
PEN & SWORD BOOKS

Please call 01226 734222

Or order online via our website:
www.pen-and-sword.co.uk